MA
MALEVOL

"This is a superb read, darkly funny and
sharply written. Anyone curious about the spiritual
history of the Western world and the vagaries of the
church over the last seventy years should read this
demonic memoir, which follows a fine tradition of
hellish imagination from Dante, through Milton, to
C.S. Lewis. Although clearly inspired by Screwtape,
this work makes its own subtle and original
contribution to an understanding of our times.
There is also, beneath the brittle surface, a deep
down wisdom here. I can only describe Magnificent
Malevolence as a fiendishly good book."

Murray Watts
Author and screenwriter

Also by Derek Wilson:

The People's Bible
The English Reformation
Reformation (with Felipe Fernandez Armesto)
A Tudor Tapestry
Charlemagne
Out of the Storm – The Life and Legacy of Martin Luther
Hans Holbein – Portrait of an Unknown Man
The King and the Gentleman – Charles Stuart and Oliver Cromwell

MAGNIFICENT MALEVOLENCE

Memoirs of a career in Hell

Derek Wilson

LION FICTION

Published by Lion Fiction
an imprint of
Lion Hudson plc
Wilkinson House, Jordan Hill Road,
Oxford OX2 8DR, England
www.lionhudson.com/fiction

Published in association with United Agents Ltd, 12–26 Lexington
Street, London W1F 0LE, www.unitedagents.co.uk

ISBN 978 1 78264 018 9
e-ISBN 978 1 78264 019 6

Acknowledgments
Front cover image: © imagebroker /Alamy
Back cover images: Ink well: © iStock/ DNY59;
Fountain pen: Uyen Le/

A catalogue record for this book is available from the British Library

Printed and bound in the UK, February 2013, LH26

Contents

*For Dave, with thanks for help
and inspiration*

Introduction

"Nowhere do we tempt so successfully as on the very steps of the altar."

Screwtape Proposes a Toast[1]

C.S. Lewis, who introduced Screwtape, a senior devil, to the world in 1942, knew that evil is powerful and personal and he understood that its main thrust is against God and the people of God. He believed that to envisage evil as a malign but vague influence located in the human gene pool is only a little less dangerous than thinking of "God" as an ethereal life force. The Bible has no truck with such formless concepts. Nor had Lewis. He took as read the biblical understanding of evil as resulting from a rebellion by fallen angels bent on mastering the human race and turning it against the creator. This erudite senior academic made no apology for propagating what many of his sophisticated compeers would have regarded as outmoded

---

1   C.S. Lewis, 1959.

folklore and superstition. "It seems to me", he wrote in a later apologia, "to explain a good many facts. It agrees with the plain sense of Scripture, the tradition of Christendom, and the beliefs of most men at most times."

That evaluation of spiritual realities remains as valid now as it was when Lewis introduced us to Screwtape, in the middle of the Second World War. The human scene has changed – profoundly – in the intervening years, but the old conflict continues to be played out on the planetary stage. It is still the same war but, as the human decades have passed, it has been fought with new weapons and different battle tactics. Every shift in international politics, every technological advance, and every development within the life of the church gave rise to new skirmishes between the forces of the Sovereign Lord and those of the "Old Enemy". There can be no doubt that Lewis would agree that Screwtape and his diabolical colleagues have not ceased their operations in the last seventy years. Holding mankind in bondage and throwing numerous spanners into the works of the Christian church continues to take up all their energies. And, knowing this, the great Christian apologist would want twenty-first-century humanity to be aware of the wiles practised by the forces of Hell from the time that Screwtape laid down his pen right down to the present day.

Therefore, the fiftieth anniversary of Jack's (he hated his baptismal names of Clive Staples) death seems to be an appropriate occasion for a "Hell update". How fortunate, then, that the following account, rescued from the archives of the Low Command's Ministry of Misinformation, has fallen into our hands. This remarkable manuscript outlines the career of the prominent devil Crumblewit, SOD (Order of the Sons of Darkness, First Class). It was in a much-mutilated state and has only with difficulty been cut and pasted together to make a reasonably coherent narrative of the activities of a post-Screwtape generation of devils. It is not, of course, "true" in the sense of being an objective appraisal of the struggles between good and evil which have dominated human affairs in the period from 1942 to the present. The account is distorted by Crumblewit's truly diabolical conceit and also his ability for self-delusion. However, it does shed fresh light on the ups and downs experienced by the church throughout this period. Crumblewit's energies were entirely deployed in the religious arena. Any involvement in political events and international conflicts such as wars, acts of terrorism, rebellions, and the nuclear arms race was purely tangential. He was employed exclusively in undermining the attempts of Christians to bring to bear upon world events the prerogatives of love, peace, and justice and to carry out the mission entrusted to them by Jesus.

There were critics who disapproved of the "flippancy" of *The Screwtape Letters* and insisted that there is nothing remotely funny about evil. Lewis heartily agreed, but pointed out that humour is a divine gift and had been used in the service of religion by, for example, G.K. Chesterton, the performances of medieval mystery plays, and, supremely, Jesus. He used the light approach in dealing with spiritual profundities because, as he explained in one of his interviews, "There is a great deal of false reverence about. There is too much solemnity and intensity in dealing with sacred matters; too much speaking in holy tones." Lewis believed that humour was a legitimate weapon in the Christian armoury and he used it to great effect in helping us to recognize our enemy and penetrate to the core of his numerous, subtle stratagems. This fresh exposé has the same objective, and I believe he would have approved. At least, I hope so. I am just one of the millions of Christians who have been helped by his lucid, imaginative and insightful writings, and this book is a small gesture of homage. [2]

* * * * *

2   Editor's note: Crumblewit had little interest in human chronology, and this has presented an editorial challenge. Dates have been inserted at the top of every chapter in an attempt to help the reader relate Crumblewit's story to contemporary events in the human world.

CHAPTER 1

How My Brilliant Career Began

(1942–1944)

In that time–space sphere of existence in which our great leader has set us to work for his glory there was an era the mortals called "the Second World War". Of course, it was not anything of the sort; the real struggle to wrest control of that minuscule fragment of all the universes from the miserable creatures the unmentionable one has put in charge has been in progress ever since the beginning. Earth is our place, the only scrap of timeless immensity we have asked for. And yet we have been forced to wage war for it, and to go on waging war until we have completed the task of enslaving the pathetic little darlings the unmentionable one sets so much store by. Oh, the monstrous unfairness of it all! The enemy claims to be the very embodiment of justice but what could be more inequitable than to deny our kind the right to enjoy our way of life and establish our culture on one infinitesimal speck of creation?

I was a junior tempter then, but even in those days I showed phenomenal promise – a promise which, as all who

13

read this will know, has been amply fulfilled throughout a career of quite unprecedented guile, deviousness, and magnificent malevolence. Those who were present at my infernal investiture will recall the words of His Lowness, Prince Lobzubble, as he conferred on me the Order of Sons of Darkness, First Class: "Rarely in the annals of the Lower Dominion has so much been owed by so many to one demon." Old Lobzubble certainly has a way with words.

I was at that time still a student at the Training College for Young Devils, then under the directorship of Principal Slubgob, a thorough, if unimaginative, pedagogue. It was, however, Slubgob who was responsible for introducing to the syllabus the Advanced Certificate in Enemy Literature.

Only the most sound and clear-headed students from each year were admitted onto this course. The material allocated for study was classified and potentially very dangerous. Naturally, Slubgob and his staff were under no doubt about my suitability for the ACEL. And what a fascinating field of study that library of hideous but seductive sedition turned out to be. No wonder these works have to be locked safely away in the archives of the Ministry of Misinformation. No wonder the direst penalties are imposed on any of our people found guilty of handling items on the List of Prohibited Books. No wonder it remains a top priority of all tempters to prevent their subjects from actually reading what the enemy has written. Remember the mnemonic we all learned at school – OIL. It is as important now as it ever was to convince humans that the Bible is Old-fashioned, Illogical and Laughable. But in order to achieve this particular objective those of us who can claim higher demonic intellect must actually be exposed to the unmentionable one's propaganda. Familiarizing myself with his nauseatingly pious poems and moralizing mischief-making has helped me to become the great lie-monger I am today.

I remember, as though it were yesterday, the flash of inspiration that set me upon the path to my later celebrity. In one of the letters written by the traitor Saul of Tarsus in the years after the disastrous Battle of Golgotha, he revealed to the enemy's recruits one of the great secrets about our magnificent leader. "Satan", he said, "can disguise himself as an angel of light." Oh, the rapturous moment when that revelation came upon me! I was filled at once, not only with renewed admiration for His Supreme Lowness but also by a determination to emulate him. Fellow pupils and school staff had frequently commented on my acting ability and I always took the lead role in our dramatic productions. Why should this talent not be turned to a lower cause? I began immediately to construct a plan which would enable me to infiltrate the enemy citadel, to become a mole, to discover his secrets, to frustrate his objectives.

Having devised a plan, the next task was to sell it.

I knew that there would be no point in taking my audacious concept to Slubgob. He lacked imagination and would have been quite unable to grasp the exciting scheme that was steadily developing in my mind. At first I thought of seeking the advice of Drigwizzle, head of the Demonic Strategy department. We are all familiar with, and grateful for, his knowledge of Advanced Tempting. His inspiring biographical and analytical studies – *Masters of Infernal Warfare*, *Distortion Tactics for Beginners*, etc. – are unlikely ever to be surpassed. I actually got as far as going to present myself in Drigwizzle's office. But, as I turned the corner into his corridor, I saw him coming the other way with his arm round the shoulder of that insufferable ass Sharfly-Bickendrop, my contemporary student and arch-rival. I had never been able to understand how, term after term, "Sharparse" (as we called him) was always a few points ahead of me in Demonic Strategy exams. Now I knew. I also knew that any confidences shared with Drigwizzle would not remain secret for long. The thought of Sharparse stealing my brainchild was unbearable. Where, then, could I turn for support in laying my brilliant scheme before the Satanic Secret Service (SSS 666), for I was fully aware that it would need resources which could be sanctioned only at the lowest level of our intelligence service?

I needed a patron in low places. Only the most gifted of strategists would be able to recognize the sheer brilliance of my proposal. I decided to go to the very bottom – First Minister Blubwarp. Inevitably, my initial letter went through the bureaucratic mill of being passed from one unimaginative, plodding functionary to another. I was quite resigned to my brainchild being crushed beneath the weight of meaningless memoranda in tedious inter-departmental despatches in some dreary official's in tray. Every great artist has to do battle with crass incomprehension, and in me the art of malevolence had reached depths rarely plumbed in the history of the Infernal Regions. It was therefore a pleasant surprise when I received a brief, handwritten, personal note from Blubwarp himself. He summoned me to an informal lunch at his club.

I duly arrived at that impressive and exclusive rendezvous and was shown to an alcove where His Eminent Lowness sat at his private table. We are all familiar with Blubwarp's much-publicized visage: the oily sheared brow, the needle-sharp fangs. Being close to the reality was an awe-inspiring experience. Yet the minister was affability itself. When I mumbled my thanks for his condescension in seeing me, he replied that he was always on the lookout for promising young devils and was impressed by my ambition and self-confidence.

The lunch was superb; Blubwarp, as I have since learned, is an acknowledged connoisseur. I particularly recall that this was the first time I ever tasted compote of politicians' promises with a cynicism coulis. My enjoyment was, however, somewhat dampened by those shrewd eyes, which fixed themselves on my every move and facial gesture. Our amiable chat about Hellish affairs in general was merely a polite prelude, and it was not until we had retired to the library and were sipping vintage acrid feminism that Blubwarp sniffed the pungent bouquet appreciatively and stared at me across the rim of his glass.

"In your letter you spoke of your – what was the precise phrase? – 'master plan'."

I took a fortifying gulp of the wine and began the speech I had practised over and over again. "What I have in mind", I said, "is a solo undercover operation, which will make a significant contribution to the war effort."

"Go on," Blubwarp said, in a tone of manifest dubiety.

"Well, the infuriating foe we're up against claims to know everything."

"He *does* know everything!" he snapped, in a sudden change of mood. "If you haven't learned that, your education has been wholly wasted."

I took a quick sip of wine and pressed on under the old devil's unblinking gaze. "But has that ever been put to the ultimate test?"

"What kind of nonsensical question is that?"

It took all my nerve to stick to the plan I had conceived.

17

"What I am suggesting is not nonsensical, Your Awfulness. Bold, certainly, but not nonsensical. I think I know how to lay a smokescreen that will confuse the enemy for long enough to enable us to launch an important attack, unseen."

Falteringly at first but with mounting passion, I outlined my plan. My host did not interrupt and when my galloping eloquence eventually slithered to a halt he merely sat back in his armchair with a long-drawn-out "Hmm".

In the silence that followed I could almost hear the cogs whirring inside his bulbous head. Eventually he said, "If you have done your research properly you will know that the enemy keeps a very close watch on the leaders of human affairs. It takes much more experience than you have to gain access."

"Yes, but… "

Blubwarp halted me with an impatient wave of his hand. "You will know from your research how apparently foolproof schemes can come unstuck. Take the shocking Judas Iscariot affair. That is one of the most shameful episodes in our history. Everything seemed to be going so well. A public holiday had even been announced throughout Hell in celebration of our victory. Then it turned out that the enemy was fully aware of our stratagem and had actually turned it to his own advantage. Many heads rolled over that." He glared at me and I could see the flames dancing in his eyes.

"Heads rolled, young Crumblewit, heads rolled. Think on that. I, for one, intend to keep my head firmly in place. I have no intention of risking it by aiding and abetting the hare-brained scheme of an overambitious junior devil."

My balloon had been well and truly pricked and I was, as you can imagine, shattered. All I could think of was to mumble my thanks for the lunch and make my escape. I rose to my feet with whatever dignity I could muster and had just opened my mouth to make my farewells when Blubwarp spoke again.

"Sit down!" he snapped. "I have not finished. I said I would not be connected with an *overambitious* junior devil. However, if a level-headed and intelligent young tempter able to control his zeal... " He sat back in his chair and closed his eyes. There was another long silence. It was almost as though he had succumbed to that odd state humans call "sleep". Then, "Arspissble," he murmured.

"Sorry, Supreme Deviousness, I didn't quite catch... "

"I said, 'the art of the possible'. It was an aphorism of one of my best subjects, Otto von Bismarck. He lapped up the thoughts I put into his mind so completely that he became one of the leaders of human society – a master of betrayal and subtlety. Oh, the wars he started! The souls he hastened on their way to our dominion! He had a short way with the kind of idealism the enemy likes to encourage. 'Politics', he said, 'has nothing to do with justice, or helping the poor, or creating a society in which individuals can develop freely. It's the art of the possible.' In other words, it's about compromise between good and evil in the interests of whomever happens to be in power. Oh, yes, I did an excellent job with Bismarck."

"You are a master... "

"Of course I am! And you do well to seek my guidance. Now, as it happens, I could use... that is to say... I could help your career – on two conditions."

"Anything you say, Abysmal Awfulness… "

"Number one, you agree to be guided by me. Number two, no one must ever know of our professional connection. If you are ever questioned about this meeting it was purely an example of my well-known encouragement of young tempters. You will not contact me again."

Of course, I agreed readily to the minister's terms. And, of course, I was determined to break free of his tutelage at the earliest possible opportunity.

A few moments later Blubwarp dismissed me, and it was some time before I heard from him again. Then a letter arrived by special SSS 666 courier with "Top Secret" stamped all over it. It summoned me to a special briefing at a secure location somewhere in the Lower Depths. I was to place myself in the hands of the courier, who would arrange transport.

"Kidnap" would have been a better word. Two more SSS 666 agents appeared. They blindfolded me and, for good measure, thrust me into a sack. There followed a long and bumpy journey before I was finally released in a featureless, windowless room. Its only furniture consisted of a table and two chairs. In one of them sat an emaciated, grey, lizard-like devil whose skin emitted a pungent smoke. He glared at me for several seconds after the door had been closed behind me.

"Sit," he said eventually.

When I had taken my place opposite him, he continued, "You are nothing. Who are you?"

"Crumblewit, Sir," I faltered.

"Are you deaf?" I was stunned by the thunderous bellow that came from his spare frame. "I said, 'You are nothing.' Now, who are you?"

"I... I am nothing," I mumbled.

"Good. I am Instructor. We do not use names here. The enemy has infinite resources. We can never be sure that even here, deep in Hell, he has not planted listening devices. So anonymity is the first rule."

Of the period that followed I can, for obvious reasons, report nothing. The training was hard and thorough. I learned invaluable lessons in infiltration techniques. However, I must make one thing clear: the career plan which I subsequently executed so brilliantly was utterly mine, MINE, and don't you forget it! Pay no attention to the jealous talk of devils whose niggardly achievements are shown up by my brilliant successes. Hell would be a better place if these disruptive elements concentrated their efforts on teaching humans how to envy, backbite, and criticize, instead of wasting their abysmal talents on each other.

Those weeks in the Lower Depths were very useful. They enabled me to refine my strategy, but I had already worked out my objective – had even set my sights on specific targets. The instructors in the Lower Depths were able to advise on the "How" but I was already very clear about the "What".

In keeping with the plan outlined to Minister Blubwarp, the first thing I had to do was disappear. Crumblewit would have to be destroyed.

* * * * *

CHAPTER 2

Manipulating a Preacher and a Politician

(1944–1948)

Thanks to Blubwarp's behind-the-scenes activity, my first assignment was to a suitable young male subject. He was an intelligent (by human standards) mortal who enjoyed intellectual debate. As a soldier in that world war I have mentioned, he faced so many delightful horrors that he was forced to ask fundamental questions. The prospect of church leaders on both sides in the military conflict praying for the success of their armies and insisting that they were meting out death and devastation in the name of the unmentionable one made it difficult for my subject, like most thinking people, to discern the ultimate realities behind the miseries we were unleashing on the world. When he emerged into civilian life he found himself in company with contemporaries who were disillusioned. Some of his friends were pseudo-Christians who had been well tutored by their assigned tempters into "progressive" interpretations of the enemy's designs. These pedlars of fashionable theology could produce only slick, facile answers to the questions my subject was asking. All in all, therefore, my assignment was an easy one.

This was altogether an exciting period for probationary tempters – deceptively exciting. The pickings were easy and Hell experienced a bonanza of men and women who had either dedicated themselves to evil lives or been distracted from pursuing the paths of goodness. Many devils of my generation launched successful careers during those brief years, only to discover later that the battle against our adversary is never that easy. They were unprepared for his counter-attacks, unlike myself. I had more important things in mind than the easy capture of one soul.

The first step in my plan was to *fail*. I had to let my subject be captured by the enemy and then make lamentable efforts to induce him to relinquish his faith. I had to make a series of elementary blunders which would convince the agents of the unmentionable one that little Crumblewit was a bungler who had learned nothing from his education and who suffered the ultimate humiliation of seeing his subject snatched from his grasp by death and welcomed into the enemy's realm. I need not go into the details of my "bungling". Suffice it to say that my subject was lured into Christian faith by enemy agents and, soon afterwards, died in a road accident. My incompetence was well publicized and I was ultimately summoned before the Retribution Tribunal. The sentence was in no doubt: destruction. Crumblewit ceased to exist.

I don't mind admitting that it was an uncomfortable experience. The taunts I suffered from the likes of Sharfly-

Bickendrop were scarcely supportable. I became the laughing stock of the junior devils. They were delighted to see the brilliant Crumblewit brought down. And what a performance I put on for their entertainment! I grovelled. I pleaded. I made excuses for myself. I threw the blame onto others. But all the time it was I who was enjoying the charade. For I knew what those addle-brained idiots did not. While they stumbled along notching up petty victories but never successfully evading the enemy's intelligence system, "Poor Crumblewit", by seeming to disappear, had got under the enemy's radar. As far as all Hell and the other place knew, I was no more. That meant that I had become a free agent. I was answerable only to "Z", the head of SSS 666, who, apart from Blubwarp, was the only one who knew of my secret existence. In the aftermath of the global war I travelled widely, seeking situations which could be turned to advantage in our long-term strategy. The planet was in a delightful state of chaos and the humans were making an excellent job of maintaining confusion and suspicion between and within countries without our direct intervention. However, I understood the enemy's tactics too well to become complacent. He has this tiresome habit of winning insignificant people to his cause and then propelling them into positions of leadership in governments and churches, where they work unceasingly to promote peace, justice, and concord. Well, two can play at that game. I decided to use an insignificant human to achieve a major shift in the affairs of the planet.

The person I groomed to be the spearhead of my attack was the pastor of a small-town church in the Mid-West of the United States of America. When I found him he was a drearily conventional minister with a nauseating veneer of humility. I say "veneer" because it was a pose he assumed, unconsciously, to cover frustration at his own failure. His moderately large congregation had not grown in size or energy for several years. They were satisfied with his preaching and contributed cheerfully to his maintenance. A lesser devil would have concluded that his little bunch of turgid Christians could be left well alone. They were doing us no harm and were certainly not advancing the enemy's cause. But I realized there was potential here. This minister, Pastor Bratt (his hatred of his own name was something I was able to use to great effect, as I will explain later), was seething with ambition. He longed to be what he called "more effective for the Lord". It was a desire the unmentionable one's agents might well have exploited, if I had not beaten them to it.

By suggesting to him courses of action that any of the enemy's agents might have promoted, I induced him to lower his guard. First of all I drew his attention to radio evangelists. These rabid spouters of the enemy's propaganda were a nuisance to us because they were able to get their sick-making message into every home to which their networks had access. Some of our colleagues had managed to use the novel phenomenon of radio (just as they more effectively used television years later) by insinuating into the preaching slots religious charlatans, who used their air time to make energetic appeals for money. Only I saw that the medium of radio could be used even more effectively. I induced Little Bratt into spending more and more time listening to the radio evangelists. I got him to analyse their techniques and then try them out in his own pulpit. It was not long before he was paying more attention to the method than to the message. He would practise his delivery over and over again, often standing before a mirror. He filled notebooks with anecdotes. He even attended a drama course at a nearby university. The result was all that I could have wished. His fame spread. Within a year he had trebled his congregation – not with people who wanted to worship the unmentionable one, but with people eager to hear this "performer", who was, by now, calling himself "Pastor Jim" (so much more appealing, as I pointed out to him, than "The Reverend Bratt"!).

My clever incognito had achieved its objective and, by the time the enemy realized that he had been duped, it was too late. When his enemy's agents *did* grasp what was going on, they naturally fought back, but even then they had no conception of the daring scheme taking shape in my brilliant mind. For months I had quite a battle on my hands. Pastor Jim had not entirely lost sight of the purpose for which our unspeakable foe had appointed him. However, I was able to fill the preacher's mind with other concerns, such as using the money that was pouring in to design and build a new church. I had a major triumph when my subject was offered a regular preaching slot on one of the radio networks. *Pastor Jim's Hour* rapidly gained in popularity. He was becoming a national celebrity. It was time to put phase two into operation.

Apocalyptic speculation about the enemy's plans for the end of the world has always served us well. It seems to me that the enemy made a tactical blunder when he announced that he would return to earth in person to engage with us in a final battle, from which he and his cohorts would emerge victorious. Sheer bravado! I suppose he wanted to convince his supporters that, whatever difficulties they were facing, they were on the winning side. Well, as an example of inspirational pep talk it was certainly flawed, and we have been able to exploit its weakness. The enemy was vague about when this "last battle", this Armageddon, would take place. He even warned his cannon fodder not to speculate about it. So, of course, that's exactly what we frequently persuade them to do. We have, over the human centuries, convinced thousands of the enemy's followers that they are prophets to whom details of earth's end have been revealed. I decided to make Little Bratt my prophet.

He was becoming daily more malleable. As letters (many containing donations) poured into his "office" (a spacious suite of rooms whose furnishings alone cost more than most of his supporters earned in a year), thanking him for his inspiration and help, and as his staff of sycophantic acolytes grew, Little Bratt convinced himself that he was in a privileged relationship with the unspeakable one. It never dawned on him that I had almost completely jammed the enemy's channel of communication. He was ready to become the private audience for one of my better performances.

One of the elementary lessons we all learn in tempter school is to keep our subjects busy. The more time they devote to the trivia of their petty lives, the less time they have for contact with the enemy. Little Bratt was, by now, becoming totally obsessed with running his growing organization. He frequently grabbed his meals between meetings, worked into the early morning hours, and took breakfast at his desk. One delightful side effect of all this was growing friction between LB (as I shall now call him) and his wife. Mrs LB complained that her husband was more interested in his work than in his marriage, and he responded by telling her that she was being used by Satan to deflect him from "the Master's work". Oh, the delicious irony of that! It was me the self-righteous fool was working for, and I was grooming him for one world-changing performance.

For several months I steered LB down the apocalyptic blind alley (my specialist knowledge of the enemy's manual was invaluable here). At last I saw that he was ready for an impressive "revelation". I chose a time when he was involved in a particularly exhausting whistle-stop tour of several American cities. One night he was on a long train journey and tossing and turning in his berth in the sleeping compartment. I went to my costume trunk and took out a shimmering white robe and a beatific mask. By the way, I *do* recommend these facial disguises. They are available from Central Demonic Supplies (CDS), and are vital to any demon attempting the full-frontal "angel of light" routine. It is an aggravating fact that no amount of make-up or expression training can achieve for us a fully convincing transformation. We can never quite replicate the disgustingly joyful smiles, the grimaces of love, or the penetrating stare of genuine sympathy the enemy's agents can turn on. In fact, only the most experienced tempters should essay vision deception. If it goes wrong, the results can be disastrous. Subjects have actually been lost to us by overambitious devils who appeared to humans in unconvincing disguise. The seraph with a squint, the archangel with an uncontrollable leer may actually be regarded as figures of fun. Their appearance may be put down to too much cheese at last night's dinner or the after effects of a scary television film. Worse than that, such ill-prepared charades may cause alarm and send subjects rushing back to the enemy in a frenzy of grovelling repentance. My own performance for the benefit of LB was, of course, well rehearsed and faultless.

As the train rattled and jolted through the night, I entered his jumbled dreams in my radiant guise and solemnly announced, "New Israel is my stepping stone!" Some humans love riddles. It can be very useful to present them with enigmas to unravel. They then get caught up in the question, "What does this mean?" and overlook the question, "Is this true?" Just to nudge LB in the right direction, I added, "When this stone is laid I will come quickly." Then I vanished. It was a cameo performance, but quite brilliant.

I do not expect you, attentive reader, to understand the long-term strategy of which this was a vital part. I must, therefore, describe the international background of the times so that you may appreciate just how wide-ranging and devious my campaign planning was. I certainly was not deploying all my skill and labour in grabbing the miserable soul of one self-important little preacher.

All this time, in the troubled aftermath of that world war I told you about, one bone of contention between leading politicians was Palestine, a small but strategically important region ruled by various Arab groups. It was vital to the major world economies to remain on good terms with the Arab nations because some of them were rich in crude oil, on which their industry and commerce depended. Right in the middle of this region there was a newly founded state – Israel. Yes, the name sends a shudder down the spine, does it not? Through much of human history Israel has been the enemy's favourite people. He chose this insignificant tribe as his fifth column in order to subvert our sovereignty, and the Israelis (or Jews) have been a constant irritant to us for generations. You will not need me to remind you of the heroic battles we have fought to exterminate these pests. For lengthy periods they controlled Palestine. Time and again we raised up other nations to throw them out but always they wormed their way back again. Not long after the Golgotha debacle we launched a major counter-attack against the enemy and his little Jewish darlings, using the Romans, a powerful, militant people who dominated the region. We tore the heart out of Israel, destroying its worship centres and killing or driving into exile most of the people. That should have been the end of them. But no! Despite all we could do by stirring up the hatred and resentment of other nations, we could not obliterate these pestilential "chosen people". Time and again we launched campaigns which appeared to succeed, but always the unmentionable one protected them. Even a vast anti-Jewish purge throughout Germany and its European empire by one of our human champions, the dictator Hitler, failed. He exterminated millions of Jews and fanned the embers of race hatred into a blaze, but the long-term result was a backlash of sympathy for the "victims of oppression". It was as though there was an invisible wall around them. While other nations were busy with war, the , the "chosen people" sneaked back into Palestine and set up a new nation state.

This created a dilemma for the world's political leaders. Should Israel be officially recognized or not? The problem was particularly acute for the United States of America. It had a large and vociferous Jewish population but its economy was dependent on copious supplies of oil and it could not afford to alienate the Arab world. The government was divided. There were bitter arguments and threats of ministerial resignation. Here in Hell the infernal Low Command were scarcely less divided. It was clear that, whatever the USA decided, most other countries would follow. So, what influence should our tempters be instructed to exert? The old guard, who could not see farther than their snouts, were all for continuing the Jewish exile. They had learned nothing from the history of our long struggle with the enemy over this issue. They persisted in believing that, given time, his "chosen race" would disappear – dispersed among the nations and culturally absorbed. Fools! While they and the progressives in infernal government argued, I put my long-prepared plan into action. And that was where LB came in.

His "beatific vision" had convinced him that the re-establishment of a Jewish state in Palestine was a sign of the imminent "end of the age". It sent him scurrying to the Bible to discover support for this dramatic revelation. He wrenched words out of context to prove that the enemy was about to return to launch Armageddon and that the establishment of a new Israel was part of his plan. LB then set about preaching this with vigour. The result could scarcely have been more gratifying. His congregations were seized with apocalyptic frenzy. His radio audience doubled in size within weeks. He was called on for interviews in the national and international press. Magazine features hailed him as "America's new prophet".

All this had a political impact, as I had known it would. Yet even I did not anticipate what happened next. I was all prepared to get LB and his supporters to lobby their representatives in government on behalf of Israel. But there was no need. My subject actually received a summons from a close confidant of the current president. The head of state was under pressure from all sides. His advisers were divided over whether or not Israel should be recognized. And he had to make a decision quickly. Naturally, it all came down to domestic politics: which policy would be the more popular. That was why he took a personal interest in LB and sent his aide to discover how much support the preacher enjoyed.

Most humans are overawed by authority. We have done our work well over the centuries. We have conditioned them to confuse greatness with power. Successful leaders are those who are regarded by their supporters as little gods who can do no wrong. For this reason PR machines provide them with superhuman images. Some rulers have even claimed that they are the personal representatives of the unmentionable one. Little Bratt had no such illusions because the self-important fool was in the grip of a stronger illusion. I had firmly planted in his mind that *he* was the spokesman of our enemy, and entrusted with giving clear instructions to the president of the United States of America. He was taken to meet the designated intermediary at a secret location and they talked together for fifteen minutes. However, it was not a conversation. The aide found himself on the receiving end of a fervent LB sermon. It was all very amusing – though I was anxious that LB might have overplayed his hand. The last thing I wanted was for him to antagonize the nation's leaders. But all ended satisfactorily; only a few hours later the president of the world's most powerful state declared that the USA would recognize the state of Israel. What a moment of personal triumph for Crumblewit!

Do I need to explain my long-term strategy? Surely not. The subsequent history of Palestine and the surrounding area has fully justified my actions. At the time there was much wrangling in the Low Command. Three ministers were dismissed from office and disposed of in the usual way for their failure to have Israel removed from the world map. None of our leaders were as far-sighted as I was. Of course, when they saw the continuous warfare into which Palestine and its neighbours were thrown and the conflicts which inevitably drew in all the leading nations, they fell over themselves to take the credit for not preventing the establishment of Israel. We have been able to foment an extremely agreeable atmosphere of hatred that has led to wars, massacres, assassinations, diplomatic confrontations, failed peace talks, and suicide bombings.

Even more personally satisfying to me was LB's gradual realization of his error. There was a patriotic American backlash within his organization – small at first, but growing in size and vigour as the promised Armageddon did not happen. I was able to sit back and enjoy the spectacle of LB's increasing agony of doubt. His health broke down and he aged rapidly. I looked forward to welcoming him here and showing him just how I had encompassed his downfall.

I could not possibly have known that the enemy would sneak in and upset everything just when LB was at his lowest ebb. When a fellow Christian minister offered him "counselling", I took little notice. The next thing I knew was that LB was wallowing in repentance and begging the enemy's forgiveness. Of course, he received it – the intellectual flabbiness of the unmentionable one never ceases to amaze me! The most devoted follower of our own great leader has only to turn to the enemy and say "Sorry" and the turncoat is welcomed with open arms. Such a pathetic, disgusting spectacle! So, yes, I know what you are thinking: I let LB slip through my fingers. Well, the reality is that this incident was not a defeat; it was a tactical withdrawal. LB had served me well. His defection was a small price to pay for all the havoc he had caused.

* * * * *

CHAPTER 3

Siege Warfare

(1949–1956)

After such a high-profile triumph it was necessary for me to lie low for a while. My cover had, of course, been blown, and enemy agents were assigned to keeping an eye on me. There was no question of my rushing into a new assignment.

Z allocated me a guest house on his Nethereach estate, where I had access to his fine, extensive library. As far as any other devil or Heavenly snoop knew, I was now employed as a member of the SSS 666 research team gathering archive information about holy sinners – those who have left the enemy's camp to wander down the pathways of "religion".

This is a fascinating and a fruitful area of study. It reveals the many and varied ways in which Christians can be deflected from their allegiance by becoming absorbed in peripheral matters. There are schismatics who excommunicate one another over minor points of doctrine. There are ritualists who draw attention to themselves by dressing in gorgeous robes, genuinely believing that the tawdry elements of earthly colour and form bear some resemblance to that unspeakably eye-searing radiance which prevents any of us from ever getting a clear look at the enemy. Then there are the philosophers. Being a scholar myself, I particularly enjoy the philosophers. How they love to define the indefinable! How they squabble over the minutiae of their own ignorance! And all because they have been duped by us into believing that what they call "reason" or "logic" can grasp the realities of eternity. The enemy made a real tactical blunder when he equipped humans with brains and the freedom to use them in whatever ways took their fancy. This is a weakness we can exploit constantly.

The choicest delight of Nethereach is Z's menagerie. He keeps a fascinating collection of tortured souls in his grounds and their remorseful, self-pitying writhings are a never-ending source of pleasure. How they squirm and slither over the arid ground of their enclosure, shrinking with terror when one approaches. An even greater source of enjoyment, however, is observing them from the hides Z has constructed. The way they behave towards each other when they think no devils can see them is a highly entertaining spectacle, and also instructive. It was while watching a furious fight between the souls of an atheist academic and a liberal theologian that I began to formulate the plan for my next audacious exploit. Their conversation, before they flew at each other with fists and clawing fingers, went something like this:

LT: I told you, time and time again, that humanity was made for more than terrestrial existence.

AA: Well, that knowledge hasn't done *you* much good, has it?

LT: I'm here because of an administrative blunder. I shall appeal, of course.

AA: Appeal? Huh! After all the damage you did to the church on earth, what makes you think you're a special case?

LT: I devoted my life to helping Christians make sense of their religion. I worked hard to strip away the accretions of superstition.

AA: Superstition? You mean the resurrection and such like?

LT: I always believed – and taught – that resurrection was a spiritual concept. Clearly, there was rather more to it than that. You rubbished the whole schema of Christian faith. Don't accuse *me* of undermining the church.

AA: Faith? That was a closed-minded, emotional response to certain propositions put forward by your spiritual ancestors. I proposed a logical counter-argument. I see, now, that I was somewhat mistaken... I...

LT: Somewhat? Oh, I wish I could still laugh! How many Christians abandoned their belief as a result of reading your books?

AA: Very few. My attacks stirred lots of them to explore their beliefs more carefully or simply to go on the defensive.

LT: Posing now as a champion of Christian truth, are you? You hypocrite!

AA: Why, you religious fraudster! I'll show you who's a hypocrite!

LT: Intellectual poseur!

AA: Pious popinjay!

LT: Idiot!

It really was a delicious spectacle. But it set me to thinking.

In the aftermath of war there was a brief resurgence of Christianity in the victor nations. Of course, we had made enormous strides during the years of conflict. Not only were millions of souls projected into eternity, quite unprepared for what lay before them, but we had sown widespread hatred, fear, and suspicion, which would fester for years.

However, not everything was beautifully black. The enemy was soon observed to be sowing his despicable seeds among the rubble and ashes and shell holes. I'm not referring to the obvious bravery and self-sacrifice which are the unfortunate concomitants of war. The humans had a passion to, as their leaders put it, "build a better world". Nauseating ideas such as "international cooperation" and "a fairer society" were bandied about. That would not have been so bad if the churches had not also been inspired by the same spirit of reconstruction and reconciliation. There were many in the Low Command who believed that the destruction and dislocation we had created would sweep away all vestiges of Christianity. I never fell for this simplistic analysis. Major disasters always provoke some humans into asking questions, to wonder why such "terrible" things happen, and even – ugh! – to pray. Honest doubt is always dangerous to us, but when it leads to serious enquiry and prayer, well, that lets the enemy's agents into their minds. They may become victims of his brainwashing.

Anyway, in the years after the conflict the enemy's churches actually grew. Families eagerly attended their weekly meetings. It was quite common for them to gather twice every Sunday and also on weekday evenings to be willingly subjected to the unmentionable one's propaganda. Then he brought out his big guns. Every so often throughout the human centuries, just when things are going nicely our way he unleashes a massive counter-attack. The Christians call it "revival". It is always associated with one or more forceful orators, persuasive goody-goody poseurs who hold mass rallies and persuade many people to think about their eternal destiny. Some of these "evangelists" have been guilty of undoing years of patient work on our part. We skilfully build walls around our subjects' minds, brick by brick – family preoccupations, business responsibilities, pursuit of wealth, worship of celebrities, pleasure seeking, etc., etc. Then, one rousing speech by some nauseatingly sincere evangelist turns our ramparts into so much rubble. The "converts" see clearly for the first time – and, infuriatingly, often see more clearly than we do.

All this calls for new strategies on our part. It was no use trying to stop the enemy's ranting rabble-rousers. If we raised up critics to engage them in open debate or used the humans' new toy of television to challenge the revivalists, their followers would only become more aware of the spiritual warfare we are constantly waging and would regard such attacks as proof that they were in the thick of the cosmic battle.

The need was for a quieter, more gradualist approach to the problem – siege warfare. If new churches were being founded and old ones revitalized, we had to employ every possible tactic to destroy them or, at least, sap their energy. We needed to undermine their spiritual ramparts, poison their theological wells, block the supply lines the enemy used to provision them, and detect unguarded postern gates through which we might gain access to their citadels. The argument I had witnessed in the menagerie had shown me one way of infiltrating churches and weakening them from within, as I hastened to explain to Z as soon as I could obtain an appointment.

"It was a masterpiece of choreography to put those two intellectuals in the same compound," I told the intelligence master as I gazed up at his throne. Z's "office" consists of a series of platforms, arranged one above the other and surmounted by an ornate couch on which the master reclines, constantly attended by slave souls who minister to his needs. Those wishing to gain favour with him are assigned to one or other of the levels. Newcomers begin on the lowest platform and are subsequently promoted to or demoted from the higher stages. I had gained level 4 by this time, only two steps away from the summit. This meant that I could converse with Z without shouting above the babble of other devils who were also trying to be heard.

"You found it instructive?" he enquired.

"Oh, enormously. It was a brilliant juxtaposition. It has inspired me to see how I – er – *we* can render some of the enemy's more vigorous churches really ineffective."

"That sounds interesting," Z said in that deceptively languid tone of his. "Come up to level 5. Have an inquisitor."

As I stepped excitedly up to the next platform, one of Z's attendants held out a dish full of the master's favourite delicacies. The deliciously squirming, cringing souls huddled together on it were some of those who had exercised power in Christian churches and used it to enforce their own ideas. Some had employed naked threats backed by torture and execution. Others had simply relied on their own celebrity to establish what was or was not "sound" doctrine. Either way, Christians were discouraged from thinking for themselves and their direct channels of communication with the enemy were effectively blocked. I popped one of the scrumptious creatures into my mouth and savoured its astringent flavour as I outlined my plan.

I do not need to tell you how impressed Z was. He did not, of course, utter ringing congratulations, but I could tell from the fast, flickering glints in his eyes and the hisses bursting from his long snout that he admired my audacity and wished that he, himself, had come up with my brilliant plan. He had no amendments to suggest and when I left I had his backing and the promise of whatever resources I might require.

All new strategies are simply old strategies in modern dress. This is one of the key points I am always careful to make in my public lectures and it is important to stress it because many devils fret themselves into oblivion by trying to out-think the enemy. Fools! To imagine that the subtlest tempter can come up with an idea that has never occurred to the unspeakable one is the profoundest absurdity. Never forget that he is omniscient. To take him by surprise is virtually impossible. The masquerade which had launched my own career had been of short duration – as I had always calculated. The enemy is, of course, vulnerable. If we did not know this, His Supreme Lowness, Lord Satan, would long since have surrendered – and then where would we be? The chink in the revolting one's armour is his attachment to his human creatures, and they continually let him down. We all know the seven basic ways of undermining them: Anger, Sloth, Pride, Envy, Lust, Avarice, and Gluttony. These stout pillars have always supported our work and they will continue to do so until final victory is ours. Never despise tradition.

One of our most successful ploys has always been to take Christian truths and distort them. The enemy has laid down various ground rules for his fawning followers. He has caused them to be recorded in writing so that they can readily discern what they should believe, what they should do, how they should behave, and what they should aspire to. This writing, this Bible, is appallingly permanent. It is – it would be futile to deny it – the enemy's most effective weapon. We cannot destroy it. We cannot stop Christians reading it (filling their time with other activities is the best we can do in this regard). What we *can* do is distort their understanding of it.

This is where logic comes to our aid. Humans have developed this intellectual discipline to help them make sense of their existence. It is an imperfect tool manufactured by imperfect creatures, but it is important to them to prevent their minds from spiralling into chaos. It is, of course, one of our objectives to ensure that their minds *do* spiral into chaos.

The easiest way to achieve this with most of our subjects is to discourage them from thinking. If they apply their minds to unravelling what seem to them to be the "big issues" – "Why are we here?" "Is there a rational mind behind the universe?" "Is there life after death?" "Why do people suffer?" and so on – we can usually divert them by filling their minds with day-to-day trivia or convincing them that such things are far too profound for their tiny minds to cope with.[3]

With intellectuals we have to employ different tactics. The development of terrestrial science and technology depends largely upon the application of logic. The micro-biologist seeking a cure for cancer performs thousands of experiments, carefully noting the results of every one, comparing them, and making deductions based on the application of logical principles. He observes the effects of a particular drug on a malignant cell. He repeats the observation. He concludes that the effects are invariable. He deduces that the drug is efficacious. He announces to his peers his "proof" that the drug can slow or prevent the multiplication of specific types of cancer cell. Logic serves many purposes the humans find valuable. It has always been a major plank of our strategy to make them think that logic has universal application; that it is the answer to everything; that it can rule their lives; that it is, in effect, a god. Ever since what their philosophers call the "Enlightenment" we have successfully induced many of

---

3 Because this is a simple path for tempters to follow, I must issue a warning against complacency. When we have created a vacant mind in a subject we should not assume that the subject can be safely left to his or her own devices. The enemy is just as capable of filling a vacuum as we are. It takes only a personal tragedy, an "inexplicable" act of kindness, a direct challenge by a Christian friend, or simply the overwhelming impact of a beautiful flower or a star-filled sky on a frosty night to oil the mental cogs and set them turning. The enemy has a myriad ways of revealing himself to his creatures. Be constantly on your guard.

their leading thinkers to believe, like the micro-biologist, that everything can be, as it were, put under the microscope and either "proved" or "disproved". It really is hilarious to observe their arrogance.

It was while watching the theologian and the atheist clawing and screaming at each other that I came to a clearer understanding of what I now call "logic lust". Both of them, I realized, had, in their terrestrial lives, been affected by this same disorder. They had both placed Christianity under their philosophical microscope. One had disproved it; the other had disproved parts of it and had tried to change it into an intellectually respectable philosophy. Which of these two, I asked myself, had been more use to us? The answer was not difficult to deduce. As the atheist himself had pointed out, his challenge had raised the issue of Christian teaching in many minds and provoked believers and non-believers into examining his claims. Of course, some had been "impressed" by his arguments, particularly when they came dressed up in the trendy garb of prevailing fashion. Many humans, thanks to our efforts, find religion – any religion – distasteful and are only too ready to believe that the atheists have rendered it intellectually untenable. However, when a clear challenge is thrown down, the opportunity is given to Christian apologists to take it up and they can be just as compelling in their arguments as their opponents. For this reason, stirring up religious controversy seldom does us any favours. Scarcely a human decade goes by without some ardent non-believer producing the "definitive" book which will, once and for all, put an end to "religious nonsense". Numerous Christian apologists then rush into print to expose the weak methodology of the exposer. The end result is that few genuine believers have their faith shattered, while many people are prompted to enquire seriously into the enemy's claims, and that can do no end of damage.

You see, the ice upon which the atheist skates is deceptively thin. The assumption that all human experience can be subjected to logical analysis is absurd, and it really should not be as easy as it is for us to keep them from seeing it. The humans are not mere walking brains. They have emotions, aesthetic sensibilities, and intuition. Their poets, painters, musicians, and architects, their mystics, martyrs, and self-sacrificing humanitarians have provided intimations of our enemy's existence which are more eloquent than the atheists' "proofs" of his non-existence. No, we get on far better when we work within the Christian church. A fallen saint or an ardent heretic is much more use to us than a gifted humanist scholar.

With this in mind I set out in search of a Christian philosopher who could be developed into a weapon for a major attack on some of our enemy's strongholds. It occurred to me that I could employ tactics similar to those that had proved so effective in my Little Bratt campaign. Someone widely accepted as a talented Christian scholar could be used to work against the church from within. While atheists battered the ramparts, my fifth columnist would open up postern gates for us to infiltrate the citadel.

It took a long time to discover the right tool for the job but at last I tracked him down at a British provincial university. Dr Xavier Oliphant, widely known as "XO" and, to his intimates, as "Brandy", was a theology faculty lecturer with a considerable student following, particularly among the females of that species. He was tall, raffish, and well below middle years. His lecture style was entertaining and contrasted sharply with the dry solemnity of his faculty colleagues, most of whom regarded him with mingled jealousy and disdain as a maverick showman. XO thrived on their criticism. What they dismissed as "flashy oratory" he defended as "making religion interesting and intellectually respectable". His often very public confrontations with more senior academics only enhanced his reputation among students and, beyond them, with Christians who regarded themselves as "liberal" and "progressive".

XO's lectures and seminars were very agreeable to behold. He had developed into an art form the mental bullying which only quick-witted academics can fully cultivate. His technique was to encourage debate among his tutees and then crush their arguments with devastating one-liners. Young people struggling to understand our enemy's deplorable activities and clinging to traditional doctrines were accused of "walking in other men's worn-out shoes". They were challenged to engage in "joined-up thinking". *Joined-up Thinking* was, in fact, the title of XO's first attempt at a "popular theology" book. Its debunking of such "myths" as creation, virgin birth, and resurrection showed great promise. However, it failed to reach a mass market because it was little more than XO's tidied-up lecture notes. I now got to work on him by encouraging his belief in his own literary gifts and by putting him in contact with someone who could help him market his ideas.

Lydia Ames-Benson was the person I had in mind. Since leaving university some ten years earlier she had entered publishing and gone, with equal rapidity, through a succession of jobs and "relationships". By the way, we must always be grateful to our linguistics department for coming up with that superbly deceptive word, "relationship". It enables us to convince men and women that their casual, short-term liaisons are grounded not on the gratification of basic, selfish interests, but on genuine mutual care. They seldom do actually *relate* to one another by merging needs, desires, and identities, but as long as we can keep the idea in their minds that they are "in a relationship" we prevent them from exploring that nauseating, self-giving affection that the enemy really wants them to feel for each other.

By the time I added Ms Ames-Benson to my portfolio she had forsaken the hurly-burly of publishing and set herself up as a private literary agent. Her client base consisted originally of well-known authors she had lured away from their previous representatives, and she was slowly adding to it by taking on a handful of lady novelists and biographers who shared her own aggressively feminist views. *Joined-up Thinking* would, I knew, appeal to her sophisticated non-religion and I made sure that her attention was drawn to it by a fellow guest at a dinner party. She acquired a copy and began to read it. Then, when my back was turned, she grew bored with it and left it at the bottom of a pile of more "promising" volumes.

Of course, I did not give up the campaign after one disappointing skirmish. I determined to bring Ms A-B and XO face to face. XO's publishers were arranging an anniversary party to which they were inviting all their authors, and I knew that Ms A-B would be there, stalking new prey. My task was twofold: I had to persuade XO to make the journey to London for the event and to ensure that Ms A-B was in the right frame of mind to be attracted to my subject and his ideas.

The lady was very malleable. Having been brought up by over-indulgent parents, she had always been accustomed to having her own way and to being intolerant of the needs, desires, and opinions of others. Setting in train the break-up of her current relationship was easy – a trainee tempter could have accomplished it. An argument over whose turn it was to buy the groceries turned into a slanging match – and goodbye partner number four. I followed this by inducing in her a mood of angry self-pity. Then I engineered a "chance" encounter with an old friend who happened to be a Christian. This zealous follower of the enemy listened to Ms A-B as she poured out her resentment of her latest lover and the male sex in general. In response she blundered in with an invitation to hear Jimmy Aldwich preach.

I must explain at this point that Britain was being plagued by an epidemic of evangelists. Most of them were Americans who arrived with large entourages, organizing slick, well-funded campaigns. They attracted hundreds, sometimes thousands, of people to their rallies and, for a few years, they did considerable damage. Individuals were won over to the enemy. Moribund churches were revitalized. The media could not ignore this phenomenon and Christianity became a high-profile talking point. We put up sophisticated commentators and comfortably ensconced church leaders to refute the simplistic message of the tub-thumpers and their emotionalistic appeals, but for the time being we could do little to extinguish the fires started by our unscrupulous adversary. In such circumstances it is advisable to play the waiting game. Religious revivals always peter out. Converts discover that the Christian path is not strewn with roses and that the unspeakable one makes heavy demands on his followers. What we have to do is sow disillusion and pick off the converts one by one.

Now, where was I? Ah yes, Ms A-B. There was no way such a smart, "modern" woman was going to fall prey to some "rabble-rousing Yankee", as she told her friend in no uncertain terms. She denounced her friend as a prig, departed abruptly, slamming the door behind her, and added all Christians to her hate list.

Getting XO to my planned rendezvous was not as easy. Teaching duties and faculty business kept him well occupied and his ambitions lay in the academic field more than in the popular market. He had set his sights on gaining a professorial chair and, with that in mind, had organized a lecture tour in the USA which threatened to clash with the publisher's party I wanted him to attend. I drew his attention to fellow academics who were using the press and the new medium of television to turn themselves into money-spinning "celebrities" (another word coined by our linguistics department), but all to no avail. When the day of his departure for America arrived it was obvious that I would have to resort to more drastic measures. His taxi had arrived and he was carrying a heavy suitcase downstairs when I zapped him with a momentary giddy spell. He tumbled to the foot of the staircase, sustaining concussion and a broken leg. The taxi driver summoned an ambulance and the result was that XO spent two days in hospital, was released with his leg in plaster, and was ordered to rest. Of course, he soon got bored with that. It was vacation time. His students and several of his university friends were away. It was now a simple task to persuade him that a trip to London would be an amusing diversion.

The party was, from my point of view, a roaring success. A personable, youngish man on crutches could not but be a centre of attention and XO found himself seated (I might almost say "enthroned") in a comfortable chair and plentifully plied with wine and nibbles by his solicitous hosts. He held court with great aplomb, his anecdotes of university life and his acerbic one-liners keeping his circle of hearers well amused. Ms A-B lost no time in thrusting herself into this circle and telling the raconteur that she had "absolutely adored" *Joined-up Thinking*. "So honest; so clear; so devoid of pseudo-religious claptrap; so timely," she enthused. By the end of the evening she and XO had exchanged cards and agreed to meet again.

When they did so a couple of weeks later it was to plan a theological book that would be "popular", "relevant", and "hard-hitting". Their plan was to commend Christianity to "intelligent men and women of the twentieth century". *My* plan was to distort the text into something bland, argued with clinical logic, and totally devoid of the mystery that, as we know, veils our adversary's designs. It was to be called *Yours Truly* and was to take the form of an apologia from the unmentionable one himself. Of course, from our perspective, the very idea of Heaven's plans being revealed in such a way is utterly absurd. If only we *did* know what the enemy really thinks and intends to do! Try as we might, his strategy remains obscure. We do not even know how long we have to bring the war to a successful conclusion. He has made vague threats about returning to earth with his whole army for a final showdown. We would certainly welcome that, for the victory would, undoubtedly, be ours. But, no, he resorts constantly to the infuriating tactics of minor battles, skirmishes, and guerrilla warfare.

The hours I spent with XO in his study and, frequently, as his companion in his non-working hours bore excellent fruit. He really had a fine literary talent and it was very enjoyable to turn it against the creator who had bestowed it upon him. As he dismantled some of the basic tenets of the enemy's belief system he really believed he was making it more accessible to "the man in the street". He saw himself as putting Christian doctrine through a fine sieve, which strained out all the elements of "superstition", "myth", and "tradition" which had rendered it unacceptable to "modern rationalists". What emerged from this process was a residue as harmless, tasteless, and ineffective as it was smooth. Had XO been as harshly critical of the philosophy of Kant and other thinkers of the Enlightenment as he was of the basic Christian writings, he might have made an unwelcome contribution to the application of Christian thought to contemporary problems. Fortunately, he had long since abandoned any such even-handedness. I had only to tweak his ideas in a few places to ensure that any vestiges of the enemy's so-called grand design were completely lost to sight.

Meanwhile Ms A-B was preparing the ground for the launch of *Yours Truly* onto the market. She cleverly whetted the appetites of publishers' marketing men by hinting that she had something exciting up her sleeve. She deployed to excellent effect those words media men love to hear: XO was a "new voice"; his ideas were "challenging" and "controversial"; they would "rattle the cages" of the religious establishment; they would "connect" with thinking people. Ms A-B understood well the importance of expectation. The substance of *Yours Truly* was secondary to the media hype which preceded it like a trumpeting herald. It did not matter what XO actually *said*; her responsibility was to titillate the publishers and, through them, the public. Humans like to be told what to think. They will, of course, always deny that fact, but fact it is. Just as they slavishly follow fashions in dress and music, so they lap up avant-garde ideas. Tell them that a new novel is a "bestseller" and they will rush to buy it. Persuade them that a new philosophy is "hip", "trendy", or "cool" and they will eagerly embrace it.

With a book deal in place and the manuscript almost ready for delivery, I grew nervous. At any moment I expected the enemy's counter-attack. It was unlike him to see his propaganda being undermined without doing anything to stop it. However, the publication process went through smoothly. *Yours Truly* was well publicized. There was an impressive launch at a London church. XO gave interviews on television and radio. And all this was followed up with an agreeably heated television debate between the author and a bishop, which almost turned into a slanging match. As a result, sales of *Yours Truly* were brisk. I had, I thought, every reason to be pleased with myself.

That was when I received a summons from Z, who demanded to know what in Hell's name I was playing at.

* * * * *

CHAPTER 4

A Narrow Escape

(1956–1958)

This time when I reported to Z's office I began on level 2. I had to share the platform with a crowd of shuffling, barging supplicants all trying to scramble upwards and push their neighbours down. Being well endowed with a strong frame and a slippery skin, I was successful in the contest and managed to kick and claw my way to level 4. There I managed to attract Z's attention.

"Ah, Crumblewit," he snarled, making his enunciation of my name sound particularly menacing. "You took your time."

"I came as fast as I could, Your Lowness," I grovelled.

"You've some explaining to do."

"I don't understand... Has someone been telling tales?"

"Do you think I need tittle-tattlers to keep me informed of what my agents are doing?"

"Of course not, Your Lowness."

"You recall our last meeting?"

"With clarity, Infernal Master."

"Did I, or did I not, describe to you in great detail a plan I had devised for sowing confusion among the enemy's followers?"

"You did," I conceded. Foolish, of course, to argue that it had been *my* idea.

"So why did you not execute it properly?"

"I did, I did! I swear I did!" Two of Z's guards were edging uncomfortably close. "I have had a book published distorting and contradicting several cherished items from the enemy's core curriculum. It will make many of his followers question what they really believe and convince others that a more rational and ineffective corpus of teaching is what the repulsive one actually intends."

"Fool!" he roared, and a half-chewed heretic fell from his slavering maw. "You underestimated our adversary. Did you really imagine he would sit back and do nothing?"

"I... I ... "

"Shut up and listen. I've had some of my best assessors following your progress, and what they report to me is slipshod planning and lack of foresight."

You can scarcely imagine my shock and bewilderment at this sudden reversal. How, I wondered, could Z possibly have formed such a distorted impression of my brilliance and my patient labours? Then it was that I caught sight of a familiar, smirking face among the small coterie of Z's darlings on level 6 – Sharfly-Bickendrop! Instantly all became clear. That talentless buffoon, Sharparse, had only ever fully mastered one aspect of the demonic craft: he understood well the cultivation of jealousy. He had obviously had the effrontery to practise his skill on Z. Doubtless, he had insinuated in our master the fear that I was a threat to his position. I can just hear his whining voice: "What a great asset young Crumblewit is, Your Lowness – so clever, so *ambitious*; obviously destined for great things." That would have been quite enough to turn the head of SSS 666 against me. He would then have set his "assessors" (Z's word for spies) on my trail and Sharparse would almost certainly have been one of them. There and then I vowed that Sharfly-Bickendrop would have to be dealt with – finally.

But vengeance would have to wait. Somehow I had to extricate myself from my present predicament. Z was still speaking.

"What did you hope to achieve by dismembering the Christians' sacred cows?"

That was a question I could easily answer! "It will make many of them doubt what they've been taught. When they become uncertain about what the enemy requires them to believe, their allegiance to him will quickly falter. Then, as they lapse, we will pick them off, one by one. Your Supreme Lowness will be aware that this is a tried and tested technique."

Z's eyes flamed and his voice roared. "Don't lecture me on demonic history. If you had one tenth of my understanding you would realize how decimating churches plays into the enemy's hands. When we remove immature Christians from their assemblies this leaves the remnant stronger. They band together more tightly and become even more convinced by Heaven's propaganda. They proclaim it with greater conviction and make thorough nuisances of themselves. We do far better to encourage churches which are made up of people who attend for a variety of reasons. That keeps them delightfully vague and wishy-washy."

"But I thought Your Abominableness approved this plan," I pleaded.

Z held up a claw to silence me and bent forward to hear something Sharfly-Bickendrop was obsequiously muttering.

"Hmm. Yes. Good idea. Listen to this, Crumblewit, and learn how we do things around here."

Sharparse slithered to the edge of the platform and leered down at me.

"Our sagacious master has placed me in charge of Operation Insipid," he began. "You must have heard of it. No? Ooh, my poor Crumblewit, you really are too much of a maverick, a loner." He beamed condescendingly. "Operation Insipid is part of a long-term strategy to knock out centres of enemy resistance in the European war zone. The Christians have been losing ground steadily since the major terrestrial conflict a dozen earth years ago but they still command several strongholds which the enemy keeps well supplied with weapons and other spiritual materiel. I won't go into detail about our counter-measures. You probably wouldn't understand; they lack the bravura and showy panache you go in for. We prefer results to self-glory."

If I could have reached the odious wretch I would have torn him to pieces. I contented myself with dissimulation. "I'd be fascinated to hear about your modus operandi," I said through clenched teeth. "I'm always ready to learn." I would allow Sharparse his moment of triumph; in the long term he would pay dearly for it.

"Our inspirational and clear-headed master has correctly revealed the weakness of your strategy," my foe continued. "We should not be removing ineffective religious people from the Christians' churches; we should be encouraging them to join and, having joined, to gain control. Let me give you a typical example."

It would be tedious in the extreme to record Sharparse's speech at length. He was inordinately fond of his own voice and the torrent of words that gushed forth from him amounted to – nothing. The "example" he chose to illustrate his own tactical brilliance was laughably mundane and insignificant. On a scale of originality of 1 to 10 it would have scored minus 5. I will relate the bare facts, and you can judge for yourself.

There was, somewhere on the south coast of England, an aggressively active Christian church. Its members were forever interfering in the local community – running youth clubs, visiting old people's homes, organizing missions, and making thorough nuisances of themselves. Just countering the activities of this one Christian community gobbled up enormous demonic resources.

But the demographic nature of the area was changing. As the country began to prosper, this pleasant stretch of coastline became a honeypot for wealthy retirees – bankers, military officers, property tycoons, and the like. Several of them joined the church. Sharparse absurdly took the credit for this influx of what he called the "G and T Brigade" (gin and tonic water is a beverage favoured by the British social elite). The newcomers transported their own urban and suburban culture to their new "colony", and church membership was one feature of it. Just as it was de rigueur to belong to the Conservative Party and the golf club, so supporting (and occasionally attending) the parish church was a distinguishing feature of the local elite.

Life now became very much easier for our agents. They were able to manoeuvre suitable people onto the church council and, through them, to "blandify" the tone set by the clergy. The existing vicar was their first major target. He was an effective propagandist (what the Christians call a "gifted preacher"), but the newcomers found his populist style vulgar and "emotional". As for his subject matter, some members of the congregation complained to the bishop that their vicar was obsessed with money being the root of all evil and was always insisting that the church should give away most of its income.

To cut a long story short, tempers flared, the church was divided, the new ruling clique used their friends in high places to get the vicar removed, and, when he left, several members of the church followed suit. "All", you might say, "very satisfactory." The trouble was that the insufferably smug Sharparse was trying to pass this activity off as brilliant new strategy. It was, of course, nothing of the sort. In that old classic *Distortion Tactics for Beginners* there is a whole chapter on dilution strategy. It was infuriating to see Z being taken in by a demon totally lacking vision. But, for the time being, I had to endure it.

"You see, Crumblewit," Z declared, with a congratulatory grunt at his latest darling, "infiltration not confrontation – that's the way to render the enemy's citadels ineffective."

I longed to point out that my plan and Sharparse's were not mutually exclusive. We were fighting a war on numerous fronts and each called for its own campaign plan. But I bit my tongue and allowed the pompous incompetent (as I now knew Z to be) to believe that he had browbeaten me into submission.

"I bow to Your Atrociousness's superior wisdom," I muttered.

Z hissed his pleasure. "So I should hope. Well, then, I am prepared to give you a second – and final – chance."

He turned to exchange a few words with one of his secretaries, who produced a thick dossier. This was handed down to me.

"Here is your new assignment," Z said. "Study it and follow your instructions — *to the letter*. None of your fanciful innovations. Don't imagine that any more of your maverick ideas will go unpunished. You may depart."

I turned to scramble down the levels. Z called after me, "One more thing: you will report regularly to Sharfly-Bickendrop."

It was some time before I had calmed down sufficiently to open the file and discover my new task. The first page bore a title in large, untidily scrawled letters: "Destroying the Ecumenical Movement". Of course, I knew a great deal about the pathetic attempts of several Christian churches around the globe to resolve the theological differences which had grown over the centuries in order to present us with a united opposition. However, for the benefit of readers who lack my grasp of human history I quote some passages from the dossier I had been handed. (By the way, you must not think that I had forgotten about or abandoned my work with XO and Ms A-B. It would have taken more than Z's threats to force me to relax my hold on them. More of this anon.)

The introduction to my dossier read as follows:

A clear indication that we have the enemy on the
run is the frantic effort he is making to bridge the
chasms we have painstakingly dug throughout
Christian history. We have ensured that his followers
devoted considerable energies to encasing in rigid
dogmas mysteries that human minds can never
embrace, let alone define with precision. Then we
have set them at war with each other in defence
of those dogmas. The gratifying result of this

brilliant strategy is thousands of denominations all calling themselves "Christian" and regarding each other with suspicion or hostility. This has been a win–win situation for us. Those within churches have been easy prey for tempters projecting hatred and exclusivity. Those outside the churches look at all the backbiting and mutual hostility and see no reason to go over to the enemy's camp. It has taken a drastic decline in church membership to alert Christian leaders to this situation and to make them heed – or even hear – the enemy's repeated calls for unity and treacly, saccharine "love".

The Low Command in their collective wisdom realized, of course, that our run of good luck could not last for ever and they developed contingency plans to deal with the situation that is now emerging. "Ecumenism" has become the new fad among the ecclesiastical top brass. An increasing number of leaders are calling for priority to be given to unity. Some have set up a monolithic organization they call the World Council of Churches. That is a grandiose title for a body which can certainly lay no claim to "world" status. Its core is the longer-established Protestant churches. That fact alone means that the Catholic Church wants nothing to do with it. This WCC represents only a couple of hundred Christian communities. At the same time individual churches, such as the Presbyterians, Methodists, and Anglicans, are engaging in their own private dialogues to discover doctrinal compromises which will enable them to patch up some sort of "brotherly" relationship.

Our response, as defined by the Low Command, is to keep the Christians at loggerheads. Resources have been earmarked (see Appendix B) for infiltrating the church bodies set up for ecumenical discussion in order to frustrate their endeavours. A deadline of ten earth years has been set to destroy all these initiatives and thus to demonstrate clearly that the enemy does not possess an organization capable of taking effective control of the planet.

I tossed the dossier aside in contempt. It had Sharparse's shallow reasoning and lack of imagination written all over it. His only answer to the question, "What should we do if a policy is not working?" was, "Pursue the same policy with more vigour." "Divide and rule" had been a major plank of our strategy against the churches for a very long time. It worked because tribalism comes easily to humans. It takes very little effort on our part to divide them into competing gangs, fighting one another on the basis of racial identity, national pride, political ideology, territorial ambition, or, as in this case, theological precision. We have always been able to keep many of the best Christian brains preoccupied with *definition*, encasing the enemy's unsearchable designs in doctrinal straitjackets. At least Sharparse had got that right. We in Hell do not know what our infuriatingly cryptic foe is up to and we are obliged to acknowledge the fact, but humans are obsessed with the desire to probe mysteries. This quest for truth is something our exasperating enemy has implanted in them.

Why? Why? Why? In the name of everything unholy, what is he up to? He could so easily have put a limit to their speculative ability. He could have stopped them wandering down pathways that lead only into the impenetrable forest of unknowing. But, no, he has given his little darlings the intellectual ability to combat most of the diseases and mental afflictions we have thrown at them. They have evolved all manner of sciences to figure out how everything works on their infinitesimal speck of space dust. They even peer beyond their own planet in their feeble efforts to understand EVERYTHING. And the appallingly indulgent creator actually encourages them, though he knows that intellectual endeavour will never enable them to penetrate the aura of his dazzling incomprehensibility. He even permits some of their cleverest men to reach the conclusion that he does not exist. What does he think he is doing? It is ludicrously easy for us to sow intellectual pride and persuade humans that they are the cleverest beings in all the universes; that nothing more splendid than themselves exists throughout the reality they call "space"; that the hypothesis of a "creator" is unnecessary – even absurd. Sometimes I wonder if it is not all *too* easy. Is there a subtle strategy at work here that SSS 666 has failed to uncover?

But I digress. The divide-and-rule strategy has served us very well indeed ever since the enemy established the organization designed to reassert his authority over planet earth. We have set rival theologians at each other's throats. We have exaggerated cultural variants into inflexible customs. We have encouraged church leaders to make such arrogant claims for themselves that large numbers of their followers have seceded. Whether in local congregations or in international church organizations we have convinced malcontents that they have such a superior understanding of the enemy's purposes that they must form their own "true" churches. In the good old days we promoted numerous heresies and then filled "orthodox" leaders with a zealous indignation that made them hunt down, torture, and murder the heretics using a delicious array of cruel and ingenious instruments of torment. Those were great times. But they are over.

The world has changed. Human politicians are fond of pointing out that it has become "smaller". Scientists and technicians have developed communication systems which have enabled governments, businesses, and private individuals throughout the world to speak to each other instantly, to express their thoughts clearly, and to exchange ideas without recourse to written documents, which took weeks or months to cross continents and oceans. It was even as I was dealing with Sharparse's challenge that one of the more astute human commentators coined a phrase which has since become a cliché. He observed that his planet had become a "global village". This trend raised for us the appalling prospect of mutual understanding and cooperation gaining a vice-like grip of human affairs.

The ecumenical movement was one aspect of this odious togetherness. Z was certainly right that the enemy was behind the World Council of Churches and other reconciliation initiatives. His precious worldwide church had become hopelessly fractured and ineffective, but instead of despatching angelic security forces to knock some sense into the leaders and staging show trials of a few chosen dissidents, he persisted with his baffling policy of non-intervention. He really has not the first idea of how to enforce his authority. When Lord Satan's rule is finally established we will certainly run a much tighter ship. However, at the time I am describing, the unmentionable one had dinned into the heads of several of the leading Christians that their mutual hostilities were playing into our hands and that they should start talking to each other. All this was so blatantly obvious that even Z could not fail to grasp it.

Where he blundered lamentably was in his failure to understand – thanks, no doubt, to the influence of Sharparse and his cronies – that the way to combat the enemy's new initiative was not to disrupt all the ecumenical discussions and keep the Christians at loggerheads. Any attempt to put the clock back could not possibly succeed. New situations call for new tactics. It needed someone with my brilliant grasp of eternal affairs to devise an effective policy, and within a very short time I had outlined such a policy and the means to implement it.

I now found myself faced with a dilemma. If I obeyed orders and tried to carry out official strategy, the result would be failure. What then? Would Z accept responsibility for his complete misjudgment of the situation? There was as much chance of that as of darkness in Heaven! No, His Sulphurous Incompetence would fasten the blame on a scapegoat – and there was no doubt who that scapegoat would be. On the other hand, if I tried to tackle the task in my own, superior, way, I ran the risk of being stopped in my tracks and punished for my disobedience.

As I applied my mind to the problem, one thing became clear. However I proceeded to implement my instructions, Sharfly-Bickendrop would take the credit for any success and make sure that I took the blame for any failure. There was, therefore, a fight to the end between us. In short, Sharparse would have to go. Concocting a plan to outwit and destroy the snivelling toady was far from easy but I worked at it with utter relish. The best tactic, I concluded, was to use Sharparse's own ambition against him. If I threw him some bait cleverly enough disguised, I felt sure he would take it. And I knew just how to do it.

Phase one of the operation was to send him a long, a tediously long, report. In it I presented my initial observations on the ecumenical problem and obsequiously requested his instructions on how I should proceed. I went into minute detail on every aspect of the operation I could think of. How many devils should I allocate to WCC headquarters in Geneva? Who did His Ignobility consider to be the key members of the organization? What specific weaknesses could I exploit? Etc., etc. In the middle of all this useless verbiage I slipped in my bait:

"Your Deplorableness is, I understand, taking over management of XO and his book in order to minimize its impact and prevent a popular debate on Christian propaganda. Unfortunately, *Yours Truly* is selling very well and there is scheduled to be a major television debate soon, which will, undoubtedly, boost sales further. You will presumably want to prevent this taking place – perhaps an accident to XO or a minor illness which will put him out of circulation? Cludbone is, as I am sure you know, an expert in human medical matters and he has done valuable work for Z in the past. Of course, I would not dream of telling Your Despicableness how to conduct your business. I simply offer this suggestion in the spirit of furthering our infernal cause."

For the benefit of those who have not made his acquaintance I must explain that Cludbone is a master practitioner. What he does not know about the human anatomy is not worth knowing. His enormous head is twice the size of his squat frame and stocked with information on every topic from boils and dyspepsia to bubonic plague and the more delightfully excruciating forms of abdominal cancer. He has undermined many robust human constitutions and put out of action several of the enemy's effective agents. More importantly, he was at this time in my pocket. He is an acerbic devil, ever ready to take offence and not in the least inclined to cultivate members of the Low Command – particularly those he considers his intellectual inferiors. For that reason many of our leaders are wary of him. Some would be very happy to see the back of him, but he is too valuable to be discarded. Nevertheless, there have been times when he has needed support and I have been careful to interpose myself between Cludbone and his detractors. In short, he knows that I can be useful to him and I know that he can be useful to me. An occasion had now arisen on which I needed his services. I took Cludbone – partially – into my confidence and waited for Sharparse's response to my report.

It was not long in coming. The snivelling little sycophant naïvely adopted my suggestions as his own in order to court favour with Z, and sent instructions to Cludbone to render XO bedridden for several weeks. Cludbone conveyed this information to me and we discussed in detail the type of affliction which would best suit my purposes. It had to be something life-threatening but not fatal. Thus it was that, a few days later, XO collapsed in the middle of a lecture and was rushed to hospital. After exhaustive tests a benign brain tumour was diagnosed. Sharparse, of course, reported this little victory to Z and took personal credit for it. What a simpleton!

XO was frightened, as I had intended he should be. His doctors assured him that the growth was not large and that it was of a type from which most patients recovered. However, the experience of CT scans, medication, and discussions with hospital staff over the relative merits of surgery and chemotherapy was very unnerving for a man who was accustomed to being in complete control of his own destiny. Every severe headache induced panic and he convinced himself that his bouts of dizziness were becoming more frequent. He found it difficult to distract himself with work because reading had become difficult and he was, of course, temporarily relieved of his university duties. His media engagements had to be abandoned and *Yours Truly* became a nine-day wonder. Sharparse congratulated himself on having scored a minor victory over Crumblewit and rose even higher in Z's favour. So far, so good!

What happened next did not go entirely to plan. I relate events as accurately as I can because, although they worked out well for me personally, they do illustrate important lessons all devils need to learn about Advanced Temptation Techniques (ATT). We have all been taught the cardinal rule, "Never Underestimate the Enemy", and you will see from Sharparse's fate just how important it is to keep it in mind at all times. He became so obsessed with internal, Hellish affairs – principally getting rid of me – that he took his eyes off the broader picture. Be warned, O reader! The unmentionable one sees all and will catch you unawares if you are not eternally vigilant.

The next phase of my XO operation was to make him do some serious rethinking. Abstract theological certainties are all very well, but when humans come up against the realities of life and death they often re-evaluate their convictions. My plan was to force XO back to some semblance of Christian orthodoxy. As he contemplated his own eternal destiny I wanted him to acknowledge that the concept of resurrection had its attractions. This, you must understand, was to be a purely *intellectual* response; I had no intention of allowing XO to follow it up with actual commitment. What I envisaged was that he would retreat somewhat from his previous liberal position. I would then ensure that his about-turn was well publicized – with suitable exaggeration where necessary. This would appear to encourage the Christian community without doing any real damage. It would annoy the Low Command, who would call Z to account, and Z would make sure that Sharparse took all the blame.

There was among XO's students an obnoxious young woman – a member of a particularly active and irritating Christian undergraduate group. One of my subordinates had been having some fun with her and I had indulged him. This woman – Amy was her name – stood up to XO in tutorials and refused to be fazed by his attempts at ridicule. What my young protégé had rather cleverly done was induce Amy to fall in love with XO. She felt pity for what she called XO's "spiritual blindness". She prayed for him regularly. (I have developed various techniques for jamming this most pernicious of all the enemy's communication systems but it cannot be denied that it presents us with our most consistent challenge.) And she determined to carry out a one-woman crusade. She visited XO in hospital and then, with increasing frequency, at his home.

After my fall from favour Sharparse assumed control of my junior, but the young devil had a healthy fear of me and I had no difficulty in persuading him to provide me with duplicates of his official reports and to keep me secretly informed of any interesting developments. He was very pleased with his progress. He complicated the XO–Amy relationship with mutual sexual attraction and Amy's loyalties were soon torn between her affection for XO and her dedication to her Christian friends. Her mentors warned her that she was playing with fire and that she risked losing her own faith. From my vantage point I could see that there was little likelihood of that. The enemy had got his hooks very firmly embedded in her. But it was a real pleasure to behold her spiritual anguish and I allowed my subordinate to prolong the game longer than, as I now realize with the benefit of hindsight, was altogether wise.

Two events now happened, in quick succession, that I certainly could not have foreseen. The first intimation of possible problems was a panicky message from my junior. He reported a conversation that was getting out of hand and asked for my help. I went immediately to a park where XO and Amy were sitting on a bench in the autumn sunshine. They were obviously engaged in a very intense conversation. Amy, it seems, had been crying.

"What's going on?" I demanded of my pupil.

"He's asked her to marry him and she's told him she can't marry a non-Christian," came the reply.

"So, what's the problem?"

"Well, Sir, I think he might... convert."

"Think? THINK! You should *know*."

"But, I can't... "

I brushed his excuses aside and concentrated on XO's mind. Immediately, I saw the problem. I couldn't get into his thoughts.

"What does it mean, Sir?" my trembling assistant asked.

"Access is denied. We've been blocked."

"But how… "

"It's almost certainly a prayer-lock. We don't come across them very often, but when we do... What are her close Christian friends up to?"

"I don't know, Sir." The young tempter was frightened and mumbling almost incoherently.

"Then find out!" I bellowed.

He disappeared and I devoted all my attention to the humans. It was infernally frustrating being shut out from their thoughts and compelled simply to listen to their sotto-voce conversation.

XO was angry, struggling with rejection. "The only conclusion I can reach is that you've been toying with me all these weeks... leading me on."

"No, no!" Amy gripped his hand tight. "I'd jump into bed with you tomorrow… *today*, but it would have to be something permanent."

"But that's exactly what I'm offering you."

"Brandy, I love you. You know I do. But I love God more. If you can't share my faith... well, it just wouldn't work... not in the long run. I don't want to have to choose. It's tearing me apart. I hate it."

If I could have got into XO's head I'd have told him what to say to the nauseating, goody-goody little madam. As it was, I could only watch and derive some satisfaction from the silence of shared misery that now followed. At last the couple left their bench and walked, hand in hand, down to the lake. It was at that moment that my crestfallen assistant returned.

"Well?" I demanded.

"You were right, Sir. There are three of them over there in one of the student rooms. They're praying. What can we do?"

"For the moment, nothing. The enemy's put a force field around your two subjects. You must wait until you can get XO alone again."

"Me?" The little devil squealed his terror. "But, Sir, they're not *my* subjects. I was only carrying out your orders. You said this was a training exercise. If XO goes over to the enemy it won't be my fault." He grovelled before me, clutching one of my forelegs. "Please, Sir, you can't blame me if anything goes wrong."

"Can't I? You'd better just make sure that nothing *does* go wrong. And remember that if there is an enquiry into your progress – or lack of it – I will be asked to provide a report. Now, off you go. I have some thinking to do."

As I reflected on the evolving situation I had every reason for satisfaction. XO was well on the way to abandoning his liberal convictions, which was precisely what I intended. My plan was that fear of death would make him reconsider orthodox Christian teaching. If lust for this insipid Amy creature served the same end, all well and good. I would ensure that his intellectual volte-face received wide publicity. This would have the appearance of a propaganda coup for the enemy, for which Sharparse would take the blame. But what if, as my gibbering junior feared, XO should go the whole hog and make a head-and-heart commitment to the enemy? My experience of what the unmentionable one's agents call "conversion" is that it is frequently of short duration. As XO's health improved and his infatuation for Amy ran its course, he would come back to his senses. Anyway, by then Sharparse would have been disgraced, and once I was back in favour I would make short work of dealing with XO.

Over the next few weeks my junior came to me frequently for advice. He was reduced to a quivering wreck as his stratagems failed, one after another. XO began attending Amy's church and, on the day that their engagement was announced, he asked to be received as a member by baptism. The moment had come for me to strike.

I summoned my junior and subjected him to a severe grilling. The loss of a valuable human ally to the enemy was, I reminded him, a crime carrying the direst penalties. I just might be able to save him, I said, but only if he obeyed my instructions to the letter. I then sat him down to write a full report of the whole sorry business, at my dictation. When he had done that I made him do it again. And again. When he had written − and signed − all three copies I told him to send one to Sharfly-Bickendrop.

"What about the other two?" he tentatively enquired.

"They don't exist," I said. "You understand?"

He nodded.

"Good. Let us hope that you hear no more about this. However, if you do − if you are summoned by lower authority to answer any questions − you will come straight to me and I will school you in how to deal with interrogation."

As soon as he had gone I addressed one copy of the report to Z, marking it "Personal" and "Confidential" and being careful to do so in an excellent copy of my junior's handwriting. Whatever backlash occurred, it would not sting me.

It was while I was waiting to hear Z's reaction that the second, totally unexpected, event occurred. XO's brief earthly sojourn came to an abrupt end. In an instant all his doubts fizzled out, his questions were answered, his speculations were swallowed up in certainty. He was wrapped around in the enemy's ghastly brilliance and disappeared from sight. Exactly what happened is not altogether clear. He was crossing a road near his home and was struck by a speeding motorcyclist. My junior told me that XO seemed to stop in the middle of the highway with his hand to his temple. Did he suffer a sudden headache or giddy spell? Cludbone later assured me that he had been rapidly reducing XO's symptoms. He insisted that he had no part in the human's death. But I believe there must have been some connection. If only we could understand the enemy's tactics! Some demonic theorists would describe XO's "accident" as an intervention by the unmentionable one – a lightning strike from Heaven. Others insist that the enemy does not work in such direct ways. They warn that he is actually manipulating us; that we are not the free agents we claim to be. The argument runs thus: if Cludbone had not smitten XO with a brain tumour, Amy would not have had the opportunity to bring about the man's conversion and he would not, subsequently, have got in the way of the motorbike and thus been snatched out of our hands for eternity. I have no answer to these frustrating riddles. If only the enemy would play fair!

Of course, I suffered the pain we all experience when a human soul is taken out of our hands. The sensation was more excruciating for me because I had been closely involved with XO. I shall carry the scar of this little triumph of the enemy until the day we inflict our final revenge on him. However, in respect of my own career, things could scarcely have fallen out better.

"Tragic Death of Uni Celeb" – so ran one headline in the local newspaper, and I made sure that the event received suitably emotional coverage in the national press as well. I pushed a tearful Amy in front of television cameras whenever possible, knowing that, even in her grief, she would take the opportunity to tell the world that her lover had ended his days as a "true Christian believer" and that he had gone to "be with the Lord". Oh, if only I could have seen Sharparse's face when he first heard the news. He must have realized immediately that it was all over for him. How I would have enjoyed witnessing his interrogation by the Retribution Tribunal. For allowing the escape of a high-profile human there could be only one punishment. I could imagine Sharparse's terrified shrieks; his insistence that he was not to blame; that he was the victim of a plot. The last stage in the fool's existence I did not need to imagine. It was a spectacle I would not have missed for all the souls in Hell. The prisoner was taken from Low Command HQ under close guard. He was marched through screaming crowds all the way up to the border. There the massive light-proof doors were dragged open just enough to thrust Sharparse through. I got as close as I dared to witness his last moments. He staggered into the all-consuming brilliance and turned his head for a last glimpse of Hell. Never shall I forget the indescribable anguish on his face in that brief moment before the portal was closed. Those near the gate heard his one last despairing wail. Then Sharfly-Bickendrop was no more.

My next call to Z's office was not slow in coming. This time I was ushered directly to level 6 and greeted cordially by the intelligence chief. It was as though the whole business of XO and Sharparse had never happened.

"Ah, Crumblewit." Z's features screwed themselves into the grimace that was the closest he could get to a welcoming smile. "Good to see you. I thought we might have a chat about the anti-ecumenism campaign. How is it going?"

"I regret to report, Your Lowness, that I have encountered certain – how shall I say? – conceptual infelicities in the policy document with which I was supplied. I have the distinct impression that Your Hideousness's subordinate lacked your grasp of the subtleties and intricacies of the situation."

Z nodded. "I feared that might be the case. I never trusted little... Whatsisname... "

"Sharfly-Bickendrop?" I ventured.

"Yes, yes. Not up to the job. Between you and me, he only got it because he was related to a certain well-placed figure in the Interior Ministry. How do you see things, Crumblewit? Speak freely. I've always appreciated your refreshingly independent viewpoint."

I grasped my opportunity, while at the same time choosing my words carefully. "The pathetic Sharfly-Bickendrop, as Your Loathsomeness rightly points out, was small-minded. He would not have recognized an original idea if it had stood up and smacked him on the snout. When he saw Christians displaying shame for their doctrinal and liturgical differences and expressing a desire to reach a new accord, all he could think about was stopping them."

"Foolish," Z muttered, though I could tell from his expression that he could not grasp the direction of my thoughts.

"As you and I know well," I continued, "church gatherings of all kinds – assemblies, synods, conclaves, council meetings, and such like – can, if properly handled, often serve us very well. Christians enjoy nothing more than getting into exclusive huddles. Now, they can, of course, be a nuisance, particularly if they indulge in that kind of prayer which permits the enemy to steer their discussions. Fortunately, this is rare; they revel in the sound of their own voices and their freedom to reach their own decisions."

"So, you think that these ecumenical gatherings pose no real threat to us?" I could tell from the tone of Z's voice that he was not yet convinced.

"They certainly have the potential for harm but they also have the potential to serve us well. Everything depends on how we handle them."

"Indeed," Z muttered cautiously. "Go on, Crumblewit."

"Well, Your Abhorrence, our primary task in dealing with the church, as you have so often remarked, is to prevent its members from actually doing anything. As long as the more active among them are bogged down in discussing their own internal matters they are not engaged in the activity the enemy has set them on earth for – what he calls 'extending his kingdom'."

"Hmm! I see what you mean, but doesn't this new move towards church unity suggest that the Christians have realized that they've been obsessed with their own sectarian and denominational concerns?"

"Indeed! Indeed! Your Appallingness has hit the nail on the head, as usual. They have realized how much damage we have done by our 'divide-and-rule' policy. That is precisely why we must now change our tactics. Our new motto must be '*unite* and rule'."

"Interesting. Interesting. Go on."

"Revising the centuries-old trend of fragmentation will mean an enormous amount of work for church activists. Just think of the number of meetings that will be involved – all the committees and subcommittees that will have to be set up. There will be gatherings of sage theologians discussing doctrinal minutiae. There will be mass conventions for the Christians to celebrate their newfound togetherness. There will be a proliferation of subgroups concerned with... oh, I don't know – anything we can dream up: social reform, women's issues, moral regeneration, and that good old time-waster, 'mission'. We can keep them busy talking for years and years and years. And while they are absorbed in their inward-looking deliberations we can get on quietly with our steady, soul-by-soul takeover of the planet."

I could read the relief on Z's face. Relief because here was a positive plan he could adopt as his own. He knew full well that the eyes of the Low Command were upon him. He had readily sacrificed Sharparse to appease their anger but he was by no means certain that that would be enough. Now he could pose as the originator of a bold, imaginative strategy that had all the hallmarks of a brilliant mind. The fact that it was *my* superior intellect that he would be passing off as his own was something I could put up with – for the moment. By taking the credit for my brilliant ideas Z was putting himself in my power. Henceforth he would have to take seriously anything I suggested. Eventually, if I played my cards right, I would be able to step out of his shadow and claim my rightful place in the leadership of the Satanic kingdom. However, not for one moment did I underestimate Z.

Now he nodded sagely, his long antennae quivering. "Good, good, Crumblewit. Clearly and succinctly put. I'm glad you agree with me on our overall strategy."

"It will, of course, not be a cheap strategy," I ventured. "We will be fighting on many levels, from local to international. That will demand a great deal of devil power. I will need an experienced and talented team to coordinate our efforts."

Notice, reader, that word "team", insinuated into Z's thinking at such an early stage in our relationship. It was the seed from which something large and impressive would grow. There comes a point in the building of any career when it is vital to develop a caucus of dedicated supporters. A team has the potential to evolve into an influence group, which becomes a pressure group, which becomes a gang, which becomes a party, which finally metamorphoses into a movement.

Z thought long and hard about my observation and I waited nervously for his reaction. Had I tried to go too far, too fast? Would he see through my stratagem? His long snout hovered in my direction as though he was trying to sniff out my hidden thoughts.

At last he said, "Of course. This will be a major operation, demanding careful oversight on a continual basis. I'll have some office space cleared for you here at the Ministry. And I'll assign some of my best devils to help you."

This was not what I had in mind. I had to think fast.

"I'm obliged to Your Awfulness. Just one little observation, if I may… "

"Yes?"

"As Your Malevolence knows, major initiatives can sometimes lose their momentum as a result of too much red tape. There are times when field agents need to be able to act quickly without waiting for confirmation from below… Might I suggest we aim for a subtle blend of centralized planning and operational fluidity?"

There was another long silence before Z spoke again, fixing me with a cold stare from his three eyes. "We are all accountable, Crumblewit. Never forget that. I answer directly to the Satanic First Under-secretary – just as you answer to me. We must never allow chains of command to become weakened by... what was your expression?... 'fluidity'."

"Oh, I couldn't agree more, Your Treacherousness. It's only those, like yourself, in overall command who can see the big picture. We all rely on your wise guidance. The sort of organization I have in mind is five or six groups, each led by one of your most trusted subordinates, who will report regularly to you while having the freedom to respond creatively to changing situations."

"I see." Z shrewdly considered the proposal, his ferret-like mind trying to discover any concealed subplot. "And where would you fit into this scheme?"

"I? Oh I, perhaps... if I don't presume too much... could be Your Vileness's eyes and ears. You are far too busy to visit every battlefield in person. I could travel widely, supervising each of our groups to make sure your orders were being carried out, checking, probing, arriving unexpectedly, keeping all our agents up to the mark, inspiring wholesome fear and obedience. This would be a cost-effective way of ensuring control; I would require only a very small commissariat."

This was, more or less, the plan that was eventually agreed – not all I might have hoped for, but more than I needed.

* * * * *

CHAPTER 5

Unite and Rule

(1958–1960)

The anti-ecumenism project was a mess. That is to say, the problem we were tackling was vast, hydra-headed and unwieldy. It was certainly not a task I would have undertaken of my own volition; it had been thrust upon me. However, I was stuck with it and it was vital to my career prospects that I should at last score some successes – the more spectacular, the better.

The proliferation of Christian unity projects took even me by surprise. The enemy poured prodigious resources into unifying his followers. He has always been very adept at turning our successes to his purpose. It is lamentable to record that he did just that at a time when we had good reason to believe that ultimate victory was within our grasp. Our Strategy Department had done an excellent job of maintaining international tension. As the devastation of the world war faded into the past they skilfully ignited minor military conflicts in several parts of the planet. The leading nations could no longer ignore these trouble spots. Whereas once they would have left African tribes or Latin American juntas or Asian political ideologues to fight their own battles, statesmen in America, Europe, China, and Russia now saw such disturbances as opportunities to extend their own influence and impose on the world their own philosophies and systems of government. The result was a state of confrontation the humans called "Cold War". It involved denunciatory and threatening speeches, infiltration of neutral regions, espionage, assassination, propaganda, and the erection of physical as well as ideological barriers, which prevented whole populations from communicating with and understanding each other. The sight of the world being divided into rival "East" and "West" camps, whose leaders hurled abuse at one another and whipped up widespread fear and hatred, was a delight to behold. But the greatest achievement of our Low Command was the development and proliferation of weapons of mass destruction.

Our technology experts revealed to human scientists how they could harness some of the more powerful forces employed by our enemy in creating the world. Very soon the leading nations had turned this knowledge on its head. They had devised and stockpiled weapons of unprecedented power and pointed them at each other in the name of "national defence". They had the capacity to launch, at a moment's notice, nuclear devices which could span continents at lightning speed and inflict devastation on a truly heroic scale. Oh, the excitement that gripped Hell! The kingdom held its breath. Emergency training sessions were hastily arranged in preparation for our complete takeover of the planet. Hell was on red alert, poised and ready to march at short notice. It was widely believed that the call could come at any moment. It would only take a statesman or military commander to panic and press a button and there would be a nuclear holocaust. We could then scoop up and process billions of human souls, deploy our front-line troops to clear out the remaining pockets of resistance, and make preparations for our abysmal Master's coronation.

I, of course, was not infected with this mass delusion. It was obvious to me that the enemy would never abdicate his responsibility so easily. The freedom he had bestowed on his wretched, undeserving creatures would not extend to allowing them to blow up what he had made. Regrettably, in their euphoria our leaders failed to make allowance for the unfathomable deviousness of our enemy. When the great disillusionment came I was among the small minority whose superior wisdom was recognized. Unfortunately I was too busy to take full advantage of this at the time. As you know, the great terrestrial destruction did not happen. What *did* happen was that Christians, the world over, were galvanized into action. In unprecedented numbers they prayed, demonstrated, made speeches, and wrote books – in every possible way they went public with the enemy's plan for planet earth. One by-product of all this activity was a heightened concern for Christian unity. Hence my department found itself far busier than expected.

Fortunately, while more senior devils were indulging in self-congratulatory plans for the final "big push", I was quietly deploying my own forces against the enemy's bastions. I had to fight for my programme. Z was under pressure to close down Operation EQ (my code name for the anti-ecumenism project) and to free up my agents for the anticipated "final" campaign. It was by no means easy to stop him caving in under pressure. It was only as time passed and frightened statesmen began desperately to talk themselves out of the crisis their own cleverness had got them into that he came to a proper evaluation of the situation. Reports from our intelligence agents made it clear that behind the belligerent posturing of world leaders lay a realization that they could never use the unprecedented power they had been handed.

Building my departmental organization (I gradually replaced the word "team" with the word "department" in all communications with the Lower Command; it created an impression of stability and permanence) kept me very busy. I divided my demonic resources into divisions in order to cover all the activities of the humans' churches. It was no easy task to keep up with them. They developed a positive frenzy for ecumenism that went on for many years. Every unity project they planted soon threw out new shoots which rooted themselves, so that, almost without the aid of my agents, a veritable forest of councils, assemblies, committees, study groups, and synods appeared, each one seeking to bring together Christian denominations and demonstrate that all the enemy's people were of one mind on a whole range of issues. Of course, they most certainly were not of one mind. That meant that ecumenism generated a positive snowstorm of paper – discussion documents, reports, minority reports, seminar agendas, and policy statements. Our task was to encourage this process – to keep the enemy's followers employing all their energies in a range of concerns subsidiary to what the enemy had actually commissioned them to do – worship him and recruit as many of the humans as possible to worship him as well.

My fertile brain teemed with ideas of topics that Christian leaders and their delegations could be kept discussing and arguing about. The implementation of my inspired concepts was carried out by a well-structured organization. I set up three major divisions: Political, Social, and Theological. The

Political Division was, in many ways, the easiest to originate and keep running. Thanks to our activities throughout the course of earth history, most humans have a love of power and influence. Nothing satisfies them more than forming themselves into establishment groups to organize and control the lives of their neighbours. Some of our most enduring successes have included, for example, bringing businessmen together in trade guilds, freemasons' lodges, civic corporations, and the like. Such bodies are adept at keeping themselves in power. The prime function of any establishment is to establish — itself. Under the pretext of serving their communities they pursue their own sectional interests and magnify their own importance. They adore uniforms and regalia. They love symbolism. They embrace anything which enhances their own exclusivity. Because they decide who is "in" and who is "out", they are able to prey upon the ambitions and insecurities of each rising generation. Young men and women anxious to "get on" long to be admitted to the charmed circle of the dominant gang or club or council. Because the psychological groundwork has been so well laid it has never been particularly difficult to give this lust for power a religious complexion. Readers will be well aware that, for several human centuries, we successfully maintained Christian theocracies. Cities such as Rome, Constantinople, and Geneva have become associated with religious establishments which wielded immense power over millions of lives. They controlled kings, they dominated parliaments, they outlawed (by what they called "excommunication") citizens who presumed to question their decrees. They could, and did, hound to death persistent "heretics" — that is, anti-establishment individuals.

It is very important for us to prevent humans from actually learning anything useful from their own history. We have several ways of doing this. We can convince them that the story of the past is irrelevant. We can persuade them to think of it in terms of human progress, making them believe that mankind is on an upward path of technological achievement, social well-being, and moral excellence. We can set them searching the past for evidence to support their fashionable modern convictions. We can use selective annals to support jingoistic nationalism, racial prejudice, or political campaigns of all hues. What we must prevent at all costs is allowing them to gain psychological insights from a study of history – a deeper understanding of their own motivations from reflecting on how their ancestors thought and behaved.

Now, where was I? Oh yes, the Political Division. What I directed my agents to concentrate on was getting Christians to divert their energies into political activity, to believe that their *raison d'être* was to establish ecumenical bodies to campaign for constitutional and political change in various countries.

In short, we got them to play the power game. They backed and, in some instances, actually formed political parties. They allocated prodigious amounts of time and money to fact-finding missions. They organized protests. They supported demonstrations – some of which turned delightfully violent. They staged huge conferences and rallies aimed at expressing a united Christian voice on issues of global concern. It was amusing in the extreme to induce them to attack some of Hell's favourite regimes, renowned for injustice, cruelty, and oppression. They knew that our enemy was opposed to these totalitarian dictatorships and corrupt oligarchies.

What they overlooked, thanks to the ingenious devices of my agents, was that by entering the political arena they were abandoning the strategy the enemy has always employed to appalling effect – the patient endurance of suffering. When he encourages his followers to confront oppression with passive resistance the oppressors all too often respond with false imprisonment, rigged trials, torture, and execution. This undermines their credibility and, in the long run, weakens them. As the reader will know, we constantly need to restrain our human allies, but, sadly, when they have the bit between their teeth the rulers of evil regimes sometimes get out of control. Some of our most promising demagogues have been overthrown as a result of massacring demonstrators, assassinating critics, or provoking armed intervention from other states. They fail to learn that wickedness is most effective when it is covert or even when it is tempered with goodness. Fortunately, some of the enemy's activists are equally obtuse and spoil their own cause by fighting with the weapons that we put into their hands.

My Social Division worked to a similar agenda. Their prey consisted of those Christians who feel strongly that religion should be *practical*. As the reader will know, it has been one of our major triumphs, ever since the beginnings of the church, to create confusion and division between those who insist on the exclusive importance of *faith* and those who demand the performance of *good works*. Both groups constitute a nuisance, but if and when they come together and realize that, from the enemy's point of view, faith and works go hand in hand, why then they become a real menace. Our abhorrent foe deploys many of his vast resources in stirring his followers to – ugh! – *love*. Fortunately, this is not easy for him. His precious humans are so dim-witted that they find it difficult to think simultaneously about theory and practice. This is a weakness we can and do exploit.

The Social Division worked among those Christians dubbed by their opponents as "social gospellers". My agents encouraged the setting-up of numerous charities, aid agencies, and relief organizations, many of which were avowedly "Christian". They then ensured that the activists became so involved in do-goodery that they lost contact with the enemy and his wider aims of world domination. Their "practical Christianity" became nothing more than humanitarianism. As long as we kept up a steady supply of wars, famines, refugee problems, oppressive political regimes, poverty, injustice, etc., it was comparatively easy to originate ecumenical bodies pledged to relieving the victims of such situations. We had them devoting all their energies to carrying out field studies, writing reports, lobbying politicians, organizing charity stunts, raising money, and making media appearances to publicize their activities. In all of this enthusiastic, high-pressure business there was very little mention of the enemy; indeed, some activists stopped believing in him altogether.

I was very proud of my Social Division. They were able to distort events that might have provided the enemy with dangerous propaganda advantages.

But the most effective wing of the operation was the Theological Division. The political and social aspects of the campaign needed very careful handling because there was always the danger that, as a result of Christian meddling in the affairs of people whose lives we had made splendidly unpleasant, the idea might spread that the enemy actually cares about his creatures. Hell forbid that acts of Christian do-goodery should actually cause humans to think about the ultimate do-gooder! Those running the Theological Division had no such obstacle to overcome. The religious experts whose minds my agents manipulated were gloriously insular, inward-looking, and obsessed with theoretical minutiae. When they met in interdenominational study groups and committees we made them believe that they were "healing the divisions in the universal church". Oh, the glorious irony of it!

The poor dears had to give their attention to issues of labyrinthine complexity: what constitutes a *true* church; what imparts *validity* to an ordained minister; who has the authority to develop and sanction *proper* liturgy; whether women can ever be priests (and, anyway, what *is* a priest?); how many *sacraments* there are and what they are for... the list of topics to be argued over was long enough to keep theological experts busy for decades. This was certainly not what our enemy had in mind when he encouraged the development of the ecumenical movement.

These ivory-tower ecumenical junkies were largely out of touch with what was happening in the real world. Millions of people were defecting from the old Western churches. While we were able to regain our hold on many of these deserters, there were some who set up their own denominations. Meanwhile, there was a disastrous surge of Christian growth in Africa and Asia. We worked hard to turn those seeking genuine spirituality onto non-Christian byways. Some developed syncretistic cults. Some looked to other religions; Eastern mysticism became particularly fashionable at this time. Some fell for one of our most creative innovations called "New Age spirituality", a subtle combination of old pagan beliefs, crude superstition, free love, and fashionable popular music. While all this was going on we kept the ecumenical experts talking and talking and talking. It was all very satisfactory. At this time I was working extremely hard to build and control my expanding empire but I always drew strength and encouragement from my visits to the Theological Division's centres of operation.

There was, of course, nothing new about this; we have always very successfully encouraged doctrinal rivalry. But the ecumenical movement provided an excellent stimulus to this kind of distortion. In particular it provoked new fundamentalisms. I found these particularly useful as a training exercise for junior devils. Because fundamentalist projects demand little real skill or advanced knowledge, I could safely assign probationers to them. The puny humans cannot grasp a one-trillionth fraction of the real conflict in which we are engaged and in which they play only bit parts. Because most Christians are too spiritually immature to realize their ignorance, it is a simple matter of applied pride to make them refuse to acknowledge this limitation. Having convinced them that they *do* understand the *fundamentals* of their faith and that they can encapsulate them in a few simple dogmas, we instil what they take for religious zeal but which is, in reality, stubborn and potentially violent dogmatism, which can be directed by any halfway competent tempter into denunciation of any other Christians who do not see things in exactly the same way. The whole objective of our strategy is, of course, that they should become so obsessed with defending doctrinal minutiae against the enemies of "true religion" that they cease paying attention to the enemy and what he requires of them on a daily basis.

On this issue of fundamentalism I summarize here the basic elements of the Crumblewit Method, which has been used successfully by my own trainees. Its basis is a simple alphabetical mnemonic:

A is for Authority Source. The subject must be induced to give total, unquestioning obedience to someone or something other than the enemy (he/she will, of course, be convinced that this authority source has been provided by the enemy).

In my experience the majority of church people fall into one of two categories: controllers and controlled. Those within the second category who are intellectually restricted find it helpful to have someone – "priest", "shepherd", "pope", "apostle", "team leader" – to do their thinking for them. Their neighbours who are equipped with mental acuity may need to be injected with a good dose of sloth. Either way, the tempter's objective must be to induce his subject simply to accept what is dished out from the pulpit.

Now, what is dished out from the pulpit is frequently directed by a still-higher authority. The existence of would-be controllers means that we have been able to provide churches, denominations, and sects with superbly monumental power structures. These top-heavy edifices in the older churches have, over the human centuries, achieved truly Byzantine complexity and their very elaborateness (the grand buildings, the fancy titles, the colourful costumes, the multiplicity of bureaucratic departments, and the acres of office space designated to them) provides them with an aura of permanence and certitude which seems to defy contradiction. But it is not only in organizations in which we have had long earth centuries to build up spiritual autocracies that we have carefully nurtured authority figures. There is a plentiful supply of humans susceptible to the development of a power complex and it is not a difficult task to insinuate such people into any religious organization, large or small. A couple of examples will show how this can be achieved in both old and new churches.

At the time of the ecumenical movement I have described, the leader of the biggest Christian body, the Catholic Church, summoned a deliberative assembly to meet in Rome, where this church has its headquarters. He and his immediate successors in office demanded some serious rethinking of several major issues, including ecumenical relations (if memory serves me well, they called it the Second Vatican Council). Hitherto, Catholic fundamentalism had insisted that all other churches were in error and that their only chance of being accepted by our enemy was by being "reconciled" to the Catholic Church. On this and other issues new reforms were introduced which radically changed old traditions. The decisions of the congress had the specific approval of the leadership, and all members of the Church were obliged to accept them. Millions of Catholics were called on to abandon some of their most cherished convictions and their most ingrained attitudes in order to accept the new fundamentalism now being imposed from the top. To say that many were bewildered, shocked, or angry would be an understatement. In Hell, all was watched with gleeful anticipation as our agents stirred up resentment.

Our adversary's namby-pamby, milk-and-water attitude to ecclesiastical power politics really does beggar belief. If one creates – as he does – sentient beings with widely differing abilities, it is inevitable that some will use their superior intellectual or physical strength to lord it over those less well endowed. This has been a salient feature of the entire history of the human race. Innumerable have been the occasions when our job has been made easier by leaders who have asserted authority over others to achieve their own objectives or simply for the sheer love of power. What has the supreme goody-goody-in-chief done about this? Nothing. Less than nothing; he has actually instructed Christian leaders to regard themselves not as masters and disciplinarians but as servants! Reluctantly I have to confess that it is his folly rather than our brilliance which has enabled us to raise up numberless petty princelings, wallowing in luxury and surrounded by fawning acolytes, who enjoyed personal power – all in his name.

We did, however, use our best endeavours to orchestrate the Catholic backlash against the reforms instituted by that convention in Rome. We sought out and equipped priests who were clever enough to appeal to the discontented and confused and bold enough to challenge the leadership. They denounced as heretics the popes responsible for abandoning the *fundamentals* of Catholicism and making friendly overtures to rival Christian bodies. They loudly preached that the Rome Council was the "worst catastrophe ever to have befallen the Church". As a result, a sizeable number of priests and congregations refused to implement the changes authorized by the leadership. The principal flag-waver of dissent we thrust into the limelight was a Spanish extremist by the name of Bartolomeo Barragon. At first his defiance was necessarily low-key, but as thousands of traditionalist Catholics responded to his literature and invited him to preach at various locations throughout the world he became the head of a movement the official hierarchy could neither control nor afford to ignore. Barragon had become a rival authority source whose diktats were obeyed as unquestionably within his own movement as those emanating from Rome were by the Catholic majority. Thus we had successfully created a church within a church.

We had established, within the one organization, rival fundamentalisms.

The situation was not essentially different within the rag-tag-and-bobtail world of Protestant evangelicalism. This brand of Christianity had seldom, if ever, acknowledged the need for one universal, visible "church". Membership of the local assembly was, in their view, what really mattered. It is not, therefore, surprising that bifurcation was almost second nature to them. Unlike in the major denominations, it was no "big deal" for a tiny breakaway group to leave a church that had, in their opinion, compromised the truth or simply become complacent and ineffective, and set up shop down the road in order to pursue a "purer" faith and a more dedicated mission.

I have always stressed how important it is to keep a close watch on such developments. You see, fundamentalism is by no means always our friend. When a group of Christians in any church, large or small, stage a protest and decide to "get back to basics", they can become quite menacing. Most of the major defeats we have suffered have been inflicted by just such rebels. A body of comfortable Christians set in their ways and enjoying their weekly routines of what they suppose to be "worship" pose no real threat. But when a protest movement gets under way – be it in a Catholic, Orthodox, Protestant, or whatever context – that is not the time for us to sit back and rub our hands with glee. Such initiatives must be diverted into more destructive fundamentalist channels.

An example that comes to mind concerns a breakaway church in Britain with which I had personal dealings. The sequence of events began when Bob Windling walked out of his Baptist church after a disagreement with the minister. He was one of those people who manage to rub authority figures up the wrong way. I had seen what was coming and instructed my agent, an eager-to-please, simpering probationer called Snagwort, to be sure that Bob shared his discontent with other church members. So successful was this ploy that when Bob left he took a dozen others with him. The point at issue was the outbreak of ecstatic religious experience known as the "charismatic movement", about which I shall have more to say later. Bob's minister was highly suspicious of what he dismissed as "arm-waving, miracle-chasing fanatics", but to Bob this opposition seemed to show that his church was stuck in an unproductive rut and refusing to accept the exciting new initiative being taken by our foe. So caught up was Bob in his discovery of a fresh religious experience that it was not difficult for my subordinate to persuade him that he was possessed of rare gifts and that he was being called to found and lead a new church, the Divine Covenant Assembly.

Bob and his followers got off to a flying start. Inspired by their leader's energetic zeal and excited oratory, assembly members proselytized enthusiastically and made genuine converts. In its early months the DCA grew dramatically. My agent panicked. He knew only too well what would happen to him if this new gathering of Christians became well established. I took my time before intervening, and ignored poor little Snagwort's pleas for advice. Keeping Hell's lower minions in a state of fear is the best way to ensure their obedience and, in any case, the DCA problem was not one whose solution could be rushed. This was the sort of situation which, as I have said, needs to be monitored closely. We could not allow "Bob's Mob", as I dubbed them, to prosper indefinitely but we had to know the precise moment to prick their balloon. When I judged the time to be right I intervened personally, being sure to let Snagwort know that this was inconvenient for me and the result of his own incompetence. How agreeable it was to observe the fawning simpleton's relief and grovelling apologies! What I did was play the success card.

This involved making Bob believe that the rapid development of his church was proof that he had the full backing of our enemy. In actual fact, he had been consulting the enemy less and less as his prestige grew in his own little world. He became his own god and exercised ever-increasing control over the lives of his worshippers. Bob Windling was merely another manifestation (albeit on a much smaller scale) of the personal fundamentalism exemplified by Bartolomeo Barragon. The mesmeric hold he exercised over his followers was criticized by other Christian leaders at the time as "heavy shepherding" – a particularly apt metaphor, as the next sequence of events demonstrated. I now drove Bob fast towards the precipice. I persuaded him that his "empire" was ready for dramatic expansion. This would involve planting new assemblies in different parts of the country. To achieve this, chosen followers would need to move several miles to fresh locations. Some of them demurred about changing jobs, selling and buying houses, moving away from families and friends, and shifting their children to new schools, but Bob overrode their objections and so strong was his hold over the church that six families made the move to a new neighbourhood. The results were agreeably disastrous. Two of the men failed to find work. One marriage broke up. Resentful children became difficult to handle. When the wretched guinea pigs turned to Bob for help all he could do was condemn their lack of faith and urge them to persevere through their trial by fire. All I had to do now was wait while enlightenment dawned on the uprooted members of Bob's Mob. Gradually their minds cleared and they saw that their idol had feet of clay. The transplanted church collapsed, spreading far and wide the dust of disillusionment, resentment, and hostility towards Christianity in general.

There is one other type of fundamentalism, which is not directly connected with personalities. It relates to the Christians' *fundamental* writings, the collection of poetry, songs, philosophy, history, biography, and personal letters known as the "Bible". This subversive text is, indeed, *fundamental* to the enemy's strategy. It contains all the essentials that his slaves need to know. As one of the few devils qualified to study this pernicious literature, I can assure the reader that it is highly dangerous. Apart from anything else, it reveals to its readers our existence and many of our battle tactics. Therefore, a major element of our counter-strategy has been to prevent Christians from reading it.

We have enjoyed a reasonable degree of success in this. The humans have an adage, "familiarity breeds contempt", and the fact that this "Bible", often finely printed and elaborately bound, is a familiar object in the homes of believers and many non-believers means that it is widely ignored. I have certainly managed to ensure that most of my churchgoing subjects consign it to a shelf alongside dog-eared paperback novels, old cookery books and once-loved tomes of children's stories. Regrettably, however, there are exceptions. There are those of the enemy's followers who consult this book on a regular basis – some even daily. And the situation gets worse as scholars translate the text into every conceivable human language and colporteurs smuggle it into lands where it was hitherto unknown. The reader will not need me to point out how devastatingly effective this can be from the point of view of our tirelessly persistent foe. Free access to the Bible has won him more new adherents than any of his other underhand stratagems.

However, our arsenal of wiles and contrivances is not devoid of useful counter-measures. We can actually turn this zeal for the Christian writings to our advantage.

One ploy is literary fundamentalism. Just as slavish following of a charismatic leader lifts from some Christians the arduous responsibility of thinking for themselves, so strict adherence to the *letter* of the Bible text (in whatever language the reader happens to be using) removes the necessity for grappling with its inner and deeper meanings. I find myself in some difficulty explaining this point, since access to these writings is strictly banned by the Low Command to all devils outside the Hellish elite. What I can say is that they consist of a wide variety of literary types, from historical sagas and poems to intimate letters, each of which calls for a different approach if its meaning and application are to be properly understood. Now, the intelligent tempter does not need to familiarize himself with the enemy's pernicious material. The correct procedure is to inspire in the subject excessive zeal for the *words* of the text. He/she needs to believe that every linguistic nuance and grammatical detail is equally sacred and not to be understood, interpreted, or believed other than literally. You need to convince your subject that any deviation from this fixed rule leads to compromise and, therefore, heresy.

You must always be quite clear about your objectives when inducing literary fundamentalism (or, for that matter, any other kind of fundamentalism). What matters is not what the subject believes but how he/she responds to that belief.

Fundamentalist attitudes must either create division in the Christian ranks or hinder the enemy's mission (preferably both!). Ideally your subject should be more committed to brainwashing potential converts with his/her own particular brand of fundamentalism than to getting across the enemy's core message. Real success will produce the following phenomena: (a) the story of the enemy's supposedly deep concern for his creatures will become obscured by issues of biblical "inerrancy"; (b) the subject will not be able to work with Christians who are not like-minded; (c) he/she will appear to the world at large as obscurantist and irrelevant. By drawing the attention of the enemy's potential converts to such "oddballs", you will be able to suggest that *all* Christians are stupid and arrogant.

B is for Blinkered Vision. Having provided your subject with an authority source, you must ensure that he/she refuses to look anywhere else for inspiration, guidance, or support.

The other elements of my invaluable mnemonic will take less time to explain because they all hinge on the choice of authority source. Once you have manoeuvred your subject into putting total trust in someone or something other than our enemy, your task is more than half done. Our self-obsessed foe will brook no rivals, make no compromises, do no deals. (That is why the contest we are locked into with him is a fight to the death.) His prime objective is total control of his adherents and this depends, in large measure, on maintaining direct and regular contact with each one of them so that he can direct what they think, say, and do. He regularly uses the Bible, church leaders, and other Christians to this end, but nothing is more effective from his point of view than personal direction.

Now, when you have frustrated him by interposing some subordinate authority, you would be foolish not to expect him to fight back. He will certainly make use of a variety of communication media to correct your subject's distorted vision. You will need constant vigilance to prevent your subject from falling prey to the advice of friends or the impact of sermons, books, etc. You must at all costs reinforce his/her prejudices. Make sure your subject consorts only with like-minded Christians. The basic reason why he/she clings to an infallible guide is insecurity. He/she lacks the confidence to rely on independent thought or, rather, on thought that is under the sole direction of the enemy. Only the word written in the sacred text or spoken by the chosen guru can be depended on. Prey on the subject's fear of paying attention to any unfamiliar communication channel. This is what I mean by Blinkered Vision.

C is for Censoriousness. Not only should your subject shun all potentially dangerous influences; he/she should become actually hostile towards them.

You will have realized from the examples I have quoted that one aspect of what we may term "advanced fundamentalism" is criticism of all Christians of other persuasions. This can and should, whenever possible, become outspoken and vitriolic. Induce your subject to denounce fellow believers as "antipopes", "heretics", "backsliders", "compromisers", "woolly liberals", "raving charismaniacs". If you can engineer actual confrontations between fundamentalists and other Christians, so much the better. Setting up slanging matches is one of the more enjoyable kinds of temptation. However, a word of caution: such head-to-heads must never be allowed to degenerate into actual debate. The object is to show up the enemy's followers in a bad light. Onlookers must see nothing but supposed Christian brothers at each other's throats and quite unable to agree on what they believe. So be careful to steer all arguments. They must always generate heat, not light.

D is for Disdain. While censoriousness involves a clash of conflicting ideas, disdain is often more effective within each fundamentalist community. Criticism is a weapon of attack; contempt is a defensive shield.

Any intelligent fundamentalist leader will ensure that his followers do not understand the convictions and actions of mainstream Christians. It is enough for them to know that any who oppose them are just plain "wrong". Disdain follows from this assumption. It asserts that "pseudo-Christians who don't think like us are spiritually and intellectually of no account". I have always found humour to be a valuable tool for welding a defensive "ring of steel" around fundamentalist communities. Poking fun at the way "foolish" or "deluded" Christians dress or worship or the kind of music they use makes the fundamentalist faithful feel superior and, therefore, secure.

E is for Exclusivity. The more Christians we can corral into isolated and isolationist groups, convinced that they alone possess the whole truth, the more effective our own major strategy will be.

One of our accursed foe's weirdest decisions was to make all his human creatures different. He would have achieved his aim of total control much more easily if he had cast them all from the same mould. I can only assume that his motive is to have billions of slaves all fawning upon him in their own individual ways so that he can enjoy multifarious relationships. Well, on his own head be it. His folly has enabled us to recruit countless souls, and we will continue to do so. It is precisely that human variety which enables us to make his "universal church" a shambles of ramshackle dwellings, many of whose inhabitants view their neighbours with distrust. As I have demonstrated, even when major Christian groups recognize the "sin of disunity", their ability to increase cooperation is severely limited. Their problem lies in the fact that members of the human rag-bag will always form themselves into cliques and groups of more-or-less like-minded people. Now, because the creation of humanity was so slapdash, our enemy had to establish a haphazard patchwork of churches in order to reach out to various cultures and subcultures. This tactic can – and, regrettably, in many cases does – work. As long as Christians keep their eyes fixed on their primary objective and realize that differences over detail are of secondary importance, they can rub along with each other and sometimes combine their forces to oppose us. This, of course, is what we have to prevent. That is why it is vital to foster exclusivity. You must make your subjects believe that the nitty-gritty of doctrine and practice *does* matter, and that only they and their friends have got everything right. This is what fundamentalism is all about and this is why it is so useful to us.

* * * * *

CHAPTER 6

Ecstasy, Error, and Exhibitionism

(1961–1967)

My outstanding successes in counter-ecumenism could not fail to attract attention in the lowest quarters. My name was soon being frequently mentioned in government circles. Thus it was that I met and became closely involved with Squimblebag, First Secretary to the Minister for Infernal Affairs. It was, of course, extremely useful for me to have access to those who enjoyed regular contact with the decision makers. There were many occasions when having to wait upon Z for confirmation of a policy initiative or the granting of more resources threatened to slow down the work of my department. Therefore, I developed the habit of bypassing the Ministry of Misinformation and going straight to lower authority.

Needless to say, this procedure had to be carried out cautiously. I could not allow Z to discover, until my own position was absolutely secure, that he had ceased to be of use to me. In Squimblebag I found an ally of finely honed deviousness and well-matured ambition. Like myself he was a forward-looking devil, impatient with the bumbling hesitancy of the old guard whose instinct for self-preservation undermined their capacity for creative thought.

From Squimblebag I sometimes gleaned information long before it was generally released. I have good cause to remember one particular conversation that occurred when my anti-ecumenism campaign was at its height. We were looking at earth from a vantage point of a few thousand miles.

"Why do you suppose our Infernal Master chose this planet? There are several others more spectacular." Squimblebag's scales glowed with a multi-hued, oily iridescence as he waved a wing around the crowded pinpoint lights of stellar space.

I stared down at the revolving blue ball beneath us. "I've always assumed it has something to do with the creatures the unmentionable one has put in charge. Our Master needs them as slaves. We cannot be expected to run the planet all by ourselves."

Squimblebag fixed me with his big red eye. "That is, doubtless, what most devils think. It's only partially true. I have it on very good authority that there's a much bigger plan in our great leader's mind."

"Go on," I urged.

"Well, these human creatures, as we know, are the enemy's special favourites. If that were not so he would not have tolerated their ingratitude and frequent rebellions; he would have abandoned them a long time ago. One flick of his wrist. I speak figuratively, of course. We don't know what he looks like. I don't suppose he actually has a wrist. Perhaps I ought to say 'one word' or even 'one thought' and humankind would have disappeared just like that." He clapped his wings together. "Humans would have gone the way of the dinosaurs. But no – he puts up with them stubbornly, however much mess they make and however much control we exert over them."

"That is certainly true."

"The government is convinced that the reason for the enemy's perseverance is that he has a bigger plan for his humans – a universal or, rather, an eternal plan."

For some moments I pondered the implications of what Squimblebag had said. "You mean he intends to make them equal with us?"

"More than equal." Squimblebag's big head nodded.

"But that's… " I scrabbled around for the right word.

"Absurd?" Squimblebag suggested.

"Well… yes."

"On the contrary. Our political analysts assure us that the enemy's secret designs involve making us redundant and replacing us with a race of super-humans – creatures that he's somehow developed or evolved from these dreary, stodgy mortal lumps."

"But surely this is an old story, a fiction invented long ago to put heart into Christians at times of persecution. As you know, I have read some of their apocalyptic writings. They are jumbled and bizarre… incoherent. A new Jerusalem floating down from the sky! Angels dashing around on horses! Plagues being poured out of bowls! I mean… *really*! Even most Christians have stopped taking these fantasies seriously."

"Yes, indeed," Squimblebag agreed, and I had never seen him look more solemn. "It's up to us to encourage their scepticism. But that doesn't mean that we, too, should ignore these stories or stop trying to fathom their meaning. What it comes down to in the long run is that it's either them or us.

That's why our Master in his wisdom has staked a claim to earth and that's why we must never relax our hold on it."

"Look," he continued, in a confidential whisper. "I probably shouldn't be telling you this and you mustn't repeat it. We commissioned a major internal report from a committee of Hell's best brains. Prince Blagender himself chaired it."

"Blagender? The Master's right-hand devil?"

"Just so. You can see how important it is. Well, this committee has just produced an interim report. Restricted circulation, of course. I can't go into details... but... "

"Yes?" I urged.

"It seems that the enemy is embarking on a major offensive and we believe it's in preparation for the final showdown. He has been delivering a new range of weapons to Christians in different places."

"What sort of weapons?"

"Prophecy, healing, angelic communication, miracle-working... "

"Oh, come, come, my dear Squimblebag," I scoffed. "There's nothing new about them. They've been available to Christians as long as there has been a Christian church."

"You think so, Crumblewit? You really think so? Take a closer look at the records. You will soon see that such enemy initiatives have taken place only at moments of crisis."

"Well, I grant that they happened at the beginning. There was that notorious Pentecost cataclysm in Jerusalem that caught our ancestors off guard. But since then... "

"Since then such events have been the signs of major enemy offensives: North Africa in the fifth human century of the new age; the monastic assault on Europe in the eighth century; the Reformation bombardment of the sixteenth century; North America in the eighteenth century (what Christian propagandists crow about as the 'Great Awakening'). Need I go on?"

I was silent for several moments as my mind embraced the enormity of what was being suggested.

"And you say it's happening again?" I asked at last.

"No," Squimblebag muttered mournfully. "This time it's worse."

"How so?"

"Come with me and I'll show you."

We relocated to a point closer to the earth's atmosphere. "There!" Squimblebag waved a wing. "And there!" He pointed with another wing. What he indicated were two metallic "birds" that I instantly recognized.

"Satellites," I said.

"Communication satellites, to be more exact. There are several out here and there will soon be many more. You can see their implication for us. The function of these contraptions is to bounce telephone, radio, and television signals back to earth. Hitherto the enemy's assaults have always been geographically contained – missionary expansion in China; monastic revival in France; that sort of thing. Now, thanks to the satellite technology the humans have developed, there's no stopping the impact of what is happening. An outburst of charismatic activity (that's what some Christians are calling it) in some insignificant town in the American Mid-West is reported – and copied – in a fashionable church in London. The next thing we hear is that priests in Italy are witnessing strange manifestations in their congregations. Blagender's committee is warning us that what we have on our hands is a global movement."

"How awful! What can we do?"

"Contingency plans are being put into operation but we will have to wait for the committee's final report before we can fully develop our strategic response. But I tell you this, Crumblewit, when the time comes there will be important new appointments for all our most talented devils." Squimblebag's glowing eye fixed me with a meaningful stare.

This was the broadest of hints that I could expect a summons from the Ministry, and it was not slow in coming. I was ordered to present myself before a selection committee of senior devils, some of whom I recognized as members of Hell's elite inner council. They bombarded me with searching questions. Had I familiarized myself with the humans' latest communications toys? Thanks to Squimblebag's forewarning I had done my homework and was able to hold forth on the most recent developments of telephone, radio, and television relays via satellite. The panel were impressed. What implications did I think these new developments might have for our war effort? I replied that all advances in terrestrial communication techniques had propaganda possibilities – both for us and for the enemy. That seemed to satisfy them. What was my assessment of the enemy's current activity? Here I had to be cautious; I did not want to create problems for Squimblebag – not while he could still be useful to me. I put on an act of pondering the question deeply and then ventured the cautious opinion that I thought I detected signs of a new offensive. My agents were reporting disturbing developments in various locations, I said. Some Christian congregations were experiencing a new enthusiasm and excitement fuelled by direct spiritual intervention on the part of the enemy. I could tell by the nodding heads that that answer had gone down well. They went into a huddle and the chairdevil himself fired the next question. If that was the case, how did I think the enemy's latest initiative could best be counteracted?

I replied promptly. "Infiltration has always been our most devastating weapon." My study of infernal history led me to believe, I suggested, that the enemy's organization was always most effectively damaged when it was undermined from within. Jealousy sown among leaders, the arousal of power-hunger, the insinuation of a desire for the worldly trappings of fame – such, I suggested, were still the best ways of corrupting the enemy's most devoted leaders and dividing Christian from Christian, church from church.

"Come, come, Crumblewit." The panel member at one end of the row shook his head and his antennae waved around frantically. "That may work in a local situation but what we have to develop is a global strategy. We must stop the enemy using extravagant and glamorous manifestations of his power to launch a worldwide recruitment campaign."

I now went into "statesmanlike" mode. "If the situation is, indeed, as grave as Your Lownesses have determined, I certainly would not want to underestimate it, but we have just as much access as the enemy to this new technology." I paused for effect, then went on. "If I may, off the top of my head, offer a hypothetical situation: picture a church in the grip of feverish new enthusiasm. Such a church inevitably contains many unstable relationships. The faster it grows, the more difficult it is for the leadership to maintain control. Suppose that we promote an internal scandal – sex and money are usually our most effective tools. Now the leadership might, fairly promptly, get a grip on the situation. However, if in the meantime we ensure that this internal problem receives maximum publicity worldwide, we can destroy the credibility of that church and halt the enemy's advance."

More nodding of heads and whispered conferring. Then the chairdevil addressed me. "Do you think you could handle such a strategy, Crumblewit?"

"I have an excellent team of personally trained agents," I replied. "They can be put into the field immediately. Judging from Your Lownesses' perceptive appraisal of the situation, time is of the essence."

My success was never really in doubt. Thus, to cut a long story short, I was appointed Assistant Director of the Anti-Charismatic Bureau with special responsibility for North America. I was sorry to see my creation, the Department for Combating Ecumenism, placed in other hands. We had just reached an important point in the development of our strategy. Our success in building up inter-church monoliths had provoked a sneaky reaction from the enemy. While we were creating among the Christian top brass an obsession with unity for its own sake, he was sowing frustration at the lower levels of church life. Reports were beginning to come in of local ecumenical projects. In several towns and villages Christian leaders, impatient with their respective hierarchies, were getting together to *do* things rather than *talk about* things. This presented my organization with a whole raft of new challenges. When churches combined to share buildings and Christians of different denominations began worshipping together they did not pose too much of a threat, but when they began combining their resources for mission and rediscovering the purpose for which the enemy had chosen them, we had to find effective counter-measures.

This was what I was working on when, thanks to Squimblebag, the opportunity for promotion came along. I could not, of course, turn down the new appointment but I did sometimes ask myself why this high-profile role had been dropped in my lap and wonder whether it made the best use of my talents. Initially I was very excited by the challenge of frustrating a major enemy initiative. I have since realized that displays of what I call "spiritual fireworks" are sometimes employed by our squirmy, clever-clever foe as diversions. We must always be on the lookout for his low-key undercover activities. He is so infuriatingly subtle! A whisper here, a nudge there, an unexpected answer to his darlings' desperate prayers, the arrangement of a sequence of "coincidences" and long-ignored Christian embers burst suddenly into searing flame. Let me give you a brief example.

There was once a little church in a quiet French village, supported by a dwindling, elderly congregation. The struggle to maintain their building and churchyard was getting beyond them. They were having to share a priest with several other churches. One day he was rushed into hospital with a heart attack. It was all very satisfactory and the devil in charge of the area thought that he could safely file the case away while he got on with more pressing work. Some parishioners dutifully visited the priest in hospital and sat round the ailing man's bed. Their concern was the chink which allowed the enemy in. Before we knew what was happening they were praying for him (hitherto it had always been the other way round). The duty devil intervened by hastening the priest's death. Wrong tactics! The little group kept on visiting the hospital. They spent time with other patients. Worst of all, they kept on praying. Of course, that was all the enemy needed to interfere. Some of the patients made remarkable recoveries.

"Miracle! Miracle!" people exclaimed. Our devil-on-the-spot panicked. He called for reinforcements but it was too late. The congregation was boosted by ex-patients and their families and some of the hospital staff. As their numbers grew they decided to abandon their crumbling church. A local farmer made one of his barns available. The whole community rallied round to refurbish and decorate it. The national press got hold of the story. Funds poured in. They used some of the money to attract big-name preachers... I can't go on. It was all too disgusting for words. And all because a devil who should have known better took his eye off the ball. The moral is clear and cannot be stated too often: never, never, never underestimate the enemy. Be vigilant. He and his agents can pop up anywhere, at any time.

But, to return to the next episode in my brilliant career, my first task was to assess the situation. I read the interim report of Blagender's committee and visited three or four of the worst trouble spots in North America. What I saw confirmed the official assessment. The charismatic movement (the name had already achieved permanence) was a major incursion of the enemy directed against a weak point in our defences. For three or four generations of human history we had concentrated on undermining the enemy's propaganda with the weapons of scepticism and cynicism. His creatures were so proud of their scientific and technological achievements and the intellectual disciplines underlying them that we were able to spread the belief that "truth" consisted of what could be proved in logical terms. Conversely, religious belief based upon revelation of realities completely beyond human understanding was "irrational", "old-fashioned", and "superstitious".

Christian apologists had, for the most part, fought back using their adversaries' weapons. They had tried to demonstrate that religious belief *could* be founded on logical arguments. While the academics were preoccupied with their dialectic, what filtered down to "the man in the street" was the assumption that the religious certainties which had undergirded many human societies were passé, unfashionable, untenable. Church attendance dwindled. Christianity ceased to be the bedrock of education systems. Public morality (often enshrined in lax new laws) abandoned the restraints imposed by the creator. The humans exulted in the newfound freedoms licensed by their "permissive society". It was all highly satisfactory.

What we had neglected was the humans' *emotional* needs. We were well practised at afflicting them with pain, grief, disillusionment, despair, anxiety, and fear, but had not made sufficient allowance for the enemy's response. We routinely enjoyed the anguish attendant upon the death of a child, the onset of a terminal illness, or the failure of a business, and we knew that our devious foe might suddenly interfere by providing a comforting new relationship, a cure, or an unexpected infusion of capital. These sallies are, as you know, the very stuff of our ongoing conventional war.

But the charismatic movement was different. It was an onslaught on a much bigger and potentially disastrous scale. Put simply, what the enemy was up to was this: he designated certain individuals through whom he could more directly manifest aspects of his power and personality. Through them he performed miracles, he healed the sick, he issued spiritual revelations which went way beyond what the speakers could have understood by mere human intellect, he taught them the rudiments of the language his fawning, obsequious, angelic courtiers use. This sort of underhand behaviour put us at a temporary disadvantage because, when the enemy revealed to his selected agents more of himself than the vast majority of his human adherents normally saw, we were unable to get a glimpse of what they were seeing. Small wonder that our devils-on-the-spot felt that they were fighting in a fog.

Now, of course, these charismatic manifestations caused an enormous stir among the enemy's people. Churches normally quiet, passive, and pleasantly respectable in their worship suddenly became excited, extrovert, and noisy. Outsiders noticed what was going on. The number of Christian converts rose alarmingly. This was the scenario that greeted me when I made my initial tour of battlefield hotspots in the North American sector. If I offer you one case study it will help you to grasp just how alarming the situation appeared.

* * * * *

CHAPTER 7

A Hard-Won Victory

(1968–1975)

The Episcopal church in a little town called Yellow Rapids had caused us no major problems. Its members were largely middle-aged or elderly farming folk and small traders. They were nice to each other and their neighbours in a non-committal sort of way. Any threatened outbursts of spiritual fervour we were able to quash by the normal means of arousing jealousies and inspiring backbiting. Then a new pastor arrived, the Reverend Jasper Corraine, a self-assured, fresh-faced young man with a reputation for pulpit oratory. He had come from a large Californian church which was one of the first in the country to show signs of the charismatic epidemic. Having infected Corraine and his wife, Bethany (a sugary, simpering blonde of the type currently made fashionable by film and television actresses), with a virulent form of the disease, the enemy had sent them to spread contagion in this peaceful, rural community.

Initially, Corraine's impact was divisive. His sermons majored on sin, judgment, and the enemy's determination to purge the church of nominal Christians. A few long-established church members left and this lulled our devils-on-the-spot into a false sense of security. But just as many people were attracted to the Corraines as were offended by them. Their meetings for prayer and study were well attended. Sunday worship figures increased. In order to put a stop to this our infernal rep in charge of the area organized a showdown. A group of elderly church members went in a body to present their complaints. The leader was a formidable lady by the name of Eliza Braddick. The meeting became very heated and ended in a delightful slanging match, after which the protestors declared their intention of going off to report Corraine to the bishop.

Then came disaster. Mrs Braddick, screaming invective at the vicar, stood up to lead her delegation out of the room. As she did so, she suddenly gasped, clutched her chest, and slumped to the floor. She had a long history of heart disease and it seemed that all the excitement had brought on a final seizure. We were all set to convey her here to Hell. Meanwhile, the humans clustered round in a horrified group. Someone sent for an ambulance. Another telephoned the doctor. A third attempted resuscitation. While this was going on Corraine took charge. He knelt beside the stricken woman, laid his hands on her, and prayed. Our reps were caught off guard with no time for a counter-attack. I was told that they were actually driven out of the building by a cosmic wind, which held them at bay for several minutes. When they were able to return they found Mrs Braddick sitting up and sipping a glass of water. They did their best to recover the situation. While Corraine called on the group to give thanks to the enemy for this miraculous deliverance, one man was prompted to suggest that there was nothing miraculous about it; the afflicted woman had responded to mouth-to-mouth resuscitation. But Eliza Braddick herself silenced him. She had felt the full force of the enemy's wretched interference and recognized it for what it was. She did not hesitate to describe her experience to her family and friends, and her interpretation of the event received confirmation days later when, after exhaustive hospital tests, the patient was declared to be in good health.

The news, of course, spread rapidly, as bad news always does. Locals who had not been to church for years turned up on Sundays, curious to see Corraine the "wonder-worker". In particular the sick and the handicapped appeared in the church or called at the vicarage hoping for miracles.

Corraine now began regular healing services. Within a few months people were flocking to Yellow Rapids from a wide area and the small community church could not cope with the increased congregation. Corraine, who could now do no wrong in the eyes of his adoring parishioners, launched an appeal for a new, elaborate church complex and demanded donations from the people as proof of their faith. On the third anniversary of their arrival in Yellow Rapids Jasper and Bethany Corraine welcomed their bishop for the opening of an impressive and expensive church centre, including offices for the church's growing professional staff, a large preaching arena, committee rooms, a baptistery, and an annexe for children's work. You can see from this the sort of thing we were up against by the time I arrived in my new post and began to set in motion an effective strategy.

I summoned a meeting of regional controllers and demanded their assessment of our major issues: 1. Where was the enemy concentrating his forces? 2. What, precisely, was he doing? 3. How much success was he having? 4. Where was he most vulnerable? The response to the first question was depressing on two counts. My agents – a particularly lethargic and unimaginative crew – bewailed the fact that from its origins in two or three flash points the charismatic movement was spreading nationwide with alarming speed. The Yellow Rapids pattern was, fortunately, not universal, but there were very many churches, of all denominational hues, where members were excited by the new phenomena and were introducing them. My second concern was that our workers, many of whom carried the scars of disastrous battles with the enemy, were despondent. "We've never come across anything like it," one of them whined. "We're not just dealing with flabby humans, with their confused thoughts and emotions; we're up against naked spiritual power."

"And just how is this power manifested?" I demanded.

The reply came in a jumbled cacophony of screams and shouts: "Healing!" "Yes – body *and* mind!" "Direct communication!" "We can't intercept the messages!" "Visions!" "Emotional release!" "Prayer vigils!" "Massive financial support!" "Frenzied preaching!" "Prophesying!"

"We've seen all this before," I said, trying to calm them down. "Why, we've even manufactured some of these effects ourselves. Think of the pagan cultures we've had worshipping us by using magic and even crude conjuring tricks."

"Oh, yes, we know all that," one bloated and grizzled demon replied. "I got a leading journalist to do a television exposé of the movement, in which he compared it to what he called 'the superstitious demon worship of backward peoples'. That only raised the charismatics' profile and got more curious or desperate humans flocking to their meetings."

I was determined to keep the meeting positive. "That brings us to the fourth item on the agenda," I said. "Where is the enemy most vulnerable?"

Silence. There was much casting-down of eyes and shuffling of hooves.

It was time to assert authority. "What?" I screamed. "Not one idea among the lot of you?" I pointed to a demon whose third arm had been severed at the shoulder. "You, there, don't think you can expect special treatment because of your war wounds. You're going back into battle immediately, so you'd better know what you're doing!" I lashed at him with my talons and enjoyed the feeling of my claws sinking into the soft tissue of his face. "Get out!" I paused to glare at the row of frightened features. "That goes for all of you! We'll adjourn for lunch – *my* lunch, that is. You had better spend the time thinking very hard. Anyone who doesn't come back with some sensible suggestions will be shipped off immediately to the correction centre."

Galvanized by fear, my "team" (Hell preserve us!) did thereafter show some semblance of strategic thinking. Of course, I was the one who had to come up with the brilliant initiatives, but at least my subordinates were now amenable to being licked into shape.

The strategy I put in place was based on the simple principle that confrontation was ineffective. (If the charismatic leaders were challenged they would denounce their critics as "worldly" and "lacking faith".) These high-profile Christians would have to be attacked from within. Once that ground plan had been established it was simply a matter of deciding the most effective modus operandi in each case. Humans, as we all know, are particularly vulnerable in three areas: there is not one of them who does not crave sex, or money, or power. Some desire all three, but that was unlikely to be the case with our chosen victims, who had experienced close encounters with the enemy. Accordingly, I set up three training camps to provide crash courses in Obsession Temptation (OT). These turned out specialists who could be despatched to deal with various of the more prominent charismatic leaders once our research workers had discovered their specific weaknesses.

The first temptation my trainees were all set to master was busyness. The Christian celebrities they were to deal with were much in demand by a host of acolytes, followers, and admirers. Their initial success led, inevitably, to more activity. Their churches grew. They planted offshoots. All of them were faced with an increased administrative burden. If they were expanding their church "plant" there were fund-raising projects to be organized, architects to be consulted, building contractors to be hired. As well as their own church meetings the leaders were in demand to speak to other congregations, to engage in the new phenomenon of "televangelism", and to write books and articles. When a tempter did his work properly all these activities took priority in a subject's daily schedule. The objective was to push the subject's private devotions into ever smaller corners, to ensure that he spent less and less time talking with the enemy.

Another important technique was to lure the charismatic heroes into seeing themselves as magicians. Of course, they never used that word and would have been appalled to consider themselves as cheap mountebanks, and wonder-workers, but when a leader began to think in terms of *his* healing service, *his* effective prayer, *his* demonstration of spiritual power, then a magician was what, in reality, he was becoming.

A magician is, as you well know, one who tries to use spiritual power for his own ends. We have raised up millions of such sorcerers, shamans, witch doctors, voodooists, wise women, and such like in every culture throughout human history. The enemy, as far as we can fathom his plans, appears to deploy his more spectacular effects sparingly and for specific purposes. To be sure, he is not above making a vulgar show of his concern for his favourites by healing diseases or frustrating us when we have mounted a particularly effective attack, but he avoids "routine" miracles and that is precisely what we wanted the charismatics to stage. Managed properly, a "healing service" could become nothing more than an emotionally charged show, a religious entertainment. With diligence a talented tempter could trick a charismatic leader into role reversal with the enemy: instead of being a servant, whose task was solely to do his master's bidding, he could become the master, demanding fresh tricks and power surges from Heaven.

The enemy's immediate response was to withhold his spiritual energy. This led to a decrease in the special effects on which several charismatic leaders relied and a gradual falling-away of their following. That, you might think, is precisely what my organization was aiming at. Not so. There was always a danger that a leader who found his popularity waning might call upon the enemy in humility and repentance – and we all know how the enemy responds to such pathetic grovelling! Fortunately, we have better techniques at our disposal, as I always impressed upon my staff. Handled carefully, success can be turned into a most effective trap.

The Corraines – in whom I took a personal interest – are an excellent case in point. Their healing ministry had soon attracted an enormous following. People were bussing in from far and wide for their weekly "Festivals of Deliverance". So large was the attendance at these meetings that not even the auditorium of the new church complex could cope with it. The Corraines, therefore, hired the town's largest public hall and hither people came or were brought by concerned family members. Every kind of human disorder was represented. There were epileptics and cancer sufferers, diabetics, and the mentally deranged. There were those who entered the hall on crutches or in wheelchairs. Sometimes hospital patients arrived by ambulance and were brought in on stretchers. The one thing they all had in common was a desperate desire for "deliverance". By that word Jasper Corraine meant release from demon possession. What he taught his flock was that every human ailment and disease, every lapse from perfect health of mind and body, was the result of demonic activity (I wish!). It was very flattering for us to be credited with such unlimited power. How very much simpler our task would be if that were the case. We would be spared the ceaseless tactical calculation of when and how to prey upon the humans' physical and mental limitations for our own purposes.

The threat posed by the Corraines' activity was twofold. There were genuine healings. The enemy, for his own – wretchedly obscure – reasons, did use the Corraines and their ever-growing staff of "associate ministers" to effect cures, which were sometimes spectacular.

The second danger was the effect on others. The Corraines' festivals had become elaborate and emotionally charged. The stage was occupied by a robed choir of some twenty or so singers and a band of musicians who led the audience in songs and encouraged demonstrations of fervour such as clapping, cheering, and arm-waving. Associate ministers offered heartfelt prayers (some of my less-experienced staff members found this painful in the extreme to endure). Then a few selected speakers were brought to the microphone to testify to what were billed as the "miracles of grace and power" they had experienced. Some of these revelations were genuine. Others were the result of self-delusion-sufferers who had convinced themselves that their symptoms had disappeared as a result of deliverance ministry. But whatever was said, whether true or false, had the cumulative effect of rendering the audience receptive to the preaching that followed. When the frenzy was at its height Jasper Corraine appeared at a spotlit rostrum and subjected the audience to a lengthy display of histrionic tub-thumping. My agents worked hard to close the hearers' minds but the enemy's minions were equally active. The end result of every such skirmish was that several members of the audience went over to the enemy. Some, of course, we were able to reclaim shortly afterwards, but the majority remained lost to us. When an individual has made a very public declaration of a change of life it is difficult for him/her to retract without losing face among friends, family, and workmates. This was another reason why it was important to discredit the Corraines: a convert could more easily wriggle out of his commitment if he could claim that he had been duped – along with many others – by a band of religious charlatans.

To say that my staff were dispirited would be an understatement. Only my experience and superior understanding kept the campaign on course. By a tireless round of front-line visits and a barrage of policy directives I hammered home the need for persistence and vigilance. I impressed on my flagging troops that we were close to achieving a breakthrough. And, at last, it came.

The Corraine organization invested heavily in the latest technology, such as relays of meetings to other venues by means of television link-ups when their hall was full to capacity. One necessary piece of equipment for crowd control was a wireless communication system. The Corraines were linked by small transmitters and receivers to all their associate ministers and to their stewards throughout the auditorium. It took me very little time to see the potential of this arrangement. One technique that never failed to make an impression was Jasper Corraine's identification of strangers who turned up with particular problems. The enemy indicated to him – directly – people he wanted to heal, and Corraine would summon them to the stage. "There's someone here with an uncured abscess on the left leg," he would declaim, and, with a gasp of astonishment, the sick person in question would stand up and hobble forward to receive the laying-on of hands. This was an important part of the show and the audience came to expect it. And I realized it was the vital chink in the Corraines' armour.

As the preacher's assistants showed people to their seats, made space for wheelchairs, and generally attended to the well-being of the audience, they naturally became aware of their afflictions. With a little prompting from my staff they probed sufferers for their medical details. With a little more urging they passed on such information to the team on the stage. For a few weeks Corraine resisted making use of such information. Then, on an evening which was unusually quiet, he revealed "hidden knowledge" about a serious arthritis sufferer. I had him! From that moment Corraine relied increasingly on the messages relayed by his own agents, rather than by the enemy. His spiritual vision had already been dimmed by the successful application of busyness temptation, so he really could not see that there was any harm in taking "short cuts" to acquisition of knowledge about his audience members. I had manoeuvred him into compromising his integrity. Healing miracles were gradually being replaced by conjuring tricks and psycho-suggestion. The next stage of my operation was simple. I got an investigative journalist to do a feature on the Corraines' activities. He took great delight in exposing the couple as fraudsters and confidence tricksters.

I now had the pathetic pair neatly trapped. Their devotees demanded that they stand up to their accusers and challenge them in the law courts. To remain silent would look like an admission of guilt. But to initiate a long-running legal battle would invite major media attention, cast doubt on their integrity, and prolong the scandal. My tactics were spectacularly successful. I was able to bring groups of trainee tempters in to watch Corraine's disintegration. He would have succumbed to a complete nervous breakdown if his bishop had not ordered him to take a sabbatical rest and then moved him to a post at diocesan headquarters, where his recovery could be carefully monitored. Meanwhile, the Festivals of Deliverance came to an end. I made sure that my triumph gained the attention of the Low Command and I received a personal commendation from the Minister for Infernal Affairs.

Equally important was the effect of the Corraine case on the morale of my own staff. It was a great encouragement to them to realize that the enemy's activists are often at their most vulnerable when they seem to be most secure. They find it very difficult to sustain that complete dependence on the enemy that he demands. His biggest blunder was endowing them with free will and, as we all know, this can so easily be turned against him. Even his most fanatical adherents – like the Corraines – maintain lingering vestiges of self-reliance.

This allows us to implant minute seeds of rebellion. We can make them *feel* that they can cope with any situation; that any suggestion to the contrary implies a degree of humiliation.

Christian leaders are looked up to by their followers as men and women of spiritual stature who are direct intermediaries between earth and Heaven. What the sycophantic acolytes fail to realize is that their adulation can be used to undermine their heroes. Any leader who actually comes to believe in his/her own power and authority is ready to be toppled. We have seen this happen over and over again throughout human history, and I demonstrated it once more in the Corraine case.

I must point out that I had nothing to do with the subsequent career of the Corraines. Any blame for their return to the ranks of the enemy's tenacious warriors cannot be laid at my door.[4] I was appointed to close down their operation in Yellow Rapids, and that is precisely what I did.

* * * * *

---

4   What Crumblewit alludes to here is the founding of Bethnimrah. In 1980, five years after their departure from Yellow Rapids, Jasper and Bethany Corraine set up a residential centre, which they named "Bethnimrah" ("House of Living Waters"). They called it a "spiritual health farm". In a low-key atmosphere, devoid of the razzmatazz that had characterized their previous ministry, people received counselling and conventional treatment as well as the laying-on of hands. Many can now testify to the help they received at Bethnimrah. It is hardly surprising that Crumblewit should want to dissociate himself from the Corraines' later history.

CHAPTER 8

How I Achieved Celebrity Status

(1975–1985)

Inspired by my leadership, the Anti-Charismatic Bureau went from strength to strength. Thanks to our outstanding success in North America I was in great demand as a speaker and seminar leader in other regions. It was as a result of my increasing exposure that I developed my celebrated talents as a public speaker. Many readers will be familiar with such motivational slogans as "Pervert and Publicize" and "Distort and Denounce". What may not be realized is that I originated them. In recent times rivals and plagiarizers have tried to claim the credit for the pioneer work I carried out in devising techniques for the manipulation of the press and television. It was I who developed MAIM (Moulding and Infecting Media) techniques. I, Crumblewit; no one else!

As I have already intimated, the possibilities of planet-spanning information services fascinated me from the start. In fact, my preoccupation with using the media as a powerful weapon against the church was the cause of my being passed over for a top ministerial post. I had always seen myself as an infernal strategist of the top rank. I had the potential to be a manipulator of human affairs at the highest level. If my advice had been heeded the rivalries between nations would long since have resulted in nuclear devastation. For example, there was an incident known on earth as the "Cuban Missile Crisis", involving rivalry between two heavily armed nations – the Soviet Union and the United States of America. Thanks to the activities of Hell's leadership at the time, these countries came within an ace of blowing each other to pieces. That would have been a really splendid triumph. It might have finally given us control of the smouldering remains of the planet. At the very least it would have been one in the eye for the enemy. I wrote a paper describing in precise terms how to sustain the self-destructive impetus. Unfortunately, at the time, I lacked the contacts which would have brought my ideas to the attention of the Low Command. As a result the opportunity was missed. Our leaders allowed the enemy to drag his darlings back from the edge of the abyss by the scruff of their necks.

I could have achieved the lowest possible depths of infernal government had I not been such a brilliant exponent of media manipulation. I realize now that I have Squimblebag to thank for my career getting stuck in a rut. He was one of the few senior devils who recognized – and therefore feared – my full potential. It was he who steered me in the direction of developing unique knowledge of human communication systems and it was his patronage which brought me to the attention of the Low Command. At the time I assumed that he had Hell's interests and mine at heart. I later realized that he was determined to sideline me. Oh, what I could have achieved... [5]

However, I can claim to have done Hell considerable service in the important area of frustrating some of the

---

5   Editorial note: Here followed several, largely indecipherable, notes of what seem to be schemes, plans, and initiatives which came to nothing.

enemy's major plans. The activities of our strategic planners in promoting wars, racial tension, economic crises, and political scandals attract the attention and plaudits of the infernal population but they can distract us from the underlying day-to-day, rough-and-tumble contests with the enemy and his agents, which are being fought in the cockpit of humankind's spiritual and moral awareness.

While populations had been decimated by wars and revolutions, Christianity had been spreading in parts of the world we once considered safe. In Africa half of the population soon belonged to Christian churches. In several Asian countries we witnessed at least a tenfold increase in adherence to the enemy. In China, the most heavily populated country on the planet, Christianity became the fastest-growing religion. The charismatic movement, which we had done much to disarm in the USA and Europe, continued to make a major impact in parts of South America. Not only was the enemy winning more adherents in all these countries but his deplorable ethical ideology was infecting education systems and even government institutions. It pains me to have to remind my readers of these facts, but no useful purpose is to be served by closing our minds to reality. The main battlefield was and continues to be in the religious domain.

It is for this reason that I am proud of my achievements in frustrating the enemy's attempts at religious revival. My Anti-Charismatic Bureau did sterling work in undermining the credibility of selected Christian leaders. Our Pervert and Publicize campaign was a particular success. We trapped various prominent Christian celebrities into sexual indiscretions or financial mismanagement and ensured that their failings received maximum publicity. This contributed significantly to a steady decline in church membership. My achievements in North America were emulated by colleagues working in Europe. It is to the credit of all devils concerned that those areas of the earth which had once been the enemy's strongholds fell, slowly but surely, under our sway. For human centuries we had almost given up on those lands where law, government, philosophy, education, art, and popular morality had been impregnated with the enemy's propaganda, but persistent toil to regain control of the prevailing culture gradually bore fruit.

The technologically more advanced nations, under our tutelage, made a god of "Progress". Or, rather, they bowed down to worship the human spirit, which, we persuaded them, is the sole source of all their accomplishments. We blinded them to the fact that it was the enemy who equipped them with a larger brain-to-mass ratio than any other animal species and permitted them to develop enquiring minds. They took the credit for themselves and consigned belief in a higher power to the realm of superstition, held only by "inferior" and "backward" races. This is, I suppose, why the enemy launched his counter-attack in what were then known as "Third World" countries. But more of that anon. To keep the events of my career in the proper sequence I must, at this point, make a slight digression.

Old Slubgob was on the point of retiring from his post at the Training College and was determined to go out in a blaze of glory. He selected some of Hell's more prominent celebrities to address the students so that they would be au fait with the current situation – and also to bask in the glory of some of his old boys who had gone on to achieve great things. Naturally, I was on his list of invited speakers. My chosen subject was "A Modern Tempter's Toolkit", and I sought to impress on my hearers the importance of keeping up to date with the techniques employed to destabilize the enemy's organization. My lecture was subsequently published and achieved wide circulation (though, unaccountably, it has long been out of print). For the benefit of any who may not have read it, I list here, in brief, the salient points.

I laid out for my eager listeners a strategy for extending our authority based on current trends in human society. I pointed out the cultural dominance of the planet being achieved by the once-Christian countries, and explained that our future success depended on continuing to subvert the prevailing philosophy of these leading nations. Every tempter was important in this process, I impressed upon my audience, because human society is composed of individuals. No devil leaving the school should consider his initial assignments unimportant. I then gave my hearers three key concepts to keep in the forefront of their minds:

1. Freedom. This political ideal, beloved of all humans and regularly exploited by ranting orators and dictators bent on enslaving them, is, at root, a myth. The humans exist to be slaves, either of us or of our overweening foe. He has always been quite open about this. He demands the allegiance of his followers, and the surrender of self is a prerequisite for anyone who becomes a Christian. We, of course, conceal our objective of keeping the humans in subjection and we do this by encouraging them to pursue personal freedom. At a national level this involves the spread of democracy, but young tempters should keep their eyes fixed on the implications of the freedom fetish for individuals.

Pseudo-psychology is a useful tool in this context. Allow me to illustrate. In order for human society to survive, certain individual desires have to be suppressed. For example, an average, well-behaved young man might meet a young woman at a party and be strongly attracted to her. However, if he is married to a different woman he will not attempt to develop a sexual relationship with her. He will *suppress* that natural desire. This is where we can use psychobabble to confuse him. We point out that *repressed* passion is harmful; it drives emotion underground and may have the direst long-term consequences. Far better, we point out, for him to be honest and open about his feelings and indulge in a secret affair. He is a free agent and should enjoy his freedom. Our trap is based on substituting *su*ppression with *re*pression. Suppression means acknowledging a desire but deliberately choosing not to gratify it. Repression is, by contrast, a form of self-delusion. So, for instance, if our hypothetical young man is a Christian he might be so appalled by the idea of lust as to believe that he is immune to it. Rather than acknowledging his desire, he denies its existence. Thus, when we dangle an attractive female before him, he has no effective defence and we may enjoy the delicious prospect of his total moral collapse, his damaging of other lives, and his eventual descent into self-loathing or, if we play our cards right, into loss of faith.

Another useful tactic is to blur the distinction between wants, needs, and rights. For example, a woman may *want* a baby. She does not, however, *need* a baby, because she can continue to function without being a mother. The skilful tempter, by causing her to dwell on her childless state, may well make her convince herself that she has a *right* to a baby, that her husband, or the government, or society, or – if we play our cards right – our enemy is denying her what is her due. This then opens up for the tempter all manner of possibilities. He can persuade her that she is free from all restraint in seeking to fulfil her own desires. Thus, according to circumstances, she may be inveigled into adultery, casual sex, or stealing another woman's child. Over and again, in several human societies, we have successfully created havoc by impelling individuals and groups into drastic action in pursuit of what they perceive as "freedom" but what is, in reality, seeking the gratification of their own desires without regard to the impact of their actions on others.

An excellent example of how this strategy can work on a global scale is provided by Operation Rabbit. The code name for this brilliant campaign was taken from a human expression, "breeding like rabbits". Scientists had developed various contraceptive devices which enabled men and women to enjoy the brief pleasure of sexual intercourse without the long-term consequences of procreation. This was a serious challenge to us. From our point of view, humans should be encouraged to flout the rules laid down by their creator, and the sooner unrestrained rutting overpopulates the planet, the better. However, since the new methods of birth control could not be uninvented, we had to find ways of frustrating their effectiveness.

The brilliant concept which gave rise to Operation Rabbit was that, rather than restrict the use of contraception, we should spread it. It had been devised primarily for use within marriage, to help couples plan the size of their family. Outside marriage, sexual intercourse was officially frowned on. Many people exercised restraint. Many, on the other hand, did not, and the highly gratifying results were underage sexual activity, illegal abortions, women left bringing up children without the support of husbands, and the spread of prostitution. Religious leaders and many politicians were all for maintaining the moral dam which was holding back the flood waters of unrestrained lust.

This attitude provided our opportunity. We persuaded liberal thinkers to campaign against the "killjoys" who were restricting human freedom. They argued that the best way to limit the effects of extramarital sexual activity was to make contraceptives as widely available as possible. So, for example, girls of thirteen and fourteen should be allowed free access to contraceptives without the knowledge of their parents. This would reduce the number of teenage pregnancies. Such arguments seem, and are, facile, but they worked. No strategic initiative has ever been more successful than Operation Rabbit. It has undermined social cohesion in many countries. Providing contraceptives to "everyone" led inevitably to the assumption that untrammelled sexual activity was OK. The collapse of the moral dam led to all the phenomena the liberals had claimed that it would eliminate. Teenage pregnancies, abortions, and single-parent families dramatically increased and, as a huge bonus, there was an epidemic of sexually transmitted disease. However, I must reiterate that the tempter who is ambitious to become the instigator of social disintegration, riot, rebellion, or war should learn his craft by practising on individuals.

2. Acquisitiveness. One of the eccentric foibles of our enigmatic foe is setting his dwarflings in a world rich with natural resources and the results of human ingenuity while seeking to impress upon them that they should not strive to acquire such things. His principal agents have denounced avarice in the strongest possible terms, and Christian history is replete with depressing examples of men and women who have closed their minds and hearts to the enjoyment of material possessions so as not to be distracted from their service of the enemy or their fellow creatures (such tiresome individuals are not immune from attack; we can, for example, use self-denial to promote pride – but that is a different story).

Most probationary tempters will find themselves assigned to subjects in what humans call the "developed" world, the more affluent nations. While it is difficult to distract poorer people from the enemy's claim to their allegiance, an abundance of material possessions offers us much more scope.

Wealthy Christians (in which category I include "comfortably off" Christians who do not think of themselves as wealthy) have to cope with a conflict between their culture, which defines "success" in terms of money and goods accumulated, and their faith, which urges them to have little regard for what the enemy's propaganda dismisses as "earthly treasure". The Christian's instruction manual denounces the pursuit of wealth in the most unequivocal terms. The best way we have found to combat this is to persuade the enemy's people that when he says it is virtually impossible for rich people to enjoy his favour, he doesn't *really* mean it. I have heard scores of sermons in which the preacher has squirmed his way through interpretations of the enemy's plain policy directives in order to assure his hearers that they may, with a clear conscience, invest in financial schemes, pension plans, and the like in order to make their earthly lives as comfortable and secure as they possibly can. Christian leaders have frequently set a personal example in this regard. Popes, cardinals, bishops, vicars, and ministers of all types have lived in palaces, surrounded by all the luxuries with which we can provide them, while enjoining their flocks to endure with patience their humbler lot.

When my anti-charismatic campaign was at its height, one of my best teams, led by Ludgeblug, a particularly promising protégé who has subsequently descended to impressive depths of achievement, scored a major coup by turning one of the Christian leaders and getting him to work for me (without realizing it, of course), and the method chosen was a radical perversion of the enemy's teaching about money. Several celebrity preachers were presiding over successful churches whose congregations contributed generously to church funds. It was not difficult to lure them into paying themselves large salaries, living in mansions, driving expensive cars, and accumulating all the trappings of wealth. Their lifestyle did not escape media criticism. To this their response was to assert that their material well-being was a sign of the enemy's favour. What my team then did was, by a process of carefully doctored logic, to develop this self-justification into a major doctrine. It was dubbed the "prosperity gospel", and I will have more to say about it later. From there it was only a short step – but a brilliantly conceived one – to the creating of a major financial scandal. Ludgeblug injected his chosen celebrity with gradually increased doses of greed until he had turned him into a confidence trickster, promising his followers spiritual rewards in return for cash. Ludgeblug allowed him a run of several years before leaving him to face charges of criminal fraud. At his trial the man's victims thronged the courtroom and would have torn him limb from limb if he had not been protected by the police. Needless to say, a worse fate awaited him when he arrived here.

3. Relativism. This is an attitude which goes hand in hand with the pursuit of individual freedom. The rules which our enemy laid down for the humans were intended to keep them in a state of dependence and servitude. He demanded, and continues to demand, their exclusive allegiance. Not only that: he dictates their relationships with each other. His slaves are directed not to kill each other or steal from each other or even to desire each other's possessions. They are to respect the institution of marriage, to honour their parents, and... well, I won't go on; the list is long and tedious. The important point is that these regulations severely limit individual liberty, or what we have always persuaded humans to think of as individual liberty. Our clever-clever foe might have thought he was providing his creatures with a well-structured environment within which they could operate safely and securely, but the degree of restraint he imposed made it ludicrously simple for us to nudge them into rebellion.

However, the rules remain in place and are still taught to children brought up in a Judeo-Christian environment. It follows that any tempter assigned to a Jew or a Christian cannot simply sweep aside the religious–moral code instilled during their upbringing. This is where relativism comes in. It is, essentially, a watering-down of the enemy's code of conduct. For example, murder is strictly prohibited but there may be circumstances when it is justifiable. War is the obvious one (oh, what fun our infernal sages must have had when they intervened in solemn conclaves of bishops and theologians convened to develop a philosophy of the "just war"!), but individuals may be lured into homicide for what seem to them impeccable reasons. Thus it may seem merciful to hasten the death of someone who is terminally ill, or to carry out an abortion on a woman for whom giving birth to and rearing a child would be inconvenient. A householder who apprehends a burglar in the dead of night might feel no guilt about bludgeoning the intruder to death. Such acts splendidly cock a snook at our arrogant enemy, who claims that he alone should determine the lifespan of every one of his creatures.

Sex remains the most effective universal tool at our disposal. Adultery, sexual experimentation by emotionally immature young people, and the unwillingness of parents to provide a firm moral framework for their teenage children are, in every human community, being justified on the grounds of "love". Oh, the delightful spectacles of misery, betrayal, desertion, cantankerous bitterness, and murder we have been able to enjoy as a direct result of inducing couples to claim (and, in most cases, believe) that "It's OK because we love each other". As if they knew the meaning of the word! It is an attribute of the enemy which remains a mystery. If *we* don't understand it, the inferior human creatures can't possibly grasp its implications. Our task is to conceal reality from them by persuading them that the enemy's hard-and-fast rules are mere guidelines, which humans are free to adapt, apply, or not apply, according to the circumstances.

Our ultimate aim is to make every human being his or her own arbiter of what is or is not moral conduct. This will be a significant contributory factor to the final disintegration of human society. In recent earth times we have pursued this policy with gratifying success. We have urged leading thinkers to challenge religious "taboos" on the grounds that the propounding of universal laws is an attack on societies' and individuals' right to develop in their own ways.

However, we must not rest on our laurels. All major religions have seen through the fallacy of relativism. Any human who has some grasp of the reality which lies beyond his infinitesimal little planet knows that the destiny of his species lies in the hands of beings beyond his comprehension. It is a lamentable fact that representatives of rival faiths which we have taught to loathe each other are increasingly coming together to expose with a united voice the ethical void at the heart of many human societies. Therefore, we must be diligent in distorting, confusing, and, as far as possible, silencing all those taking a stand against moral decay.

This is why war against the church remains, as I have always insisted, our top priority. I have sometimes heard devils who say, "Our job is closing down churches." Nothing could be further from the truth. As fast as we close churches, the enemy establishes new ones. If we were to concentrate all our efforts on reducing the size of congregations and making their buildings redundant we would find ourselves constantly playing the game of catch-up with our industrious and innovative foe. In fact, one conclusion I have reached is that shutting churches is a standard part of his plan and one he has sometimes duped us into carrying out for him. To use an earthly analogy, he is like a gardener who constantly prunes his plants, cutting out dead or unproductive branches in order to invigorate and strengthen the main stems. Our job is not to wield the pruner's knife for him but, on the contrary, to protect the fruitless limbs so that they will continue to suck life from his trees and shrubs.

The policy we adopt is despiritualization. It is one with which the reader will be very familiar. All tempters learn basic despiritualizing techniques at the primary education level. But familiarity may breed flabby thinking. Some of you who read this need to get back to basics. You must understand that nothing irritates the enemy and frustrates his purposes as much as congregations which project an image of ageing insipidity and are widely regarded as irrelevant. Therefore, it really is an important part of our task to keep weak churches alive – but only just. There are numerous ways to go about this. Perhaps I can best illustrate some of them by telling a story. It is fictitious, but I have constructed it by bringing together real incidents that have occurred in churches in which I or close colleagues have been involved. I call my story:

The Living Death of St Ailing's

Imagine an English rural community, something between a large village and a small town. Despite twentieth-century developments its ancient church still dominates the skyline. But it does not dominate the life of its people. The Sunday congregation has been steadily dwindling for years. Here we have achieved despiritualization by natural wastage. The thirty or so mainly elderly people who make up the congregation have no time or energy to spare for the enemy's work. They are too busy fund-raising to keep their 700-year-old building in a state of tolerable repair. They are quite good at this. They arrange fêtes, concerts, whist drives, and so on. And it is in our interests to see that they carry on. Their emotional commitment to their Gothic church is something we support because, should the struggle ever become too great and the building have to be abandoned, the enemy might be able to make some use of these people. He is very adept at finding work for idle hands to do. So we can come and go more or less at will among these church people.

Now, see that same little congregation a few years down the road. Their vicar has just left and they are given the unwelcome news that he is not to be replaced. The diocese can no longer afford to pay a professional pastor to care for such a small community. St Ailing's will, in future, be joined to the nearby urban parish of St Thriving's. Now this is a situation which requires careful handling. St Thriving's is an appallingly active church. It has a vicar and curate and several lay people involved in leading services, as well as running activities such as youth work, study groups, parish visiting, and the like. There is a real risk that some of their enthusiasm might rub off on St Ailing's. This calls for different despiritualizing techniques.

The most obvious is parochialism. Among the St Ailing's folk we raise feelings of resentment and fear of being swamped by the larger church. We successfully create a siege mentality – a determination to preserve their time-honoured traditions at all costs. We toughen their resistance to change. For example, suggestions that the time of Sunday services might be moved or new, up-to-date music books be used are violently resisted. But suppose the steady drip, drip of mission-oriented zeal from St Thriving's does begin to work? Suppose some of the members of the larger congregation decide to worship at St Ailing's in a deliberate attempt at infiltration? What to do?

We can certainly continue stirring up friction – complaints about the vicar's forthright preaching style, the length of sermons, the establishment of study groups, opposition to plans for a parish mission – that sort of thing. But care does need to be taken with direct confrontation. It not infrequently makes people think. And that is the last thing we want to encourage. Having prevented most of the St Ailing's folk from learning anything new about the enemy's programme since their Sunday-school days, we don't want to see them abandoning the closed-mind habit. Far better to keep their attention focused on non-spiritual religious peripherals.

Church politics presents us with varied opportunities to deflect Christians from pursuing the enemy's main objectives. Interference by the diocese or whatever regional or national body oversees local churches can be useful to us. Those at the upper levels of any religious hierarchy tend to live in a rarefied atmosphere of abstract ideas and impressive-sounding strategies. This helps us to induce a "them-and-us" mentality at the local level. Nothing infuriates churchgoers more than attempts to impose new initiatives from above. The pursuit of power is something relatively easy to inject into a church situation. Self-importance is a very entertaining vice to behold, especially when it is dressed up in religious clothes. No matter how small the pool may be, we can usually find someone who wants to be a big fish in it. If you can stimulate your imagination again, I will show you what I mean.

Thanks to a lack of money and manpower, the St Thriving's group of churches grows even bigger. St Ambling's and St Somewhere-in-the-Sticks are added to the group, to which the diocesan authorities now give the high-sounding name of "Partnership for Mission and Worship" (PMW). In fact, of course, this heterogeneous conglomerate is quite unable to work together. The lack of trained staff makes it difficult, if not impossible, to maintain all the services and meetings to which the people of these parishes had become accustomed in the "good old days". It is soon apparent that lay people will have to shoulder several of the burdens hitherto carried by clergy. This is our opportunity to get some of the best people into positions of authority, and by "best" I mean, of course, not those prompted and equipped by the enemy, but those who have other reasons for extending their own influence. They may have a particular cause to promote or axe to grind or they may simply have a psychological need for status. This is actually crucial for us because, if we are not careful, the enemy can use this shake-up to slip into influential positions men and women of his choice who can work under his close supervision. I sometimes suspect that the enemy allows a church to disintegrate in order to establish a new regime (yet another example of the way he can turn our initiatives against us). We can best thwart this stratagem by getting in first with our own candidates.

There are many humans we can employ because they consider themselves to be natural leaders. They may have achieved important positions in business or local government or in military careers and believe that, having retired from professional life, they are being "called" to direct the activities of the church. It is our task to encourage such delusions and keep them from realizing that the qualification the enemy is interested in is spiritual maturity. So we send two or three of such individuals off to diocesan headquarters to receive a smattering of instruction in church doctrine and they return with pieces of paper proclaiming them to be "trained theologians" qualified to instruct their neighbours. Up they then pop in the pulpits of the St Thriving's group and ardently proclaim whatever high-sounding but ineffective twaddle we put into their heads. And what makes the situation even more delicious is that they regard themselves as spiritual shepherds of the enemy's flock.

On the subject of church politics it is important to be aware that church people have traditionally taken the theories and practices of secular government as their models for running their own affairs. Whether they live under a tyrannical king, a squirearchy, or a democratically elected parliament, they tend to equate in their minds the governance of church and state and seem oblivious to the instructions of the enemy regarding the regular conduct of church affairs. He is, or aspires to be, a hands-on ruler who chooses not only the men and women he appoints to be the leaders of every Christian assembly, but also those who are to exercise the various necessary gifts – teaching, evangelizing, healing, administration, etc. He expects his appointees to be in regular communication with him so that he can hand down his instructions.

In a great many churches we have successfully sabotaged this schema. Thus, for example, in several places it is the norm for church councils to meet together to discuss business, to reach decisions, and then, almost as an afterthought, to direct a brief prayer to the enemy, informing him of what they have done and intimating that they require his endorsement. Our basic strategy has been to blind them to the reality of prayer. We, of course, can never know exactly how prayer works. When our detestable foe establishes direct contact with a group of his darlings it is difficult to interfere effectively. When he is talking with humans on a one-to-one basis there are, as you know, various techniques at our disposal – wandering thoughts, time constraints, telephone calls, other interruptions, etc. However, when a group of Christians come together to spend disciplined time in prayer it is almost impossible to get a look-in.

As I was saying, churches tend to emulate the political philosophy of secular regimes and that is certainly the case with the latest ideological fashion – democracy. What makes this so particularly ironical is that democracy is one of the enemy's inventions. He has let it be known to his followers that he regards all people everywhere as equals. How he could ever have imagined that such a ridiculous idea would work is beyond me, but it is a fact, and one which we have been able to distort in several ways. What the enemy means by "equality" is that he is impartial in his concern for and (ugh!) love of every one of his human creatures. In other words, he chooses to regard as equal people who are patently not equal. In several countries this absurd principle has been adopted and adapted as a basis for mundane government. All adult citizens, irrespective of age, sex, intelligence, or integrity, have been given the right to vote for the people who will govern them. It has taken little effort on our part for church activists to assume that democracy is the best of all possible systems and, therefore, the one they should adopt in church affairs. The result is that men and women of little spiritual understanding and no obvious holiness get voted onto committees which then set the agenda for their churches. Thus, instead of control being entrusted to those the enemy has chosen and trained for leadership, it is placed in the hands of men or women who happen to be popular or who shout the loudest. An army run by sergeants!

Let's take a last brief look at our PMW to see how we can use this democracy nonsense as a ball and chain to be fastened to the life of a church. The various parishes now linked together have been instructed to work as a unit. This calls for a central body to discuss all aspects of policy, make decisions, and set out a plan of campaign. What the enemy would want, as I have already suggested, is that such a leadership group would be composed of his appointees, chosen in consultation with himself. He would expect that all members would be his particularly close followers and the recipients of the gifts he had bestowed for the benefit of the "partnership". That would not have suited our book at all. Thanks to our efforts, St Thriving's is no longer the force it once was. The disruptions caused by amalgamating with other churches and the extra organizational burden imposed on the vicar and his team have taken their toll. To these problems we have added bickering between the various churches of the "partnership", each of which is primarily concerned with its own interests.

In this situation the first priority is seen to be "unity". And unity, it is automatically assumed, must be based on equality. Thus the new overseeing body is made up of representatives from each church, elected by church members. Brilliant! What better recipe could there be for introspection and stagnation? Instead of the "partnership" finding its unity in a common purpose – that of spearheading the enemy's mission in the area – we create a diverse group of leaders possessing varying degrees of commitment (and non-commitment) to the enemy. Since these "leaders" are not selected for their spiritual maturity, it follows that they cannot discern and carry out the enemy's plans. Not knowing what direction the church is supposed to be going in, they cannot lead it. Very soon they are spending all their time organizing social events among themselves, special services, and fund-raising activities. The end result is that the smaller churches in the group do not grow and St Thriving's congregation actually declines because several of its spiritually aware members defect to other, "keener" churches in the area. Despiritualization is virtually complete. Job done!

But, to resume my personal history, as I have said, the success of my Anti-Charismatic Bureau was noted in lower circles and my own achievements were being lauded by Squimblebag (for reasons known at that time only to him). Thus it was that I received a summons to the office of no less a devil than Prince Blagender. You can imagine how thrilled and awestruck I was by this rare privilege. I had often stood outside the gates of Blagender Pile, with its sentries barring access to all but the favoured few. To actually pass through those portals and have the guards salute me as I did so was an experience the memory of which I shall always treasure.

The anteroom into which I was shown was impressive in the extreme and clearly designed to induce an appropriate state of mind in all those preparing for an audience with the great devil. It was hung from floor to ceiling with portraits of Blagender. From a loudspeaker came a continuous medley of extracts from the prince's speeches. There were half a dozen other invitees in the room and they were all seated on chairs facing a large screen, onto which were projected scenes of Blagender's numerous military triumphs. I took my place among them and soon entered a trance-like state as my mind tried to cope with the competing sounds and images with which it was assailed. This was pride on a truly monumental scale. Magnificently awe-inspiring. I felt almost sorry when my turn came to be ushered into the archdevil's presence. I wondered, briefly, whether the reality of coming face to face with Prince Blagender might not be an anticlimax.

I could not have been more wrong.

* * * * *

CHAPTER 9

Communication and Confusion

(1986–1988)

The throne room into which I was escorted was long – very long – and narrow. Ceremonial guard devils were placed along it at regular intervals. At the far end, on a dais under a splendid canopy, the prince sat and watched as I approached with measured and respectful tread. As I reached the raised platform I did not dare to look up but I felt the archdevil's presence. An aura of warm, throbbing vileness emanated from the throne, embracing me, making me feel at the same time abashed and embraced. There are no words to describe my emotions at finding myself in the presence of this legendary hero of the cosmic war. Prince Blagender's greatness overwhelmed me yet I sensed with elation the brotherhood of evil which united us.

"Crumblewit." Oh, the thrill of hearing my name uttered by those famous lips!

"At your complete service, Your Inestimable Lowness."

"We hear very satisfactory reports of you."

"Your Supreme Iniquity is too gracious."

"On the contrary; you would not be here if your labours had not deservedly brought you to our attention. Your dossier makes impressive reading. We have you marked out for more important work."

My excitement mounted. "More important work" – what could that mean? A ministerial post perhaps? I mumbled my appreciation.

"Tell me, Crumblewit," the prince continued, "you have familiarized yourself with terrestrial communication systems, so what do you consider to be the most important from the point of view of increasing our control of human minds?"

I replied promptly. "Television, Your Majestic Abominableness. In many countries there will soon be a set in every home, even in the poorer ones. This provides us with immense opportunities to fill the humans' minds with… "

"Yes, yes, to be sure," the prince interrupted. "Television presents interesting possibilities. But what do you know about computers?"

"Computers?" I had to think quickly. "They use them for business purposes and children's games… "

"Our information is that they will become the most important vehicles for human interaction in the very near future. There are several experts working now on projects that aim to place satellite-linked computers in every home – perhaps, even, in every pocket."

I tried not to show my surprise.

"Do you see what this means, Crumblewit?"

My mind went into overdrive. "Instant brainwashing, Your… "

"Precisely. As usual, Crumblewit, you get right to the heart of the matter. Billions of humans, all in instant communication

147

with each other. We plant a Hellish idea in a man's mind in Beijing. He presses a button, and immediately thousands of people read it in Baltimore, Birmingham, and Beirut."

I could not stifle an involuntary gasp.

"I see the implications have not fully impacted even on your keen mind, Crumblewit."

"Your Superlative Awfulness, I... "

"It is, of course, obvious that we must take control of this technology before the enemy gets his claws on it... "

"Oh, absolutely, Your... "

"... which is why we are setting up a government commission to gather information and to make recommendations as to policy. We need Hell's best brains on that commission. It must be chaired by a devil of exceptional ability."

Suddenly I saw, with a rush of excitement, where this conversation was leading. Prince Blagender wanted me to head up a commission of vital importance, a commission responsible directly to him. "That is why", the prince continued, "we have appointed Squimblebag as chairman. We instructed him to draw up a list of devils he wanted on his team. Your name was at the very top."

Squimblebag! Squimblebag! I felt as though a goblet brimming with vintage hypocrisy had been dashed from my lips as I was on the point of tasting it. My "dear friend" Squimblebag, I realized in an instant of revelation, was determined to interpose himself between me and the promotion which was my due. My head throbbed with resentment. My limbs trembled with rage. It was all I could do to listen to the prince as he outlined the remit of the new commission. He concluded the interview with congratulations and instructions to report to my new boss without delay.

Without delay? Never! Crumblewit to go crawling to Squimblebag? Certainly not! If he wanted me on his "team" *he* could come to *me*. That much I had irrevocably decided before the gates of Blagender Pile closed behind me.

Well, the summons was not long in coming. Squimblebag's note was brief. "Curt" would be a better word. He was delighted, he wrote, that my appointment had been confirmed by lower authority. The first meeting of the commissioners had been arranged. He gave the time and place. He felt sure that I would accommodate myself to these arrangements and expected me to be present. I did not trouble to acknowledge this directive.

I took care to arrive slightly late for the meeting. It had already started and Squimblebag was in full, self-important flow as I entered the room and took my seat at the end of the table opposite the chairman. I gazed round at my fellow commissioners. There were seven of them. All nonentities. Not an original, creative mind among them. As Squimblebag rambled on I fixed my thoughts on working out his game plan. My colleagues were all yes-devils who would follow the chairman's lead and back his decisions. Why, then, had Squimblebag involved me? The answer was clear. I was to be the brains of the outfit. My now-extensive network of agents would be put to work gathering information. My brilliant mind would sift it all and make policy recommendations. My literary skills would be called upon to draft the report. And when it was hailed as an excellent piece of work, who would receive the plaudits? Certainly not Crumblewit.

Thwarting Squimblebag's stratagems would call upon all my resources of deviousness and cunning. He had – or so he thought – wedged me into a corner. By commending me to the lowest authorities he had tied me to official policy. It would be extremely difficult to undermine him without spoiling the work of the commission. If Blagender ever got to suspect that I was being "uncooperative" – well, the reader will not need me to point out the dire consequences of that. Throughout our first meeting I was cautious in the extreme. I made a point of applauding Squimblebag's initiatives and whenever my opinion was solicited I deferred to "our chairman's superior understanding". I tried hard to keep all hint of sarcasm out of my voice, though I doubt whether the pompous narcissist would have noticed my darts even if I had not blunted them.

The trouble was that Squimblebag was absolutely right about the importance of computers and all the associated technology. Television, as I knew well and had always urged, was an excellent tool offering numerous possibilities. At the lowest level it provided an endless stream of trivia with which we could fill people's minds and divert their attention from issues concerning their eternal well-being. Handled properly, TV could even prevent them from thinking at all; they could simply take their ideas and opinions from the screens which dominated their living spaces. But there were more creative uses to be made of this medium. Particularly valuable were the related fields of soap opera and celebrity worship. It has been one of our greatest long-term achievements to ensure that most humans live drab lives. Over and again the enemy attempts to break through their humdrum existence by offering glimpses of his greater reality. We, of course, cannot see the pictures he is presenting to their minds, the "visions" he is imparting. No matter; what we can do, and have done consistently with great success, is keep the pathetic creatures preoccupied with the mundane: working feverishly to earn money to buy those trinkets – clothes, gadgets, motor cars, jewellery, houses – which give them social status and bolster their sense of self-worth. If this leaves them craving "something more", we offer glamour. We have schooled a whole industry to dangle before the populace images of men and women whose wealth, fame, and exciting lifestyle suggest what, with luck, ingenuity, or extra effort, their fans, too, might achieve. We have manoeuvred them into a delightfully jumbled state of mind in which fact and fiction, reality and dreams are splendidly confused.

Perhaps I should explain how we have used television to achieve this. There are three phases of operation involved.

Phase 1. Persuade viewers that what they see on their screens is "reality". We allow news broadcasts, factual documentaries, and educational programmes. We even permit the enemy a little air time. My own concentration, and that of my team, has been on manipulating Christian usage of the media. We have, for example, created a situation in which "televangelism" has become a dirty word in mainline churches.

Phase 2. Originate programmes which distort and exaggerate human life. The best example of this is the soap opera – a serial drama which offers a delicious menu of violence, deceit, envy, greed, lust, anger, hatred, and broken relationships.

Phase 3. Encourage viewers to identify with the fiction played out on their screens. Let them really believe that normal behaviour involves extramarital affairs, drunken rowdyism, shouting angry abuse, and deliberately inflicting pain or humiliation on others.

When viewers subconsciously begin to behave in their own situations like their favourite television stars, we have achieved the confusion to which I refer. It is then up to us to ensure that the resulting lowering of moral standards spreads throughout human society.

Television – and, of course, cinema, radio, and the press – remain important battlegrounds. However, Blagender and Squimblebag were quite right to focus Hell's attention on the latest tools for human interconnection, and I applied myself to accumulating information on this fast-developing technology.

I immediately perceived that evolving a strategy for making use of what its enthusiastic pioneers later called the "internet" or the "information superhighway" would be an enormously complicated task. Hitherto we had had to concentrate only on gaining control of a relatively small number of programme-makers. We successfully induced many writers, producers, and editors to rebel against moral restraint in the interests of "artistic freedom" and this, as I have said, further weakened the enemy's grip on the ethical agenda. Within a human decade of the terrestrial spread of television the portrayal of physical and mental violence, sexual licence, and obsession with wealth had become norms of television output. However, the vestiges of restraint remained. Regulatory bodies were still partially influenced by the enemy's agents. We could not gain complete control of the media in order to ridicule the enemy and promote the rejection of his rules.

Computers, by contrast, presented us with an embarrassment of riches. Their use was unpoliced. Anyone could promote whatever ideas and beliefs he or she wanted. Even before the development of the internet and the laptop I could see the possibilities for disseminating information across our entire range of subversive material, from local gossip-mongering to attacks on revered institutions. The time was rapidly approaching, I realized, when we would be able to spread child pornography, atheistic doctrines, and political nihilism, to relay instructions for the manufacture of terrorist bombs, coded arrangements for the distribution of drugs, or plans for sexual orgies. The time was coming when nothing and no one would be beyond the scope of our propaganda. This unfamiliar new world was, I realized, almost upon us.

What was worrying was the sheer scale of the operation which would be necessary to gain control of every computer outlet and inlet. Not only would we need to propagate demonic ideas and initiatives, we would also have to keep a tireless watch on all the enemy activists, who would be equally energetic in promoting their slave-master's insidious schemes. I decided that it was this aspect of our strategy that I should focus on initially. My fellow committee members and Squimblebag himself were being swept along by a tide of unquestioning enthusiasm for the new technology. Experience and my own superior analytical skills had made me very wary of the enemy's subterfuges. I knew only too well that we must never underestimate him. He has this aggravating habit of popping up anywhere and at any time. Indeed, he seems to revel in making his appearance in situations which we thought we had under control...[6]

---

6   Editor's note: This seemed the most sensible place to incorporate Crumblewit's notes on Christian music. His text becomes increasingly disorganized from this point on, for reasons concerning his later career and which are not difficult to deduce (see below, pp.238–39). There are places where the narrative breaks off in mid-flow and others where notes have been incorporated which are out of sequence. There have been times when my attempts to follow the author's twists and turns of thought have ended up in cul-de-sacs of incomprehensibility. Crumblewit's rambling reflections on Christian music cover several decades but they do, eventually, connect with his explanation of how the Squimblebag Commission sought to counter the spread of new devotional and inspirational songs being made universally available via the internet (see below, pp.159–160).

Few subjects divide Christians more effectively than music, and we have for many human generations exploited aesthetic differences to create splits in churches and drive worshippers into irreconcilable factions. We have achieved this despite being under the considerable handicap of not understanding what music *is*. The unmentionable one has endowed his creatures with a profound sensitivity to various sounds and combinations of sounds and he obviously uses this as a means of communication with them. He can bypass their mental processes to induce a variety of emotional states. Most tempters have experienced the following frustrating sequence of events: you spend time and effort tying up a subject's mind in intellectual knots; you have him or her sick with worry about a particular problem or reduced to inactivity by conflicting possible courses of action or boiling with rage at some perceived slight. Then, while your back is turned, the wretched mortal suddenly comes into contact with music. It might be a deliberate act, such as switching on a radio or an iPod, or contact might be involuntary – a street busker churning out tunes (whatever they are!) or background music in a restaurant. Before you know where you are, the subject's mood has changed – anxiety is soothed, anger is calmed, decisiveness replaces torpor. Then all your hard work counts for nothing. We've all been there!

Thanks to the tireless efforts of our research teams we have learned various techniques for turning music to our own advantage. Thus a patriotic song evoking love of home and country can be made into a nationalistic rant sung with aggressive fervour by armies marching to war. Teenagers can be prompted to channel their anger and frustration into frenzied sounds carrying hostile lyrics to challenge the shortcomings of their parents' generation. By subjecting humans to combinations of sounds that they find distressing ("discordant" is the technical term for this), we can drive them to distraction, even suicide. Languorous "melodies" (another technical term), when combined with visual images of an erotic nature, easily arouse sexual passion. The chanting of ancient religious music in ancient religious buildings, instead of tightening the enemy's grip on minds and hearts, can be used to induce in both hearers and performers a feeling of self-satisfied religiosity far removed from what the composers of the music originally intended. And when we get crowds of sweaty humans together in darkened rooms to wriggle their bodies in time with very loud, monotonous rhythms bashed out by drums and guitars, we can induce them to abandon mental activity altogether.

However, this is all run-of-the-mill tempting. What is more demanding and more valuable as a part of Hell's overall strategy is interfering with the enemy's uses of music to raise the spiritual awareness of his devotees. I have made a particular study of this and covered the basics thoroughly in my discussion paper, "Disharmonization for Beginners". Rather than repeat the arguments rehearsed there I will quote a couple of examples of disharmonization in action.

It was during my probationary period at college that I was sent on assignment to a church somewhere in Britain. It was a conventional set-up in a small town at a time when churchgoing was still a respectable pastime of the middle class. My tutor introduced me to the principal activists. The Revd Dominic Rainbird was the vicar – youngish, enthusiastic, and worryingly open to new, creative ideas. His wife, Sarah, assisted in running the youth club, whose leader, Richard

Hackshaw (widely known as "Rickshaw" or "Ricky") was a single male, fresh out of college, with a passion for all kinds of sport. The choirmaster and organist was George Bourdon, a retired teacher who had been in charge of the music at St Simpleton's-in-the-Mire for longer than most people could remember. He it was who had raised the musical standard of the choir to a high pitch. Scarcely a Sunday passed without the performance of an anthem and George sometimes took his singers to perform at choral events elsewhere. He was proud of his achievements and had long since substituted worship of what he thought of as "beauty" for worship of our enemy. In fact we had done such a good job on him that he saw no distinction between the two. As far as worship was concerned George ruled the roost at St Simpleton's. It was all very satisfactory.

George's problems began with Dominic's arrival in the parish. The new vicar insisted on choosing the congregational music (hymns), something his predecessor had been content to leave to the organist. It was Dominic's intention, as he said, to encourage "new music and new thinking". This, of course, we could not tolerate. However, the devils in charge at St Simpleton's turned the situation to advantage by fanning aesthetic disagreement into a feud between the old guard and the new. What was more worrying was Ricky Hackshaw's influence over the local young people. Many joined his youth club and had to suffer Christian indoctrination. He took parties to camps where skilled enemy agents played on their emotions. Several went very decisively over to the enemy. This was the situation in the church when I was brought in.

I quickly mastered all the salient points and realized that our priority was to stop the revitalization of the church, which was well in progress. The demographic of the congregation was changing as more teenagers and young married couples joined. What we needed to do was widen still further the gulf between the "oldies" and the "trendies", as the rival camps were now labelling each other. Loyalties were focusing on George and Ricky respectively. What would deepen their rivalry? The answer was obvious: music. I suggested to Sarah Rainbird, a moderately accomplished pianist, that she might form some of the young people into a popular religious music group. My tutor was far from pleased. He demanded to know why I was providing the enemy with more ammunition. He was not wholly convinced by my explanation but he gave me my head and was very impressed with the result.

Hot Gospel, as the band called itself, soon acquired a considerable following in the area. Two of its members also belonged to the church choir and it was not difficult to provoke a conflict of interest, particularly when George made fun of Hot Gospel as "unmusical" and "irreverent". Such jibes lost him the support of three choir members. My strategy was working perfectly.

There was one more move to be made and I lost no time in planting a new idea in Sarah's mind – a family service in the church, at which Hot Gospel would perform. Dominic took some convincing, because he knew how George and his friends would react, but he gave the youngsters his support and steeled himself for the inevitable conflict. It was not long in coming. An angry George Bourdon stormed up to the vicarage and protested loudly at this invasion of "his" territory. A truly delicious row ensued. George insisted that his years of faithful service deserved better than this "betrayal". He threatened to resign. Dominic replied that the church would be sorry to lose him but that, if George felt so strongly, perhaps the time had come for him to retire. The old musician was shell-shocked. He marched off, threatening all manner of reprisals, including denouncing the trendy Rainbirds to the bishop. It was all delightfully nasty.

This was the point at which my placement ended. What I heard later about subsequent events at St Simpleton's made me wish that I had continued to be involved. Bungling devils assigned to the project seriously overplayed their hand. Resentment in the congregation led to Hot Gospel and their supporters joining the local Baptist church. This then became a seriously strong centre of our enemy's activity. An attempt to create scandal by pushing Sarah and Ricky into a sexual relationship failed lamentably and won widespread sympathy for the vicar and his family. Although George Bourdon and a few others defected to St Spike's on the Mount, the congregation at St Simpleton's actually increased and there was growing cooperation between the parish church and local Nonconformist assemblies. I can state most emphatically that this was none of my doing!

We really do need to be subtle about exploiting cultural differences. It is important, for example, to keep those involved in formal worship from really analysing what they are doing. They should be encouraged to assume that what they find pleasing is even more pleasing to our wretched foe who, whatever else he is, is the author and instigator of all that rubbish humans label as "beauty", "art", "spirituality", and "holiness". I sometimes think musical purists actually believe that the enemy has nothing better to do than sit on a cloud and listen to their oratorios, anthems, and sacred songs, with a copy of the score in front of him. On the other hand, Christian ravers seem to envisage the awful one as an indulgent paterfamilias whose heart is touched by the spectacle of crowds of exhibitionists lustily belting out inane jingles and waving their arms about as proof of their devotion.

Such subconscious misconceptions are precisely what we should be fostering. Once Christians realize that the enemy has given them music for their benefit not his, that it is an offering from him to them, and not vice versa, that's when the trouble starts. Heaven intends music to be a conduit feeding into human minds and hearts concepts, ideas, impulses, and spiritual titbits. It is an appallingly powerful means of communication and one which we must block or divert at all costs.

The advent of new recording techniques provided me with the opportunity to scupper one potentially dangerous Christian music initiative. The proliferation of religious jamborees, as the reader will know, has been a major strategy of the enemy for several earth years. The bringing together of thousands of – mostly young – excitable enthusiasts to submit themselves to various kinds of Christian brainwashing has regularly required enormous Hellish resources to be deployed in counter-measures. Music plays a major part in these gatherings and many "Christian pop" groups have emerged. They deliberately mimic the style of contemporary secular bands which are part of a highly sophisticated entertainment industry. They have huge followings worldwide and attract all the trappings of wealth and fame. They receive the adulation of millions of mindless fans and serve a very useful purpose in encouraging the expression of basic emotions without reflection on the responsibilities and restraints the enemy desires to impose on them. What Christian groups aim to do, as some of them have said, is "redeem pop culture" by marrying contemporary musical styles and Christian lyrics. In attempting this they tread a difficult path, and we have enjoyed frequent success in tripping them up.

Take the case of Tony and Tina. This teenage brother and sister were accomplished singers and guitarists who performed folk songs and had set their sights on a professional career. They were of no consequence to us until, as a result of certain distressing difficulties, they were hoodwinked into going over to the enemy. I forbear entering into details. Suffice it to say that Tony had to struggle with a debilitating illness and Tina found herself in an unhappy sexual relationship. An agent of the enemy infiltrated their situation when we were not looking and they surrendered to his blandishments. One result was that, drawing on their own emotional experiences and the enemy propaganda they were eagerly absorbing, they began to write their own religious lyrics and, within a short time, found themselves much in demand at Christian jamborees. They were very effective. They did a great deal of damage. They had to be stopped.

I put one of my best operatives on the case. He persuaded Tony and Tina (they always performed under their own names and resisted our efforts to persuade them to adopt a more trendy stage title) to sign up with a commercial agent. He obtained a contract for them with a recording company who put their songs onto cassette tapes and, later, onto compact discs and video discs (techniques of sound reproduction were changing rapidly at that time). My rep was alarmed at their initial success and wanted to create friction between the performers and their agent, but I forbade him.

"The long game is always more effective," I counselled. We could afford to allow the enemy a few minor successes in the process of working towards ultimate victory. Thus Tony and Tina became a sensational "hit" in the worldwide Christian community. They toured in many countries and their tapes and discs sold in millions. They prospered – exactly as I had hoped they would. Their lifestyle changed with bewildering rapidity. First-class travel, the best hotels, pleasant houses, and, within a couple of years, marriage – all this came their way. Then, having achieved such a degree of material well-being, they easily fell prey to the temptation to sustain it at all costs.

The way to do that was to go on producing new songs. It may well be that the enemy had fresh lyrics to teach them and suitable tunes to carry his message, but now Tony and Tina had less time to listen to him. The fans demanded a constant flow of new material and their agent was energetic in keeping them up to the mark. The result was an output increasingly strong on emotionalism and weak on devotional content. Songs that had hitherto served to deepen the commitment of many Christians were replaced by ditties which could be sung with fervour but contained little by way of religious challenge. We had thus turned a hostile source of inspiration and Christian morale-boosting into a purveyor of insipid religious blandness.

So, to summarize, we can minimize the threat of religious music in three main ways: 1. We can encourage the use of various musical styles as badges that Christians use to distinguish themselves from one another. 2. We can ensure that it expresses feelings rather than inculcating doctrines. 3. We can make enjoyment of the sensual thrill of music a substitute for the excitement bestowed by the enemy on those who are enthusiastically active in his service.

* * * * *

CHAPTER 10

Highways and Byways

(This rambling section of the narrative introduces various episodes from the period up to 1988)

The tireless work of the Low Command has many facets and the activity of the Squimblebag Commission was, of course, only one of them. However, all aspects of policy have to be integrated and it may help the reader to understand where my contributions fitted into the bigger picture if I summarize the main priorities of Hell's strategy at that time.

Essentially, what we had to do was respond to earth situations which changed drastically from decade to decade. The "world war" was an important achievement. It had created destruction and distress on a scale far greater than the humans had ever experienced. But it did not achieve all we might have hoped for – the permanent division of the planet into rival armed camps hurling at each other weapons of such destructive force that the created order of which our industrious and imaginative foe is so proud would have been reduced to a ball of dust spinning through space. We did manage to sustain for several decades a conflict known as the "Cold War" between two rival power groups armed to the teeth with nuclear weapons, but somehow the enemy managed to bring about a rapprochement between the heads of government. The best we could do as far as human conflict was concerned was to provoke minor wars, revolutions, violent demonstrations, and massacres. These pleasant diversions brought us in a fairly steady harvest of souls but they were just that – pleasant diversions. We clearly needed a new global strategy.

That word "global" provides the key to our next brilliant policy shift. The development of the communication technologies to which I have already referred transformed life on the planet. "Globalization" became the new buzzword among politicians. It was supposed to signify growing understanding, harmony, cooperation, and peace between nations. I suppose that was the enemy's intention; it certainly smacks of his naïve belief in the ability of his creatures to subsume their national and sectional interests in the quest for the general good. What it actually meant was that the dominant nations had discovered new ways of extending their control. Old-fashioned empire-building had come to a halt because scientists had equipped rival armies with weapons of such destructive force that governments were frightened to sanction their use. But war had always had economic objectives – loot, taxation, control of natural resources. Now the leading nations had the means to achieve their economic ends without recourse to military intervention. Commercial corporations opened factories in poor lands where they could exploit a low-paid workforce. They bribed local officials in order to gain trade concessions. Diplomats vied with each other to secure favourable business deals.

But what lay behind all this was political evangelism. There were two rival ideologies competing for world domination. One was democracy/capitalism. The other was communism/socialism. Each appealed to the material ambitions of its adherents and claimed to be able to create Heaven on earth. In reality, there was little to choose between them. Both ensured that the many were controlled by the few, that disparities of wealth remained firmly in place, that the planet's human and other resources were mercilessly plundered, and that the "haves" (as has been the case in all human societies) exploited the "have-nots".

Communism was a philosophy of centralized political and economic control based upon power. We persuaded its theorists and advocates to believe that only firm government control over every aspect of national life could deliver a just society which would meet the needs of all citizens by a process of forced equality. Any philosophy which called this into question was suppressed. This, of course, included religion. The Low Command was very satisfied at having brought a large proportion of the human race under atheistic regimes. I always felt that we should be careful not to become complacent – and I was proved right.

The rival system was more complex and seldom failed to present us with strategic challenges. Democracy/capitalism had at its root the Judeo-Christian ethic. We had, of course, managed to distort it, but religious thought forms frequently thrust themselves into political speeches and manifestos. There was a long tradition of democracy/capitalism going hand in hand with militant Christianity. In earlier times armies and colonial administrators despatched from Christian lands had usually been accompanied (or even preceded) by preachers

– troublesome busybodies intent on changing indigenous cultures and winning converts for our enemy. This was where the real battle lines were drawn, and Hell's resources were seriously stretched as church after church was set up in lands where the enemy's insidious message had never before been heard. It is to the credit of our ancestors that they fought hard and, ultimately, successfully to divert much of this energy into the proclamation of a new religion – democracy/capitalism. Formerly, colonial takeovers had been justified by the claim that "Christianity and civilization" were being brought to backward peoples. Now, thanks to the activities of Hell's misinformation experts, the religious aspect of colonial expansion has been abandoned in favour of the preaching of a secular gospel. Nation after nation has been won over to the Western ideals of universal suffrage and the market economy in the deluded conviction that this will ensure human happiness. If power was the motive force for communism/socialism, what fuelled democracy/capitalism was that magnificent core sin that continues to serve us so splendidly – greed.

The two political systems rest squarely on the same assumption (which we have securely established) that the humans' material world is the only reality. Its rich resources exist solely for their benefit and are theirs to exploit at will. This is, as we all know, a typical Hellish distortion of the enemy's real intention. He *has* supplied them with a richly stocked planet and he *does* intend them to enjoy it. In his absurd overgenerosity he has spoiled his creatures in the hope, one must suppose, that they will respond to his open-handedness and use his gifts intelligently. Materialism provides virtual immunity to intimations of immortality. It keeps the humans unaware of their eternal destiny so that they can happily concentrate on improving their material well-being. As a result they will do anything, devise any argument, frame any policy, pursue any strategy whose aim is the accumulation of wealth and the trappings of wealth. Individuals, commercial companies, and national governments have dedicated themselves to greed. Latterly, our strategy has come under some attack – and not only from Christians. An international conservation lobby has appeared and is pointing out what should always have been obvious – that the earth's resources are finite and that pillaging them irresponsibly will not only exhaust them but will also disturb the ecological balance and thus accelerate the rate of decline. Campaigners hold conferences and bombard governments with statistics about deforestation and the poisoning of the atmosphere with those gases which are an inevitable by-product of industrial and technological "progress". Moralists, meanwhile, are adding their voices to the cacophony of do-goodery assailing the ears of world leaders. They clamour for a fairer distribution of planetary resources. They point out that, despite the mushrooming human population, it is still possible to feed all the people adequately. It calls only for the "haves" to assume responsibility for the "have-nots". Wealthy nations, it is claimed, must recognize an ethical responsibility to restrain their own consumption, thus creating surpluses for distribution among the majority world population, which is undernourished and vulnerable to disease.

Readers should not be unduly concerned by these developments. The Low Command has the situation well in hand and ensures that national governments always put their own interests before those of the planet. In totalitarian states any protest against materialistic philosophy is easily stifled, while democratic governments always have to pander to the clamour of their electorates for constant improvements to their material standard of living. Thus, as long as we continue to promote individual greed, we can be sure that politicians, who depend on their popularity, will always support what they call "national well-being" against humanitarian consensus. One way or another, the steady flow of souls through Hell's portals will continue, and it matters not whether they arrive as a result of famine and corruption in the poorer regions of the earth or of overindulgence in the materially affluent nations. Admittedly there are more gourmet delights to be savoured in the soul of an obese banker succumbing to a heart attack at a Manhattan party than in that of a lean and hungry revolutionary in a failed African state, but, when all is said and done, a soul is a soul is a soul.

So, in brief, we have kept humans obsessed with their short stay in the material world and devised for them political philosophies and economic theories with which they can justify to themselves sheer acquisitiveness. My own contribution to this strategy has lain in giving greed a religious gloss. The enemy could not have made clearer his opposition to the accumulation of wealth for its own sake. In his abhorrent human form he either earned a modest living with his own hands or, as an itinerant preacher, relied on the charity of his adherents. He championed the cause of the poor, and degraded himself by wallowing among the dregs of society. He was so outspoken in his opposition to the rich and powerful that, as you know, there seemed to be a possibility, at one point, that our Master might divert him from his course and turn him into a social revolutionary. Numberless Christians have sought to emulate him by deliberately espousing poverty.

However, for the rank and file of the enemy's followers things have never been quite that simple. Their problem stems from their owner's generosity. He has created a planet brimming with delights. He has equipped them with the skills necessary to turn natural resources into all manner of cunning inventions. And he has enabled them, by their own skills and industry, to earn the money to acquire many more things than they need for survival. For the Christian who takes his or her religion seriously, this creates a dilemma. How should he/she use the gifts bestowed by the enemy? Is it permissible simply to accept and enjoy them, or should consumption be limited so that money can be given to the poor? Can a bigger house, a better car, or an expensive holiday be justified while homeless people still litter city streets and an ever-increasing number of charities clamour for support?

And, of course, Christians have a more fundamental problem: security. The enemy has provided clear instructions: his followers are to concentrate on serving him day by day and to trust him to take care of their future needs. This demand puts their faith very much to the test. Total dependence involves taking the enemy at his word and casting aside self-reliance.

This, as even the most bungling tempter knows, provides us with numerous opportunities to create anguished dilemmas and even to undermine faith completely. Every day numerous Christians are asking themselves, "Should I saddle myself with a huge mortgage in order to have the security of owning my own house?" "Should I invest in a pension plan?" "Should I put money aside for a rainy day?" We can make them worry about not having enough money and we can make them worry about having too much. Best of all, we can encourage them to ignore altogether the problems created by surplus wealth and to give in completely to selfishness. Of course, they don't realize that that is what they are doing. I have often seen prominent devotees of the enemy get hot under the collar when obliged to listen to sermons on "The Christian Attitude to Money". They are extremely sensitive on this issue and it is easy to make them suspect that any exposition of the enemy's demand for sacrificial giving is merely another attempt by "the church" to part them from their hard-earned cash.

Something that helps our cause enormously in this regard is propagating false theologies of wealth, and this is a field of expertise in which I have particularly excelled. The secret of success in this, as in other spheres of temptation, is to grasp firmly the fact that essentially humans believe what they want to believe. That being the case, when they are faced with a head-on clash between their own fundamental desires and the demands of the enemy, Christians are open to persuasion that their master's words need not be taken at face value. By way of illustration I will relate how I devised and propagated "prosperity-gospel" theology.

There are phases in the rise and fall of earth empires when one nation has the upper hand. Its people enjoy a material standard of living which is the envy of other countries. For several years after the "Second World War", the United States of America found itself in this position. Europe had been ravaged by the destructive march and counter-march of armies. State treasuries were empty. Rebuilding shattered cities and re-establishing sound economies occupied most of the combatant nations for a generation or more. During this period the USA, whose home soil had been spared, was seen by many as the land of promise. Unbridled capitalism and the opportunities provided by its expanding economy enticed a steady flow of immigrants, many of whom prospered. So commonplace were rags-to-riches stories that people referred to the pursuit of wealth as "the American Dream". Most citizens were very proud of their nation's status as the world's richest and most powerful nation.

This, of course, suited us very well, because we were able to keep millions of people preoccupied with making and spending money. However, this period also witnessed a serious onslaught by enemy forces in the USA. Thousands of men, women, and children became Christians and numerous churches were founded. One inevitable result was the emergence of preachers who challenged the doctrines of self-reliance and the pursuit of riches which were fundamental to the prevailing philosophy. Converts were confronted for the first time with the black-and-white demands of the Christian writings and asked themselves the age-old question; how could an affluent lifestyle be squared with the enemy's insistence on a simple life and total dependence on him?

It was important for us to counteract such soul-searching, not least because of America's worldwide influence. I have already drawn attention to the political evangelism which was a feature of this period: the fervent activity of diplomats, statesmen, and commercial tycoons to extend Western influence, preaching a gospel of democracy, capitalism, and the pursuit of wealth. The Christian revival in the USA and, to a lesser degree, in Western Europe produced a simultaneous surge of religious evangelism in other lands.

It began in quite an unthreatening way. Individual Christians and small groups were despatched to newly independent nations as teachers, agricultural advisers, doctors, and nurses in order to display what the nauseating do-gooders called "practical Christianity". For a while the enemy got in under our radar. The Low Command underestimated the potential of such apparently insignificant operations. Fortunately, some of us perceived only too clearly the harm such activity could do. We banded together to form a pressure group. We lobbied our leaders, issued discussion documents (see my "Half-truths – Their Dissemination and Effectiveness"), and, wherever the opportunity arose, we infiltrated some of the more troublesome Christian movements. It was clear to us that the most effective way to stop people round the globe benefiting from the spiritual water the enemy's agents were distributing was to poison the wells.

Perhaps "muddying the wells" would be a better metaphor. If we could stir up the silt of political and economic philosophy so that it clouded the Christian message, our objective could be achieved at source. This would be a more effective use of devil-power resources than deploying thousands of operatives round the world to counteract outbreaks of unadulterated Christianity. Accordingly, we set in train several pilot schemes. Some were successful in diverting individual churches from the enemy's core teaching but by far the most outstanding – and the one in which I was, for a time, involved – was Operation Modern Magic (OMM).

We gave our initiative this name because it was simply a new manifestation of ancient battlefield tactics. Our ancestors often gained adherents by prompting humans to believe in what we call "magic". The basis of magic, as I have already mentioned, is the attempt to manipulate spiritual forces to produce desirable material objectives. What pleasurable sport it must have given devils of old to watch greedy humans uttering bizarre incantations in the hope of discovering buried treasure, or gabbling meaningless formulae over their freshly planted crops, or offering jewels at dusty shrines to ensure business success.

Well, the American Dream provided us with both the opportunity and the means to launch a new magic mania. As I have said, the USA had become the home of a glamorous materialism that was the envy of people around the world. In America and elsewhere the poor and the not-so-poor desired the trappings of wealth enjoyed by many in the land of promise. What they either did not know or chose to ignore was that most wealthy men and women had built their success on developing skills, working hard, and making sacrifices. The starry-eyed hopefuls we had spoon-fed with generous helpings of envy and greed were looking for short cuts to the glitzy lifestyle. They wanted a new kind of magic. So we gave them the "prosperity gospel".

Basically what we did was select some preachers and writers and fill their heads with a new "theology" which was a jumble of basic Christian teaching and the American Dream. I can best illustrate how this worked by narrating some incidents in which I played a major part.

It all began on an American golf course. Ben Cremovitch, a moderately successful businessman, was playing a round with his friend Abe Grekheim, minister of the local Pentecostalist church. Ben was a member of Abe's congregation. He also had political ambitions and had decided to contest a forthcoming election for the United States Congress. Both men needed money – Ben for his campaign and Abe for the development of church work. Greed was their prime motivation, though, of course, we did not allow them to realize this. Their conversation, as they worked their way around the velvet greens of Ben's exclusive club on a radiant summer morning, went something like this:

Abe: How's the campaign coming along, Ben?

Ben: Competition's tough, as you know, but we're building slowly.

Abe: Well, the church is right behind you, as you know.

Ben: Thanks for your backing, Abe. I really appreciate what you said in your sermon on Sunday.

Abe: It was no more than the truth. We need more born-again Christians like you in our politics if we're to rid our great nation of atheism, socialism, and wishy-washy liberalism.

There was a pause as the two players teed off on the next hole. As they set off down the fairway, conversation resumed.

Ben: There's so much I could do, and want to do, as the representative of this community.

Abe: Sure you do, Ben, and I just know the Lord's waiting to bless you. Are you praying about it?

Ben: Sure I am.

Abe: No, Ben, I mean *real* prayer – prayer that lays hold of Scripture promises.

Ben: I'm not sure I...

Abe: Look, what's your biggest need right at this moment?

Ben: That's easy – money. My rival has more wealthy backers than I do.

Abe: And you've been praying for more funds, more patrons – right?

Ben: Yeah.

Abe: Vague! Way too vague! How much money do you really need between now and the next election? Exactly!

Ben: Well, my campaign manager's looking for $350,000.

Abe: Now, you know that getting elected is part of the Lord's plan. So it's only your lack of faith that's holding you back. Look, you see the next green way up there?

Ben: Yeah!

Abe: Well, if you get everything right – posture, grip, swing, allowance for wind – your next slot will land right up, real close to the pin. It'll happen. It's inevitable. The laws of physics and aerodynamics say so.

Ben: I guess so.

Abe: It's exactly the same with your three hundred and fifty grand. Do the right things and the money's yours. It's inevitable. The laws of divine provision never fail.

Ben: What do you mean by the "right things"?

Abe: First off, you have to use faith imagination. Envision yourself sitting at your desk with bundles of dollar bills covering the surface – four hundred thousand dollars' worth of bills.

Ben: Hang on there, Abe. I said $350,000.

Abe: I'm coming to that. The second thing you do is pledge $50,000 to the church as a thank offering. You can write a post-dated cheque when we get back to the clubhouse.

Ben: Hey, wait a minute! I don't *have* fifty grand.

Abe: Faith, Ben, faith! You don't have because you don't ask. That's what Scripture says. The Lord intends you and the church and our great country to prosper. All the resources for this are sitting in his bank vault. And the key to the door is faith. We

have Scripture's promise that money donated to
the church will be returned to the donors sevenfold.
That's why your fifty thousand will be turned into
three hundred and fifty thousand.

Now, as you will realize, we had been doing a lot of work behind the scenes before this particular exchange could take place. And it certainly was not an isolated event. Numerous theological wells had been muddied as we built up a movement based on a distortion of the enemy's teaching about wealth. Affluent Christians tended to feel uncomfortable about the growing gap between rich and poor. Many responded to the plight of their fellow human beings by founding and supporting charities as well as devoting time and energy to practical schemes of social welfare. The danger of this was that they learned more about that nauseating activity of the enemy – sacrifice – and were drawn closer to his perverted way of thinking.

The strategy that we more radical devils proposed, and which was gradually endorsed as official policy, was to persuade as many Christian opinion-formers as possible that the love of money (clearly condemned by the enemy) was actually a good thing. We turned the enemy's lavish overindulgence of his people to our advantage by planting the thought that he actually wants his people to be rich. The message went out via pulpits, books, and TV screens that a Christian's faithfulness could be measured by the size of his bank balance. The world's poor could be helped only by the world's rich. Therefore, it was incumbent on Christians to become rich.

The originators of OMM took this strategy a stage further. We instigated "miracle incantation": Abe Grekheim was just one of many Christian pastors we persuaded to adopt a mechanistic attitude towards prayer. The enemy, as we know to our cost, instituted this particular form of communication in order to bring his sheep-like followers round to his way of thinking (that's why it will always remain a vital part of every tempter's activity to sabotage his subject's prayer life). OMM turned this process on its head. It used prayer as a form of spiritual blackmail. We convinced the subject that he had a *right* to certain favours and was fully justified in claiming them. In a word, "magic". I only wish I could have seen the enemy's reaction to the mounting cacophony of demands that assailed him. He must have been infuriated!

But we had one more trick up our sleeves – miracle incantations. These took various forms but were usually performed in emotionally charged meetings. As worshippers placed their offerings in the collection bowl they might "sprinkle" them in dumb show so that they would grow. Another device was to get every member of the congregation to hold their hands aloft and imagine them holding the specific sum of money they were demanding from the enemy. Of course the only people who really benefited from all this hocus-pocus were the pastors and church leaders. They grew richer and richer from the offerings of their duped followers and were not remotely hesitant about flaunting their wealth with palatial houses, expensive motor cars, and luxury suites in the best hotels when they went on preaching tours. To their devotees such a glamorous lifestyle seemed to be proof of their leaders' faith and vindication of their doctrine.

At this point I can almost hear you thinking, dear reader, "Surely this could not last. The enemy cannot have responded positively to all the preposterous demands being made on him.

When earnest prayers were not answered, would disillusion not set in?" The answer lies in Phase 2 of OMM. We engineered a few apparent miracles. Not many; just enough to keep the prosperity-gospel pot simmering nicely. For example, to return to our two golfers, Ben and Abe. You will recall that the businessman was gulled into parting with $50,000 by the promise that it would be turned into $350,000. I was the one who "answered" this particular prayer. It was a stroke of pure genius. I increased the temperature of the electoral battle Ben was engaged in and when the rival candidates were almost at each other's throats I provided Ben's opponent with some damning but false information about him. He hastened to go on television to expose Ben's moral failings. Ben, of course, indignantly sued him for defamation. The result was an out-of-court settlement for $400,000. Not only that, the debacle swung the election in Ben's favour. What better proof could he have had that the prosperity gospel really worked?

* * * * *

CHAPTER 11

Ꮒotting Ꭷp the ꝑace

(1989–1995)

It was about this time that a radical change overwhelmed the political scene. It took the humans completely by surprise. It even threw a spanner in the works of our Low Command. Of course, this should not have been the case; our leaders ought to have made contingency plans for a major shift in the balance of power on earth. I had certainly been warning against any complacent continuation of Hell's traditional policies, but no one listened to Crumblewit.

Briefly, what happened was as follows: as I have explained, the major nations were divided into two camps – communist and democratic. In the former, tight, centralized control was maintained by appeal to national pride and an ideology that promoted subservience of individualism to the interests of the state. Democracy, by contrast, prided itself on personal freedom, encouraging greed and the accumulation of material goods – usually with the aid of credit facilities. Both philosophies claimed to hold the secret of human happiness, a fallacy we had become well practised in exploiting. The weakness in this arrangement was that communism and democracy were both secular ideologies, which urged the human herd to regard their earthly existence as the only reality. Since official state propaganda either denied the possibility of life after death or declined to involve itself in metaphysics, ordinary people could evaluate their own worth only in terms of their possessions.

Now, people in industrialized democratic states were better off materially than the majority of their counterparts in the communist world. This was no problem politically as long as the latter could be kept largely in ignorance of the former. For this reason communist leaders censored the press, controlled radio and television channels, severely restricted travel, maintained tight border checks, and even, in one instance, erected a concrete wall to prevent citizens from escaping. Such restrictions, as I clearly foresaw, could not remain in place for ever. Information oozed across state boundaries and, with the advent of satellite information technology, the trickle became a flood. Inevitably, the subjects of totalitarian regimes began to ask why they, too, could not have houses and cars and fashionable clothes and all the supposed benefits of capitalist society. Pressure on governments built up until, very suddenly, several leading communist states simply collapsed. Dictators were swept aside. Power caucuses were forced to yield to demands for new, more democratic, constitutions. Relations between once-hostile states took on a friendlier hue. Capitalist corporations set up operations in former communist countries. It was this series of political revolutions which demanded a major rethink of Hell's overall strategy.

However, the more fundamental revolution was the one that was taking place in the field of human communication. Political regimes come and go. Ideologies evolve and dissolve. But the tidal wave of technical innovation was unstoppable.

Its effects were diverse and, to those who, unlike me, did not keep a vigilant watch, bewildering. It presented so many opportunities. I have already referred to the help the internet provided for all tempters. Pornography, sedition, drug dealing, terrorism – every conceivable kind of crime and vice could now be propagated and nurtured internationally via the World Wide Web. Yet there were less obvious, but equally delicious, ways of despoiling human society using computer technology and its derivatives.

The greatest achievement the Squimblebag Commission can claim is the creation of the technonerd. This was – and is – a human subset so totally infatuated with information technology that its members lived in a world of virtual reality. Oh, the fun we had withering the brains of young men (it was almost always the adolescent and post-adolescent males of the species who were most susceptible to our activities). We induced them to spend most of their waking hours in front of computer screens, playing mind-numbing games and devising new ones. They withdrew steadily from the real world and became as aliens to friends and family. They communicated almost exclusively, through their little square screens, with those who shared their obsession. By focusing their minds on the possibilities of computer technology, we induced a state of heightened self-regard. They became, in their own estimation, little gods, creating a myriad of new ways of exerting power over their fellow humans. They set up businesses to sell people all manner of goods and services, thereby accelerating rampant consumerism. Once we had established an almost total slavish dependence on computers, we urged technonerds to demonstrate their cleverness by sabotaging whole networks (by introducing what were called "viruses") and creating widespread mayhem. It goes without saying that the relationships established within the technonerd community embraced every human emotion, from admiration and comradeship to jealousy and hostility. We had no end of enjoyment showing these pathetic subjects how to attack each other through the information highway. Thus was born "hacking", a means of gaining access to internet systems (hitherto regarded as secure) and creating all manner of distress thereby.

This was all very diverting – so much so that Squimblebag and his cronies failed to see where the real battle was being fought. The enemy also had his technonerds and they were using their skills to spread his wretched "good news". As well as communicating with each other to encourage nauseating do-goodery, provide information about Christian activity worldwide, and initiate bombardments of prayer against some of our strongholds, they disseminated Bible versions, sermons, other Christian writings, songs, and all manner of tawdry religious trappings. It fell to me to spike the enemy's guns. This was an extremely demanding task but I was the only devil equal to it and I set about it with my usual efficiency and energy.

I set up a subcommittee of my best operatives to gather and systematize all available information about enemy internet activity. We despatched research teams, which reported back regularly. From this data I was able to compile a concise but all-embracing report for Squimblebag to digest and pass on to his bosses. My analysis made it clear that our ever-vigilant foe was using the new technology in three basic ways which threatened our worldwide operations: he was spreading *Information*. No longer could we rely on subverting Christian individuals and groups by keeping them ignorant of each other's existence.

He was encouraging *Interrelation*. Weak enemy groups were able to attract support from stronger organizations in the form of prayer, financial aid, and human resources. And he was supplying *Inspiration*. Not only did he disseminate the latest insipid religious jingles, he also spread news of his paltry military successes. I spelled out in such simple terms as even Squimblebag could not fail to grasp that we could not stop this insidious traffic. What we could and should do was distort it. To my considerable satisfaction – and Squimblebag's chagrin – the Low Command gave me carte blanche to organize the entire internet counter-offensive.

I always encouraged my subordinates to take initiatives and contribute freely to policy discussions. There are several advantages to this kind of leadership. It creates the illusion that the leader is interested in furthering the careers of his agents, and thus encourages loyalty. It enables him to take the credit for all good ideas and provides useful scapegoats for projects that fail. At my next subcommittee meeting it was my little protégé, Snagwort, who proposed an interesting policy initiative. Could we not, he suggested, replicate within the Christian community the kind of divisions we had spread among secular technonerds? Jealousy, pride, and self-importance might serve us just as well in one area as in the other. My own thinking had already been running along similar lines but I knew that such an operation would be a tricky plan to pull off and would be expensive in terms of devil-power resources. I was, therefore, pleased to hear the idea put forward by another member of my group whose name I could attach to the proposal in any subsequent reports. Accordingly, I complimented the proposer, agreed to implement *his* suggestion, and moved the adoption of a pilot scheme to be known within the committee as "the

Snagwort Plan". We selected a church in Brazil as our target and I took personal control of the operation, with Snagwort as my Number Two.

For some time an enemy initiative in Rio de Janeiro had been causing us considerable problems. South America has many churches, displaying varying degrees of syncretism between orthodox Christian teaching and animist beliefs imported long ago with the slaves who came from West Africa. One such was the Assembly of the Sacred Spirit (ASS for short!). It operated in the backstreet slums of the city, offering false hope to the human detritus whose lives we had ruined with drugs, alcohol, stupidity, the indifference of society, and the negligence of the government. ASS presented no challenge to the control we had established in that area of the city. Until the arrival of José de Entrada as the new minister. He had returned to his home town after acquiring a degree at a university in the USA and attending a charismatic student church. It should have been obvious to our agents on the spot that Entrada was trouble. Unfortunately, they were sloppy and complacent. It was some time before news reached the lower echelons of command that ASS was growing and becoming more active. Entrada's histrionic preaching was galvanizing his people into undertaking various initiatives – food distribution, repair of decrepit dwellings, employment bureaux, and the like – always, inevitably, accompanied by dissemination of the enemy's message of supposed concern for his downtrodden creatures.

I made a close study of Entrada's tactics and his burgeoning career. I observed that he was making considerable use of his North American contacts. He had established a group of supporters in affluent US churches and kept them informed of the needs of his community. They protected his activities with an appallingly effective prayer shield, sent gifts of money, and frequently supplied him with young volunteer workers who went about in the slums, preaching and doing nauseating "good works". All our incompetent agents could think of doing was to have some of these helpers attacked. When I arrived on the scene one teenage girl from New York was actually in hospital, fighting for life, having been set upon and raped by a backstreet gang. I immediately put a stop to such behaviour. The last thing we needed was Christian martyrs!

And there was, as I soon perceived, a better way to undermine ASS and to do it permanent damage. Entrada spent an increasing amount of time in internet contact with his foreign supporters. He sent out newsletters, prayer requests, and appeals for money. He received advice from leading figures in North American churches, invitations to speak at conferences and seminars, and copies of the latest fashionable Christian songs. In short, he was becoming a technonerd. As his church developed closer international links its distinct character changed. There was a steady shift in Entrada's theological position; he was bringing ASS more into line with North American Pentecostalism and shedding its animistic accretions. He established a training college and recruited US lecturers to teach there. He was fast becoming a celebrity within the charismatic sphere, and his influence was spreading, largely via the World Wide Web, to other lands. He sent preachers and missionaries to the USA, to parts of West Africa, and even farther afield. Within a few earth years his organization had grown from its Brazilian origins into an international network of churches within which he enjoyed the status of a mini-pope.

All this I encouraged – and attracted no little criticism for doing so. But brickbats and backstairs gossip did not worry me. By now I had the support of several members of the Low Command who had come to realize that Crumblewit was master of the long game. My plan was to get Entrada more and more embroiled in the pseudo-reality of the internet. Then, when the time was right, I would tighten its coils around him and squeeze. The time was virtually ripe for my next move when little Snagwort made his proposal. Shortly afterwards I took him with me to New York. Here we set up our position one evening, close to a disused warehouse in the depressed area of the city known as Harlem. Sounds of raucous music came from inside, supposedly in praise of our enemy. How he can take delight in such strummed and screeched cacophony I find totally bewildering. Even from our distance poor Snagwort found it almost too much to bear. His snout curled and he clapped his paws over his ears. Large numbers of people were soon streaming into the building, which was, as I explained to Snagwort, the latest ASS church to be founded. I led my disciple a little farther away.

"Try some of this," I said, handing Snagwort the flask I always carry. "It's a blend of drug dealer and tyrant. I have it specially prepared for me. It will revive your spirits."

The young devil drank greedily and was profuse in his thanks. I was gradually forming the impression that he had the makings of a useful, subservient lieutenant.

"How are we going to infiltrate here, Sir?" he asked as he returned the flask. "I've studied your notes on the use of celebrity seeking, financial maladministration and sexual misconduct, and, of course, your handling of the Corraine affair is famous, but I can't see that any of these approaches helps us here. This Entrada fellow is hideously sincere. He lives simply, is devoted to his wretched followers, and inspires the same attitudes in others. As to his regular contact with the enemy, our reps here are in despair of ever being able to break that down."

"Well observed," I replied. "You have just described what the Christians call a 'saint'."

"Yuk!" Snagwort's scaly body trembled all over at the very thought. "Saints have always caused Hell no end of trouble."

"Indeed they have," I agreed, "but not half as much trouble as they have caused the church."

The young devil looked puzzled.

I catechized him. "Are most Christians saints?"

"No," he responded firmly.

"Why is that?"

"Because the enemy has not finished changing them from their old selves."

"Who hinders that transformation?"

"We do."

"Of course we do. We work on them day in, day out and we achieve varying degrees of success. We blunt their effectiveness. And – mark this, young Snagwort, for it is important – we ensure that they remain painfully aware of their failings."

His uncertain frown returned. "But doesn't the enemy inculcate feelings of guilt so that his slaves will repent and adhere to him even more firmly?"

"Yes, yes!" I waved the quibble aside. "But guilt is also something we can make use of. When a saint turns up he makes those around him even more acutely aware of their shortcomings. Think of it as someone coming into a dimly lit room with a bright lamp. The dust and cobwebs, hitherto almost invisible, are suddenly shown up. Now, how does the average, run-of-the-mill Christian respond to that?"

Snagwort looked crestfallen. "From what I've seen, Sir, they find the saint inspiring and try to learn from him."

It was not the answer I had hoped for. "Well, yes, sometimes that does happen," I admitted. "It's certainly what the enemy has in mind. But if we do our job properly we can engineer a very different response. What we should be doing in these circumstances is making the less-than-holy feel threatened by the holy."

Snagwort looked doubtful. "I see. At least, I think... "

My patience was wearing thin. "For example," I said with as much calmness as I could muster, "a saint has a disciplined prayer life. Some of Hell's greatest champions have wrestled in vain to divert saints from their regular – in some cases constant – contact with our oh-so-communicative foe. Now, those who live in the shadow of a saint are inevitably aware that their own prayer activity is skimpy by comparison. This intensifies their feelings of inadequacy."

"But, Sir... "

I hurried on. "This is a vital chink in their armour. With a well-aimed thrust we can turn admiration into resentment and jealousy. What thoughts might we effectively pop into their minds?"

Snagwort closed his eye to avoid my penetrating gaze. I could almost hear the cogs in his brain grinding slowly into action. At last he said tentatively, "I suppose we could prompt them to make excuses for themselves."

The moment was right to treat my disciple to some faint praise. "Not bad, young tempter, not bad. But we should be able to go a step farther. My preferred plan of attack would be to suggest the following line of thought: 'It's alright for him. He can get up at four o'clock in the morning to pray. I've got a busy job; I need all the sleep I can get.'"

"Oh, Master, you are brilliant!" Snagwort exclaimed (sometimes the simple-minded can see those truths that elude their cleverer fellows!).

"That is only the first step," I explained. "What we should do next is whisper to the subject suggestions of jealousy and suspicion."

"What sort of suggestions, Master?" Snagwort's eye was now fixed on me in a look of deepest admiration.

"Something like this, perhaps: 'I wonder if all that self-denial is just a way of drawing attention to himself?' Or this: 'We only have his word for it that he spends three hours every morning in prayer.' Or this: 'He tells everyone how holy he is and they are all dazzled, like rabbits in headlights.'"

"Yes, yes!" Snagwort responded eagerly. "So how can we use this technique in Entrada's case?"

"I've given that question a great deal of thought, and it has become clear to me that the internet is our best tool. Entrada has used it to great effect to build up his international network of admirers, the vast majority of whom have never met him. For that reason many of them have not become ensnared by his personality. They are simply following his reputation at second hand. This is one of the major advantages of the internet; what is glibly referred to as 'communication' is in reality a much-debased form of human interaction. Even Entrada cannot transmit holiness by satellite! So, young Snagwort, mark this and learn: I have persuaded Entrada that he can do just that. He is so much in love with the new technology that he believes that he can reduce his spiritual experience to emails and internet sermons. When I say 'believes', I do not mean that he has come to this conclusion by careful thought; he has simply assumed it to be true. At this very moment he is in the middle of drafting detailed rules for all these new churches of his. The likes of Squimblebag are dismayed by Entrada's missionary zeal and his accomplishments. It takes someone of my genius to turn apparent defeat into resounding victory."

I paused for a pull at my flask and, in a moment of absent-mindedness, handed it to Snagwort to enjoy a comradely drink. "Specifically," I continued, "what I have done is convince our nauseating Heaven-hound that his formula for mission is the *only* formula for mission; that what works in Rio de Janeiro will work in New York or Lagos *in exactly the same way*. The wretched clever clogs is supposed to have learned a smattering of church history but I have blinded him to one of its constant themes. How has the enemy managed to spread his pernicious teaching into every place on the planet? By making that teaching cross-cultural. No other religion or philosophy has ever managed to escape completely from the thought forms and customs in which it was developed. Only our enemy's precious Christians have managed, without deviating from his core message, to present it in different ways as culture and local circumstances demanded. Over and again he's stymied us, sneaking his wretched 'good news' into regions we thought we had made quite impervious to his propaganda. Of course, it is always a tricky job for his emissaries to get the balance of essential message and other beliefs quite right, and this does make it possible for us, if we are vigilant, to turn the situation to our advantage. At the moment Entrada is totally hostile to the slightest departure from his mission package. That means that he is treading on the toes of potential Christian allies who believe that they know their local people better than he does and that he is insensitive to their needs. Have you grasped all that?"

Snagwort nodded sagely.

"Good, because I'm putting you in charge of the next stage of this operation. Pick half a dozen of our more reliable devils and install them in each of Entrada's new churches. Six earth months should be sufficient for the cracks to begin to appear in the worldwide ASS movement. I will expect an interim report on my desk then."

I knew that the time limit I had given the eager-to-please little devil was unrealistic, but by imparting a sense of urgency I ensured that he would put every ounce of energy into the job and, in his turn, inspire a suitable degree of anxiety and fear in the other members of his team. In fact it took three times the six months I had allotted before Snagwort and Co. made a real breakthrough but, when they did so, results were gratifying. Briefly, what happened was this: the ASS minister in Lagos expressed concerns to other church leaders (secretly, using the internet!). This led to demands for the setting-up of a central ASS council with real policy-making powers. By the time Entrada had rallied his most dedicated supporters it was too late. The council decided that he had been pushing himself too hard and that he needed a sabbatical.

Snagwort dedicated a long passage of his report to a colourful description of the bitterness and anger to which Entrada succumbed when he realized that he had been sidelined. The founder of the movement took some of his disciples and made desperate efforts to set up a new church, to be called the "Christian Reformed Assembly of the Sacred

Spirit" (CRASS). There followed an acrimonious war of words – on the internet (!) – between the two bodies, which was followed with dismay by Christians worldwide. There was subsequently some criticism of the fact that some of the churches continued to flourish, but I was able to let Snagwort take the blame – and the punishment – for that.

* * * * *

CHAPTER 12

Lies Ancient and Modern

(1996–2000)

Every intelligent strategist knows the importance of choosing battlegrounds carefully. Beware of populist propagandists who want us to take on the enemy over every single issue. Hell's resources are not limitless, and to fritter them away confronting the enemy in skirmishes we are unlikely to win without committing disproportionate forces would deflect us from our primary objective and weaken our endeavours where success is really important.

Take, for example, the measurement of time. There are in our midst obscurantist agitators who campaign against the Christian calendar. They would have us believe that we have sold out to the enemy by allowing him to establish in most earth societies the dating of events from his catastrophic personal intervention. They say it constantly draws attention to the DI.[7] They want us to stir up resentment among non-Christian religious communities and have them fight for

---

7   Editor's note: We have been able to establish that in Hell "DI" stands for "Disastrous Initiative", and refers to the incarnation of God in Jesus Christ, one of the blackest days in infernal history.

"equal calendar rights", so that all dates would have to be written with every conceivable alternative included. This, it is claimed, would permanently assert that all human religions are just that – "human" – and that there is nothing to choose between them. Like all heresies, this sounds plausible, but if the Low Command had allowed themselves to be swayed by equal-rights agitators they would have diverted resources from really important conflicts, such as fighting for control of the internet. What a time-wasting business the Dechristianize Dating lobby involved us in when they persuaded some in the Low Command to back their efforts to have the conventional dating designations "BC" and "AD" dropped in favour of "BCE" (Before Common Era) and "CE" (Common Era). What did they achieve? Atheist spokespersons and a handful of non-Christian religious leaders complained that the age-old system was an example of religious discrimination. Several Christian leaders countered by claiming that scrapping the traditional system was, in itself, religious discrimination. The result was a few bad-tempered debates. Pathetic little triumphs! Most humans were either ignorant of the campaign or indifferent to it. Those who did show an interest found the proposed change confusing. This was a classic case of choosing the wrong battleground.

However, that said, there are times when we can make use of calendar issues. Of particular value are anniversaries of the DI. In past epochs we were able to stir up apocalyptic frenzy every time a "significant" date drew near. It is, sometimes, a pleasant diversion to reflect on the old stories of infernal heroes and battles long ago. (By "diversion" I do not, of course, imply that I ever permit myself to be deflected from our eternal purpose. It is legitimate to draw inspiration from the more glorious episodes in our history only if this spurs us to greater effort.) In the year 1300 we induced a cash-strapped pope to proclaim a year of "jubilee". It is, by the way, particularly satisfying to note that the church had got its dates wrong. They had miscalculated the DI by four years so that 1300 and any other century-end according to the Christian calendar bore no relation to the event it was supposed to celebrate. However, in that year delicious sermons were preached throughout Europe describing in lurid detail the fiery vengeance our enemy was about to exact and the way people could escape his wrath by filling the coffers of the pope and his court. Thousands upon thousands of terrified Christian pilgrims flocked to Rome in the belief that they would thereby receive absolution of all their sins and thus be safe when the imminent return of our enemy and his Heavenly cohorts occurred.

In those days it was easy to induce fear in the humans because we could substitute superstition for Christian commitment. Life was short for most people and death was an ever-present reality. The church offered a realistic picture of terrestrial life as a speck in the ocean of eternity. People were, therefore, concerned about the question, "What happens next?" This gave us ample opportunity to distort the enemy's message by emphasizing his role as judge. Whenever he tried to persuade them that he cared for them on both sides of the grave, we could superimpose visions of Hell as a gaping monster, ready to gobble them up if they did not confess every last sin and secure (by appropriate financial incentives) the prayers of the religious professionals. Of course, we *were* waiting to receive souls as soon as they departed their bodies and, of course, the enemy *does* judge people on the basis of their response to him on earth. Our tactic, as ever, was not to substitute falsehood for truth, but to promote half-truths which would replace the image of a deity longing to forgive with one of a deity obsessed with punishment. Thus, instead of approaching the enemy with gratitude and loyal service, his potential followers were likely to be paralysed by fear. So, whenever a religious anniversary appeared on the horizon, we took the opportunity to ratchet up end-of-the-world panic.

The situation today is very different and more complex. We have enjoyed considerable success in banishing from human consciousness all ideas of final judgment. In those countries we have encouraged to think of themselves as "advanced", the church has lost its hold on the prevailing culture. We have made it unfashionable for "sophisticated" people to believe that there can possibly be any life beyond their current state of being. If they do – vaguely – acquiesce on the existence of a supernatural realm, they assume that whoever rules in that realm will look kindly on them, whatever their merits or demerits. This, of course, is all to the good and we can compliment ourselves on the secularization of society.

It is, also, a singular achievement that we have brought about the despiritualization of a large section of humanity without eliminating fear. We have removed the concept of life after death but we have given them many other things to worry about. The destruction of the enemy's darling planet has been brought nearer by the invention of nuclear weapons. Our leading strategists are ensuring that the necessary technical know-how for producing ballistic missiles is spreading to as many nations as possible and the time cannot be far off when one of them uses them in a disproportionate attack on an enemy state. This raises the possibility of escalating warfare and destruction on a hitherto unprecedented scale.

How ironical it would be if we could forestall the enemy by provoking his creatures into destroying the planet before he gets round to launching the final war against us, which he has promised for so long.

Of course, when it comes to the annihilation of the planet we do have another string to our bow. If the humans do not blow up their home we can induce them to make it uninhabitable. Overpopulation and ruthless exploitation of natural resources are rendering the planet steadily more hostile to the majority of its occupants. Governments and ecology campaigners meet frequently to discuss long-term solutions to these problems but it is usually quite easy to ensure that short-term greed blocks any initiatives that threaten to be effective. All thinking people are fearful about their planet's future and, while this is not the same thing as the old apocalypse mania, it is a useful standby. Never forget that the creation of fear, by whatever means, is very much our business.

So what do I mean when I say that we can still make some use of DI anniversaries? Well, they might not have the ability to evoke widespread fear. Any self-appointed prophet who announces the imminent end of the world now only provokes derisive laughter. But such activity is valuable to us, because it can dislocate churches and engender conflict among Christians.

As all Hell knows, biblical fundamentalists are, by definition, Christians who take their basic text very seriously. They tend to be assiduous in winning recruits for the enemy and this, of course, means that we have to keep our sights firmly fixed on them. One reason for their success is that many people are looking for certainty in a world they find puzzling and, sometimes, unnerving. Scientific and technological advances have enabled them to defer for several earth years the moment when they confront us and the enemy in that revelation of dazzling clarity which decides their real fate. In the interim we fill their fleeting days with myriad distractions – joys and toys, working and shirking, pain and gain, leisure and pleasure, affection and disaffection – but the enemy is also active among them, and blocking out his nagging, whining voice is our major objective.

Unfortunately, nothing we can do can conceal from humans the knowledge that the "time of no more choices" will inevitably come. It takes only a sudden illness, the unexpected death of a friend, the trauma of a broken relationship to make them ask those questions we would rather they continued to ignore: "Why do people suffer?" "Is there life beyond death?" "Does the universe exist by chance or is it designed for a purpose?" (Yes, incredible as it may seem from our viewpoint, many of the humans cling to a belief in the pointlessness of creation!) It is when they are at their most vulnerable that the enemy often plants a zealous Christian in their path, ready with a bagful of answers to their questions.

Now, of course, not all Christians are biblical fundamentalists, "Bible-bashers" whose trite "solutions" to the "big questions" convince nobody. But, by the same token, not all Bible-bashers are insensitive clods who do more harm than good to the enemy's cause. Would that everything were that simple! I stress this obvious point because some devils are guilty of slipshod thinking when it comes to dealing with Bible-toting fundamentalists. Never oversimplify; Bible devotees ARE NOT ALL TARRED WITH THE SAME BRUSH. They do not even all believe the same things. We are not dealing here with a Christian subspecies, clearly recognizable by their spiritual markings. Devotion to their sacred text is, certainly, a universal trait among them, but interpretation of that text varies quite widely and it is precisely their differences of emphasis that can provide us with cracks into which to wedge our levers.

When the year AD 2000 loomed up on the horizon several churches turned their attention to the "end time". A significant number of Christians were asking, "Is this it? And, anyway, what is 'it'?" As individuals and church leaders tried to deal with such questions, sermons and lectures abounded, books began to flood the specialist Christian market, and the internet hummed with a variety of "revelations" offering promises, warnings, and threats about the imminent end of the human experiment. The main points at issue were, "What does the Bible say about the end of the human world, the enemy's judgment of all his creatures, and the positions his followers will be allotted in the post-terrestrial age?"

Well, we would all like to know the answers to those questions, wouldn't we? If the enemy had revealed his battle plans in advance we could muster all our forces for the final showdown. He is not that stupid. Every creature in Heaven, Hell and earth has been kept in the dark. Even the Bible, which contains his manifesto, offers only veiled hints about the end time (you will have to take my word for it that I have subjected this pernicious document to the closest scrutiny and learned nothing of value). All he has told his Christian sycophants is that the end will come unexpectedly and that, therefore, they should live as though it were going to come tomorrow. This is the only point on which the enemy and our own great Master agree! We all have to be ready for the final confrontation.

By this time I had begun to form my own little group of devoted lieutenants into a secret caucus ready to grasp any initiative to mould policy in Hell's greater interest. It was becoming steadily more obvious that Squimblebag's ambition was insatiable. He was interested only in his own advancement and was using our commission to notch up spectacular successes which would attract the attention of the Low Command. Instead of developing a strategy for gaining total control of the internet and preventing the enemy's people from making effective use of it, he was trying to dazzle his superiors with the multiplication of pornography TV soaps, sensational revelations about the private lives of major politicians, and suchlike trivia. It would be to Hell's advantage that this egocentric incompetent should be removed from office. That, I knew, would take time and would require careful planning, since Squimblebag had considerable influence in low places – hence my private reform group.

It was at one of our meetings that clever little Snagwort, in his routine report, mentioned, in passing, the emergence of the Twice-born Church. This was a community established in a remote part of northern India which, through vigorous use of the internet, was growing quite rapidly. Like many sects inaugurated by us throughout Christian history, it was premillennial. That is to say that its theorists had set out a mathematically calculated timetable for the enemy's activity, which ordained that, prior to the enemy's return to earth a second time to establish his rule in the terrestrial sphere, he would call out his people so that they could share in his thousand-year reign. There are numerous versions of premillennial theory. According to the Twice-born bunch, the appalling one's visitation has already occurred but they are the only ones who know it. They assert that the creator has chosen to set up his kingdom on earth exclusively among them and not worldwide. Expressed in those simple terms the very idea sounds – and, of course, is – ludicrous, but it is worth reflecting for a moment on how we still manage to divert some Christians into such spiritual cul-de-sacs.

The more zealous a church becomes and the more committed it is to mission, the more hostility it provokes. We ensure that persecutors apply strong pressure, not to destroy such a church – that very rarely happens – but to distort its message. Briefly, this is how our strategy works: our subjects become so alienated from society that, instead of persevering with their message of the enemy's concern for their persecutors, they turn their backs on them. They develop what we call a "stockade mentality", withdrawing, either metaphorically or literally, into closed communities. It is not difficult to get them obsessed with the idea of *vindication*, even *vengeance*. They long for their persecutors, or even unbelievers in general, to get their comeuppance. This, of course, is the exact opposite of the role for which the enemy has chosen them. Therefore, they desperately need to justify their exclusivity. The most effective, well-proven way for us to (apparently) salve their consciences is to get them obsessed with millennial speculation. This, as you will know, is the job of our Special Antiliterature Service (SAS). This unit of highly trained demons is skilled in imposing on feeble human minds incorrect interpretations of those poetic and prophetic parts of the Bible relating to the enemy's future intentions. As I have already mentioned, these are obscure – and deliberately so. Oh, if only we could read his mind! No, I don't really mean that – such an experience would be too awful (literally) for words.

But to get back to the Twice-born Church. It initially comprised Christian families and congregations who had suffered persecution at the hands of militant Muslims. Our agents persuaded their leaders to withdraw into a self-sufficient commune that identified itself as the enemy's kingdom on earth, the harbingers of the millennium. Its members would (so they believed) enjoy perfect harmony as they prepared themselves to receive the enemy when he returned, physically, to set up his thousand-year rule among them and, through them, over the planet. The Twice-born Church was merely the latest example of those exclusivist sects of which, as I have said, there have been many throughout Christian history. Left to its own devices, it would, like them, fracture along its own theological fault lines, career downhill into extremist lunacy, self-destruct in an orgy of violent extremism, or dwindle into harmless obscurity. Such was Snagwort's analysis.

However, I realized that these fanatics and others like them offered more potential for disrupting the enemy's international operation. Again it was the internet which had changed the situation. The Twice-born loonies had not abandoned their terrestrial mission; they continued to reach out via the World Wide Web to the "unsaved" masses and to those churches which did not share their own "revelation". They urged people to flee the "domain of the Antichrist" and join them in their Indian haven. It was Snagwort's opinion that we should encourage this activity so that the "holy" community would be so swelled by the influx of a heterogeneous throng of converts as to become rapidly ungovernable. I realized that we had within our grasp the elements of an altogether more subtle and corrosive strategy. I therefore had a series of discussions with contacts of mine in the SAS and we devised a plan of campaign. At the appropriate time I invited the head of the SAS (whose identity must, of course, remain concealed) to address my little band.

When this meeting had been called to order I gave a brief introduction. "As we all know," I said, "the enemy intends that his sycophants should not bother their heads with the ultimate destiny of the human race, but get on with the job of serving their neighbours in the here and now. That is why we have always reacted by encouraging apocalyptic calculation and speculation. Your average Christian, for all his/her ardently mouthed cant about winning others for the enemy, is basically only concerned about 'what's in it for me'. He/she wants to be sure of being on the right road to eternal glory, on the winning side when you-know-who blows the final whistle. For this reason end-time scenarios have a constant fascination for many of the enemy's followers. Exploiting this fascination has frequently served us well but now we have an opportunity to launch millennial misinformation in a much-enhanced form."

Around the table, eyes were fixed upon me and my mystery guest. Snouts quivered in anticipation. "Premillennial fantasy", I explained, "comes in many forms and it is, itself, only one version of the end-time phantasmagoria we have implanted in Christian minds. There are other beliefs which are held with no less ardour."

"By people like Jehovah's Witnesses and Theosophists," an eager disciple interjected.

"Yes, yes! No need to state the obvious!" I waved him to silence (I do dislike being interrupted). "Such sects are widely recognized as heretical. Their usefulness to us is very limited. It is differences *within* the mainstream churches that we have to cultivate. That, as I have said, is the specialist work of the

SAS, which is why I have invited their chief of operations to describe some of their activities. It is important that we understand more fully what our experts are doing, so that we are better able to support their invaluable work, but also so that we can join with them in an exciting new initiative."

My guest, a thin devil with shrewd eyes glistening from a mat of black hair that effectively masked his features, made his presentation, using a timpace transporter, which enabled him to involve us directly with the events and people he was using to illustrate his lecture.

"As Crumblewit has said," he began, "the Service's work in this area is all to do with diversion tactics. We have to prevent any group *calling* itself a church from actually *being* a church. That is to say, we have to make them abandon their mission. There are many ways of doing this; an enemy unit can be diverted into any of several areas of activity – maintaining old buildings, defending specific forms of what they are pleased to call 'worship', confusing spirituality with culture… "

"What exactly do you mean by that?" one of my less able lieutenants asked.

"I mean that we instil confused ideas about 'beauty'. One of the Christians' favourite ditties speaks about the 'beauty of holiness'. Now there is nothing more abhorrent than holiness; it sets up an almost impervious barrier to temptation. Beauty is a quite different matter. It is a word people apply to a painting, a piece of music, or any other human artefact that moves them emotionally. When such an item has a religious theme – a cantata or a cathedral, for example – they can be induced to venerate – or even worship – the object. We so confuse their thinking that they actually end up believing in the 'holiness of beauty', and imagine that they are drawn closer to the enemy by wallowing in their emotional responses. But that is not what we're considering today. The diversion I want to focus on is theological argument. You all know what a wide spectrum of belief Christian theology covers and you also know that, in all their feverish gropings after eternal reality, the enemy's people have achieved only the dimmest understanding of who he is and what he intends. One of our most effective ways of exploiting this ignorance is TDT, Theological Diversion Tactics. We divide this subject into seventeen subheads. The one we will be looking at is TDT/9a, Chiliasm. You will find that fully defined in the notes accompanying this lecture."

Our speaker paused while I distributed the sheaf of papers he had brought with him.

"Briefly," he resumed, "chiliasm is an obsession with the idea that the enemy plans to return to earth and rule there for a thousand years. It is based on various poetic passages in the Christian writings. Now, no one knows exactly what these visionary ravings mean. I don't, you don't, and all Christians don't. BUT", his eyes gleamed and everyone present was hanging on his words, "the first rule of TDT is, 'Persuade them that they *do* understand'. For example, here is the Twice-born Church, in which you have taken an interest." He fingered the controls of the timpace and we were all in a dusty Indian compound watching an elderly, white-haired Christian addressing a group of women and children with the aid of a complicated chart. "So, you see," the aged speaker was saying, as he pointed with a stick to the intersecting lines and dates, "what we call the 'rapture' will occur on 27 July 2000, when Christ will return to us... here... and begin his millennium reign... here. Christ will rule" (the weaker members of my team whimpered and covered their ears at the mention of that terrible name) "through us, his chosen twice-born, and gradually all mankind will see him... and know that we are his lieutenants. Many will then accept our leadership. Alleluia!" The cry was taken up with enthusiasm by all the class. "It will be their last chance," the speaker continued. "At the end of the designated time, he will go forth... from here... at the head of his angel host to destroy the cohorts of evil and all people who are not among the twice-born and to receive us into his glorious, eternal kingdom." The little assembly erupted in an inane frenzy of alleluias.

Our SAS guest took up his commentary. "Now let us go to a different gathering." He tweaked the controls again and we found ourselves in an austere stone building where some thirty or so men in black robes were seated on benches, listening to a tall speaker, similarly clad and with a large, bushy beard. "St Athanasius' Orthodox Seminary in Greece," our guide announced. "Listen to what this fellow has to say about end-time theory." We all paid close attention to the hirsute priest.

"Something you will need to be aware of in your parishes, especially in the major towns," he announced, "is the spread of premillennial heresy. As I have explained, the church teaches that what the Scriptures say about the second coming must be interpreted symbolically, spiritually. When we read that the Lord will reign for 'a thousand years' we should understand this as figurative language for the present age. Our Lord reigns now, in Heaven, with the blessed saints and does spiritual battle with the forces of darkness. We are caught up in this conflict whenever we encounter evil. It is vital that your people cling to this belief, for how else will they be able to cope with temptation? The second coming will happen when it will happen, and we should not trouble our minds with complicated calculations based on poetic Bible passages or attempt to identify in contemporary events things prophesied long centuries ago. 'That way madness lies' as some poet or other has said.[8] Take, for example, what these obsessed millenarians call the 'rapture'. Because they take every jot and tittle of Scripture literally they have convinced themselves that the Lord will come and whisk away all his elect, from wherever they are, up into the sky – bodily. What does that mean in practice? Well, we would all be well advised never to travel by aeroplane or ride in a taxi. Just think what would happen if the pilot or the driver turned out to be one of the chosen ones! All over the world there would be planes falling from the sky and the street chaos in Athens would be even worse than usual!"

This brought hoots of laughter from the bearded one's audience. When it had subsided, he went on. "However, the arguments of these obsessed millenarians can be very persuasive because they seek to persuade believers that they are a cut above non-believers and even above Christians who do not share their own eccentric viewpoint. Like the Gnostics of old, they claim that only they understand the more difficult passages of Scripture; that they have, so to speak, 'cracked the chiliastic code'. That is why you must be prepared to confront these subversive elements on their own ground. Over the next three lessons I will take you through the salient Bible texts. We start with… "

Our guide brought us quickly out of the seminary. "That information is classified," he explained, "but I think you can

---

8   From Shakespeare's *King Lear*, 1605.

get the general drift of what we might call the traditionalist attitude towards end-time speculation. We have one more visit to pay." Again he fingered the control buttons. Now we were in a huge library. In the reverential hush that pervaded the atmosphere scores of readers sat at desks set in rows like miniature cubicles. Each had its little pile of books, which were being studied with the utmost concentration. "London. The British Library," our guide briskly informed us. He led us along one of the aisles and we stopped beside a gaunt, white-haired figure who was writing vigorously, pausing from time to time to consult two leather-bound volumes on special stands either side of his notepad. Our speaker motioned us to look over the earnest student's shoulder. The hurried scrawl was not easy to decipher, but this is what we read:

ISRAEL AND THE SECOND COMING

Chapter 9

Let us summarize the facts as we have so far
ascertained them from the inerrant Scriptures.
The prophecies of Ezekiel, Daniel, and John
make it crystal clear to any who approach
them with committed, obedient minds that
Israel will be both purged and preserved
during the final tribulation. This began with
the re-establishment of the state of Israel,
which involved conflict with its neighbours
from which it emerged victorious. Greater
suffering will, however, follow in the immediate
prelude to the Second Coming. There will be

a tumultuous period of three-and-a-half years.
At first Russia (the "Kingdom in the North")
will invade and be utterly crushed. Then the
USA (the "Ruler of the Ten Kingdoms") will
renege on its support for Israel and make
a bid for planetary domination. No earthly
power will be able to stand against this world
dictator, which is why the Lord will return at
the head of his angelic host for the final battle
– Armageddon. In this chapter we will describe
the phases of that conflict and the fate of its
various participants.

The scene faded as our speaker returned us to our meeting room. "That is just a taster", he explained, "of the varied activity of some of our units. You can see, thanks to our work, how obsessed all these subjects are with two things – the past and the future. They devote enormous energy to grappling with ancient prophecies and they then try to second-guess our enemy's intentions regarding the end time. Not so long ago, few Christians were interested in apocalyptic. It seemed almost as though the golden age of fiery preachers and wild-eyed heretics pronouncing the imminent destruction of the world had passed for ever. It has taken us years to revive interest in these things and, as you can see, our efforts are now bearing fruit. We are on the verge of a real breakthrough.

"This is where your team can help us. I have been discussing with Crumblewit ways in which we can exploit the internet to increase the friction between the advocates of rival chiliastic theories. Crumblewit, perhaps you'd like to brief your team on what we are calling 'Operation Dead End'."

"Certainly," I responded. "Operation Dead End is essentially a three-stage manoeuvre. We will use our expertise to locate Christian individuals and groups committed to the use of the internet. From them we will select those potentially susceptible to TDT. SAS will then assign personnel to work with us on developing rival chiliastic websites."

"Is the objective to generate major conflict among Christian activists?" someone enquired.

"That would certainly be highly desirable," I responded, "but it must remain a long-term objective. For the moment, don't lose sight of the fact that the 'D' in TDT stands for Diversion. As long as Christians are indulging in speculations about the end time and using the latest communication techniques to air their views, two things will happen. One is that unbelievers will increasingly dismiss them as wacky, head-in-the-clouds cranks. The other – and this is more important – is that the chiliasts will focus all their attention on their dramatic end-time scenarios and ignore the down-to-earth, everyday, humdrum business the enemy has assigned them of striving for the welfare of their neighbours."

Thus was born one of the most effective campaigns in recent infernal history. We managed to entangle thousands of Christians in the coils of useless speculation. Some of them were men and women endowed by the enemy with considerable intellectual and even spiritual gifts. Of course, it did not take the all-seeing meddler long to realize what we were up to. Then he lost no time in alerting his preachers and teachers to the danger posed by our brilliant strategy. He had internet sites set up to recall Christians to the central elements of his message but, in its time, Operation Dead End was a spectacular success. The point needs to be made and made firmly in the light of later infernal events. Rivals jealous of my success will seek to persuade you that Operation Dead End was of little consequence, a mere sideshow. DO NOT BELIEVE THEM.

* * * * *

CHAPTER 13

Incompetence!

(2001–2006)

We were losing the battle for the internet. That was the stark reality facing those of us who did not delude ourselves with minor triumphs. Squimblebag trumpeted his "achievements" so loudly that we could scarcely make our own warnings and misgivings heard by the Low Command. When atheists published their blogs he made sure that copies were sent to Prince Blagender's office. When churches fractured over subjects such as child abuse by priests, homosexuality, or women bishops, he hyped the divisions and secured maximum coverage in the infernal press. While my team concentrated on issues which really went to the heart of Christian belief and had long-term impact, he drew attention to himself by spreading sensationalized stories through interviews and lecture tours. And all the time the enemy was using the latest technology to encroach steadily on our territory. Everywhere he was encouraging, stimulating, and inspiring individuals and groups, and this was proving much more subversive than the high-profile clashes Squimblebag set so much store by.

Much of our success over the human centuries has been based on the relative isolation of Christian communities. We were able to keep churches and denominations focused on their own problems and petty disagreements because they could not see the bigger picture. But, by the beginning of the new millennium, any Christian anywhere could "surf the net", as it was called, and discover within seconds what his co-believers were doing in any part of the planet. A pastor at his wits' end because of the opposition we had stirred up in his congregation could swap experiences with his counterparts in other towns. An African diocese afflicted by drought could summon aid from its "partner" church in the affluent West. Christians whose commitment to the enemy we had been carefully eroding might be revived by an internet sermon. Leaders driven to the brink of despair by widespread apathy and the failure of their mission could draw encouragement from reports of evangelistic successes elsewhere.

But these were not the only tricks our devious and industrious foe was up to. My team drew up a list of his more aggravating stratagems. I have a copy before me, and it makes depressing reading.

1. Mushrooming Mission Movements: New propagandist enterprises are being set up in Asia, the Middle East, South America, and Africa. At the same time vigorous churches in the underdeveloped world are sending mission teams to secularized societies in Europe in an effort to reclaim areas where we had successfully eroded Christian belief. All these endeavours attract support from churches round the globe, thanks to the internet.

2. Mayhem and Martyrs: In several places aggressive Christian activity is provoking response from adherents of other faiths, predominantly Islam. Churches are being burned and worshippers slaughtered. Such events should NOT be considered as victories for our cause. News of Christian suffering, spread by the internet, actually strengthens the stubbornness of the enemy's people and provokes them into supporting their co-religionists with material and spiritual aid.

3. Messaging and Manipulation: There is a steady increase in the subversion of modern media by Christian activists. The enemy's agents are setting up radio and television stations to propagate his despicable "good news". They use catchy music and trendy language to infiltrate hitherto unresponsive cultures. Internet operatives offer courses of instruction and engage in direct communication with individuals they are seeking to seduce.

4. Moving Movies: The era when we enjoyed virtually unchallenged control of cinema and television film-making is past. Christian production companies have muscled in on our territory and are using the medium of film to tell modern parables and to present the Christian argument in ways accessible to those very people we have trained to respond to visual stimuli, rather than to think for themselves.

5. Mass-Marketed Meditation: By far the most
alarming aspect of the enemy's latest strategy
is his pestering of his adherents to concentrate
their minds on him. The exchanging of
information by Christians, vastly increased by
the internet, is provoking worldwide prayer.
If we attempt to undermine a church in, say,
Chile, we immediately find ourselves hampered
by a prayer shield thrown up not only by
those directly concerned, but by supporters in
many other lands. Of late there has emerged
a movement dedicated to ensuring that
communication between earth and Heaven
is maintained non-stop. This jamming of our
signals and blocking of our access is a crisis
which demands urgent attention.

This report was sent direct to Low Command. It provoked an
immediate response – but not the one I had hoped for, and
certainly not the kind of response which might have resulted
in an effective rethinking of Hell's strategy. I was summoned
to Squimblebag's office. He was furious.

"After all I have done to advance your career," he ranted,
"I did not expect you to go behind my back in this way."

"A copy of my team's report was sent to your office," I
replied calmly.

"Do you really think I have time to read everything you
send in?" he demanded. "The sheer volume of paper you
generate is enough to swamp my overworked staff."

"I have a conscientious and hard-working subcommittee,"
I said. "We do our job to the best of our ability. If your office

cannot cope, perhaps you need to consider some departmental reorganization."

"Don't you dare presume to teach me!" he screeched. Suddenly he soared upwards, wings flapping furiously, and then swooped towards me with outstretched talons. I ducked in the nick of time. He flumped onto a side table, scattering papers everywhere. He was gibbering incomprehensively and for a moment I thought he would explode. Gradually, however, the fit subsided and his eye glowered at me with concentrated hatred. "I know your plan, Crumblewit," he hissed. "You want to undermine me and take my place. Well, I warn you that I have more influence right now than you will ever have. Persist in your disruptive schemes and you will only destroy yourself."

"My dear Squimblebag," I responded calmly, "I fear you must have been working too hard. Either that or some jealous devil has been feeding you with conspiracy theories. My only concern is, and always has been, to serve Hell to the best of my ability. I genuinely believe we are facing a real crisis at the moment. Of course, my analysis may be flawed, but if I had concealed the disturbing evidence my team has uncovered... well, that would be treasonous, would it not?"

Squimblebag stood fuming – literally. As he tried to control his rage, his whole body trembled and smoke seeped from between his scales. At last, all he could do was gasp, "Get out! You have not heard the last of this."

It was this demonstration that finally convinced me that, in Hell's best interests, our incompetent departmental head had to go. His failure to present to his superiors an accurate picture of the enemy's activity was seriously undermining our readiness for the final showdown, which was, as far as my best intelligence could determine, almost upon us. But, of course, he was right when he drew attention to the support he enjoyed in low places. He had worked long and hard to smarm his way into the good graces of several senior devils close to the throne. It would take every ounce of cunning I could muster to dislodge him.

Meanwhile, with many senior figures now closely watching the conduct of my department, I had to find new ways of using cyberspace to our advantage and spiking the enemy's internet guns. As the new millennium got under way, fresh global crises dominated the humans' political agenda. All too clearly I saw that they could also dominate the demonic agenda. Our leading strategists were whipping up religious and political conflict between the Muslim world and what had effectively become the "ex-Christian" world. They engineered a series of wars in the Middle East, that area of the planet where we have so often successfully created mayhem in the past, and ensured that confrontation there poisoned wider international relations.

In this they were certainly successful. What they created was, in effect, a second crusade era. Islamic and Christian cultures clashed spectacularly. Wars aside, our agents provoked a constant sequence of lesser atrocities, from attacks on embassies and minor riots to spectacular acts of destruction and mass murder. One technique I particularly admired was the brainwashing of impressionable young Muslims to become suicide bombers. They were seduced into strapping explosives to themselves in order to detonate them in places where they would kill large numbers of their enemies. What was so delicious was that those carrying out these acts of bizarre martyrdom had been deluded into believing that they were going straight to Heaven, where their religious zeal would earn them spectacular rewards. Many readers will doubtless have enjoyed Disillusionment Parades at which some of these deluded political dupes have been displayed squirming and writhing in their eternal agonies of betrayal.

Pleasurable as some of these diversions were, they were, nevertheless, just that – diversions. Moreover, they could very easily backfire. For example, they could interfere with the general slide into secularism and non-belief which we had been engineering for several decades. The spectacle brought to the world's TV screens of Christian and Muslim leaders denouncing each other certainly strengthened the commonly held illusion that one religion was as good – or as bad – as another. However, by highlighting the differences between rival systems of faith and ethics, it prompted many thinking people to examine carefully the claim over their lives advanced by our enemy. Just as high-profile confrontation between atheists and believers appears to work to the disadvantage of the latter but, in the longer term, draws more attention to the enemy's manifesto, so bringing Muslims and Christians head to head often has the same effect. I have said it before but, because it is vitally important, I will say it again: we gain infinitely more by persuading people to ignore our implacable foe than by prompting them to reject him.

What my team and I had to do in the precarious situation we now faced was to develop the potential of the internet to undermine faith. This would involve working in subtle ways on individuals and groups. By sapping their spiritual energy and tampering with their communication lines with Heaven we could spread a kind of religious "mushiness" which would hamper the effectiveness of many churches, including some of the enemy's strongest bastions. We are always at our best when we play the long game. By the steady drip, drip of temptation we can deflect Christian athletes from their spiritual training programmes. This weakens their commitment to mission. It also (and this is highly important) lessens the chance of the baton of faith being passed down the generations. One of our under-acknowledged policy successes has been the watering down of family religion. We have created a mindset among millions of Christian parents which convinces them that, while it is their duty to see that their children are well educated and to inculcate in them moral awareness and social responsibility, they should not "impose" their religious beliefs on them. This is one of the main ways in which we have managed to loosen the enemy's grip on areas, such as Europe, where Christianity was once hideously dominant. I believed we should concentrate our energies on this kind of, admittedly unglamorous, activity. My difficulty was that it lacked strong PR potential. It would be difficult to present our successes to the Low Command in such a way that they would appreciate our true worth. This problem greatly exercised my mind as I drove my team ever harder to produce results that could be maximized in the reports we sent to our superiors.

We had, by no stretch of the imagination, exhausted the possibilities of the internet in sapping spiritual energy. I perceived early on that we could turn to our own advantage some of the ways the enemy used this technology. Cyberspace is only *virtual* reality. Now, dismantling a *real* Christian's faith or undermining the life of a *real* church demands solid hard work, usually over a period of earth years, but tampering with the pseudo-realism of the internet can offer a very useful short cut. Time, I think, for a simple illustration. The following story is, in itself, undramatic, but it does show how we can use the enemy's communication lines against him to excellent effect.

There lived in a small Australian township a late-teenage girl called Tanya. She had, regrettably, slipped through the fingers of her attendant demon and become a Christian. She found her local church of little value in the development of her spiritual life – not surprising, since that group of wishy-washy semi-believers had long since been neutralized by our forces. But she demonstrated a persistence in studying Christian writings and in prayer. I received a request from her distraught demon – Grunkwich by name – could my team do anything to help? He explained that Tanya was addicted to the internet and wondered if there was some way in which this could be used to uproot her tender faith (and, thereby, save his bacon). I assigned one of my juniors to the case.

We soon had a fuller picture of Tanya's life. Clearly, she was lonely. She had few friends – even fewer since her conversion. This was why she relied on the internet for companionship. She spent much of her time downloading pop music, as well as occasionally reading online sermons. We decided to introduce her to a Christian chat line. For those who may be unfamiliar with the term I should explain that a chat line is a means of carrying on conversation, through the computer screen, with other users who may be hundreds or thousands of miles away. Tanya "chatted" with various Christians around the globe and was very quickly drawn into this unreal world. She could scarcely wait to return from work every evening, when she would rush to her screen to share more of her own thoughts and feelings with her new "friends".

Now, I must emphasize at this point that such activity could be dangerous. There are many "Tanyas" whose religious delusions have been encouraged by chat lines or who have been lured into closer contact with the enemy. However, used properly, chat lines can have the opposite effect, simply because they conjure up a make-believe world, where nothing is exactly as it seems. When humans speak face to face they gather more from visual and aural signals, such as body language and tone of voice, than from the actual words spoken. Words themselves, when stripped of such aids to interpretation, can be very deceptive.

We manoeuvred Tanya into an increasingly closer pseudo-relationship with one particular correspondent, called Björn. The real Björn lived in Sweden, was some twenty years older than Tanya, was divorced, and was as insecure in his Christian faith as she was in hers. This was not the Björn that Tanya met. From their earnest conversations she developed an image of him as a vibrant, mature Christian man on whom she could rely for sound advice and knowledgeable help in studying the Bible. In his earlier years Björn had attended an active Lutheran church and though, thanks to intelligent work by our agents, he had settled into another congregation which was safely mediocre, he had a basic knowledge of the Christian writings and, more usefully, an extensive vocabulary of evangelical jargon. Tanya was thrilled to read his reports of "anointed" speakers who had "blessed" him by "opening the Scriptures" and drawing forth "treasures" of "deep" meaning therefrom. Such pious flim-flam impressed her greatly. Within months her dependence on her spiritual "guru" had become total. All her other Christian contacts, including her few local friends, seemed tame by comparison with Björn. She was obsessed by this fictional personality of her own creation, who now stood firmly in the way of any direct communication the enemy tried to establish.

So far, so good. Her demon was now being guided exclusively by my team – in other words, by me. What we had to do was bring about Tanya's disillusionment and, with it, the abandonment of her faith. We implanted in her a passionate desire to meet Björn. She had, on a couple of occasions, asked for a photograph of him but he had put her off by warning her against "earthly vanity". She accepted this without question. In the early stages of their relationship she might have been suspicious of Björn's reluctance to provide a visual image. Now it only heightened her regard for his holiness, a regard which was beginning to take on romantic overtones.

I should make it clear that Björn was not consciously seeking to seduce his young correspondent. What was truly delicious about this situation was that he was as innocent of evil intent as she was. He saw himself merely as Tanya's mentor and regarded her as a young disciple, whom he was trying to help. She, by contrast, was emotionally incapable of such detachment. What was happening was that their cybernet personas were drawing closer together and Tanya believed that she had discovered a real-life soulmate. She was determined to meet him, and we built this into an obsession. Her desire for physical contact was, of course, frustrated by the fact that she had no means of discovering Björn's address. This was not an insurmountable problem for us but we did have to ensure that any encounter in real space occurred under circumstances which could be of greatest benefit to us.

Our first step was to introduce Björn to a lady of a similar age and to draw them into an intimate relationship. Because his earlier experience had soured his feelings about matrimony, he and Ingrid began living together without bothering to get married. Once that relationship was safely under way, we induced Björn to make a slip-up in one of his messages to his Australian friend; he told her something about his church in Stockholm. This was enough for Tanya. She located the building (with the aid of the internet, of course) and resolved that she would pay her guru a surprise visit. She booked a flight to Stockholm and even learned a few words of Swedish to aid her in her enquiries.

The trap was set. It needed only to be sprung. On a fine Sunday morning in June Tanya arrived at the church and took her place in a back pew from where she had a good view of the sparse congregation. No one fitted the image of Björn that she had formed in her mind as she spent most of the service scrutinizing the other worshippers. As soon as the ritual was over she asked her neighbour if she knew the man she had come to see.

"Oh, yes," was the bright reply. "He's over there. I'll take you to him." The stranger led Tanya down the aisle to where a bald, middle-aged man stood, holding hands with his female companion. I can hardly find words to describe the immensely satisfactory wave of misery that flooded over Tanya. With the greatest difficulty she held back tears of disappointment as Björn smilingly introduced his partner. He invited the visitor to lunch but she made an excuse: "Other people to see... return flight tomorrow... sadly no time to get to know you properly... Just happened to be in Stockholm... had a sudden impulse to say hello." She turned and fled without another word.

You can see from such examples how picking off the enemy's adherents one by one – especially his younger followers – can be more advantageous in the long run than much-trumpeted spectacular victories. The enemy is well aware of this, which is why we always have to be on the alert for counter-attacks. Grunkwich did not learn this lesson. He was so euphoric at the outcome of the Swedish trip that he took his eye off the ball. The miserable corollary to this tale is that on Tanya's return flight to Adelaide the enemy slipped a Christian young man into the seat beside her. During the long hours of the journey Grunkwich could not prise them apart. Tanya poured out her heart to the sympathetic stranger and... well, I need not go into the distressing outcome. Suffice it to say that Grunkwich was summoned to give an account of himself to lower authority. He had only himself to blame. I had done all I could for him. Anyway, I was too busy trying to rescue the department's reputation from Squimblebag's mishandling.

Somehow, I had to make his incompetence so obvious that not even all his cronies in the lower echelons of the service could protect him. I brooded long over this and eventually came to the conclusion that some small sacrifice would be necessary. It would be more expedient for one soul to be lost to Hell than to endure continued seepage to the enemy as the result of one devil's stubborn commitment to sloppy methodology. The only question was whom to choose for our guinea pig. It would have to be someone fairly high-profile, whose decision to become a Christian would create quite a stir. I paid several visits to the central registry office, personally going through the "Current Operations" section of the soul files. Eventually I whittled my choice down to three individuals. One was a prominent Asian politician. Though technically Muslim, he was secretly troubled by the extremist antics of some of his co-religionists. I thought we could make him so disturbed by the "atrocities" being perpetrated in the name of Islam that he might be forced to reconsider his own allegiance. He had received his early education from Christian missionaries and still had connections among enemy activists, which might be useful to us. The second was a Canadian sportswoman with a huge personal following, especially among young people. Her conversion would certainly make an impact which would reverberate through the lower corridors of power. My third possible choice lay with a popular singer of Jamaican origin. His publicity machine had built for him an image as the "Bad Boy of Pop", and stories of his addiction to drugs, fast cars, and even faster women were intermittently fed to the press. In fact, much of this was a façade. His childhood years had been spent in a nauseatingly enthusiastic churchgoing family, and his sisters still sang in a gospel choir. He was a keen, if not particularly bright, student of philosophy, psychology, and religion, and had his own set of hybrid beliefs. We had always managed to keep him muddled about ultimate reality but, if we were to relax our hold on his mind, it was a safe bet that the enemy would go barging in. I eventually decided to run with this third alternative and Joseph Grafton, aka "Graffiti Joe", became the lever with which I intended to dislodge Squimblebag.

For this highly secret operation I needed a very small team of devils I could trust. I selected Snagwort and coupled him with Grunkwich, whom I had now seconded to my department. The latter choice might strike the reader as strange, but the fact is that Grunkwich was totally dependent on my support at his forthcoming enquiry. I was confident that he would do exactly as I told him – whatever that might be – without question, in the hope that I would put in a good word for him. I therefore arranged for his interrogation to be deferred on the grounds that he was needed for a confidential mission. Of course, once Grunkwich had served my purpose, he could be delivered back into the expert hands of the unholy inquisitors. With my two assistants I relocated to Switzerland, where "Graffiti" had his Alpine hideaway, and together we went to work.

* * * * *

CHAPTER 14

Recognition at Last

(2007–?)

We were able to lay and carry out our plans undetected because all Hell's attention was focused elsewhere – on the "big" issues. There was a general sense of euphoria throughout our kingdom, a widespread feeling that, at long last, things were going our way. Despite repeated warnings by scientists, the summoning of numerous international conferences, and ardent "Green" demonstrations, we were driving the humans, lemming-like, towards the aridization of the planet our adversary had provided for them.

Our principal tool was good old-fashioned greed. If I may mix my metaphors, greed acted like sand in the political machine and also as a universal blindfold ("universal" at least throughout the industrialized nations). World leaders, intent on maintaining their grasp on power, or even genuinely convinced that they had the answers to the world's problems, were, in reality, paralysed by their political systems. They needed, above everything else, to sustain public confidence. Public confidence depended on a general feeling of well-being. Well-being was interpreted by all populations as the uninhibited accumulation of "things".

We persuaded millions of humans that their "worth" was measured in terms of shiny motor cars, second homes, designer clothes, and an array of other status symbols. Citizens and nations plunged themselves into debt. Banks and financial institutions tumbled over themselves to lend money and accumulate the accruing interest. Throughout most of the industrialized nations people grew accustomed to mounting prosperity. The steadily increasing ownership of material possessions acquired an apparent inevitability and the dim-witted humans persuaded themselves that this state of affairs would continue ad infinitum. We successfully blinded them to the reality that planetary resources are finite, that disparities of wealth lead inevitably to social upheaval, and that some sacrifice of personal comfort and convenience might, in the long run, be to the benefit of all. The dolts could see no farther than the next step on their materialistic treadmills. All their efforts were concentrated on keeping the wheels turning, and Hell could rejoice on two counts: the feverish pursuit of wealth brought the humans very little satisfaction, and it kept their minds well away from any consideration of eternal realities.

It would be appropriate here, in passing, to pay tribute to our Semantics Bureau. Their directives on language distortion lie at the root of many of Hell's successes. I have already referred to the extremely productive fudging of meaning between "want" and "right". This tool has become increasingly useful of late. Your typical citizen of a democratic country may "want" to own his/her house, or to enjoy an annual foreign holiday, or to have his/her ailments cured by top-quality medical staff. When we subtly substitute the concept of "right" for "want", so that he/she is convinced that, without any personal effort, government or society or simply some vague "they" should make these things available, we sow the seeds of discontent, disillusionment, and potential political instability.

So, as I say, Hell was *en fête* at the prospect of terrestrial ecological suicide and economic meltdown. The trouble was that there was little or no forward planning. I was almost alone in realizing that our adversary was not going to stand by and watch his precious planet and its inhabitants spiral into chaos. I am amazed that our leaders, for all their long experience of evaluating the enemy's tactics, seem to have gained only a partial understanding of his fundamental relationship with the humans. *He lets them make their own mistakes*. Domination and control are so much part of our political philosophy that we are afraid to let the earth creatures think for themselves in case they should decide to throw in their lot with the creator. He, on the other hand, takes a morbid delight in letting them almost reach the point of self-destruction before he intervenes and says, "Now look what you've done." Western politicians in search of popularity openly embraced greed. They became notorious for corruption. They were aided and abetted by newspaper editors who were supposed to be the public watchdogs. Western culture became a dog-eat-dog free-for-all in which the ethical principles so beloved of our adversary were routinely disregarded. It all looked wonderful. So, as I say, Hell hung out the flags. And while we were all patting ourselves on the back, human opinion-formers looked at the mess and began to see it for what it was. They began to ask, "What's gone wrong?" And, of course, the enemy, like a scolding nanny, replied, "You've broken all the toys I gave you and I'm the only one who can help you mend them."

This was why I changed my tactics. By warning anyone who would listen about the dangers of short-termism I had simply earned a reputation as a maverick. So I stopped making public appearances and employed subtler methods to nudge policy in a different direction. And the first step was to get rid of Squimblebag.

The demonic security around Graffiti Joe ("Graff" to his multitudinous fans) was appallingly lax. His duty devil – Thrax by name – was lazy and, consequently, considered himself overworked. He was delighted when I informed him that he had been reassigned and that his place would be taken by Grunkwich. Thrax unsuspectingly handed over all his case notes to my nominee and we went through them methodically. It was as we were laying out our plan of campaign that I received an unexpected summons from the Low Command. I was to attend a meeting of the Policy Committee at Blagender Pile to discuss some "urgent matters" which had recently come to light. With a certain amount of foreboding I paid my second visit to that impressive residence.

This time there was no waiting in anterooms; I was escorted directly to a high-vaulted council chamber where a collection of senior devils were clustered in small groups, sipping aperitifs and nibbling canapés. I accepted a glass of bubbling vintage hypocrite and selected a scrumptious-looking glutton tartlet from the tray presented to me, and strode into the room with an air of confidence that I certainly did not feel.

"Ah, Crumblewit, here you are. We have been waiting eagerly. Couldn't start without you, eh?" The greeting came from the maw of none other than Prince Zublub, Head of the Statistical Bureau and Minister Without Portfolio.

"I came as fast as... "

"Of course, of course. Good old Crumblewit, meticulous as ever, eh?" His multiple chins wobbled in unison. "I'll just let Blagender know that you've arrived. Then we can start. Ceremony first, discussion after." He indicated the long table in the centre of the chamber. "You will be sitting there on the left of the presidential chair. Blagender will be presiding, of course. Always personally attends important occasions such as this."

"I'm not quite sure..." I began, but the prince interrupted.

"Nervous? Don't be. Don't be. I'll be next to you. I'll guide you through the ceremony."

He went out and returned moments later escorting Prince Blagender, before whom we all prostrated ourselves. We were then bidden to take our seats and I found myself in the place of honour next to His Unutterable Lowness. I wish I could remember the polite conversation that passed between the prince and me but I was so bewildered and overwhelmed that the details remain hazy.

Then the prince called for order.

"Your Lownesses, Your Disgracefulnesses and Dishonourablenesses, this is very far from being a routine council meeting. Earth affairs have taken an important turn and we need to consider carefully our response to the changed state of things. The consensus of this policy committee, endorsed by our Emperor, is that our great task is on the verge of completion: we have wrested control of most human societies from our adversary's grasp. By the application of greed, pride, jealousy, and anger we have brought them to the brink of collapse. Their banking systems have broken down, several of their governments are bankrupt, extremist politico-military groups are gaining power, religious strife is rife, and national leaders are searching in vain for solutions, because, of course, there are none.

"We have propelled them so far down the road of materialism that they cannot turn back without acknowledging decades, nay centuries, of Hell's control. International peace-keeping endeavours are frustrated by governments unable to throw off the shackles of national self-interest. Too late, whole populations have come to realize that their politicians, financial institutions, and communications media are not to be trusted. Corruption, political scandals, and sheer incompetence are now commonplace and we have been able to engender widespread indignation, anger, and despair. So we can justifiably compliment ourselves on what we have achieved and we can look to the future with renewed confidence.

"However, we must never confuse confidence with complacency. Too often in the past we have seen defeat snatched from the jaws of victory. We need to keep our eyes open for whatever cunning stratagems our unscrupulous and unflagging adversary may devise. His stubborn refusal to admit defeat means that we will have to press home our attacks right to the very end. Someone who has never failed to remind us of this is the devil we are dishonouring today. No one has made a closer study of the enemy and his human agents than Crumblewit. His has been a strident and sometimes lone voice, informing us of the wretched interferer's tactics and urging us to vigilance. Today we recognize his contribution by electing him to this committee and by awarding him the Order of the Sons of Darkness, First Class. I call upon His

Imperial Lowness, Prince Lobzubble, to make the award on behalf of our Satanic Master."

In a daze I was led by Prince Zublub to a dais before the conference table. Prince Lobzubble, that grand infernal veteran, approached, aided by two attendant demons.

"In dishonouring you," he declared in his reedy, wheezing voice, "we dishonour a devil who has given long and loyal service to our Lord and to all Hell. Rarely in the annals of the Lower Dominion has so much been owed by so many to one demon." He then placed across my shoulder the sash of the Order, to which was pinned the medallion of the Burning Globe. Trembling with pride, I was led back to my seat, with the applause of Hell's greatest ringing in my ears.

I was not allowed long to bask in my glory, for the meeting now moved, as Prince Blagender had said, to consideration of the current situation. When my opinion was asked I tried to gather my thoughts together into some kind of coherent order. I made a good start by warmly commending all present for engineering the encouraging situation to which His Despicableness, Prince Blagender, had referred. Then I cautiously pointed out that our adversary could, would, and had already begun to turn this very situation to his advantage.

From the far end of the table a booming voice demanded, "How, exactly? What evidence have you got?"

"Well," I replied, thinking fast, "we have unfortunately witnessed defections to the enemy's ranks as a direct result of confrontation between atheism or Islam and Christianity. When the arguments for rival beliefs are brought out into the open some people who have never given our adversary's trumped-up claims any serious thought begin to do so."

"Surely the numbers involved are insignificant?" someone else protested.

"It seems that our enemy has always been more interested in quality rather than quantity," I responded. "Your Learned Frightfulnesses will be familiar with his 'faithful remnant' theory. Even individual turncoats can pose problems. There have been some spectacular desertions from our ranks, people who have made themselves appalling nuisances to us. Only recently a one-time drug smuggler (a splendidly violent thug) went over to the enemy. Of course, his Christian mentors made considerable propaganda use of this, parading him on public platforms and issuing a video disc telling his story. Their tactics were, I regret to report, quite effective."

I was aware of a ripple of reaction along the table. Before more questions could be fired at me, I hurried on. "As we are all aware, our unscrupulous foe has implanted something of himself in every one of his human creatures. We can never scrape out the last vestiges of this *imago dei*, which is why every tempter has to be on the lookout for situations which risk fanning into flame what some Christian theorists have called the 'divine spark'. Our hideous president has rightly applauded the collapse of human institutions and the undermining of political and economic systems. All this has spread excruciating human suffering, and of this we can be justifiably proud. However, this in its turn also evokes a measure of response from that wretched *imago dei*. The humans set up charities and go out of their way to help their unfortunate fellows. Often Christians take the lead in this and use it as a means of spreading their own poisonous propaganda."

A devil opposite glowered at me and growled, "Are you trying to tell us that our current success is all a delusion?"

Momentary panic seized me. Had I overstated my case? "Not at all," I hurriedly replied. "All you distinguished analysts round this table see much more of the picture than I do. As you may know, my own specialism is control of terrestrial communications media. Any conclusions I draw are based on my study of the messages humans exchange with each other through television, radio, internet, mobile phones, and the like. What I can report is that Christian activity is becoming networked. Formerly, much of our activity was concentrated on infiltrating local churches, but now Christians increasingly study and even worship through their computers. We should not congratulate ourselves too heartily over dwindling and ineffective congregations or denominations overburdened with staffing problems and the maintenance of antiquated buildings. The enemy now has myriad ways to bring together his people. The limitations imposed by ministerial hierarchies no longer inhibit his initiatives. He is liable to pop up anywhere and set up ad hoc groups and organizations for specific purposes."

Several committee members now tried to speak at once but Prince Blagender intervened. "Our colleague Squimblebag is in charge of that department, and I was hoping that we could have had his input today. Unfortunately, he has sent his apologies. Without his assistance in this matter we had better move on to other business."

It was no surprise to learn that Squimblebag could not face being present at my moment of triumph but I felt a twinge of disquiet at his unexplained absence. However, thoughts of that incompetent buffoon could not be allowed to spoil my time of glory. That evening a banquet was held in my dishonour and over the next couple of days I was feted by several of Hell's most distinguished citizens. My anxiety did not resurface until I returned to Switzerland. Grunkwich was there but of Snagwort there was no trace. "Where has he gone?" I demanded.

"Squimblebag took him back to HQ," was Grunkwich's nonchalant response.

"Squimblebag was HERE?" I shouted.

"Yes," the dolt replied. "You just missed him. He came soon after you left."

My mind went into overdrive as I re-examined recent events: the unexpected summons to Blagender Pile, Squimblebag's unexplained absence from the meeting, his earlier angry discovery of my confidential report to the Low Command, and, further back in time, his introduction of Snagwort to my group of "trusted" agents. Could it be that I had underestimated...

* * * * * *

Postscript: The manuscript breaks off at this point. In fact, the last surviving page is torn. The file containing it bears the label "Prisoner C" and has been well thumbed. Crumblewit's autobiographical notes are dog-eared, some sections have been scrawled through with thick pen strokes which have, in places, torn the paper, and there are numerous scurrilous annotations. It should be stressed that the foregoing narrative is the result of a laborious editorial process. Some entries existed only in note form, while others were extended passages in the author's bombastic and self-congratulatory style. Crumblewit seems to have jotted down his experiences and reflections over a long period of time and then, periodically, attacked the task of turning them into a coherent whole – a task which remained unfinished.

There are a few other papers in the file, some of which made it possible to fill in minor gaps in Crumblewit's career. The only one that throws any light on the author's ultimate fate is the following:

Document 137/B – Snag.

I was employed by His Disgracefulness
Squimblebag to infiltrate the organization of
the traitor Crumblewit and report back any
irregularities in his behaviour. I quickly observed
that Crumblewit was a creature of huge ambition
and almost unlimited guile. Excellent though
these qualities are, it became obvious to me that
they were being employed to further his own
career, rather than for the welfare of the Infernal
Dominions. In particular, I noted at least three
occasions when he appeared indifferent to the fact
that subjects had defected to the enemy. He was
prepared to acquiesce in the escape of human slaves
if such tragedies furthered the implementation
of his own agenda. Latterly, he attempted to
turn me against our supremely malevolent chief,
Squimblebag. Unfortunately, my suspicions
remained unsubstantiated for a long time. Only
when I had managed to obtain a duplicate key
to the strongbox in which the traitor kept his
private papers did I light upon the evidence of his
unHellish activities. I discovered what appeared

to be notes for a detailed account of his career in
Our Infernal Majesty's service. When these were
confiscated after Crumblewit's arrest I was able
to identify them beyond any shadow of a doubt. I
have the satisfaction of knowing that the traitor was
condemned by his own pen and that I was able to
play a significant part in his discovery. I trust that
my diligence and zeal will be suitably rewarded.

Signed

Snagwort

הספרדיה

The ArtScroll History Series®

Rabbi Nosson Scherman / Rabbi Meir Zlotowitz

General Editors

SURVIVAL

Inspiring accounts of heroes and heroines of the Holocaust

by Renee Worch

Published by

Mesorah Publications, ltd

FIRST EDITION
First Impression . . . November, 1992

Published and Distributed by
MESORAH PUBLICATIONS, Ltd.
Brooklyn, New York 11232

Distributed in Israel by
MESORAH MAFITZIM / J. GROSSMAN
Rechov Harav Uziel 117
Jerusalem, Israel

Distributed in Australia & New Zealand by
GOLD'S BOOK & GIFT CO.
36 William Street
Balaclava 3183, Vic., Australia

Distributed in Europe by
J. LEHMANN HEBREW BOOKSELLERS
20 Cambridge Terrace
Gateshead, Tyne and Wear
England NE8 1RP

Distributed in South Africa by
KOLLEL BOOKSHOP
22 Muller Street
Yeoville 2198, South Africa

ARTSCROLL HISTORY SERIES ®
"SURVIVAL"
© Copyright 1992, by MESORAH PUBLICATIONS, Ltd.
4401 Second Avenue / Brooklyn, N.Y. 11232 / (718) 921-9000

ISBN
0-89906-872-3 (hard cover)
0-89906-873-1 (paperback)

Typography by Compuscribe at ArtScroll Studios, Ltd.

Printed in the United States of America by Noble Book Press Corp.
Bound by Sefercraft, Quality Bookbinders, Ltd. Brooklyn, N.Y.

Acknowledgments

My heartfelt thanks to all who entrusted me with the task of recording these mind boggling events, in one of the most heart-breaking eras in Jewish History. And if I have succeeded in some measure in fulfilling the trust vested in me, I am grateful to Hashem. For me, it has been an enriching and rewarding experience.

I am deeply grateful to one of the principals of the book's major story, Mrs. Tziviah Rothbart. With infinite patience and graciousness, she made herself available at all times to clarify facts and add details. I hope she will forgive me the times when my enthusiasm for this project would make me oblivious to the lateness of the hour. Rabbi Berish Weiss generously supplied me with a translation of his father's memoir, a manuscript to which I referred constantly. May I add that it is indeed unusual that a *gaon* and leader of his stature recorded his wartime experiences. Thank you to Rabbi and Mrs. Shloime Josephovitz for their welcome contribution to the Rothbart story. A special thanks to Mrs. Rochel Spitz of Brooklyn for her invaluable translation of Dayan Weiss' original manuscript. I am grateful to the dear friends who supplied me with their own experiences which were the basis of the other two stories: I am deeply indebted to my dear friends, Bertle Halberstadt and Ziggy and Lotte Gluckstadt. Sincere thanks to Toni Grossberger for allowing me access to her own manuscript. A special thank you to my dear Libu. Thanks to Mr. and Mrs. Weinberger of Boro Park, to my very dear Miriam Stern, and her brother Eli for their help and to my dear family for their continued encouragement. Heartfelt thanks to my editor, Anne James. We appreciate the gracious help of R' Yitzchok Tzvi Kohn, and Mr. Michah Oppenheim.

A special thanks to Rabbi Nosson Scherman, whose constant advice and encouragement helped me to continue, and Ethel Gottlieb of Mesorah Publications who shepherded the manuscript to publication with love, taste, and skill. To everyone else at Mesorah, whose association was not as personal but equally indispensable. My sincere thanks to Yehuda Gordon, Chavie Friedman, Nichie Fendrich, Mindy Kohn, and Zissi Landau of the typesetting department.

To my dear husband, my love and gratitude for his continued support and for understanding my need to write. I pray Hashem will allow me to retain this privilege.

Renee Worch

Introduction

A participant in the harrowing and inspiring events described in this book must have mixed feelings upon reading the narrative. On the one hand, one's blood boils upon reliving the fear and constant terror. On the other hand, one is uplifted by the pure faith and unselfish heroism of those who risked their lives to save more people than seemed to be humanly possible. Most of all, one feels renewed gratitude for the Divine Providence that enabled us to survive, and that made it possible for my father ז״ל to go on and serve as a leader of Klal Yisrael in Manchester and Yerushalayim. Though my mother ע״ה was not strong enough physically to survive the endless ordeal, the image of her saintly faith and uncomplaining courage remain with us always as a model of the eternal Jewish wife and mother.

I am grateful to Mrs. Renee Worch for her magnificent effort in reconstructing the story and capturing all of its drama. Though I was but a teen-ager at the time and was shielded by my parents as much as possible, the memory of those months remains with me and to have read Mrs. Worch's account makes me feel as if I were looking into a fifty-year old mirror. She is a friend of our family and of the other families who went through that ordeal. We confided in her and she has been loyal to our trust.

Like most of those who lived through *Churban Europe*, I realize that unless the lips of the survivors are unsealed painful though it is generations to come will never know how it was. Equally tragic unless those who remained loyal to Hashem tell *their* stories, posterity will have the accounts only of those who deny or fail to see any *hashgachah* at work in those awful days.

Mrs. Worch and Mesorah Publications are to be commended, therefore, for bringing these experiences to the general public.

Berish Weiss

·§ Table of Contents

Part One
Kristalnacht

Chapter One

eipzig, Friday the 26th of October 1938 began no differently for Bea than any other day. The early mornings were getting perceptibly colder, but frost was still some weeks away. The alarm clock shattered the silence of her bedroom; sleepily Bea reached towards her bedside cabinet and silenced the offender. She was anxious not to disturb Frau Geller, her elderly landlady, a genteel widow who shared the rest of this comfortable apartment with her only son. She switched on the light. Only six o'clock! Enjoying the luxury of a few extra moments in bed, she looked lovingly at the delicate china trinket dish on her dressing table, a farewell gift from her favorite aunt.

How their hearts had ached that day in Fuerth in the summer of 1935, when Tante Rosie brought her this dish, lovingly wrapped and tied with a satin ribbon. What tears they had shed! This was a double farewell: Bea was leaving home to start a two years' teachers' training course in Nurenberg, and Tante Rosie was emigrating to Paris with her husband Moritz and their children.

Life in Germany was no longer peaceful or prosperous. Jack-booted youths, inciting hatred with anti-Semitic songs, goose-stepped through the streets, after hours spent drinking in the local taverns. The first pangs of fear struck quiet, law-abiding Jews, but it was all too easy in those early days to believe the youths were merely indulging in a passing craze. Had not Jews in the past often survived amid hostile nations! At home and in their meetings, they argued among themselves.

"This is home, where else! Surely we German Jews have nothing to fear from these hot headed boys!"

"The decent majority of Germans will surely defend us! They will remember the thousands of Jewish youths who fought and died for the Fatherland in the Great War!"

But the egg laid by Germany's symbolic Eagle was about to hatch; the monstrous fledgling would grow to spread its terrifying wings across Europe, destroying and mutilating all who opposed it. However, its sharpest claws were reserved to tear at the very heart of the Jewish people.

All this was yet to come. Tante Rosie and Bea, who so much resembled her slim, elegant aunt, were exchanging gifts and saying a tearful farewell to each other, as Tante Rosie stroked Bea's beautiful auburn hair. Bea's frail and vulnerable appearance belied her inner strength.

Shortly before her twentieth birthday, Bea had applied for permission to emigrate to Palestine, then a British Mandate, as a nursery school teacher. To obtain a visa, one had to bring proof that one would not be a financial burden in that country, and while waiting for the necessary documents, she enrolled at a teachers' training college in Nurenberg. The city was only a short distance from Fuerth, her hometown, and to earn a little extra money, she gave math lessons. This money enabled her to pay for Ivrit (modern Hebrew) lessons. Life was exciting, precarious: the limited number of visas allocated to German Jews were soon snapped up, and she was not among the lucky ones. At the end of her two-year study she received her teacher's diploma, but could not get a teaching post; state schools had stopped employing Jewish teachers.

So in the spring of 1937 she accepted a place at an agricultural training center (*hachsharah*) in Belgium, a short distance from Antwerp, which at that time had one of the largest Orthodox Jewish communities in Europe. These *hachsharos* had been founded in many countries to prepare the urban Jewish refugees for the rigors of a mainly agricultural life in Palestine, and to teach them modern farming methods. Bea hoped that by joining a *hachsharah* she would improve her chances of getting a visa, but it was not to be. Now, here she was in Leipzig, an assistant teacher in a Jewish kindergarten, glad that she at least earned enough to support herself.

She glanced at the clock. Six thirty! How silly, to have wasted so much time daydreaming over the past! She hastily jumped out of bed and began to wash and dress. After tidying her room, she went to prepare her own breakfast in Frau Geller's kitchen. She looked at the large noisy clock on the wall. Kurt, Frau Geller's only son, would soon be returning from morning service in the synagogue. Bea felt acutely embarrassed in his presence; he was tall and very thin and intensely shy. He never spoke to her unless first spoken to, and blushed crimson before replying, so she contrived always to have breakfasted before he returned home.

Bea was fond of her landlady and was grateful to have been offered accommodation in this comfortable apartment at a reasonable rent. The family would occasionally invite her for an evening meal, and she had formed warm friendships with girls from local families with backgrounds similar to her own.

This evening, she was to visit the home of one of her friends. Friday night was always a special time; the family would linger at the supper table, the father with the other male members would sing the beautiful haunting Shabbos songs, while the flickering Shabbos candles spread a soft warm glow around the room.

Humming to herself, Bea straightened the cover on her bed; a quick glance around the room assured her that everything was in its place; a clean freshly ironed blouse neatly folded on the chair was ready for her to change into in the evening. She picked up her jacket and, closing the door quietly behind her, hurried down the stairs and out into the street. It was twenty minutes past seven. No need to hurry, the kindergarten was but a short distance away. It was her turn to be on early morning duty from seven-thirty onwards, when the first of the toddlers would be arriving, brought by a parent, or an older child on their way to school.

Bea enjoyed taking the longer route through the park. She paused for a moment, taking a deep breath of the balmy morning air. She loved the quiet and to watch the effects of the changing seasons on the park: the falling leaves carpeting the ground in the autumn, the transformation into a white wonderland in the winter, with just the occasional footprint to spoil the dazzling white expanse; an eerie stillness when even the sparrows seemed subdued as they tiptoed across snow-covered grass. Suddenly it is spring: the magical re-awakening of all that the earth brings forth. The laughter of children playing on the muddy embankment, calling to each other as they watch a swan gracefully glide past in the pond, followed by a line of cygnets. Summer follows swiftly, in a blaze of brilliant colors.

Slowly, as the days get shorter and the nights grow cooler, the trees and shrubs don their coats of many colors, the magnificent oaks and chestnut trees blazing with bronze and golden hues. Bea looked on benignly as a boisterous gang of urchins climbed up the trees for chestnuts. She wanted to shout at one boy who was swinging dangerously from one branch to the next, but quickly drew back. She turned away; in her desire to save a child from injury, she had almost forgotten that it was a grave offense for a Jew to scold or upset an Aryan child! She hurried through the park and sighed with relief as she left it and approached the school.

Bea strolled across the street towards the school building, her thoughts dwelling in pleasant anticipation on joining the Schonberg family for the evening's Shabbos meal. She hurried up the stairs and into the bright airy playroom which was also the classroom, ready to receive the first of her early morning charges. As the children started arriving during the next hour, neither the matron nor Bea was unduly concerned that so few came. There could have been so many reasons for their absence, especially on Fridays, when some working mothers would stay at home. There was nothing to suggest that this day was to be different from any other, but *Operation Abshieben* (Operation Deportation) had already begun.

The following morning in the synagogue, the rabbi mounted the *bimah*, indicating that he wished to speak. Tension rose; in shocked silence the congregation listened. He began, "Some of you will already be aware of the plight of the Jews who have been rounded up and detained since Thursday night, the 25th of October. They had no warning, and were given no time to prepare. These families are in urgent need of food and clothing. We have been told that many have spent the night in the open air. It has been raining incessantly; help must be given urgently. Since this is a case of *pikuach nefesh* (the requirement to save lives that are in danger overrides the restrictions of the Sabbath laws) we must do whatever is necessary to help."

When the rabbi had finished speaking, he remained on the *bimah* as solemn little groups formed in earnest discussions. One by one they respectfully approached him for more details.

It transpired that *Operation Abshieben*, as it became known, began when the Polish government recalled its own nationals who were at that time domiciled in Germany. They issued a declaration from October 31, 1938, that any Polish citizen still in Germany would be deprived of Polish nationality and become stateless.

This edict released a flood of returning nationals that the Polish government had not bargained for. They soon realized that the trains crossing their frontiers were not bringing back their own prodigal sons; the Germans had seized the opportunity to transport thousands of Jews across the frontier. These were the so-called 'Ostjuden' — Jews of Polish origin, and faced with this influx, the Polish government closed the border, leaving those already rounded up stranded between the hostile countries.

At the synagogue, no time was wasted in setting up a rescue operation. Everyone volunteered to help. Bea, with other young women, was assigned the task of contacting the Polish Consulate where, it was rumored, some of the families were being held. They walked the short distance, and were wholly unprepared for the sights that greeted them there. At no time were any of the arrested Jews allowed into the consulate building. They had been herded into the open courtyard without shelter from the wind and rain. About two hundred souls had been kept there since the previous day, without food, drink, or sanitation. Babies in soiled diapers cried pitifully under their coverings of soaking wet blankets. Wet, cold, and hungry children could be heard wailing in every part of the enclosure.

The volunteers immediately sprang into action, and hurried back to the Jewish quarters to collect large baskets of bread and other foods. Some begged from door to door until their baskets were full, while others collected thermos flasks filled with hot drinks. Others collected dry clothing and waterproof covers from the homes of those imprisoned at the consulate, who handed over their house keys to the volunteers. In spite of the rabbi's sanction, Bea was determined not to break the laws prohibiting writing on Shabbos. She recalled many years later, "I put a key ring on each finger and tried to memorize the address of each one. This was a challenge and I repeated each individual address, as I went back and forth in the driving rain!"

In the late afternoon the consul relented and gave permission for the babies and young children to be taken away. Once again the volunteers searched for families willing to take children into their homes, then hurriedly collected carriages for the babies. Bea made the journey three times, gathering as many little ones into the borrowed carriage as it would hold.

She was pushing the carriage with two babies inside, one sitting on either side and three tired little ones holding onto her, when a man drew up at the curb beside her. Leaning out of the window, he shouted "Fraulein, where are you going with those children?" Terrified, she decided to ignore him and urged the weary children to walk faster. He called again, this time much louder. Quivering with fear, she answered, "I am taking them to be looked after by families, until their own parents are released." Her heart pounded in her chest as she tightened her grip on the carriage handle.

"Come here, I will take you," he said, stepping out of the car.

"Oh no, you won't!" she answered with a boldness born of fear and the need to protect her charges. She quickened her pace, dragging the children along. Never trust an Aryan! But by now he was walking beside her.

"These children are cold, wet, and hungry," he remarked gently. "They will need food and clean clothes. Since you don't want me to help you, let me give you money," and saying this he placed a roll of bank notes in the carriage. Long before Bea had recovered her wits, he had returned to his car and driven away. Suddenly, the rain seemed to have stopped: with those kind words and generous gesture, he had magically raised her spirits. There were still some Germans left who did not hate the Jews!

It was quite dark when she knocked at the last house with the remaining child. The lady of the house ushered them into the living room exclaiming, "You are soaked!" To Bea, she added "Come along into my bedroom, Bea, you can change into something dry."

Eva, their young daughter, took charge of the little girl. Not until she had changed from her own wet garments into the warm dry clothes did Bea notice that she felt ravenously hungry. She had not eaten all day! Everyone gathered around the dining room table to listen to the husband as he recited the short *Havdalah* prayer ending the Sabbath, their son Moritz holding aloft the special plaited *Havdalah* candle. Then, the lady hurried into the kitchen and soon emerged with a meal for her unexpected guests.

Comfortable in dry clothes, and enjoying a steaming bowl of soup, Bea recalled the events of this long day, marveling at the warmth with which she was welcomed in each household as she brought along her little charges. Now she longed to relax and close her eyes, but first she had to make a list of the children's names, and the families they had been placed with. She asked for pen and paper and was soon absorbed in this final task, setting out in her neat rounded handwriting all the relevant information, taking great care to spell the names and addresses correctly. She wondered if all the children had settled in their foster homes; care and food perhaps would make up for the strange surroundings. Frau Geller would no doubt understand her unusual absence, for she too had been in synagogue that morning.

Refreshed by the hot soup, she saw it was time to leave. She felt an overwhelming desire to be alone in her own room and to shut out the days events. She found the Geller apartment in darkness, undressed with relief, and sank into a dreamless sleep.

❀   ❀   ❀

Not everyone had a bed to sleep in, however, on this night of the 27th of October. Only a little better off than those forced to pass a second night in the open yard of the Polish Consulate, were the thousands still awaiting their fate, trapped between two hostile countries. The Polish frontiers remained closed; the Nazis were reluctant to allow re-entry. When they did eventually give permission, no train returned to its correct station and the unfortunate travelers were imprisoned in the coaches!

However, the moment the leaders in the Jewish communities became aware of these trains, there was once again no shortage of volunteers ready to help.

Food was collected, sandwiches and hot soup prepared. Trestle tables were set up near the railway lines ready for the trains. Those held up in the border towns of Zbaszyn and Beuthen passed through Leipzig upon their return; volunteers stood on the platform, waiting to distribute the food and hot drinks. The train slowed down and stopped in the station — but the volunteers were forbidden to board it! For three minutes, a few travelers, picked at random, were allowed to alight, then the train pulled away from the station. Outstretched hands begged for food from every window and door. The volunteers pressed around the windows, thrusting food into as many hands as they could reach, while the few lucky ones, dragging their pathetic belongings, were trying to get off. Tears of pity and frustration glistened in the eyes of the helpers as they watched the train glide away, gathering speed as it disappeared.

Chapter 2

armstadt, Friday the 26th of October 1938. Here too the day started uneventfully. Times were very difficult and those who could were quietly preparing to emigrate, but for most families this was just a dream. Visas were almost unobtainable without money. It was a constant struggle to survive, since the Nazis had deprived most Jews of their livelihood by employing Aryans in their place. But up to October 1938 there was still a measure of optimism; surely it was just a matter of time and patience before justice would prevail! But this night was to shatter that illusion for a large section of the Jewish community.

The streets were in darkness and deserted. Two o'clock in the morning was no time to be abroad. The shadow of a cat melted into a dark alley, an owl hooted as it flew across the roofs. Vehicles manned by the Gestapo in plain clothes fanned across the town, moving stealthily into the streets with Jewish families. The police were well briefed with a list of names and addresses: Here too, *Operation Abshieben* had begun. Suddenly the stillness of the night was shattered with thunderous knocking on front doors, as powerful searchlights lighted up the windows of Jewish houses.

"Who is there?" asked the terrified voice from behind the locked door.

"Police! Open up immediately!"

The door opened, and two Gestapo thugs burst in, pushing the man in his night attire against the wall.

"Get dressed!" they bark, "All males must come with us!"

The men hastily got dressed and were pushed out into the night, leaving the terrified women at home to comfort their children and pray.

Early next morning, Frau Guttman and her daughter Toni went to see their neighbors, only to learn that all families with Polish backgrounds had suffered the same fate. They decided to telephone the Polish consulate in Frankfurt and ask for help, but no one answered the telephone. Toni and two companions agreed to travel as delegates to Frankfurt, a journey of some 30 km. Arriving by 9:30 at the consulate, Toni was shocked to find the courtyard full of women whose husbands and fathers or brothers had been snatched during the night. No amount of pleading and shouting helped — the doors remained locked. The consul's staff refused to get involved.

Reluctantly, Toni returned. When she arrived at her home station two Jewish boys met her. "Don't go home," said one. "Your mother and the children have been taken away by the Gestapo."

"Ah, what shall I do?" she exclaimed, bewildered.

"Try the rabbi," suggested the boy, as the two turned away.

The rabbi in Leipzig told her that all the families of Polish men had been rounded up; first they were assembled in the synagogue hall and later taken by train to Frankfurt where the men were being held. Their destination was apparently Poland. The rabbi's wife joined in the discussion, and it was decided that the best course would be for Toni to go to Darmstadt and join the family; at least they would all be together. Before doing that, however, she should return to Frankfurt to visit her married sister, to find out if her husband too had been arrested.

Toni had nothing to take with her; she dared not go back to their apartment, so the Rebbetzin packed her a little case with a few of her own clothes and some freshly baked bread. The rabbi offered her a sum of money which she gratefully accepted.

At 4 o'clock on Friday afternoon, nearly time for Shabbos, she knocked on her sister Eva's door. Weeping, they fell into each other's arms, while the children huddled in a corner too frightened to move. It was so comforting not to be alone! Eva related her own harrowing experience. She had been told to present herself and the children at the station, no later than 8 P.M. Hurriedly, they began to pack a large case to take to Poland: featherbeds, blankets, clothing; the little food she had in the house; not much to start a new life in Poland! They were going to a country they had never seen, with a language they did not understand. The Shabbos candles were still burning on the table when they finished packing and were ready to leave. Toni hesitated for a moment, then, with a final glance around the cozy room, closed the door.

A terrifying scene awaited them on their arrival at the station. Stormtroopers in brown and black uniforms stood guard over the crowds: clearly this was to be a mass deportation. An oppressive stillness hung in the air. Sad, bewildered faces stared into the distance, as the guards watched and waited.

Toni wiped her eyes. Eva caught her hand and held it.

"We scanned the platform for familiar faces, panic rising inside us. Suppose our family was not there! Eva was the first to notice our parents with the rest of our family, huddled together with others from our town," Toni told me. "This was no joyful reunion on a station platform, just a sigh of relief from our mother as she bravely wiped away the tears she could not control. Later she told us how vividly she recalled the first time she made this journey, but in reverse!"

At the turn of the century, shortly after their marriage, Toni's parents were forced to consider emigration from Poland. It was so difficult to eke out a living in a rural Jewish community hedged on all sides by hostile Polish peasants. They heard that, just across the border, there was a land that was friendly towards Jews, where one could work unrestricted. So, with meager possessions, but an abundance of enthusiasm and faith they crossed the frontier into Germany and joined the warm, friendly Orthodox community of Darmstadt. This became their home, and the birthplace of their children, bringing blessing and prosperity as the years went by. Until the rise of the Nazi party!

Now, here they were, on a crowded railway station, awaiting deportation to a country they had left behind so long ago. Frau Guttman shivered as she looked at the SS, guard holding a revolver in his gloved hand. At last the train to take them to the Polish border steamed into Frankfurt station, hours late. Even then their ordeal was far from over.

As soon as the train came to a halt, the SS guards stepped forward, barking orders, "Hurry, Hurry!" while pushing people into the train. There was no time to collect possessions. Children shaken from their sleep began to cry. It was almost midnight. Guards impatiently herded the Jews into the smaller part of the carriage, monopolizing the larger section for their own use. There was a lack of air, and the single toilet in each carriage was totally inadequate for the needs of so many people.

It was Friday night — Shabbos. Normally, happy families would unite around the candle-lit supper table; the mother would be busy serving the traditional steaming hot chicken soup, while the master of the house would lead the singing of the *zemiros* (Shabbos songs praising Hashem). Now, the weary travelers tried to lift their spirits and comfort the crying children. Someone started to sing *zemiros*, but the song died in his throat.

A long time later, the train steamed out of Frankfurt station, and wound its way through the dark countryside. Did anyone know of their existence? A ghost train, passing in the night. It had been re-routed to avoid the towns and cities, and made long detours which added many hours to the journey. Occasionally, it stopped at a village siding, but only the guards could leave. The unfortunate Jews had to remain on board until they finally reached the Zbaszyn frontier, twenty-four hours after leaving Frankfurt-am-Main.

Utterly exhausted, hungry, thirsty and deeply distressed, the travelers finally disembarked, but not without further harassment. Once again they were ordered to move faster, faster, but how could anyone move quickly after spending twenty-four hours in a cramped carriage! They were herded into a queue for passport and customs inspection. To their horror, they were ordered to hand over all the monies in their possession: it was illegal to take more than a very small sum out of the country. The guards reveled in their power. One approached a little boy, standing quietly in the queue, and shouted, pointing his revolver at his head.

"Why don't you help this old woman carry her case!"

He then kicked the terrified child in the stomach, and laughed as he lay writhing in pain. Toni saw several such cruel incidents.

A short time later a delegation from the local Jewish community arrived. These angels of mercy (as they truly appeared!) asked permission to distribute food. Toni told me forty years later, "The memory of those sandwiches is still with me!" She was worried about the money the rabbi had given to her. How could she let it be taken from her? She whispered to one of the volunteers. He nodded, carefully glanced around to make sure no one was watching, and she slipped the wallet into his hand. He memorized the address and some weeks later the money arrived safely at the rabbi's residence!

The Nazi guards retreated to the warmth of the ticket office, and the weary travelers were able to relax for a few moments. From the Polish volunteers they learned that the Polish government had acted — by closing the frontier! What was to become of these innocent travelers? It was long past midnight, when they were finally told that they would be taken back to Frankfurt-am-Main. This time the SS guards traveled in a separate carriage, so the return journey was easier to bear, but it still took twenty-four hours, stopping at Breslau and Leipzig. The Jewish communities of these towns brought soup, sandwiches, and milk for the children, an act of *chesed* (kindness) still remembered by those on the train.

At 2 P.M. on Monday they finally arrived back in Frankfurt. Here too, they were greeted by volunteers who gave them food and arranged to drive the weary travelers to their homes. What heartfelt thanks were offered to Hashem for their safe arrival! They wished for nothing more than a bath and sleep, sleep, sleep! But their ordeal was not yet over — what was this covering the front door lock? An official seal? Toni had never seen her father so dejected as when he contemplated this new challenge. He had no choice but to trudge wearily to the police station. An officer in Gestapo uniform was seated behind the desk. As Father explained his predicament, more Jews came in with similar tales.

"Ah! ja, ja," said the officer amiably, opening a ledger. "A mere formality. You forgot to pay for your overnight stay in the prison and also your return fares to Beuthen! Prison accommodation for the men and railway charges for each member, including small children, are to be paid within a few days." Still smiling, he handed out the prepared invoices. "And now," he said benignly, "we will have the seals removed from your doors. Good day to you!"

Frankfurt's shul hall had been prepared as a reception center, so that travelers could all be given a hot meal, and any help they might need. Bea told me of the emotional reunion of a couple that had their children included in their own passports, four on the father's passport and three on the mother's, not realizing the complication this would cause. Diabolically the Nazis took advantage of this arrangement to separate the families, sending them on different trains. For three terrible days they remained unaware of each others fate. "How we all rejoiced to see the family reunited! We praised Hashem for his *Hashgachah Pratis* (Divine Providence)!

From the moment the Polish Jews were imprisoned, the rest of the

Jewish community rallied to their aid. The high standard set by the rabbis and community leaders inspired the larger community to give instinctively.

Although families were back in their respective homes, the Jewish community struggled to survive. Jewish business men were no longer able to trade with their Aryan colleagues. Jewish employees had been replaced with Aryans since 1933, even though they were less skilled. So quietly and secretly, many Jews prepared for the inevitable exodus. If only they had realized the true nature of the Nazis, more would have tried to escape before it was too late. *Auswandarung* (refuge to foreign countries) was a topic discussed wherever Jews met.

Chapter Three

November, 1938: Nothing that had happened before in the long history of persecution of our Jewish nation could have prepared us for the Holocaust. The Jews in Germany and the newly annexed Austria struggled to absorb yet another set of edicts, and brace themselves against more restrictive rules governing their very existence. They were certainly unaware of the meticulously detailed, secret plans being prepared in the length and breadth of the German Reich to drive the Jews out of Germany. Germany was to be *Judenrein* (free of Jews). Who knows how long these plans took to prepare? But they were undoubtedly ready by the 9th of November 1938. It was a Jewish youth who unwittingly was to provide the spark which ignited the blaze.

On the evening of November 9, 1938, Germany heard that Herr Ernst Vom Rath, a third secretary in the German Embassy, had died in Paris. A hysterical Jewish youth named Hershel Grynszpan had stormed into the embassy demanding to know why his parents and family, Jews of Polish nationality living in Germany, had been deported back to Poland. They had written him detailing the terrible hardships they had suffered and he was determined to avenge them — by shooting the German ambassador! He drew a gun and started shooting wildly, one bullet fatally wounding Vom Rath. This was a perfect excuse. The violence that followed was described as occurring "spontaneously, by an enraged German people," people, who in fact knew nothing at all about Ernst Vom Rath. The "rage" was planned and orchestrated by the Nazi Party in Germany. In fact, the "spontaneous" demonstrations erupted at the very same minute throughout the country.

In Leipzig, Bea continued to work in the nursery and spend her leisure time with friends. On the evening of November 9th she was walking home to her lodgings, enjoying the soft evening breeze, when suddenly she became aware of a strange quietness. Hardly anyone was in the streets. This was not a Jewish area. Where had everybody gone? Out of the silent darkness there suddenly appeared a policeman. Her initial fear left her when she noted that he did not wear the new Nazi dress, but the old police uniform.

"What are you doing out so late at night?" he asked. "Why, it is only 9:30!" Bea answered, surprised at his concern.

"Don't stand there arguing with me!" he said gruffly. "Now be quick, on your way! And don't stop anywhere until you are home!"

His sharpness alerted her. An involuntary shiver ran through her spine. She thanked him and hurried home as fast as she could. The Nazis had found the conventional police force to be unreliable during the Polish *Abshieben*. Many had secretly informed their Jewish friends of imminent deportation. So this time, the Gestapo took no chances and remained in total control throughout the ensuing night, not trusting the local police.

Bea arrived home safely and the household slept peacefully that night, in total ignorance of what was happening elsewhere.

❦　❦　❦

Not since the Spanish Inquisition and the pogroms of 1648-49 has there been such nationwide wanton murder, looting and burning of Jewish lives and property. This was the night when Germany and Austria fused and exploded into an orgy of murder and destruction, planned to the smallest detail and implemented with Teutonic precision and cold-blooded determination. A night when the self-styled "Herrenfolk" (Master Race) plunged to new depths of barbarism. No amount of money will ever compensate for the desecration of the Torah Scrolls, priceless manuscripts, synagogues and other property, and the loss of the greatest treasure of all, human life.

That night would go down in the annals of German history as *Kristalnacht*, the Night of Broken Glass, because millions of glass panes, mirrors, glass and crystal ornaments were smashed. Hardly a synagogue, Jewish shop, or school remained unscathed. The greedy flames of the bonfires in the streets were fed with holy books looted from synagogues and Jewish libraries. The *Sar of Edom* (murderous angel of Edom) was soaring to its zenith!

☙ ☙ ☙

At 7:30 A.M., next morning, Bea was greeted with undisguised astonishment by the wife of the nursery caretaker.

"What are you doing here?" she exclaimed.

"What do you mean!" Bea asked, bewildered.

"Ach, don't you know? Have you not heard that the Gestapo have burned the synagogues?" exclaimed the caretaker, adding "They broke into Herr Rabiner's apartment and beat him senseless, and smashed his furniture before they dragged him away! By his beard; they pulled him out of the house and into a waiting van!" After a pause, she sadly went on.

"They came up here too, intending to smash up the furniture, but I pleaded with them, don't do that or I have no job to go to in the morning!" She sighed and looked round the classroom with its neat rows of little tables and chairs. "This must be the only Jewish institution not destroyed." She seized Bea by the hand and propelled her towards the door.

"You must not stay here, it is not safe. Go home, but avoid going your usual way, it runs through the heart of the Jewish area."

Seeing that Bea was wholly confused and had probably not understood her meaning, she added gently, "When you come out of the building, go the opposite way from the one you would usually take to go home. Fortunately you live in an Aryan district, so you should be safe there."

Bewildered by the turn of events, Bea hurried away from the Jewish sector, merging with the early morning flow of fellow human beings. Looking around her, she suddenly felt desperately lonely and unwanted. At any moment someone might point a finger at her, shouting "Jude raus" (Jew out)! Why was she here? Turning hastily, she took a short cut through the park that separated the Jewish from the Aryan district, and she was back in the Jewish area. Nothing that had happened before prepared her for the sheer brutality in front of her eyes. Droves of people, entire families, were being driven out of their houses, straight into the waiting vans. Parents were trying to soothe their terrified children as the Nazis slammed the doors shut. Bea pressed her body tightly against the wall for fear of being noticed, and helplessly looked the other way. The synagogue entrance was littered with broken glass and charred furniture, a Holy Scroll hung out of a shattered window, one end dragging on the ground. A Nazi youth was shamelessly relieving himself against it.

The cry of an anguished woman rent the air. She and her children had been forcibly removed from their apartment and now she was pleading for her baby, still in his crib.

Destruction of a Shul on Kristalnacht.

Profanation of Torah Scrolls.

"Stop your crying!" shouted one of the guards. "I will get your baby!" A few moments passed, then he appeared at the third floor window with an infant in his arms, calling,

"Here, mother, catch your baby!"

Bea could take no more. Pushing through the crowd that had gathered, she started to run as fast as she could, not stopping until she reached her own apartment. She raced up the stairs into the safety of her own room, bolted the door, then collapsed on the bed, unable to move until her heart stopped pounding against her chest. With no clear plan as to where she could go, she hastily threw a few of her belongings into a suitcase. She must flee from this hostile place, but where could she possibly go? Her parents! She suddenly feared for her parents, she must get to a telephone and call them. Could she possibly use her Aryan friend's telephone? She wondered as she locked her suitcase.

Closing the door behind her, she walked quickly to the stairs. She heard the front door open, someone entered followed closely by a second pair of footsteps. Bea stopped; voices mumbled, but she could not make out the words. Cautiously, she leaned over the banister. Two SS officers walked across the hall towards the stairs. Trembling with fear, she began to descend without haste, as they started to ascend. Now she was almost level with the two officers. Their hard grey eyes held hers as they passed. Keep walking, keep walking, she commanded her feet, as they had passed almost touching. She heard the banging on her apartment door as she raced to the front door; her hands shook as she wrenched it open.

The closeness of the encounter, and the knowledge that she had been the target, filled her with terror. Outside, she leaned against the wall, and closed her eyes for a moment, breathing deeply to ease the pounding of her heart. In a state of shock, unable to think clearly, she walked through the park back into the Jewish sector. The streets were full of people running in all directions, hopelessly looking for missing loved ones. Suddenly someone shouted.

"Halt, or I'll shoot!" Then again, "Halt, or I'll shoot!"

She prayed resolutely but walked on, not daring to look back, as the dreaded command was repeated.

A young couple just ahead of Bea froze. The young man could not move, though his distraught wife urged him on. Years later, Bea could still hear the sound of his wife sobbing as they dragged him into the van. Once more she fled to the opposite side of the park.

Could this really be the same city? Here she watched people passing by, laughing or conversing normally. Housewives with laden shopping baskets, a boy on a bicycle whistling a popular tune, little girls skipping. Did these people have any idea of the horror on the other side of the park?

Numb and frightened, she kept on walking. Not daring to return to her own apartment, she turned towards the home of a colleague. Yet — what if Maria were afraid to befriend her — or worse! However, her need for someone to talk to proved too strong, and bracing herself, she rang the bell. The door opened and tears of relief ran down her cheeks as Maria smiled and motioned her to come in, closing the door quickly behind her. Maria waited until Bea had regained her composure.

"How can I help you?"

Bea told her of her concern for her parents in Fuerth.

"Go ahead and telephone your parents."

It was her sister Lisa who answered the phone. Relieved to hear her voice, Bea longed to tell her about the burning and looting, but held back, it was unsafe to talk in public places and she had been warned that telephone conversations could be overheard. Her main concern was for the safety of her parents.

"Is Mamma available?" she inquired.

"Yes" came the curt reply.

"Can I speak to Pappa?"

"Perhaps later" Lisa answered.

They exchanged a few more guarded questions, then the phone clicked. Bea understood from their short conversation that her mother was thankfully safe, but her father was imprisoned, and would hopefully be released soon.

Choking back the tears, she replaced the receiver. She thanked Maria, excused herself, then fled into the street. Bea walked for hours as she tried to come to terms with this living nightmare.

At the age of twenty-two, her life, her world, lay in ruins. But worse was to come. Soon all Jews had J (for Jew) stamped on their official documents; the men were also given the added name "Israel" and the women "Sara."

Chapter 4

uerth, only a short bus ride away from Nurenberg, was the birthplace of the Nazi Party, a hotbed of intrigue and the headquarters of that dreaded Jew baiter, Gauleiter Julius Streicher. Lisa's earliest recollections of the Nazi Party go back to sometime in 1926 when she was only five years old. Although the party was not yet officially recognized, it was nevertheless very popular with the working class of Nurenberg, and feared by most of the Jewish children as the party members marched through their neighborhood. She vividly recalled one early morning being disturbed by the sound of marching jackboots outside the bedroom window. She froze in terror as she heard their voices raising in unison to the refrain; *"Wenn Judisch Bluht am messer Spritzt, geht es nochmal so gut!"* ("If Jewish blood spurts from our knife how good it will be once more!") The years seemed to fall away, as she recollected that morning in Fuerth and gave a slight shiver.

"I was convinced they had come to take me away, as I had witnessed on previous occasions, when they had marched through the streets into the Jewish quarters with their burning torches." Sitting on the low windowsill, she watched fascinated as the flames from the burning torches jumped menacingly, licking the air, adding to the general air of bravado. The adoring public lining the streets egged the Nazis on. Craning her neck, she noticed her little cousin watching from the doorway. She raced down the stairs, and without a word, they clasped hands, two terrified little girls, drawing comfort from each other, as they watched the hostility of these rabble, heard their rousing, hate-provoking songs. This tableau was to remain with

Lisa all through her childhood and into her adult life. Sixty years later, it can still send shivers up her spine!

She shrugged her shoulders as if to shake off the lingering memory and told me of the times when she was caught up in the midst of one of those dreaded marches, while playing in the street. It was a situation she most feared, for what could she do? To give the Hitler salute like everyone else, and to be recognized as a Jew, meant an instant beating for insulting the Fuhrer. He did not want to be saluted by Jews. Yet to stand and not to salute was even more dangerous. So she had become adept at rising her hand tentatively and at the same time carefully shuffling backwards, letting the adoring crowd surge forward until she was safely clear. She would try to shut out the words of the songs, inciting the murder of Jews. Indoctrination was total, at work and play!

With hindsight, it is easy to see how Hitler and his henchmen captured the imagination of the nation's youth. These youngsters, mostly out of work, were offered handsome uniforms to replace their shabby clothing; the general working classes, bored and penniless, were eager to join. They not only exchanged their work overalls for expensive uniforms, but gained undreamed of power. Power to beat and harass the Jew, any Jew! The formula could not fail. At last they had an identity, they belonged to a vibrant fraternity, and if one felt squeamish at beating random Jews who happened to cross one's path — well, after a few free beers, all inhibitions would evaporate. It was good to belong to this *Herrenfolk* (Master Race)! How the world must envy them! As they listened to the man who was destined to lead them into a glorious victorious war, it was easy to fantasize about the glories to come. Our glorious, victorious Reich was destined to last for a thousand years and beyond, our Fuhrer proclaimed, amidst thunderous applause.

"But first," he told his eager listeners "We must rid all Germany and then the rest of the world, of its scourge — the Jew! We must do all in our power to rid the world of the Jews. They are the cause of all our troubles!" his voice boomed to more thunderous applause. Hitler had done his homework well. He did not need a degree in psychology to capture the imagination of a disillusioned and defeated nation. A natural flair for public oratory, personal magnetism, combined with an implacable hatred of Jews, is a formula that never fails.

"Here we were," said Lisa. "On November 9th at 1:30 A.M., there was a loud banging on the outside door, which awoke the household. The next moment a brick shattered a window and someone shouted,

"Be quick, open the door or we will break all your windows!"

It was a bitterly cold night. Mr. Leinhardt hurriedly slipped into his dressing gown and dashed to open the door. Hardly had he unlocked it, when two SS guards pushed their way into the hall shouting.

"Everyone get dressed, you are under arrest!"

Mr. Leinhardt pleaded in vain for the women and children to be spared. A highly polished leather boot kicked him in his stomach. Too terrified to cry, they struggled into their clothes, Frau Leinhardt practical as always, quietly told everyone to dress in their warmest clothing. She quickly slipped some food into their pockets. How they blessed her later during the long, bitter cold night! They had hardly finished dressing before being herded out of the house.

Cold and terrified, they were marched through the deserted streets towards the town square, which soon filled with hundred of Jews. Here they watched with mounting terror as the Nazi storm troopers brought the holy Torah Scrolls from the synagogue and started to burn them in the center of the square. Suddenly the whole sky seemed to be exploding into a brilliant glow of light and flames. With military precision, virtually every synagogue the length and breadth of Germany and Austria was set aflame.

All this time, more Jewish families were arriving in the square. Little children and old people with no shelter or even a place to sit down remained there, right through the long freezing night. At 7:30 A.M. they were marched towards the Berolzheim Gymnasium. The streets were lined with jeering hostile people.

Ironically, they were being taken to the gymnasium which had been built through the generosity of a public-spirited Jew, who had bequeathed large sums of money for the benefit of the town. Once inside the building, the men were separated from the women and children. A uniformed man mounted the stage and the hall fell silent. Lisa had no doubt that they were about to be mowed down in a hail of bullets, but with infinite relief, they heard him announce, that the women and children, were now at liberty to return home. The men were to be interned in Dachau concentration camp; many would never return.

The older men were released from Dachau that afternoon. Herr Leinhardt was among the lucky ones. On his way home he passed the town square. Nothing but a smoldering mound of ashes remained of the thousands of holy books and Torah Scrolls. He hesitated for a moment, then walked towards the fire. Perhaps he could still find something worth salvaging! He was bending down looking among a pile of charred documents when he heard someone shouting. "Look at that Jew, stealing our papers! Come, let's throw him on the fire!" Herr Leinhardt dropped the page in his hand, turning around he ran as fast as his lungs would let him. His chest was ready to burst and he could not go on. He quickly slipped into the partly opened door of a vandalized shop, gasping for breath, wiping the sweat from his brow. When he felt safe, having regained his composure, he slowly walked home. Though everyone was in a somber mood, Frau Leinhardt and Lisa could not disguise their joy at his return. Herr Leinhardt asked that the low stool he used on *Tishah B' Av* (the fast day of mourning) be brought to him. Then seating himself by the bookcase with his beloved holy books, he opened the Book of *Lamentions* and quietly began reciting the prayers commemorating the saddest day of the Jewish calendar.

Chapter Five

Moritz stared into the darkened room, wondering what had awakened him? Normally a very sound sleeper, he would sometimes fail to hear even the loud ring of the alarm clock. He switched on the bedside lamp and checked the time, only two o'clock in the morning. A strange uneasy feeling persisted, he slipped his leg from under the warm feather covers, his foot sliding over the icy linoleum floor groping for his slippers. Having found them, he stood stretching and yawning, then walked to the window and pulled up the blinds. Instantly he was wide awake — the sky was lit up! Giant flames reached for the sky roaring and crackling, fiery tongues licked the stars as the black and grey billowing smoke spread across the sky. He watched with growing horror as he realized that it was coming from the direction of the *Waisen Schul* (White Shul). To get a better view, he opened the window. An icy blast of air rushed in, accompanied by the noise of breaking glass, which suddenly seemed to be coming from all directions. What was going on? He had a strange feeling that it was the sound of breaking glass that awakened him. Fear gripped his young heart. Those Nazi youths were on the rampage again. Who could have guessed that this was much more than a few thugs having fun? A night when the so called *Herrenfolk*, sank to a new depth of villainy. A night of destruction inflicting pain and misery beyond description or understanding, leaving those who witnessed and survived with indelible scars which, fifty years later, could still invoke intense pain, at the recollection of the infamous *Kristalnacht*.

Fully awake, Moritz turned away from the window. He must get dressed. His first impulse was to put on his good suit, but he changed his mind and pulled on his less comfortable stiff workman's overalls. A quick glance in the mirror to straighten his tie. Tall and slim, with twinkling blue eyes, his short blond hair neatly brushed away from his high forehead, he was scarcely the stereotype of a Jewish boy, just out of yeshivah and apprenticed to a printing works. He turned away from the mirror, feeling guilty, as always, when masquerading as an Aryan. And yet his Aryan looks and laborer's uniform were to save his life on that fateful day!

Closing the door quietly behind him, he walked along the passage towards the stairs. Muffled sounds came from behind the closed doors of the adjoining apartments, so he was not the only one to have been disturbed by the strange happenings! He felt less alone.

The acrid smell of burning irritated his nostrils the moment he stepped outside. He turned up the collar of his overall and strode in the direction of the fire. Turning a corner, he stopped: Nothing could have prepared him for the wanton destruction he now witnessed. Holy books and furniture had been dragged into the street from the shul and thrown onto a fire which had been lit in the street. Broken glass shrouded the pavement. Not a single window pane remained intact in the shul building, although it later transpired that the actual building was saved from total destruction because it was flanked on either side by buildings belonging to Aryans. Moritz turned away; his eyes filled with tears at the sight of a Holy Scroll being dragged along the pavement, lifted up and thrown on the fire. Moritz turned to escape, from the sight, but he could not get away, for whichever way he turned, he was confronted with crashing glass and burning piles of Jewish property.

By daybreak, having tired of dragging out property, the ever-growing army of Nazi hordes invaded the houses of Jewish families, wreaking total havoc before they left taking the male members with them. They searched for valuables, slashed all clothing beyond repair, and caused the greatest damage in the kitchens and pantries. They pulled all glass jars and preserves off the shelves, and smashed them against windows and mirrors.

Moritz trudged aimlessly along the glass-strewn streets, trying to comprehend how a civilized nation could do this to itself. Perhaps, he thought, their loathing and fury towards their Jewish neighbors would have burnt itself out with the bonfires in the towns and cities.

Shul in ruins.

Moritz joined the throng of people going to work. Arriving at the printing works, he noticed the startled look on the face of the foreman as he came towards him.

"Moritz," he whispered, taking him by the elbow and propelling him towards the door. "You cannot stay here, don't you know the great danger you are in? All your Jewish colleagues have been caught as they came in through the gates. You are lucky to have slipped through, but you are not safe here." Then lowering his voice further he went on, "I know you carry a sharp knife for self defense. Please rid yourself of it, for they will cut your throat with it, if they should search you." Moritz wanted to protest, but the foreman stopped him. "Listen carefully to what I tell you. I want to help you save your life. Do not go home, they may be waiting for you. Walk casually to the railway station, and there you should be able to mingle with the workers going by train to the I.G. Farben factory. Now, take care! Do not board the train until it starts moving. Then jump on and get out of this town."

Abruptly giving the required Hitler salute, he walked briskly back

Shul in ruins.

into the workshop, leaving Moritz frightened and bewildered. Quickly collecting his wits, he walked swiftly away. The knowledge that only his ability to blend with the average Aryan laborer gave him safety, did not boost his self-confidence as he furtively looked for somewhere to get rid of his knife. He entered the station with a pounding heart. A waste bin received his knife, though the muffled clang as it hit the bottom convinced him that he would be arrested. An agonizing moment later, realizing that no one had noticed, he slowly moved away, trying to control his racing heart. One hurdle out of the way, but not yet out of danger! Walking along the platform, he watched helplessly, as SS troopers hauled terrified Jews from the train. They were not as fortunate as he. Look indifferent he told himself, "act naturally, as if waiting for someone." Prying eyes were constantly on the lookout for Jews passing as Aryans. He watched from the corner of his eye as the guard closed the doors. His body tensed, now was the time to make a dash as the whistle blew, or it would be too late! Sprinting for the closed door, he grabbed at the handle and wrenched it open as the wheels began to move. The next instant he had jumped on to the moving train slamming the door behind him, leaving the astonished guard and SS colleagues to commiserate.

More composed, he walked along the corridor, always keeping an eye on the nearest exit. Thanks to Hashem, it was a short, uneventful journey to the next scheduled stop. With some reluctance Moritz left the train; the risk of being apprehended too great. He spent the rest of the day and following night in the open, sheltered under an old tree. In the end, loneliness overcame his fear: He longed to be among people he knew.

Next day, he resolved to go back and collect his car which was parked in the courtyard of the apartment block. He had left the keys in the apartment. Would they still be there? After buying a can of milk from a farm nearby, he walked to the station and bought a ticket for Frankfurt-am-Main. With renewed confidence he boarded the train, having purchased a newspaper which he intended to read to help him relax, but his peace was short-lived, for, from the far end of the carriage, he heard someone calling for identification papers. The dreaded SS! Paralyzed with fear he could not move, his hands shook as he tightened his grip on the paper, trying unsuccessfully to focus on the print in front of him.

The next moment the massive bulk of an SS officer loomed over him. Suddenly the German roared with merriment, pointing at the picture dominating the front page; a synagogue burning and an old Hassidic Jew, his hands tied behind his back, kissing the boots of a Gestapo officer. Moritz instantly copied him and also burst out laughing, daring to look his tormentor straight in the eyes. Still smirking, the latter turned away and continued his inspection. Moritz was badly shaken; beads of perspiration trickled down his forehead onto his cheeks, but he did not notice: He was staring at the newspaper. By a quirk of providence he had picked up the wrong paper! Instead of the moderately liberal paper he had intended, he had picked up the virulently anti-Semitic daily, and this apparently careless act had saved him from prison and deportation.

Cautiously he disembarked and hurried through the streets, acutely conscious of his unwashed appearance. To bathe and shave was his first priority! When he reached the courtyard, his old car was still there. Now all would be well! He tore up the stairs two at a time, but his rising spirits soon evaporated as he surveyed the shambles that was once his tidy room. Everything bore the hallmark of the Nazi 'Sturmers': drawers overturned, contents strewn across the floor, clothes and bedding slashed, but above all, they had left their mark, even in this simple dwelling place. His shaving mirror was smashed, the mirrored wardrobe door shattered, glass splinters everywhere. He could not possibly stay here. Searching among the rubble, he miraculously found the car key and with a final sad look around the room, he closed the door.

He was tinkering with the car, trying to coax it into life, when he heard a familiar voice calling. It was his old friend, Leo; their delight at meeting each other was mutual. Both had managed to evade arrest so far, but for how long? Moritz invited his friend to join him. They would drive away, hoping to find a safe place. While they were talking, Moritz had managed to start the engine. Grinning with pride, he asked Leo to jump in. At this moment an official Gestapo car drove into the yard, and screeched to a halt at the end of the courtyard. Horrified, the boys watched as the two officers opened the door and came walking towards them, shouting to Moritz to switch off his engine! That did it! With all his strength he pushed his foot down on the accelerator, the car shot forward, nearly throwing his passenger through the wind screen, and the next moment they were clear of the yard. Leo threw a backward glance and saw the two men dashing for their car; however, Moritz, with his superior knowledge of the area and the little head start, managed to elude them. They drove into the forest, some distance away, and for the next three days emerged only to buy food. The sight of Gestapo cars patrolling the roads made them realize that they could neither remain in the forest indefinitely, nor return to Frankfurt.

At last they left the forest, heading for the nearest gas station. Moritz intended to drive to his parents in Fuerth, and reasoned that in this village they would less likely be stopped by gendarmes than in a town. Leo checked the water level, and got back into the car; they waited for the pump attendant to bring Moritz his change. As the man emerged from the kiosk a car stopped directly behind their car and two uniformed military police jumped out. Whether they had just drawn up to get gas or to ask the boys for their documents, Moritz and Leo would never know, for no sooner had Moritz seen them through his mirror, then his reflexes took over. He switched on the engine, slammed the car into gear, released the hand brake, and shot forward and away, the wheels screeching their disapproval, leaving the mechanic with the change in his hand and Leo wondering what had possessed his friend. Moritz shouted above the noise of the engine, "Hold onto your hat! I must drive as fast as this old jalopy will go, or they will catch us!" Glancing anxiously at the mirror he mused, "If we can reach the intersection ahead, we have a good chance of losing our pursuers." Mercifully they reached Fuerth without further mishap.

Moritz was to remain in hiding until the end of December. On two occasions the Gestapo ransacked his father's home trying to find him. At last he got the joyful news, that his permit and exit visa had arrived, and he had been among the lucky few to be offered a place in Gateshead Yeshivah!

Chapter Six

It must be recorded, that even in a country as evil as Nazi Germany, there were "righteous Goyim," Aryans, who were willing to risk their lives to try and help their Jewish friends and colleagues. It was through the help of his righteous Aryan colleagues that Bea's Uncle Nathan was saved. He was a livestock breeder, dealing almost exclusively with Aryan farming communities, and it was a measure of the esteem in which he was held, that he was known to everyone as the "Prince." Most disputes and misunderstandings would be brought to him for arbitration.

On the evening of November 9th, a wagon loaded with hay drew up outside his house. An old farmer and his son stepped down from the high seat. Nathan, the "Prince," watched from his cottage window, as they tied the horse's bridle to the gate post. He had let it be known that he had applied for emigration to America. His heart ached, for he was loath to leave this peaceful place where he had lived for most of his life, near the farmers, yet within easy reach of Fuerth. But sadly, Germany was no longer a place for Jews. He looked around his room. Its beamed ceiling reflected the light from the brass chandelier; the little bureau in the corner had once held his treasured and much used Hebrew books, but now the shelves were almost empty. A large trunk stood in the middle of the floor, packed with most of his clothes and books. It was ready to be closed, but he had to wait for a customs inspector to come and check its contents, as it was forbidden to take any object of intrinsic value, such as jewelry, ornaments, or paintings. Since so many Jews were emigrating, there was a waiting list for the inspectors to call.

The knock on the door roused him. Johann, the old farmer, and his son entered the hall. Johann twisted his cap uneasily in his calloused hands. Nathan motioned them to follow him into the lounge. To try and break the awkward silence, he joked, "You have come too earlyto drive me to the harbor, I do not expect the customs inspector before next week!" Then he gave a short nervous laugh, when he caught the two men exchange glances. Johann spoke,

"You are right, my friend, we have come to collect you!"

"But, I cannot go yet, I have explained, my case has not been sealed with the official seal, besides, I was joking, as you know. We can hardly travel on top of a haystack!"

"My friend, you cannot wait for your case, even tomorrow will be too late. You must come with us now, you are in great danger, we have wasted too much time already." So saying, they walked to the door.

Nathan did not doubt their words. It seemed strange to lock the door behind him, but what else could he do! Turning reluctantly from the house, he watched in amazement as they silently removed a bale of hay from the wagon, revealing a large gap where he could comfortably be hidden. Heart racing, his mind in turmoil, he settled down among the hay. His friend slid back the displaced bale, and thus Nathan left his home and his life, unable even to give a backwards glance. He took nothing with him but his invincible faith in the Ultimate Provider, and so was luckier than many others who did not escape the Nazi fury that night, *Kristalnacht*.

❦ ❦ ❦

As the weeks went by, life became more and more difficult and more restrictive for the dwindling Jewish community. Bea continued to teach at the infant school, though only children from poor families remained. From being a bright, lively group of healthy children, they began to show the telltale signs of undernourishment.

The children had been given a sandwich during their morning break. For several days one little boy would run to Bea saying; "Fraulein, Fraulein, when are we having breakfast?"

She smiled at his appetite, and said, "Moishele, why do you start the day by asking me when are we having breakfast? Surely you have just had breakfast at home!"

Whereupon the poor little tyke burst into tears. "Because I have not had breakfast" he said between sobs.

"Why not?"

"And I did not have supper last night" he cried.

"Why?" whispered Bea, putting her arms around him.

"Because, Mummy has not enough for everybody, so the children who have meals in school cannot have food at home."

Bea could hardly believe what she heard. Rising from the floor, she looked around the class of eager little upturned faces. "Put your hands up, those who did not have breakfast this morning, or any supper before you went to bed last night."

The matron and Bea were horrified as they watched so many little hands being raised. Of course, they should have known! All the husbands had been imprisoned, their property confiscated, their homes plundered. How could the mothers provide for their hungry children?

Bea began raising money for these families. Every evening after work she tramped from house to house, door to door, asking people to help.

"It was a heartbreaking task," she remembered years later, "not because of any unwillingness to help, but they all had so pitifully little themselves." Even the wealthy Jews were powerless, for the Nazis had frozen their assets, instructing the banks to release only small sums for bare necessities. And yet no one sent her away empty-handed, even if they could give no more then a few pfennigs.

She recalled one gentleman, a prominent and once wealthy member of the community, who told her the good news that he was emigrating on the following day. He explained that the Nazis would not release his bank account; "but I want to help you." Putting his hand in his pocket, he took out a 100 mark note, a fortune in those days, and gave it to her. Bea was speechless. Her heart jumped for joy, for this undreamed of gift would enable her to feed so many more children.

This story has a sequel worth mentioning. Bea and her benefactor were to meet many years later in Manchester, England, where so many of the refugees had settled.

"You don't know how many hungry mouths your generous gift had provided for," she told him.

"Oh, yes, I do," he answered, "the expression on your face was enough!"

With this money and the house to house collections, every child was provided with a cup of hot cocoa and a bun before going home, in addition to the cup of milk and a sandwich at 11 A.M. Bea soon noticed the wistful looks on the faces of the older children coming to collect the little ones. From then on cocoa and buns were given to those children, too. At least they were not so hungry at bedtime.

With all their efforts, the children's diet was still insufficient for good health. T.B. was rampant, so the headmistress managed to arrange a course of sunray lamp treatment for the children. They also needed winter clothes, so on her rounds of collecting Bea added a plea for warm clothing. Jews could not buy clothes in non-Jewish shops and Jewish shops had long since been plundered. If anyone needed medical attention, they could call only a Jewish doctor, but most had long since emigrated. Barred from hospital work and not allowed to refer their Jewish patients to hospitals, it had become difficult to stay in practice. By the end of November, very few remained. This was brought home forcibly to Bea on the day she injured her ankle.

It happened shortly after her arrival in Leipzig, before she joined the staff at the kindergarten. She had worked for a short time at an orphanage which had been forced to move from its spacious detached house into an apartment on the second floor of a large building, surrounded by hostile neighbors, who constantly complained. The children were not allowed to play in the street or even in the local park. Bea offered to take them out into the countryside, so a farmer was approached for permission to play in his field. This was grudgingly given, "but only this once!" The game ended abruptly when Bea fell heavily into a ditch. Though in great pain, she managed to hobble back to the apartment with the help of two boys. It was only later that evening, when her ankle was extremely swollen and very painful that she became concerned. Someone recommended a doctor who, though Aryan, might be willing to treat her. It was only the intense pain that gave her the courage to pick up the telephone. She explained what happened.

"Come over to my surgery" he said.

"*Ich bin judin*, (I am a Jewess)" she told him.

"I did not ask you." Pausing for a moment, he then said: "Do not come directly to my surgery, enter two buildings before, then walk through the courtyard of both buildings which will bring you to my back door. Be there at 8 P.M. sharp. I will open the back door myself."

She was there at the given time. His kindness made the pain bearable, he x-rayed her foot, then put it in plaster. He stayed with her in the deserted surgery until the plaster cast had set. Bea often wondered if he survived the war. His courage must surely have endangered his life.

Just before Chanukah, December 1938, the matron finally received her long awaited 'Auswanderung' (exit permit). Her parting from Bea was sad and emotional. It had become part of the daily fabric of life, to see a friend, neighbor, or loved one, making their last journey to the railway station with hand luggage and 10 marks in their pockets, the sum allowed per person. Those left behind would pray that tomorrow would be their turn. Bea took charge of the kindergarten; there were not many children left.

She continued to provide meals for the children. One little boy once told her, "I like this acorn cocoa much better than our acorn coffee at home."

"But this is not acorn cocoa, it's just cocoa," Bea explained.

"You mean this is real cocoa?" His mother like so many, would go in the park to collect acorns, which she would then roast and grind. "Acorn coffee is 'ugh!' " he added.

At the beginning of March, Bea finally received her own exit papers. A visa to England! She could hardly believe her luck and rushed to tell Frau Geller the good news. How wonderful! She must telephone her mother. Oh, if only they could all go together! In her excitement she nearly forgot the time!

If she did not hurry, the first children would be arriving, with no one to look after them. Now she would have to find and train someone to take over in the nursery. This should not be a problem.

Only two short hectic weeks had passed since receiving her documents, and now she was sitting in this packed railway carriage on the way to freedom. Looking round, she saw other young people like herself. It was easy to tell which of the passengers were emigrating. Seals fixed on their suitcases was proof of their leaving and testimony that were taking nothing of value out of the country. She shuddered at the recollection of the frightful ordeal she had to endure before the seal was finally attached.

❦   ❦   ❦

Saying goodbye to all her friends had been more emotionally difficult than she had expected. She had become part of this warm close-knit community. Everyone rejoiced with those fortunate to receive their exit papers, hoping their own turn would come soon; though they were reluctant to leave most of their possessions behind.

Being well aware of the consequences suffered by Jewish emigrants caught with so-called illegal articles in their suitcases, Bea nervously checked and re-checked her suitcase, ticking off the items one by one. She felt sure nothing in her cases were of value to anyone, yet she could hardly sleep the night before the inspection, waiting for the customs officer to call. She prayed to be spared from the inspector whom the Jewish community referred to as the *Totenkopf* (deathhead) for even among these arrogant and cruel inspectors, he was feared more than all the others.

Suppose, he was the one to inspect her cases! Alas, he was — Bea knew it was him, the moment she opened the door and he strode into the room. Though not a tall man, he filled the room with his presence. His steel grey eyes missed nothing, striking terror in every Jew he encountered.

Bea led him into Frau Geller's lounge, where, neatly arranged, were her clothes and other personal belongings, in and around the open suitcases. He looked with undisguised loathing around the room. Not a word spoken. He examined the cases, for any hidden pockets or cavities. Satisfied, he turned his attention to the neatly wrapped packages, "What is the meaning of this?" he asked, unwrapping a silver fork, knife and spoon.

"My cutlery." Bea answered.

"You cannot take this!" he answered in a clipped guttural command.

She returned his piercing look with a boldness which surprised her landlady who was standing discreetly in the background.

"The law permits me to take one set." Bea answered.

"The law! I enforce the law, and this you cannot take with you!" he said. "You have contravened the law by attempting to take silver articles out of the country!"

He also made her remove the wristwatch, she was wearing, but finding it of no significant value, he discarded it, much to Bea's relief, for it had great sentimental value to her. At last, the inspection over, he watched as she repacked her cases, then placed the official seals on the locks.

Safely seated in the carriage taking her away, her recollection of her ordeal still fresh in her mind, she shuddered, thinking, "I will never forget that face!" There would come a time she would recall those prophetic words.

Chapter Seven

arriage doors slammed, the whistle blew, the train began to roll; the usual good humored crowd of well wishers was conspicuously missing. We're going, we're going, to freedom, to freedom, away, away, the rolling carriages seemed to be murmuring to Bea, as she watched the countryside flash by.

She closed her eyes, banishing the hostile world as she fondly remembered the events of the previous year.

In May 1937 she had traveled to Belgium to gain agricultural experience, and recalled the happy carefree weekends she spent in Antwerp. Perhaps she should have remained there, but who was to know? Are other countries really less hostile than Germany beneath their glossy veneer? It almost made her chuckle, as she recalled an incident which confirmed her suspicion of other countries.

During one of her weekend visits to Antwerp she had developed acute appendicitis and had been rushed into the hospital for an emergency operation. Hospitals in Belgium were run by dedicated nursing nuns. They treated their Jewish patients with the same high standard as anyone else. On the second day after the operation, the visiting Catholic priest stopped by her bed. Smiling benignly, he greeted her, saying, "The Jews deserve their treatment in Germany."

Shocked and amazed, she was about to protest when he continued.

"They deserve their treatment at the hands of the Nazis, for refusing to accept our Savior as the new Messiah!"

She lay there fuming with righteous indignation! Even in her weak and pain-racked state she could not let this outrageous accusation pass unchallenged! Regaining some of her composure, she answered sweetly, "Do you believe in the writings of the Old Testament?"

"But of course," he answered kindly, raising his voice for all to hear.

"Everything?" she queried in fractured Flemish.

"But of course" he loudly reaffirmed.

Whereupon she opened her little well-worn *Tanach* (Bible) which was always with her. Opening it to *Isaiah* 11:6-8 she translated from the Hebrew "You will know that the Messiah has come, when 'the leopard will lie down with the kid ... and the child will play on the hole of the asp.' " Then looking up, she told him. "I will not argue with you, but will you do something for me?"

"Certainly," he replied.

"Well, go to the zoo, take a kid and put it in the leopard's den. If the kid is still alive tomorrow morning, then I will most certainly believe in your Messiah!"

Perhaps it was just as well that Bea's Flemish vocabulary was very limited, so she was spared the full details of his virulent tirade. His face became distorted with rage, as he rained curses down on her. At last he stormed out of the ward, leaving an oppressive, embarrassing silence in the room. The woman in the bed next to Bea began to sob.

"Why are you crying?" she asked turning towards her.

"Because of the terrible curses he flung at you."

"Oh, don't worry about that." Bea told her reassuringly, gratified by her neighbor's genuine concern.

"But you don't understand," she sobbed, "he cursed you that you will not get better." Stifling her sobs, she began to pray, holding her rosary.

"Just you see, his curses cannot touch me." Bea assured her. Although the priest continued with his daily visits, he did not speak to Bea again.

Bea was still in the hospital, when she received a letter from her parents, urging her to return to Germany. Five months had passed since her arrival and unless she returned within six months, she would lose her right to go back; such were the laws, newly enacted, regarding Jewish nationals. A few days after receiving the letter, she felt sufficiently strong to travel back to Fuerth, intending to return as soon as she could. It was while she was at home with her parents that Bea was offered the post of assistant matron in Leipzig.

Suddenly, Bea was shaken out of her reverie back into the reality of an overcrowded railway carriage. The train had come to an abrupt halt. A hush fell; the faces of the passengers were drawn and anxious. Bea craned her neck to look out of the window. They had come to rest at Kehl station, the last checkpoint on German soil!

Wearily, everyone alighted for a final scrutiny of their baggage and a close examination of exit papers. With mounting tension, clutching their precious passports to freedom, they anxiously waited in the queue, as the Nazi customs officers meticulously scrutinized each document. Their cold eyes seemed to be mocking Bea as she put out a trembling hand to retrieve her papers. Finally they re-boarded the train, the whistle blew. Slowly it steamed out of the station, out of Germany, never to return!

An unusual quietness descended on the carriages. Most of the passengers were subdued and withdrawn, worried about loved ones left behind, and contemplating what the future had in store.

With loud clanging and screeching, the train came to a halt. Bea jumped to her feet and leaned her head out of the window. Hesitating a moment, she called to a man standing on the platform, close by her windows.

"Excuse me sir, could you tell me where we are?"

To her joy and surprise, he answered "Shalom, you are in the land of the free!"

She quickly put her hand in her pocket to retrieve a postcard she had prepared for this occasion. "Please will you post this card to my parents in Fuerth. This will be the signal that I have safely crossed the border!" He took the card from her outstretched hand, refusing the pfennigs she offered.

"Allow me this *mitzvah* (good deed)" he said smiling.

The train began to move. Next stop, Paris! Bea leaned back against the cushion and closed her eyes.

Her stay in Paris was brief and uneventful. Finally she reached England. Wonderful, welcoming England! Bea was among the fortunate ones, for she had a job to go to. She had been hired as a domestic by a family in Liverpool. From the moment she settled in, she put all her energy and the little money she earned to get her parents out of Germany. She was justifiably concerned for their safety. Many of the older generation were reluctant to be uprooted and journey into the unknown. They sighed with relief as they watched their children and grandchildren leave the country, but failed to grasp the great danger threatening their own existence. After all, even the most uncivilized and backward nations respected their elders! And here they were living at the summit of civilization!

Back in Fuerth Mr. Leinhardt did his best to carry on with the increasingly heavy burden of providing for his family and helping those, even less fortunate. There was a constant stream of Jews to be bailed out, some from police custody and some in more difficult cases, from Dachau. He could not refuse, yet where was he to get the money from? Tall and clean shaven with blue eyes, he did not resemble the Nazi image of a Jew. A successful commercial traveler, he was among the few still trading with non-Jewish clients. One day Mr. Leinhardt called on one of his regular clients. He had climbed the two flights of stairs confidently, in anticipation of a much needed order, but he wastotally unprepared for his frosty reception. Looking straight at him Mr. Shultz greeted him saying, "We have dealt with you for nearly twenty years. Now tell me, are you a Jew?"

Without hesitation Mr. Leinhardt answered "Yes."

Herr Shultz rose from his desk, "I will count till three, if you are not gone by then, I will personally kick you down the stairs!"

Mr. Leinhardt knew then, that Germany was no longer a place for Jews to live in.

Hashem guides our destiny! Mr. Leinhardt was still reluctant to leave his beloved community, though greatly reduced in numbers; he felt deeply the responsibility he had borne for so long. More than ever he was needed by the community. It was in this state of indecision that he arrived home that day. Mrs. Leinhardt was relieved when her husband came home; she had an urgent message from their daughter, Bea in England. The phone rang again soon after, it was Bea.

"Pappa, when are you and Mamma coming?" she asked urgently.

"Perhaps in a few weeks time" he answered.

"No, Pappa" she pleaded, "*Es brent ein fuer* (a fire is burning)!"

Then he understood that there was no time to be lost. He correctly interpreted the message to mean that the war everyone feared, but hoped would not happen, was about to erupt. He immediately finalized his exit papers, arriving in England a very short time before that fateful day when Prime Minister Chamberlain's message to the British public declared that the country was at war with Germany.

They settled in Manchester. Bea left her employment in Liverpool to join her parents.

Chapter Eight

England's declaration of war against Germany was to have strange repercussions on the thousands of Jewish refugees trying to establish new homes in England. Having escaped the most barbaric persecutions in history, they now found themselves classified as 'Enemy Aliens.' It is now part of history that all the men who suffered so much before escaping to England were now required to give themselves up for deportation. The lucky ones were interned in the Isle of Man, the others were deported to Australia.

The women fared better, together with the children; they were required to report to the local police station where a special department was set up called the Aliens Office. How well we all remember it! From the time the war broke out each Alien Identity Card needed classification to establish how serious a risk one might be. There was an interminable line of people waiting to be interrogated before classification. Of course no one doubted the fact that the government had to ensure that no spies and other undesirables should have the freedom to operate undetected. But many Jews felt that the authorities had overreacted, for it was ludicrous to imagine that there was even one Jew in the entire country who would help the Nazis. Yet even though the treatment of the Jewish men was overly harsh, it was to have the effect they hoped for, which was to flush out the odd Nazi spy masquerading as a Jewish refugee! How many were actually apprehended and caught this way, I have no way of knowing, but I do know of one case.

Bea was standing in line waiting her turn for classification. To her intense horror, she saw coming out of the examining room a man

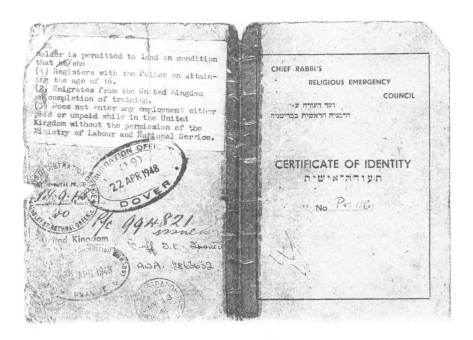

CHIEF-RABBI'S

RELIGIOUS EMERGENCY

COUNCIL

ועד העזרה ע״י
הרבנית הראשית בבריטניה

CERTIFICATE OF IDENTITY

תעודה־אישית

No. Px. 116

who would have passed anywhere as a European Jew — his hat and shabby suit were just like those of any other man in the room. But to Bea, he was *Totenkopf!*

She charged into the room he had just vacated and cried hysterically "Catch him, catch him, please don't let him get away!" By this time someone from the inner office had joined the staff trying to calm her, another sent for a cup of tea, but she insisted that they leave her alone and pursue the Nazi.

Eventually she calmed down and was asked to explain herself. An officer patiently listened as she recounted in detail her encounter with *Totenkopf.* Then he told her soothingly to go home and forget it; all would be well. Assuring the officer once again that she was quite sure in her mind that she was not mistaken, she had no choice but to leave. Her only consolation was she was not interrogated and her identity card was stamped with the lowest grade (the least dangerous)!

Some months after this episode she was asked to go to the police station. She went along, taking her identity card with her, which she presented thinking they wanted to check something, but instead she was ushered into the inner office, where a high ranking officer was waiting for her. He told her that he had been given a message for her.

"Oh, what is the message?" Bea asked, "What have I done wrong?"

"Nothing" he answered, "I was told to tell you 'thank you,' and that you would understand. Now, do you mind telling me what it is all about?"

"No," answered Bea, "but thank you for the message!"

Chapter Nine

No book about these events can be complete without a mention of the *Kinder-transport* — the children's transport that was to save the lives of thousands of children. We will join the train which began its journey at the border town of Gliwice, its final destination, Berlin, stopping at all stations in between. The first children to board were two small boys. They sat forlornly not quite comprehending why they were on this train. At least they had each other! Next stop, Oppeln, still near the border. Wolfgang, barely eleven years old, was helped onto the train by his mother. She tried to keep a brave face, even managed a smile, as she heaved the battered suitcase into the compartment. When he was seated comfortably, she gently warned him not to leave his seat, and to eat his packed lunch. Choking back her tears, she reminded Wolfgang to write home regularly. As a final parting she told him, "Remember, always be a good Jew." He never forgot those words, the last she ever spoke to him.

His mother returned to the platform and rejoined his two bewildered little sisters. They had recently been moved from the State School to the newly formed Jewish School. On the tenth of November, peace ended for the children of Oppeln.

Just as in other towns, with the destruction of the shul and the only school for Jewish children, the very fabric of Jewish life was destroyed forever. Along with other parents, Wolfgang's mother anxiously awaited notification from the organizers of those *Kinder-transporten* everyone was talking about. Fearful for the safety of their children, most households were eagerly awaiting their quota. How many children would be given places, who would be the lucky ones? At last the letter came, one place only was reserved for Wolfgang. Now here was his mother on this cold unfriendly railway station, putting on a brave face, as she waved goodbye to her precious son. His intense dark eyes strained to hold his mother's receding figure, then his eyes closed to stop the tear drops from spilling over. Soon he was absorbed in the wonders of the countryside flashing by, fascinated with the ever-changing landscape. Time passed quickly and they soon arrived at the next station, Brezlau, a town with a large Jewish community. Wolfgang watched with keen interest the many groups of families standing on the platform. Children were crying, clinging to their mothers. This was too much for Wolfgang, who had been so brave when parting from his mother; the tears now rolled down his cheeks. No fathers were there to bid their children goodbye; most of them had been interned. The pitiful scene was repeated at every station.

Finally at midnight, they steamed into Berlin where a team of volunteers was waiting for them. Whispering, they told the children to be very quiet and not to talk. Making sure each child was accounted for, they led them quietly out into the street, down an alleyway, then tiptoed through more streets and alleyways, until the tired bewildered children were finally ushered into a dimly lit hall. Here they were told to lie down on the floor and go to sleep. There must have been hundreds of young children, as Wolfgang recalls, but no one made a fuss; they all lay down in their clothes on the floor boards. How long they were able to sleep is not clear. Awakened before daybreak, their identity tags checked to make sure each child still had one, then back to the station, the way they had come.

They boarded a train which would take them direct to the Dutch seaport of Hook in Holland. Each child was given a small food box. It was not until they reached Aachen on the Belgium border, that the train stopped. German guards in Nazi uniforms came aboard, which upset many of the children. Terrified of being taken away, some began to cry, setting up a chain reaction. Not until the Nazis had left the carriages, was it possible to calm them.

The train arrived at The Hook shortly before midnight. Leaving the train, each carrying their own cases, they boarded the boat, each being given a bunk bed to sleep in.

At last they had a place to lie down, but not for long! As soon as the engines were switched on, there was a dash to go on deck; not all reached the rail before seasickness overtook them.

Wolfgang had no such problems. Comfortably ensconced between the clean sheets, he opened his shoulder bag and counted the many bars of chocolate he had been given as parting gifts. Every grown-up he had said goodbye to, had given him a bar of chocolate, along with advice and admonition to be a 'good boy.' Never in his young life had he dreamed of possessing such a hoard of chocolate. He was surprised his mother had let him keep so many.

At the thought of his mother, he smiled wistfully. Mamma was very fond of chocolate. Slowly he counted the bars on his bed cover, seventeen including the small bar! The smell made him feel very hungry. It was a long time since they had eaten. Mamma would surely not object if he ate just one so late at night? He could hear other children retching, but this made him even more hungry. He chose the one with the prettiest picture, peeled back the wrapping and popped a large piece into his mouth. He savored the rich almond flavor, then gently sucked the melting mess down his throat. That was delicious! But having finished one bar, he unwrapped another, then another . . . vaguely he wondered what he was going to tell his mother. Should he save them for Shabbos? Just one more he told himself, then I will put the rest away! . . . but which one should it be? His concentration on this problem was momentarily interrupted by the groans coming from the bunk bed across the cabin. A frail young boy about his own age, his eyes closed, hands clasped over this stomach wailing for his mother. It almost brought tears to Wolfgang's eyes, he wanted to help — perhaps the boy was hungry! Unwrapping a large chocolate bar, he offered it to the boy. "No, No," the boy cried, he did not want to eat anything, then jumped off the bed and raced on deck. What a strange boy to refuse chocolate! Wolfgang could not waste it, so he popped it into his own mouth. He was quite sorry when the last bar was gone. He counted the neatly folded wrappers. Satisfied that nothing was left, he snuggled down and fell asleep, waking up refreshed the following morning. They docked at Harwich at 7 A.M.

It was time to leave the ship, the children were counted once more. Wide eyed and uncertain, they carefully walked down the gangway, and took their first unsteady steps onto British soil. Here they were greeted by ladies handing each child a lunch box. Ushered into a hall, they all sat down to open their box. Each one contained two hard boiled eggs and two buttered buns. Wolfgang looked at the contents; it was strange, but he did not really feel hungry! Leaving the buns for later, he chose to eat the eggs. Taking one out of the box he held the shelled egg, then carefully removed the slippery white surrounding the yolk, putting it aside he repeated the procedure with the second. Admiring his handiwork, he held the two perfect yellow egg yolks in his hand, then throwing back his head he popped them into his mouth. Fortunately one of the helpers noticed a little boy with unusually popping eyes, seemingly turning crimson. In a flash, he realized what happened, he dashed over to Wolfgang and gave him a sharp slap on his back. Two perfect yellow balls seemed to shoot out of his mouth, thereby, probably saving his life.

Here, assembled in this transit hall, the children experienced their first taste of freedom. They were no longer told they must not talk or make a noise. Encouraged by the friendly approach of the helpers, the children began to talk and ask questions, but most important for the older children was the knowledge that they could now express their thoughts without fear. It was a realization so strange, it needed constant reminder.

From Harwich the children went to different absorption centers — homes set up specifically for them. Lisa Leinhardt was among the older girls who were taken directly to London, arriving at Victoria Station. Her first recollection on arrival was the friendliness of its people. They followed their guide out of the station and into the street. They must have looked like weary refugees, for they were cheered by everyone they passed, as they crossed the road to a reception center — friendly Cockney drivers perched on their coal carts, giant shire-horses clip clopping past — the incomparable British public. Where else in the world can you leave your suitcase on a railway station, return the following day and still find it in the same place! Such was the reputation of the people.

Wolfgang was among a contingent of several hundred children who were transferred to Lowestoft on the East Coast. They were temporarily housed in the deserted summer cottages along the seafront. His recollection of this summer resort, is of howling arctic winds and driving rain. Mercifully their stay at this place was cut shorter than the organizers had anticipated, when during one particularly stormy night, several roofs were blown off and the children spent the rest of the night with nothing but the beds they were lying on.

On the move again, they went back to Dovercourt near Harwich. For the next two nights they slept on the floor of the vast ballroom in a hotel. Mattress touching mattress, who cared! It was warm and dry. It was a short happy interlude for the weary little wanderers. They were treated to a concert and other entertainments which had been specially arranged for the benefit of the children. It must have been a gratifying experience for the performers, seeing row upon row of eager, upturned little faces, hundreds of waifs, each sitting on their mattress, shouting encouragement to the artists, who needed no interpreters. Two days, which provided happy remembrances to be stored with the memories of intense longing for that special place called home.

Then, time to move on. One group of 250 children were transferred to Walton on the Naze to a Jewish convalescent home. The 'Samuel Lewis' home was ideally situated on the seafront with record sunshine in the long summer days. The only snag — it was now winter! The organizers had intended to use if as a short-stay hostel, but due to an outbreak of scarlet fever, the children were to remain for three months. Out of sheer boredom, Wolfgang tried his utmost to catch the fever, but not even sharing a cup with someone infected would make him succumb. He next tried leaning over his feverish friend. A severe reprimand was all he caught. The long weeks of quarantine seemed to stretch interminably. Wolfgang longed for the world outside. Standing by the window he watched the ambulance coming, ferrying the new cases to the local hospital. He too wanted a ride in the gleaming white ambulance, attended to by gentle nurses who came wrapped against the biting wind, in strange blue and red cloaks. Perhaps, one day, it would be his turn. Wolfgang underestimated his wonderful constitution.

Then suddenly it was spring! The fever had abated and there were no new cases. At last free to explore the outside world, to walk along the pier, Wolfgang had his first encounter with his English contemporaries. He watched with wonderment a group of boys playing a game. One was holding a heavy narrow piece of polished wood, and another boy was throwing a wooden ball. What a strange game, perhaps, these boys could not afford a tennis racquet and a nice soft ball! He became absorbed in their game, growing more confused. Not until much later were the intricacies of England's national sport, namely Cricket, explained to the refugees.

A few days later the children were moved out of the 'Samuel Lewis' home and transferred to Clacton on Sea, here they stayed for the next six weeks. The weather had greatly improved and the children were beginning to settle down. It was with some regret that Wolfgang and a few other boys packed their belongings, after being told they had been accepted in the Orthodox boy's refugee hostel in North Manchester. Although pleased to be rejoining a religious community once more, it was with much trepidation that they faced the journey into the unknown. There are few places in England that could have offered a greater contrast to the bewildered young boys.

Emerging from the train at Manchester's London Road Station, they were soon engulfed by a heaving mass of humanity rushing in all directions. Clutching their suitcases they pushed their way towards the entrance, hopefully someone would be waiting to collect them. They tried to hide their apprehension from each other as they emerged from the station, with the sound of hissing steam and a voice booming over the loudspeaker still in their ears. Tired and bewildered, they stood waiting, looking around they perceived a dismal vista of grey chimney stacks belching out smoke, fine particles of soot floating in the air. This was their first impression of Manchester. The grime and drabness hiding the warmth and generous nature of the people who have made it their home. Wolfgang lived in the Manchester hostel until after his *Bar Mitzvah*. Later he was to enter the Staines yeshivah founded by the much loved Rabbi Weingarten where he remained until his marriage to the author of this book.

Lisa told me of that fateful two-day journey from Germany, through Holland, followed by a very bumpy North sea crossing. Thousands of children arrived cold, hungry, and intensely homesick for the warmth of loving parents and family whom most of them would never see again. How can one measure or even try to imagine the emotions of those parents! They sent their precious children into the care of total strangers, their destination but a name of a foreign country. Who would comfort a sick child crying for its mother? These selfless parents, in the thousands, were unable to tear themselves away, and watched the trains carrying their precious "cargo" until they had disappeared beyond the horizon.

The children soon settled down, watching the ever-changing panorama outside their window. Suddenly one of the adults accompanying them called out, "Look children, we are now leaving Germany! Those signs flashing by are in Dutch!" Lisa gave a deep sigh of relief, "We are now in Holland, we are free!" Wide eyed little ones listened to the older children calling to each other.

"We are free, and we can now say and think whatever we like."

They laughed and joked, raising their voices. Just to be able to raise one's voice was freedom, so alien that it needed practice. It provided these youngsters with some welcome diversion, free to talk, to laugh, to think!

England: The welcoming smiles of its inhabitants made up for the lack of sunshine. People opened their hearts and their homes to the refugees. The Jewish Aid Committee, based at Woburn House, worked tirelessly to find ever more sponsors to snatch young people out of Germany and Austria, before it was too late. Thousands of girls were brought over as domestics. They in turn, once settled in their new employment, used up all their resources to help other members of their families. The young men were absorbed in the yeshivahs or apprenticed in workshops.

Lisa was among a party of children who were sent to a refugee hostel in Manchester. She was overjoyed the day her dear parents arrived. As they looked out of the carriage window they observed their surroundings, which were of a drab, damp and fog-shrouded town. Little did they realize then that a time would come when they would be grateful to be there. By settling in Manchester, they were spared the heartbreak and trauma of having to flee the dreaded flying bombs which were to terrify the Londoners.

Part Two
The Bunker

Chapter One

arch 1944. Erika looked out of the railway carriage window. She was deep in thought and hardly noticed as the familiar landscape flashed by, taking her away from her beloved family, her home in Grosswardein, 'Little Paris,' as it was affectionately called. How many times had she made this same journey to Budapest, but in very different circumstances! She sighed, then glanced around anxiously. Had anyone noticed? Did anyone in this crowded carriage suspect that she was a Jew, traveling with false papers, an impostor? To her relief most of the occupants were either reading or excitedly engaged in discussions of topical events. Most agreed enthusiastically that it was fortunate that Hungary was now allied with Germany: a great victory would follow, once all Jews had been disposed of!

Erika tried to look unconcerned as she felt the comforting bulk of her travel documents in her pocket. These were her passports to safety; they testified that she was Erika Fekete, aged thirty-one, returning to her home in Budapest after visiting her husband, an officer in the army. Her beauty had always attracted admiring glances, but now they made her feel acutely uncomfortable, as she tried to adjust to her new identity. She was no longer Lola Weinberger, the elegant vivacious wife of Yidel, an influential member of the Orthodox community, mother of two sons and daughter of the wealthy *talmid chacham*, Reb Josef Zeidenfrau. At the thought of her boys, she sighed again; three soldiers across the narrow passage looked up. She prayed silently, gazing out of the window, until the soldiers resumed their conversation. Lola-Erika closed her eyes, pretending to sleep. This way she felt safe enough to retreat into her real self, and could allow her mind to wander over the turbulent events that had forced her to flee.

❧ ❧ ❧

The days, weeks and years rolled away as easily as the rushing wheels over the railway lines, taking her back to that momentous day in 1940 when Rumania was forced to relinquish her sovereignty over the land she had annexed from Hungary after the 'Great War' of 1914-18. At the stroke of a pen, Grosswardein was once again Hungary. Strange as it seemed on reflection, there was an air of celebration: even among the Jewish families. Euphoria prevailed in spite of the disturbing stories circulating; stories about pogroms in Poland and inhuman treatment at newly constructed 'Concentration Camps' in Germany. The stories were so horrifying that they were difficult to believe: Hungarian Jews thought they had been embellished as they traveled by word of mouth across the borders of Eastern Europe. Here in Hungary, the Jews had been assured that as long as they shared their prosperity and wealth with Christian/Magyar neighbors, all would be well, so Jews took a non-Jewish partner into their businesses and continued to flourish.

❧ ❧ ❧

August 30, 1940, the Vienna Conference ruled in favor of partitioning Transylvania, so North Transylvania was annexed to Hungary. How well Erika remembered that summer! She and her husband were celebrating their tenth wedding anniversary. The heady scent of the jasmine blooms wafted through the open windows. The gathering clouds of the Holocaust were but a tiny wisp on the clear blue horizon.

❧ ❧ ❧

. . . 1941. The Hungarian government joined forces with the Nazi Reich, and immediately proved that it needed no instruction in "settling the Jewish question"! 50,000 Jewish souls were rounded up and deported to Poland. Their crime? They were Polish nationals who had settled in Hungary at the turn of the century and had long since considered that country to be their home.

Once back in Poland, they were handed over to the Germans. "The Germans were ready, and welcomed them with open arms, and promptly put them to death." Wrote Rav Itzchok Jacov Weiss in his autobiography.

Some, however, did escape during the long journey in crowded railway carriages; they hid in fields and forests, scavenging for food in the back yards of isolated farms. Since Hungary was still relatively safe, these Polish Jews, armed with false passports, brought first-hand tales of the horrors of the newly built *Arbeitslager* (labor camp) as the camps were called. Hunted by the police, they lodged in the Jewish communities, and many considered their warnings of impending dangers too pessimistic. "Poland and Germany have a record of persecuting Jews, but our country has a long tradition of tolerance towards them." Deep in thought, Lola-Erika sadly shook her head. Yes, she and her husband had been among the majority of Jewish business people who had dismissed such rumors until it was too late. Here she was now, disguised as a Magyar, her husband deported to an 'Arbeitslager,' her two young sons hidden with Christian friends. If only they had listened . . . she sadly reflected; the rhythm of the wheels seemed to mock her, murmuring, it's too late, too late, too late . . .

Chapter Two

Uncle Meyer arrived one night at the home of the Schreibers. He had recently escaped from Auschwitz, which at that time was just a name on the map, notoriety still to come. Penniless and with false documents in the name of a gentile he managed to cross the border, and make his way to his brother's home.

Reb Yankel tried to reassure his brother. "Do not worry about our safety. Even if the Germans did take over Hungary, most Jewish families are well prepared. We have taken precautions ourselves. A secret bunker has been built into our home. Come, I will show you."

He guided his brother to the pantry, and removed a false partition. Crawling through an uncomfortably narrow passage, Uncle Meyer found himself in a roomy area. There were several folding beds, shelves well stocked with non-perishable food; even a tap to supply water. On a high shelf was a strong box with the family valuables. A little stove with cooking utensils and a well stocked cabinet with linen and clothing completed the arrangement.

Mr. Schreiber beamed as he surveyed his lair. "You see, we are well prepared, should the need arise!"

His brother Meyer just shrugged his shoulders as they re-entered the main living quarters. Brushing the dust from his suit, he remarked, "Who built this bunker?"

"Oh, you need not worry on that account. I have known the builder for many years, and he has been well paid for his discretion."

Meyer could only shake his head. To be at the mercy of the goodwill of not only the builder but also of his laborers! He thought of all those families in their bunkers and could not shake off his sense of foreboding.

Alas, events were to prove him right: thousands of Jews were betrayed by the people they paid to protect them. But among the multitudes of Jew haters, there were still some righteous *Goyim* (non-Jews) willing to risk their lives to help a Jewish friend.

❀   ❀   ❀

Though outwardly life seemed to continue normally in Zoltan Rothbart's household, arrangements were going ahead to prepare a hiding place. To comply with Admiral Nicholas Horthy's new law, he had to take a non-Jewish partner into his firm. This was Appan, the works manager, a tall well built middle aged man, an ex-army officer, and now the partner of his long time employer whom he held in great esteem. Mr. Rothbart was strict but fair; Appan able and conscientious. These two 'partners' were inspecting the buildings, not for possible repairs, but for something of greater urgency. Bricks were removed and then replaced.

❀   ❀   ❀

The voices of the children playing in the courtyard of the girls' school drifted through the window of the Rothbart residence. Tziviah Rothbart glided gracefully in and out of the spacious reception rooms. Her mind in turmoil, she rubbed at an imaginary spot on her polished silver candelabrum. The radio had just announced that Hungary had entered the war! There was much rejoicing in the streets of the towns and villages. It was to be a short-lived jubilation, but for the moment the Nazis were welcomed with open arms.

Tziviah Rothbart was brought back to the present by the sound of the boys. She could hear one of them crying before they had reached the gate of their home. She really must tell the boys more sternly not to bully each other! Her annoyance turned to alarm as Jonah stumbled into the garden badly bruised and bleeding, accompanied by two of his friends. She rushed through the door and down the patio steps towards the children. The older boy explained that they had been ambushed by a gang of youths from the Catholic school nearby. Jewish boys were used to being attacked by their non-Jewish counterparts, but up to now this had usually amounted to no more than a quick few swipes at an unsuspecting *cheder* boy on his way home. Organized gang attacks were a new menace! Mrs. Rothbart felt helpless and afraid as she washed and dressed the wounds, and tried to soothe the 6 year-old with reassuring words. Jewish children just have to learn the hard way that we are living through very difficult times, Tziviah sadly reflected.

❧ ❧ ❧

Life went on much as before. Certain restrictions were to be expected in a country at war. The Hungarian Jews considered it a good omen that Jewish boys and men from the age of 18 were still being called up to serve alongside their fellow countrymen; they did not know that their sons were promptly dispatched to fight and die in the frontiers of the Ukraine. Very few were to return, but that was still to come. Just as the German Jews, up until 1938, mistakenly believed that only the foreign Jews, namely, the *Ostjuden*, were at risk, so in Hungary too, the Jews imagined they would not be persecuted. It was during these turbulent times that Admiral Horthy reclassified his loyal Jewish subjects as second class citizens.

In Grosswardein, as in most other Jewish centers, the fears and uncertainties drew the community closer together. The precious children needed to be educated and sheltered from the hostile environment, while higher rabbinical studies, judicial inquiries and judgments continued to make overwhelming demands upon the Rabbinical courts, presided over by Rabbi Pinchas Zimmetbaum. Who could be sure that the Jews who managed to emigrate would be any better off?

Chapter Three

lke Schreiber and her two daughters were on their way to the fruit and vegetable market some distance away. They passed Dreher's Beer Factory which was a hive of activity, a constant stream of lorries loading and unloading the crates of bottled beer as well as large wooden beer casks. A smell of hops permanently lingered in the air. Across the cobbled road, past the abbattoir, was the matzah bakery. Here Miriam took a deep breath, she loved the smell of hot matzos. Her sister Freidle smiled at her indulgently. Past the yard of the Vizhnitz Shul, they turned the corner into Kopistran road. On the opposite side, set back from the road, was the solid brick building of Mr. Rothbart's soap factory. Then past the timber yard, and turning into 'Zarda Utca' street, they reached the fruit and vegetable market.

The stall holders greeted the family warmly. Mrs. Schreiber ordered boxes of fruit to be distributed among the poor families. Having completed her purchases she went on to visit the salons which formed part of Ullman's Palota, across the road, a world apart from the loud, brash market traders.

This mall was the ultimate in elegance; a group of exclusive little shops, where politeness and decorum were a way of life. Downstairs was a discreet cafe with a pianist in the background, where the women could exchange knitting patterns with the latest gossip. The upper floors were divided into luxurious apartments. Coming out of the dress shop, the Schreibers met Mrs. Rothbart, carrying a hat box. The two women greeted each other; a *Bar Mitzvah* was taking place the following Shabbos. All who worshiped at the 'Great Synagogue' were invited for 'Kiddush' (a toast drink) and cake — lavish Bar Mitzvah parties were not yet in vogue. The girls enjoyed these unhurried shopping trips, for one was sure to meet one's friends in Ullman's Palota. All too soon it was time to go home.

Mrs. Schreiber liked to take the short route, through the courtyard of the Palota, past the boys' school. Walking through the square,

The 'Great Synagogue;' the Big Shul, Fuchs Mór Street.

they passed the 'Great Synagogue,' and on the left the 'Small Synagogue,' also known as *Chevra Shas*. At the far end of the square stood the *Beis Din* (Rabbinical Court) building, the very heart of the Orthodox Jewish Community. Just then Dayan Itzchok Jacov Weiss and his colleague emerged from the building, in earnest discussion, walking towards his private residence. In the spring and long summer days, the Rebbetzin would watch from the open window as her husband walked home, and prepare refreshments for everyone.

Mrs. Schreiber stopped discreetly until they had passed. Now she hurried on towards the wide, tree lined road.

Chapter Four

The wisp on the horizon had billowed, into monstrous black clouds spreading their tentacles across the land, greedy for Jewish blood. The 27th of Adar, March 23, 1944, will always remain a black day on the calendar of the Jews of Hungary. On the first day that the Germans occupied Hungary, they began to round up the Jews, herding them towards the railway, into cattle trucks which would take them to internment centers set up in Kishtartsha, Sharvar, and other towns. It was the first stage of a hellish journey to slave camps. The Jews were stripped of their worldly possessions and given in exchange their 'badge of honor,' the yellow star! This star, now compulsory for every Jew, marked the "open season" for attacking Jews, in the street and in their homes.

Shortly before Pesach, the bored SS troops invented a new game. Black patrol cars would cruise the streets, vying who could spot the wearer of a yellow star first. The unlucky Jew was then beaten, to the merriment of the onlookers. Later, special torture chambers were set up in every town and village. In Grosswardein, the Gestapo took over Dreher's beer factory, where they set up their headquarters, reserving some rooms for use as torture chambers, and one section became the soup kitchen for the dwindling number of Jewish inhabitants.

❧　❧　❧

All was quiet at the residence of Dayan Weiss as he tiptoed into his study. He looked around, at the well stocked shelves filled with his beloved holy books, the *seforim*. An involuntary sigh escaped his

Dreher's Beer Factory.

lips. What was to become of these precious books and above all, whatwas to become of his warm and close knit community? It was barely three hours since the end of the meeting in this same room with the heads of the community, to discuss the worsening situation, but no suggestions had been proposed to alleviate the gloom and fear. Unable to rest, let alone sleep, he hoped to find solace among his books.

Suddenly, a very gentle knock on the window made him look up. Alert and apprehensive, he moved silently to the window, where he strained his eyes to see into the uncertain light. His body stiffened as he recognized the stunted figure of Erno, the elderly caretaker from the 'Small Synagogue' Rabbi Weiss hurried to open the french window.

Erno respectfully removed his cap, twisting it nervously in his calloused hands, his eyes darting around the room. Rabbi Weiss went to the corner cabinet and poured his guest a glass of *schnapps* and waited patiently until Erno had drunk it.

"Well my friend, have you anything to report?" Erno began twisting his cap with renewed vigor,

"Yes, Rabbi. I have come to warn you that you and your family are among those on the list for deportation."

Stunned by what he had just heard, Rabbi Weiss whispered "When?"

Erno shrugged his shoulders, "Perhaps tomorrow," then looking up at this man whom he so much respected, he whispered, "Please do not blame my son! He is a gendarme and has to obey orders." Dayan Weiss nodded and thanked him.

The caretaker left. Alone once more, Rabbi Weiss began to pace up and down. This was the news he had been dreading. A tall, aristocratic man, his shoulders now sagged and he looked much older. He was in great danger; to delay could prove fatal. Yet how could he leave the community, which was so dependent on him? A rabbi was there to serve. However, to remain was certain deportation: he had been warned! He prayed for guidance.

He had no choice but to flee. His heart ached at having to wake his frail, ailing wife Rivka. Rabbi Weiss briefly explained his plan to her, she nodded in agreement and hurried to collect some provisions. Gently opening the bedroom door of his sleeping son, the Dayan's face softened. In repose Berish looked even younger than his thirteen years.

"There is an old derelict building a short distance from the Jewish quarters," he told her. "If we can reach it undetected, we should be reasonably safe."

❦ ❦ ❦

Rabbi Weiss would have liked to walk faster; it would soon be light and he had to reach the safety of the building before the Germans resumed their car patrol, chasing Jews with yellow stars. He looked at his ailing, uncomplaining wife and young son, with a heavy heart. A few more streets, then he saw the building ahead of them. "Look!" he called out encouragingly, "here it is!" Uttering a silent prayer of thanks they quickened their steps. Suddenly they heard the sound of a car driving towards them. The dreaded SS! Had they been detected? No time to find out! In a flash, they darted across the road, into the courtyard; a door with broken hinges let them into the tall building. With the speed of mountain goats, they climbed the stairs to the top, a feat, with the Rebbetzin so frail, they could not possibly have achieved in normal circumstances. At last they felt safe. The Rebbetzin sank gratefully down on the dusty floorboards, closing her eyes; the pain in her chest she bore without complaint.

They were to remain in hiding all that day, but the following morning, Rabbi Weiss decided to return with his family, together with those of his father-in-law Reb Pinchas Cimmetbaum and his son, Reb Itche. It was Erev Pesach and he was needed: to sell the *chometz* for the Jews in his town was just one item that could not be delayed. Later that day they received the news that all the Jews captured during the last few days would be allowed home.

However, they went ahead with their plan to conduct the Seder in a hidden bunker which had been prepared, but which they had hoped would not be needed. A windowless subterranean cellar was the venue for celebrating the deliverance of the oppressed Israelites from Egyptian slavery. On this night every Jew is obligated to remember and recall the harsh treatment suffered by his forebears.

The crisp white tablecloth, the flickering light in the silver candle sticks, only added to the solemnity of the Seder. It was not easy for Rebbetzin Cimmetbaum to keep her boisterous children quiet in this crowded, stifling confinement. The two youngest were thankfully asleep, but the older children had to be gently restrained. Rebbetzin Weiss, a natural raconteur, told them stories drawn from Jewish history, but took care not to disturb the men, absorbed in the wonders that the ancient world had witnessed, dipping deep into the wellspring of our Holy Scripture. Her grateful sister-in-law marveled at her ability to keep the children spellbound. She told them of the Spanish Inquisition, and how much better off they were than those Spanish Jews, who, when captured, were burnt at the stake!

"Phew," exclaimed Raiselle, "How lucky we are today, for no one would do such a terrible thing!"

The two women gathered the children closer, nodding their head in agreement. "No nation could be so cruel today!"

And so the Seder continued well into the night. Reb Pinchas Cimmetbaum sat at the head of the table, his son and son-in-law on either side of him. It was not difficult to taste the bitterness of slavery, even before the eating of the bitter herbs.

The community leaders gave thanks to the Almighty that the eight days of Passover had been celebrated without undue harassment. Travel restrictions were severely enforced: no one could leave without a permit. Rabbi Weiss attempted to send a messenger across the border into Rumania, requesting help for those who wished to emigrate, but the messenger was caught near the border and the letter confiscated. As a result, Rabbi Weiss was once again forced to flee, and hid at the home of a shoemaker on the outskirts of the town. The search was called off a few days later, when the Germans had more urgent matters to attend to, and the Dayan was able to return to his family.

Chapter Five

May 3, 1944. Fear and suspicion lurked everywhere. The sun streaming through the open windows of the Schreiber household failed to lighten the oppressive gloom. On the previous afternoon, they had suddenly been disturbed by a loud banging on the door — it could only be the dreaded SS! Uncle Meyer, alert and fearful since his arrival from Lemberg, knew he had been denounced! In a last desperate attempt to avoid capture he ran to the bathroom and locked the door, hoping to escape through the window. The SS burst in and demanded to know where their quarry was hiding. Not waiting for an answer, they ransacked the house, smashing any closed door. The family knew Uncle Meyer had been caught, when they heard him tumbling down the stairs. A single cry escaped his lips.

Mrs. Schreiber wondered how to approach her husband regarding their own safety; having witnessed at first hand the treatment of her brother-in-law, she feared the worst. To find a safe hiding place was her paramount concern. Since the betrayal of his brother Meyer, they could no longer trust the servants. The 'secret' bunker was common knowledge among their workers and therefore useless.

In the Rothbart household too, all was peaceful on that fateful day. The 25th day of the *Omer* would remain imprinted on the hearts and minds of all who lived in this Jewish community. It was the beginning of the decline of this once famous Jewish center in Grosswardein, which was to suffer the total loss of its Jewish population, as did many other towns and cities throughout Europe.

Schreiber villa in Grosswardein.

On this beautiful warm Wednesday morning, with the first light of the day, the Jewish sector was encircled with barbed wire and watch towers were erected and manned by the Gestapo (police). The Jewish population awoke to the realization that they were trapped! The dreaded word "Ghetto" was on everyone's lips. They did not need to read the notice boards to tell them that they were now enslaved as surely as their forefathers had been in Egypt.

Rabbi Weiss woke up to a loud banging on the door. The Gestapo had come to ransack the house and rob them, but at least they did not beat them this time. The Polish refugees had warned the community that this was a prelude to mass deportation to the murder factories, but few could believe that such barbaric places actually existed. It was bad enough to walk around the new Ghetto and read the notices! In bold letters they declared that anyone caught trying to escape, would be shot. Escape? How could anyone possibly escape? Surrounded with barbed wire and the Gestapo, with the Hungarian populace now openly baying for Jewish blood!

Dayan Weiss nervously paced up and down in his study now stripped of all its valuables, the holy books torn and strewn on the floor. He bent down to pick them up carefully and re-arranged them on the shelves. Reb Yiddele had sent a message suggesting he apply for work as a wood-chopper in the forest: This was the only way to escape from the Ghetto. The army was short of wood. "The Vizhnitzer Rebbe and his family have also applied for the job," Reb Yiddele assured the Dayan. Feeling he had nothing to lose, the Dayan applied for a work permit for himself and his young son to join the wood chopping brigade and leave the confines of the Ghetto.

And so it came to pass that on Wednesday, May 10, 1944, at the crack of dawn, on the thirty-second day of the *Omer*, a most exalted team of woodchoppers were driven out of the newly erected Ghetto, accompanied by a military escort. Their destination was a forest close to the village of Tartarosh, near the Rumanian border. In the forest they joined the rest of the 'woodchoppers,' among them, the Vishever Rav, his cousin, the Rav of Riminov, the Vizhnitzer Rebbe and his son-in-law Reb Yiddele. It was now the day of Lag B'Omer, the day when in happier times the school children used to go into the forest. It was the one joyous day in the calendar, during the counting of the 'Omer.' And here they were, the children of Hashem, chopping wood in the forest. They worked for three consecutive days, leaving their sleeping quarters at dawn and returning at dusk.

On the following day, which was Friday, they received orders not to report for work, but remain indoors. Fearful of the implications, they had no choice but to comply. As they were to recall in years to come, the day was spent in prayers entreating the Almighty. With deep gratitude they watched the sun go down as they prepared to welcome in the Shabbos Queen.

Early on Shabbos morning they were ordered to report for work in the forest. Refusing to desecrate the Sabbath, they commenced morning service, fearing the wrath of their guards at any moment. After the service they sat down on a rock in the courtyard for their Shabbos meal. The peace was shattered by the noise of an approaching vehicle. The Vishever Rav walked to the archway to investigate; his body began to tremble.

"It is the gendarmes" he stammered. A few moments later, the dreaded elite with the distinctive plumes in their hats burst into the yard, shouting obscenities at the terrified men. Given no time to finish their meager meal or collect their few belongings, they were bundled into the back of the van and taken to Gestapo headquarters. The Nazis were waiting for them and they had to endure a merciless beating. The Dayan's heart cried out to the Almighty that his son, a mere child, should be spared the most vicious blows. In the end the Nazis tired of the game and barked orders for the battered Jews to

Berish Weiss; second from the right.

climb back into the waiting truck, their pain and discomfort aggravated by the lack of air and space. They solemnly recited the *Vidui* (confession), asking Hashem that if there was a heavenly decree that they must die, they should do so swiftly. In this mood they continued on their journey into the unknown. A short time later they passed the familiar crossroad which branched off towards Grosswordein. So their destination was to be their Ghetto once again!

Their ordeal was by no means over. The van drove through the Ghetto gate in the late afternoon, followed by several other trucks, disgorging their prisoners outside the 'Great Synagogue.' In all there were about three hundred tired and terrified men. Those in Rabbi Weiss' group noticed that the Vizhnitzer Rebbe was not among those lined up in the yard. He had been smuggled across the border into Rumania.

Having to stand for many hours while the SS guards unhurriedly checked each person was just one of their ordeals. A personal search followed, with more beatings, until everyone had been called.

Dayan Weiss was returning to his place when he heard his name being called again. His heart missed a beat, his knees trembled with fear; willing his legs to obey him, he slowly retraced his steps, facing his tormentor.

"Remove your glasses!" the Nazi barked. Beads of perspiration on his forehead, the Dayan waited, while the guard carefully examined the gilt frame. Throwing them to the ground, he shouted.

"It is not gold, go back to your place!"

At long last, the roll-call was over and they were herded into the Shul (synagogue) which had never been intended to hold so many people, there was barely room to sit down; to stretch was impossible. Thus they spent the rest of the evening and all night. The following day, Sunday, the public soup kitchen had been told to provide a meal — their first since being captured.

The soup kitchen had been set up to provide meals for the tremendous influx of people into the Ghetto: thousands of families, not only from all parts of Grosswordein, but also from the surrounding provinces which had been dragged in. There were no provisions to feed so many hungry souls. Dreher's warehouse had been requisitioned by the German Gestapo and was perfectly suited for their plans, as the Jewish population was soon to discover. A part of the building which housed the offices of the Dreher beer factory was now used as the headquarters for the Gestapo and some of the other rooms were being prepared as torture chambers, from which few Jews would emerge alive. It was in this same building that a soup kitchen was set up, to provide the only meal of the day that was available for the many thousands of people now forced into the Ghetto.

In the afternoon restrictions were eased, allowing relatives to visit those in the Synagogue, under the watchful eyes of the Nazi guards. Rabbi Weiss grieved that his son had to endure harsh treatment with the men, but he learned from his wife that the situation outside was little better. The distress the men suffered from the lack of food and drink and constant harassment was greatly aggravated by the refusal of their guards to allow them out for normal human functions, so they were forced to defile this holy place.

For the benefit of his men's entertainment, the SS commandment would enter shouting "Achtung!" then the Germans would laugh as they watched the effect this had on their petrified victims. They would threaten to starve anyone who did not immediately snap to attention.

After a while, crowded conditions, deprivation and uncertainty were taking their toll. Some men were ready to convert, just to be free, but the Nazis were no missionaries!

On Wednesday, the fifth day of their incarceration, they were allowed to return home, without any explanation for the change of heart. Home was of course the Ghetto, SS guards escorted them to their family reunions. The Jews were told this was a privilege and honor, but they had come to regard any civility from the Germans with deep suspicion.

Chapter Six

Normality was impossible. People were not only occupying every room of every house, but lived and slept in the gardens and courtyards. This was the scene that greeted Dayan Weiss on his return to his home, which was filled to capacity and beyond. During his absence any food in the house had long since been used up. The only way one could obtain sustenance was to join the never-ending queue for soup prepared at Dreher's factory.

My dear friend Miriam was to tell me, many years later, "The soup was only given to those people who could stand in the queue and wait for their turn. If you did not come, you did not get!"

The Germans still had some more surprises in store for the Ghetto population. They put up posters stating that no Jew would be allowed on the streets at night, and there was to be total silence from 6 P.M. to 8 A.M. Intoxicated with power, a gang of a hundred SS police stormed into the Ghetto one day, searched everyone again, ripped up floorboards and dismantled furniture, hoping to find hidden valuables.

Dayan Weiss was once more pacing his study; it was now the only room that he could still use as his own. He was determined not to succumb to the situation without a further effort. After the failure of his woodchopping scheme, he found it difficult to convince either his family or colleagues that one must never give up trying. They pointed out the virtually escape-proof fences, constantly patrolled by trigger-happy armed guards, the watch towers with searchlights, and the fact that they could be shot on sight. The Dayan listened and then patiently explained that his plan was not to risk anyone in a getaway doomed to failure. His aim was to find a hiding place here in the Ghetto, a place where they would remain safe, only to gain time.

"Who knows what the future will be?" he told Reb Yitzchok Shmuel. "We have to deal with the present. Hashem will do the rest." But even if they found a safe bunker, how long could they survive without food? Dayan Weiss did not have an answer — just an unshakable determination to try a little harder.

Wednesday, May 27, 1944, was the day the Nazis commenced the liquidation of all the Jews of Grosswordein. On that first day hundreds of innocent victims were sealed into cattle trucks. By Shabbos the system was working at peak efficiency: on that day three thousand Jews were packed into trucks. No description could do justice to the ordeals suffered inside this moving 'Gehinnom.'

The following day, Sunday, the first day of Shavuos, Rabbi Pinchus Cimmetbaum, head of the Beis Din, revered father-in-law of Dayan Weiss, was deported, together with the remaining members of the Rabbinical Court. Few were ever to return.

The Germans began locking up houses as they became empty. The long queues outside the soup kitchen were getting shorter.

Miraculously, by joining his brother-in-law's family, Dayan Weiss and his family had so far escaped deportation, and his search for a safe hiding place was at last rewarded. Reb Simcha Weiss, a member of the 'Small Synagogue' offered to share his secret bunker with the Dayan.

This bunker was in the cellar. A small hole in the wall, the size of an oven door, was the entrance. Reb Simcha took the Dayan down into the cellar and showed him the entrance; it had an ingenious device to enable those inside the tunnel to close the gap. Dayan Weiss marveled at its construction. Reb Simcha explained how he had built this hiding place without any outside help, as he could not even trust the caretaker of the building. He had secretly dug the tunnel to the large chamber beyond which was part of an unused wine cellar belonging to a tavern now demolished. The entrance to the cellars was partially hidden from view by a latticed wood partition, which divided the courtyard. Standing in the damp and cheerless cellar with the smell of mold growing on the walls, the cobwebs brushing against his hat, the Dayan turned towards the troubled face looking at him, and could not find the words to thank him. Reb Simcha urged the Dayan to be very careful as he left the building, which had a common courtyard with the adjoining houses. This was patrolled by Gestapo and the caretaker, who had been employed by the Germans because of his knowledge of the area.

Once outside in the street, the Dayan hurried to collect his wife and son Berish and return to the bunker as soon as possible. Houses surrounded by the Gestapo, the families trapped inside, tore his heart with futile pity. It was with immense relief that he closed his own front door, shutting out the hostile world, but now was not the time for rest. Delay was dangerous: deportations continued relentlessly. The Dayan considered it his absolute duty to retain his freedom, if only for one more day. He cautioned his wife to take only food or other articles that could be hidden in their pockets; they were not to carry anything that might arouse suspicion.

One last lingering look behind; was it a million years ago, when he had been a member of the respected Rabbinical Court in this prestigious Jewish community? And now here he was, sneaking like a thief out of his own home, hoping no one would see. A furtive glance up and down the street, then a casual stroll in the opposite direction; after a lengthy detour, they reached the wooden fence and dashed down the cellar stairs. They had made it! Hashem be praised. As their eyes became accustomed to the darkness they could discern the objects in the cellar by the pale rays of light coming through the partially blocked window, secured with rusty iron bars.

Dayan Weiss removed the boulder covering the passage. His wife looked horrified, but after a moment's hesitation, she dropped down on her hands and knees and crawled through. Berish looked inquiringly at his father, a tall well built man. How could he possibly squeeze through that narrow tunnel? The Dayan watched his son crawl through with the agility of a healthy youth, and then, with great discomfort and bereft of dignity, he slowly eased himself through the gap. To their surprise, they discovered Reb Alter, his family and the Rav of Tildush already present. The room was fairly large and had better ventilation than the other cellar they had just left. Shafts of light and air streamed through the gaps in the ceiling.

Reb Simcha and his family had not yet arrived and everyone was worried. "Perhaps he decided to wait until darkness before bringing his family," someone suggested.

"Perhaps" murmured the others, without enthusiasm. The minutes and hours ticked by. They prayed for the family's safety, but alas, it was not to be. The man who so painstakingly built the bunker was caught as he came out of his house during curfew. The caretaker, lurking in the dark, shouted to the Nazi guards who came immediately. The caretaker pounced near the entrance of the building, and the German took a roll call of everyone living in the house. Finding some missing, they lined the family of Reb Simcha Weiss up against the wall in the courtyard and pointing their guns at their heads shouted loud enough for anyone in a nearby hiding place to hear.

"If those who are missing don't show up, we will kill the entire family Weiss!" They shouted out the names of the missing people. Reb Itzchok Jacob Weiss conferred with the other two men in the cellar. They decided to give themselves up only if their names were called, in the hope of saving the lives of their benefactor and his family. They prayed fervently and listened trembling with fear. At last quiet was restored; they were saved for the moment. However, it was no longer safe for them to remain in this bunker — the Nazis had some devilish ways of making people talk — but to leave at night would be suicidal. They would just have to wait until the morning.

At dawn, they heard the sound of cars drawing up, doors slamming. The Gestapo were back! They surrounded the building, then roused all the residents, who were taken away for deportation to Auschwitz. Later that morning, those in the cellars cautiously emerged. They were stopped by a policeman as they tried to exit from the courtyard. He demanded to know what they were doing in that particular section since all the Jews from that area had been deported. The Dayan, answered firmly, "We are from another section, but are lost and entered this one by mistake." Incredibly, he was believed! Dayan Weiss and his family headed for the home of his brother-in-law, Reb Itche, and although they were stopped again, they were allowed to continue. With the help of Hashem, they all arrived safely at the house. It was now Shavuos. The Torah Scroll was taken out and the service was conducted. The Bobover Rebbe and Reb Yeshaya Eichenstein of Zidichov were also in the Ghetto; together the Rabbonim discussed ways to save their lives. The Bobover Rebbe, a Polish refugee, had much experience of the German tyranny. He urged everyone to try to escape, adding, "If they put you on a train to a concentration camp, you can start saying Kaddish for yourself!" He managed to survive the war himself by hiding in a bunker.

Chapter Seven

The Ghetto was scheduled to close down within days and they were desperate to find another place to hide, but where? Different locations were considered and then rejected as Dayan Weiss conferred with the Bobover Rebbe and Rabbi Eichenstein. It was mutually agreed that it was perhaps safer if they each took a different way, since a large section of the Ghetto had already been sealed off. It was becoming ever more difficult to move outdoors, and those unfortunates who were caught hiding in bunkers were rumored to be treated even worse than other prisoners.

Dayan Weiss would not give up. Darting in and out of buildings looking for a hiding place, he would hide in mere holes and cracks whenever danger loomed, then, when it seemed quiet, he would emerge and continue searching. Finally on the point of despair, he stumbled across the courtyard of the Vizhnitzer Shul. It was Friday; the Ghetto was a ghost town with the final deportation scheduled for the following day, Shabbos. What was he to do? Go back to his wife and son and await the roundup, follow his brethren into the cattle trucks? What kind of human mind is it, that can voluntarily incarcerate fellow humans packed like sardines, without food, water or provision to relieve oneself? Dayan Weiss shuddered. He prayed to Hashem.

Did he hear his name being called? He was not sure. His body tensed and he slowly looked about him. Once again he heard someone call him softly, and saw a trapdoor lifting over a manhole. This bunker had been prepared for the family of the Vizhnitzer Rebbe! Overjoyed at being offered a place, he gave thanks to

Hashem and returned to his family who were anxiously waiting for him. It was getting dark, time was of the essence: they had no choice but to try and reach the Vizhnitzer bunker that night, and they succeeded. With steely resolve, slipping in and out of the shadows, they reached the bunker. A room originally designed to accommodate twenty people was now packed with at least forty souls, men, women and children. There was ample food on the shelves, but mostly perishables; the ventilation was inadequate for the needs of forty pairs of lungs, but a pipe running along the wall was pierced to provide water. Dayan Weiss was grateful to have been offered refuge in this already crowded bunker, but he could not rest. He kept vigil through the night, and at last, as the sun rose in the sky, and the heaving sleeping bodies all around him began to stir, Dayan Weiss had come to a decision.

At the onset of the trouble, when the Germans began erecting the fence, Mrs. Tziviah Rothbart had been to see him with a problem. Before leaving, she had offered a place in their bunker for him and his family. At that time although he thanked her, he did not really consider it, for he questioned the security of a hiding place that might be known to a non-Jew. Too many Jews had been betrayed by a so-called trusted gentile. He had no reason to suppose that Mrs. Rothbart's arrangement would be any different, but now he wondered ... Having no other choice, he would seek her out and accept her offer.

Chapter Eight

Among the first victims driven out of their homes were Mr. Zoltan Rothbart's elderly parents. Their spacious villa, set in acres of gardens which gently sloped down to the river, showed their wealth. They were surprised by the storm troopers' sudden attack, and were unable to save any of their property, which was confiscated. Now they were homeless.

Their son, too, had his home confiscated, but Tziviah Rothbart had managed to hide her valuables and a large amount of currency. Now looking for somewhere to live, they were lucky to find an empty apartment in the Ullman Paloto which was well inside the Ghetto, and quite near the soap factory. Here it was that the senior Rothbarts came to join them, followed by their daughter with her family the following week. Mr. Zoltan Rothbart had many influential friends among the local bureaucracy, but he did not know whom he could still trust and turn to for help. To hide within the confines of the Ghetto did not appeal to him: it seemed far too dangerous. The Germans were systematically surrounding houses and making them *Judenrein* (free of Jews). Time and again, they would storm a building and trap everyone inside. Zoltan knew only too well what their immediate fate would be; from the windows of his factory, he had often observed the unfortunate Jews being herded into cattle trucks for transportation to the *Arbeitslager* (labor camp). But why the women and children, and why the old and infirm?

Even if they were not caught, how were they to survive without food? No, it would be far better to contact one of his gentile friends, to help him find a way of crossing the border into Rumania. This would cause his parents hardship, but to leave them in the Ghetto was not a consideration, no matter what difficulties were involved. Zoltan paced up and down his private office, looking at the ornate antique desk, the highbacked director's chair, the leather easy chairs, all symbols of a prosperous, old-established business. Suddenly they meant nothing. His bank account was frozen. He walked to one of the large windows overlooking his industrial estate sloping down towards the railway lines. On the far left, beyond his line of vision, the yard and outbuildings merged with the timber yard which, though part of Rothbart's property, had been hired out to a gentile, Toppa Joshika, a high-ranking official. Although this area was designated as part of the Ghetto, and therefore out of bounds to Gentiles, until the fences were erected, he was still allowed access to the timber yard.

Having made a decision, Zoltan talked it over with his wife. It involved his friend Toppa. He would offer a very large sum of money, in return for getting them away ... His wife looked up at him, never doubting that he would find some way to save them. After a few moments deep in thought ...

"How are you going to manage our escape?"

Nervously, he paced up and down while he explained, "I have noticed that the timber yard is still not fenced off," he told her. "I want you to come to the factory with the children. I will give you a letter, which I want you personally to hand over to Toppa, in which I pledge a large sum of money in return for helping us escape." He paused for her agreement, then continued. "If he agrees to help, and takes you to a safe house, away from the Ghetto, I will come the following day with my parents and the money, which I will hand him, when he takes us safely over the border."

It was a simple plan but dangerous, for if they were caught, they would be shot. "You write the letter, and I will go and collect the children," his wife replied matter of factly.

Her trust in his judgment and her courage made him feel uneasy. Would her self-confidence and charm be enough? She paused by the door, and said, blue eyes shining, "Don't worry about me!"

An hour had hardly passed when Zoltan heard a gentle tap on his office door.

"Enter," he called, as he continued to study the documents on his desk. Someone gave a little cough. Who was this peasant girl? Her head bowed, a kerchief covering her hair, it was difficult to make out her features. Suddenly, jumping to his feet, he exclaimed! "Tziviah! What are you doing in those peasant clothes?"

"Well, don't you think I'm less likely be noticed?" She went to the door and ushered in the two children, Rifke and Jonah; they too were dressed in the coarse fabrics of the working classes. She took the letter he had prepared; the ticking of the wall clock was the only sound as she carefully slipped it into the hidden pocket of her dirndl skirt. They parted in silence; Tziviah took the children by the hand, and walked out of the room.

Down the long corridor she went, through the vast dispatch hall, usually a hive of activity, now strangely quiet. The packing tables were stacked high with soaps. Past the loading bay, with its newly installed equipment for storing and moving the heavy cases in and out of the warehouse. Past the lorries now parked in the deserted yard. But Tziviah hardly noticed: She was fighting back the tears. She had no illusions about the dangers she and the children would be exposed to as they walked the length of the factory court and into the timber yard. Tightening her grip, she drew the children closer, and they passed under her husband's office windows. She resisted the temptation to look up.

Zoltan remained motionless, staring out of the window, long after they had disappeared from view. Would she still find Toppa working in the timber yard? Would he be willing to help her or would the risk be too daunting? Would he ever know? Unable to concentrate on the work at hand, he strode out of the room. Walking to the opposite side of the building, he passed through a smaller gate, leading into an enclosed courtyard. Here his faithful manager Appan had helped him build a secret bunker, consisting of a large subterranean chamber, enough to accommodate his family and parents, with a smaller chamber for their valuables. He stopped a short distance from the entrance, full of doubt. Here surely was a safe hiding place! He reproached himself for sending his wife on this foolish and dangerous mission. But Hashem works in wondrous ways and Zoltan would recall his decision to send her away with deep gratitude.

Only the previous day Tziviah had organized the removal of their valuables from their home, hours before the Nazis burst into the house. She had divided her jewelry and other valuables into three separate lots, entrusting one parcel to Maria, Appan's wife. Another lot was taken into the bunker, and the third parcel was buried in the ground. His sister too had brought her family's valuables for safekeeping into the bunker, and marveled at its construction. It seemed such a solid, safe place to hide.

Now he must go home and explain to his parents the absence of Tziviah and the children.

The Nazis were waiting for him. In his absence they had taken his sister away for 'interrogation.' They had found no valuables in her home, and were determined to find out where they were hidden. They tortured her to make her talk, but she refused to betray her brother's trust. Finally they sent her home on a makeshift stretcher, broken in body and mind, still insisting she did not know.

They were waiting for him in his apartment. Not until he arrived at SS headquarters, and was initiated into the torture chamber, did he know why he had been arrested. They beat him and kicked him to make him reveal the location of any hidden treasure or bunker, but as he would not give in, they left him on the floor in a pool of blood.

Semi-conscious, he heard through a haze of pain his father's name being called. With super-human effort he tried to focus on the stooped figure coming through the door.

"Pappa!" he cried out. He knew then that he must tell the Nazis what they wanted to know, to save his old father from the same fate.

Tziviah arrived in the timber yard, looking for Toppa. She was not unduly concerned that she did not find him immediately. It was noon, so he could have gone into one of the wooden huts to eat his meal of black bread and salami with garlic, and perhaps take a short nap. The children played happily between the stacks of logs. It was good to hear their childish laughter, but she warned them not to attract attention. She searched for Toppa, but two hours later she still had not found him. Occasionally, she would stop and listen to find out if he was loading timber, but hearing no familiar sound she walked on. Reluctantly, she had to accept that he was not there, so to ask for his help, she would have to go to his house. She took the letter from her pocket, and read the address: She would have to cross the railway lines to get there. With the children following closely, she started walking across the deserted lines. Suddenly she heard someone shout, "Stop, or I'll shoot!"

She froze, her mouth dry, as she heard him shout, "What are you doing in this area?" The terrified children instinctively ran to her side, clutching at her skirt. Taking courage, she looked straight at the Nazi guard, ignoring the rifle pointed at her, and answered "We are gathering firewood for cooking." "You are under arrest, follow me!" Had he noticed that they were not wearing the yellow star? He marched them back into the Ghetto.

They were surrounded by a crowd of women, wanting to know why she was under arrest. Instantly the women began jostling each other, arguing and bumping deliberately into her, giving her an opportunity to withdraw the letter from her pocket, and someone snatched it from her. She uttered a silent 'Thank You' to Hashem, then they arrived at the police station. The waiting was agony. What was to become of her children? Would she be sent to prison for not wearing the yellow star? What excuse could she make? Would Zoltan be notified? Would he be allowed to take the children home? Doubts and fears for which she had no answer gripped her mind. She tried to comfort Yonah and Rifke. At last her name was called, and she was ushered into a room where she was told to strip. Two women searched her, but finding nothing incriminating she and her children were finally released. Tziviah was puzzled that during the long hours of waiting her husband had not come. Perhaps he was waiting for her. Now she was eager to join him outside.

"Tziviah," called a familiar voice. It was her friend Elke Schreiber.

"I will walk you home," she said matter of factly.

"Why has Zoltan not come?" Tziviah asked.

"Well," Elke cleared her throat, "he is not very well." Seeing the shocked look on Tziviah's face, she tried to prepare her gently. "They took him in for interrogation this afternoon," then quickly added, "he is home again. He will need a few days' rest, and your coming home will be a tonic for him; he was very worried about you and the children."

But Tziviah was no longer listening. Leaving Elke in mid-sentence, she started running, stopping now and again to catch her breath. Racing up the stairs, she was greeted by her mother-in-law who led her into the room where Zoltan was lying. Nothing could have prepared her for this. A sob escaped her lips as she looked towards him.

Elke Schreiber paused for a moment, as she watched her friend running. What could she do to help? It was getting near curfew time, when it was forbidden to be out in the street. The Ghetto was becoming a ghost town as new sections were sealed off, but she still had not come across a place for her family to hide. She had no food for her children. Their spacious home outside the Ghetto boundary was now only a memory. Miriam Schreiber was to tell me many years later, "We were among the lucky ones who managed to find accommodation with a family. Even though we did not have much room, we were infinitely better off then those people who had to live outside in yards and gardens, because every room in the Jewish houses was full." Miriam recalled some of the impressions which had remained vivid in her mind. At the same time that the Nazis were pushing Jews into the Ghetto, they had also started the deportations. She told me of those early days and weeks: the crowds coming into the Ghetto, the cruel guards herding people towards the railway station. It was not good enough to walk, they had to run or risk being hit by a rifle butt! All day long in a never ending stream, she watched young and old running, running past the fence as the guards kept shouting, "Schneller, Schneller, (Faster, Faster)!"

Nearly everyone had a rucksack on his back with a few possessions, and even these were taken from them. Miriam watched fearfully; when would it be her turn? A little girl with an improvised rucksack ran past; her bewildered eyes met Miriam's, before she disappeared behind Dreher's factory.

A new game was invented by the Gendarmes, who were mostly Hungarians. Among the young Jewish boys, there were always some very brave, others just foolish who were willing to take great risks in the hope of escaping. Some would attempt to scale the wall in the hope of making it to a ditch before the guard spotted them. Others would try to dig under the fence. It is not known how many actually escaped, but most died, shot by the guards. Shooting at fleeing Jews was much more exciting then shooting at rabbits or chickens!

As the days passed into weeks, the flow of Jews into the Ghetto became a trickle, and by the fourth or fifth week it had almost stopped. Operation "mopping-up" was coming to an end. The last ones to arrive into the Ghetto were the patients from the Bikur Cholim Hospital. The Vizhnitzer Shul became their temporary hospital, the benches used as beds. The Nazis had no facilities for transporting thirty thousand Jews in one day or week. You can only cram so many into a cattle truck at a time. The rest joined the soup-line.

And so continued this shameful chapter in human history. The shocking chronicle gave abundant evidence that the Hungarian soldiers and police surpassed their German masters in inflicting torture on their own Jewish nationals.

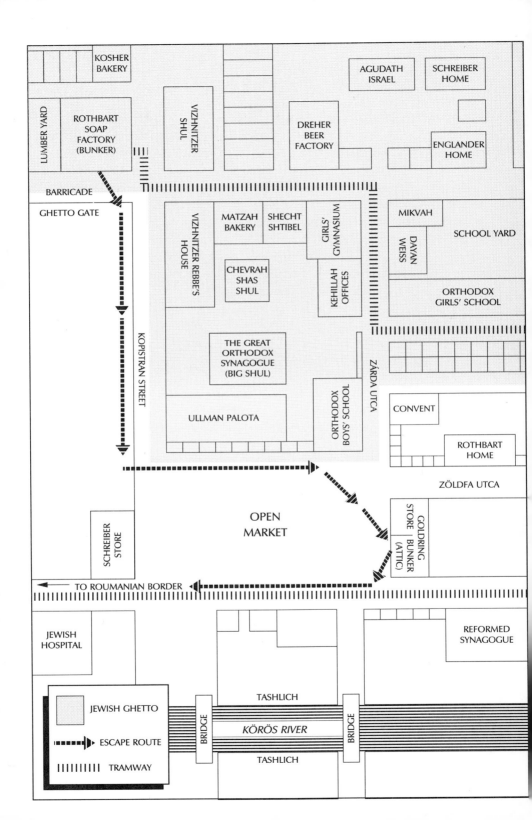

Chapter Nine

ne morning Tziviah and her trusted friend Elsa Fuchs were standing outside the soap factory in anxious discussion. Time was running out for the remaining Jews in the Ghetto. The two women had circled the whole area several times, carefully examining every nook and cranny as a possible place to hide. Finding nothing suitable, they would start again, lest they had missed a potential place. Near despair, as their hopes faded, Tziviah suggested they start in the attic once more. Elsa looked at her in disbelief.

"Why on earth should you want to do that?" she asked, unable to hide her irritation.

Tziviah shrugged her shoulders and answered patiently, as if explaining to a child:

"We have searched the grounds surrounding the factory thoroughly. Perhaps there is somewhere we have overlooked inside the building!"

She guided her tired and reluctant friend into the deserted factory. Their footsteps echoed across the hall as they tiptoed towards the staircase. Silently they climbed the stairs to the attic. Elsa looked scornfully around; she had been here yesterday, but she thought they had been wise to decide against using it as a hiding place. It was too obvious, and would surely be one of the first places the Germans would investigate when searching for hidden Jews. She was about to tell her friend that they were wasting their time, and it would be more helpful if they concentrated on other areas, when she heard Tziviah give a little triumphant cry. Tziviah was standing near a chimney stack, and was pointing towards it, her hand trembling with excitement. From where Elsa was standing she could see nothing that could possibly be of interest, but she decided to humor her friend. Coming nearer, she could still see nothing. Tziviah pulled her towards the back of the chimney stack.

"If you knock this wall towards the base, you will get a hollow sound!" She demonstrated by bending down and banging a stick she had picked up against the bricks. The sound certainly was hollow, compared to the other wall. But what did it prove, wondered Elsa? Tziviah had the answer.

"You see," she exclaimed, unable to contain her excitement, "there is a disused garage attached to this building. Perhaps we can find a way of reaching it through this wall. Perhaps we can remove some bricks!"

To Elsa it seemed a bit far fetched, but they had no alternative. Without much enthusiasm, she helped Tziviah remove some loose bricks at the back of the chimney stack, they came away quite easily. Suddenly, the two woman looked at each other in disbelief — they had come across a secret passage! Disregarding the shower of dust and soot flying through the air, Tziviah stooped and, in her fashionable suit, edged gingerly forward through the narrow gap until she reached the other side. Coughing from the dust she had inhaled, her eyes stinging, she looked incredulously around her as she emerged. The large airy room she now faced was built on a lower level than the one she had come through, but there were a few steps connecting the two levels. As if in a dream she descended the stairs and was soon joined by Elsa, trying to remove a spider dangling from her hair. In wonderment they walked around the large triangular shaped room. A thick layer of dust covered the bare, rough floor boards, plaster hung loosely from the walls, ventilation was provided by the gaps in the shattered timber walls and through holes in the ceilingless roof.

'Beauty is in the eye of the beholder!' is not just a well worn cliche. No palatial residence, with glittering crystal chandeliers, and covered with exquisite Persian rugs, could ever have appeared as magical to the two women as this mice infested loft. Taking a last look around, Tziviah quickly made a mental note of all the people she would be able to offer a safe haven to. She hurried to tell the good news to her husband and his parents, while Elsa collected her two boys, Munday and Ernsty. Her husband, a highly respected member of the Grosswardein Rabbinate, was among those who had been deported, ostensibly to labor camps somewhere in Hungary. Not until after the war did Elsa learn of his untimely death in the concentration camp.

Once at home, Tziviah breathlessly described her discovery to her husband and his parents, but to her chagrin her parents-in-law refused to consider hiding in a loft. She pleaded, but they were adamant, as the loudspeakers drove through the mainly deserted Ghetto, urging people in hiding to give themselves up.

"You have only two days left" they warned.

Mrs. Rothbart senior argued, "Even if we get deported, they would surely not force the old people to do hard labor? Being locked up in labor camps, surely cannot be as bad as hiding in a dirty loft with no privacy and sleeping on the dirty floorboards!"

"Perhaps their faith in the Almighty was greater than ours!" Tziviah was to tell me.

Leaving her husband to try and persuade his parents to change their minds, Tziviah hurried to continue her mission of mercy. She had set her heart on sharing their bunker with the Schreiber family. She had always been in awe of this couple whom she was proud to count among her friends. Their generosity was legendary. Mr. Schreiber was a prosperous furrier; his exclusive shop was a magnet for the rich and elegant, yet his business did not prevent his heavy involvement in charity work. He was a man of strong convictions who would never compromise on matters of religious principles, yet gentle and understanding with people who came for help. As she quickened her step, Tziviah recalled the time he won the state lottery. An endless stream of people representing a myriad of good causes descended on Grosswardein, hoping for, and getting a share from his lottery windfall, a fortune in those days. Rumors persisted that he continued to donate from his "lottery fund" long after this was exhausted, dipping deeper into his private account. In all his charitable work, he was gently helped and encouraged by Elke. She would not tolerate food being wasted, and personally supervised the distribution of spare food and garden produce among the many poor families.

Knocking on the door of the Schreiber residence, Tziviah was firmly resolved to have them share the bunker. To her immerse relief, Yankel and Elke readily accepted her generous offer; it was a gift from the Almighty! "But do hurry!" Tziviah pleaded, anxious to get safely back. Prior to her friend's coming, Elke had been busy toasting bread for future use; then glanced around the empty shelves of her

Reb Yankel Schreiber before the war.

larder, picking up a bag of dried beans and a packet of candles. Who could have guessed that this packet of beans would one day be a feast for twenty-eight starving souls!

Taking great care not to be seen, each in turn ran through the yard of the soap factory and into the building, whenever the guard was out of sight. Zoltan Rothbart was waiting in the packing hall, and guided them silently up into the safety of the loft. He had never envisaged having so many people here, but how could he refuse anyone? He felt uneasy that so many knew of his hiding place. What if someone confided in the wrong person! He tried to shake off this strange premonition. Elsa, covered in dust and dirt, was trying to bed down her two children on the dirty floorboards with cardigans for pillows. There were two Wiesel brothers, Yankel and David, their three sisters, Reb Moishe Leib, and now Mr. and Mrs. Schreiber and their five children. Zoltan turned to the far end of the room where the roof sloped almost to the floor. Mrs. Schreiber was busy spreading her coat on the floor for everyone to sit on. Mr. Schreiber sat on a low wooden packing case. Where did he find it? Oblivious to his surroundings, he held an open *sefer* in his hand, while his lips moved silently. Tziviah sighed as she watched her friend Elke Schreiber lying down on the dusty floorboards; even a mattress would have been a luxury! A mattress! She suddenly recalled the prophetic words of a Polish fugitive as he watched someone carrying a mattress into a bunker in readiness.

"*De narische menschen* (the foolish people)," he exclaimed in despair, "they should be preparing to flee, instead of carrying mattresses into useless bunkers!"

Alas, few were willing to listen, until it was too late. And now it was even too late to stock up with food, let alone mattresses!

Shortly before sunrise, having checked that the children were still sleeping, Tziviah indicated to her husband that they should go down.

Quietly they eased themselves through the gap and down the stairs into the dispatch room. There was no need for words; this was to be the last day for the Jews in the Ghetto. They could not stand by and watch as the Gestapo came to take their parents away. Perhaps a final plea from their son would now sway this indomitable old couple, but they would have to act quickly, before the Germans came and surrounded the Polato complex. They devised a plan of action. Tziviah would lock the outside door, while her husband slipped across the road. He would make a last attempt to persuade his parents then hopefully return together with them in a short time. Tziviah would keep vigil at the window and run to unlock the door as soon as they came into view.

Zoltan threw back the bolt and carefully opened the heavy door. Too late! Cars came screeching to a halt! Locking the door once more, they raced back to the window. Car doors slammed as the Nazis surrounded the Polata, while others went inside. Their parents emerged, followed by a Gestapo officer. He seemed to hesitate and motioned them to wait. An eternity passed before a second officer came out, shouting at the frightened old couple.

"Jews, where is the rest of your family? We know there were more people in this apartment!"

Paralyzed with fear, Tziviah and her husband held their breath. The seconds ticked by. Then the unmistakable voice of her mother-in-law was raised.

"But don't you know! They were taken away yesterday!"

Stunned at his mother's courage and calmness, Zoltan gripped his wife's hand as they waited. Would the ruse work? For a moment which seemed an eternity the leader hesitated then clicking his heels and raising his hand in the Nazi salute, he gave orders to leave.

Never would they forget watching the old couple being marched down the road and out of their lives! Tziviah turned away from her husband, allowing him a few moments of privacy as the tears ran silently down his face.

"At least they did not treat Pappa and Mamma roughly," she whispered, ignorant of the fate awaiting the old people.

It was not safe to remain downstairs; at any moment the Gestapo could come in, as they swept through the Ghetto, flushing out all the Jews, all through that terrible day. What chance did they have of avoiding detection, and how long could they remain in that limited space with so many people. Who would provide them with food?

Kalman Appan.

Having given so many people a shelter, Zoltan felt overwhelmed by his responsibility. His body was still bruised and aching from the beating he had endured; his heart ached from the sight of his parents' arrest. He strode defiantly to the front door, disregarding the possible consequences, and began to pace up and down the gravel path. He stopped abruptly as someone approached, then relaxed as he recognized his colleague Kalman Appan carrying a large parcel under his arm. Kalman's face lit up with pleasure and surprise.

"Rothbart Batshy" (Uncle Rothbart; an endearment), he exclaimed, "what are you doing here? I have been waiting for you since dawn at the railway station with this food parcel. Not seeing you, I thought I had missed you among the crowd. What are you doing here? Don't you know the consequences of being caught?"

"Kalman," demanded Zoltan "how did you know the time the Jews would be rounded up and taken to the station?"

Kalman Appan shifted uncomfortably from one leg to the other.

"You know, my son has been promoted to head of the Grosswardein police force. How can I help you? They know every hiding place, there are informers everywhere, no bunker is safe from their prying eyes."

"Kalman Appan, my friend, we have found a hiding place, but I need your help. We will need food to keep us alive. Will you help us?"

"Where is your bunker?" Appan inquired.

"Here in this building."

Appan could not hide his look of disbelief, for he knew the building intimately, but after Zoltan had explained where the secret room was, he agreed that, providing he could gain access to the premises, he would bring them food.

Suddenly, there was hope! Kalman Appan was the registered owner of the factory, he would apply for permission to re-open it. This he would have to discuss with his son.

"Now take this food parcel" he told Zoltan, "you will find enough food to last the four of you for a week."

Zoltan swallowed. How could he explain there were eighteen people, not four? Seeing his hesitation, Appan understood.

"How many people are there?"

Zoltan agonized for a moment, he did not want to alarm his friend. They could always eat less and share it with the others. So he answered 'eight people' meaning eight more. But Appan misunderstood.

"What, you are eight instead of four!"

"No, my friend" Zoltan answered gently, "we are twelve altogether. We will pay you well, please help us!" Reluctantly Appan agreed. His loyalty was only towards the Rothbart family. They kept their promise, and Kalman Appan and his wife were richly rewarded.

More cheerfully now that he had some food to share, Zoltan climbed the stairs to the attic. Reb Moishe Leib Mendlovitch was busy measuring the gap in the recess. He explained that he was constructing a camouflage to hide the entrance, lest the attic be searched. Leaving Reb Moishe Leib Mendlovitch to finish, Zoltan bent almost double to fit his tall frame through the gap. In his absence three more people had arrived: Schreiber and two young yeshiva students. Tziviah looked around the crowded room, at the grimy faces and blackened hands. Years of undisturbed dust and soot from the chimney hung in the air settling on everyone, as they tried to make themselves comfortable in small family groups. It was Friday afternoon, almost Shabbos. Tziviah looked at her children sitting on each side of her. Rifke sucked her thumb while clutching her favorite pillow, the only luxury she had been allowed to take with her. Jumping to her feet, Tziviah told her husband, "I cannot have the children so dirty for Shabbos, I am going to bathe them!" Her husband stared at her incredulously.

"Either you are joking, or you have taken leave of your senses!" he told her. But Tziviah was adamant, the children were not to be left in their dirty state.

"And how, in these cramped waterless quarters do you propose to bathe them?"

"Not here!" she answered, "Of course not. I am going to take them to the *mikvah*."

Zoltan pleaded, as to a fretful child, "Tziviah, listen to me, I will not allow you to endanger your life or that of the children. What you propose to do is foolish and dangerous!" Holding up his hand to silence her, he said firmly, "Enough of this nonsense! You know what will happen to you and the children if you are caught!"

She was beyond listening to reason. Grabbing her children in an unguarded moment, she smuggled them out of the bunker and holding each one tightly by the hand, she started running, running towards the *mikvah* at the other end of the Ghetto.

Chapter Ten

Rabbi Itzchok J. Weiss, Dayan of Grosswardein, had just emerged from the trapdoor that covered the entrance to the bunker in the Vizhnitzer courtyard. He had a sense of impending disaster. He must find another hiding place for himself and his family before the Germans returned to continue their search, for come they certainly would! If only he had accepted the offer to share a bunker with the Rothbart family! Now that the Ghetto was deserted, it would be reckless to venture into the streets to look for them. Suddenly, he froze, unable to believe his own eyes. Surely he had just seen Tziviah Rothbart running past, trailing a child by each hand! Recovering somewhat, he furtively craned his head around the entrance of the courtyard. There was no mistaking the running figure of a woman and two children. Why was she running, and where to? There was no time for speculation: she was running towards the 'Great Synagogue.' He beckoned to his wife, hurriedly explained, and she at once set off in pursuit.

Meanwhile, Tziviah and the two children had arrived in the yard of the old *mikvah*. Breathless, her adrenalin working overtime, she was intent on getting her children bathed for the coming Shabbos.

"How wondrous are the ways of The Almighty," she was to tell me. "Through this act of utter foolishness, we were able to give sanctuary to Dayan Yitzchok Yacov Weiss, his Rebbetzin and his son Berish."

As she feverishly bathed and dressed the children, Rebbetzin Rifke Weiss came running in. As they hurried out of the *mikvah* building, the Rebbetzin pleaded with her.

The Mikvah Building.

"Frau Rothbart, please take us to your bunker. My husband told me to remind you that once you offered us a place in your bunker!"

Tziviah looked at this frail, distraught lady, and hesitated only for a moment. It was true, she had offered to share their bunker. "Of course, you can come," she answered as they scurried along the deserted streets. (Perhaps the Germans had taken a temporary break).

The Dayan and Berish were standing outside the Vizhnitzer yard as the foursome approached. Tziviah paused, explained how to get to the bunker, then taking the two children firmly by the hand, she hurried away. Her distraught husband was waiting in the deserted factory. He was so relieved at seeing them that he could not be vexed with her. Silently they climbed the stairs and joined the others in the bunker.

"Zoltan," she said hesitantly.

"It's all right," he answered gently "You don't need to apologize, you're back and you are safe, that is all that matters!"

"Zoltan," she repeated awkwardly, "I have something to tell you."

Her husband turned towards her in shocked disbelief. "You did not agree to take more people?"

Unable to meet his eyes, she whispered "Yes, I did!"

"Who?"

"Dayan Weiss?"

"And who else?"

"His wife and son?"

"You are telling me that three more people are coming!"

Tziviah just nodded her head.

Chapter Eleven

ayan Weiss turned to speak to his wife. "Let us not linger even a moment."

"Perhaps I should take a few of our belongings?" Rebbetzin Rifke suggested.

"We cannot risk the delay," the Dayan answered. It was growing dark. Glancing furtively up and down the street they quickly walked towards the soap factory. Footsteps clattered behind them, they hid behind a wall, then sighed with relief when they saw it was Reb Mendel Guttman, his wife and two children. He too had been in hiding in the Vizhnitzer courtyard, and had overheard their conversation. He begged the Dayan to take them with him.

Deep in thought, Zoltan surveyed the bunker, his troubled eyes sweeping over the reclining figures on the dirty, dusty floor. Mice droppings were scattered everywhere. What a strange coincidence that had suddenly thrust so much responsibility on his shoulders! His brow furrowed as he wondered how long so many people could remain hidden within the rafters of this wooden warehouse. It had no amenities, principally, no insulation to keep out the summer heat. In late afternoon, it was like a heated oven; the lack of water made everyone irritable, and now his wife was telling him to accept three more guests! Tziviah said, "Don't worry, I will make room for the Rebbetzin near me, you only need to find a place for the Dayan. Berish can sit with the other boys." Zoltan sighed. He had always been in awe of the learned Dayan, and he must find him a place where he could observe the outside world through the open wooden wall panels. The best he could do was offer him a place near Reb

Rebbetzin Rifke Weiss. | Dayan Weiss.

Moishe Leib. Just then they heard the muffled sound of someone crawling through the narrow passageway. One by one, they slowly emerged. The first to come through was the Rebbetzin, pale and gasping for breath, then the Dayan: Zoltan marveled how someone so tall and well built could have squeezed through the narrow passage. Berish followed then another and another, until finally the last member of the Guttman family emerged! Instead of the three people they had expected, they beheld seven! Zoltan swivelled around to look at his wife.

"Did you?"

"No, I did," the Dayan answered swiftly. "Please let them stay," he pleaded with Zoltan, explaining that the Guttman family had followed him out of the Vizhnitzer bunker. "To send them away would be certain capture!"

Zoltan rolled his eyes heavenward in resignation, not quite convinced of his wife's ignorance in this matter.

A few days later they learned of the Gestapo's raid on the Vizhnitzer courtyard. They must have been tipped off about a possible bunker. Alas, no one there escaped; all that discomfort and suffering had been in vain. Captured and bundled into a waiting van, they joined the rest of their enslaved brethren in concentration camps.

That night was the first Shabbos in the bunker. No one knew how long they would remain. The food they had was meant to last four people for one week, and now there were 28 people with no certainty when the next food supply would come. The need for water was even more acute, with sanitation an added problem. Since the addition of their latest guests, there was hardly enough room for everyone to stretch their legs. Creaking floorboards made even turning over a security hazard, yet all felt privileged to be safe. The Shabbos service was quietly and fervently conducted by Dayan Weiss and devoutly followed by all present. When they finally fell asleep, Mrs. Rothbart recalls, she and her husband took turns to keep vigil through the night, and wake the noisy snorers, for fear of alerting passers-by. Every soundcould be heard through the wooden walls and floor-boards. That was just one of the many problems that were to plague them.

For the moment they were safe, but their only means of getting food was through their precarious link with Appan. To him this presented a great problem and danger. He genuinely wished to help his Jewish friend, but even his high position of chief of the local constabulary did not give him complete freedom. He requested permission to inspect the soap factory for possible damage, with a view to re-opening it. Since the construction of the Ghetto, all gentiles who lived within its boundaries were forced to move out, and were resettled in the beautiful homes belonging to Jews. Gentiles were banned from entering the Ghetto and Jews were prevented from leaving, so Appan's only hope of bringing food without arousing suspicion would be if he could go into the factory legitimately.

He was given permission to enter the deserted Ghetto on Monday morning accompanied by a German soldier, so his plan to smuggle food into the bunker was thwarted.

Up in the loft, the mood was grim. The parcel of food distributed on Friday among thirty souls, was but a fond memory. Drinking water was severely rationed. The loft became a furnace as the sun rose in the clear sky. There was not sufficient ventilation for so many people with no space to move. It surely was a miracle that the children kept quiet and did not cry out! Rifke, even at the age of four, sensed the danger. She used to stuff the corner of her pillow into her mouth whenever she felt the need to cry.

Through the gaps, they watched with mounting fear, as Appan accompanied by a soldier approached the building. They had no way of knowing why he had come, and why the Nazi soldier? Were they about to be betrayed? Following Dayan Weiss' example, they recited *Tehillim* (Psalms) their lips moving silently, entreating the Almighty for help. Mothers held their children tightly so no one would move. Reb Yankel Schreiber was engrossed in his beloved *Mishnayos*, apparently oblivious to the drama around him.

At last the footsteps echoing from the factory floor ceased. They heard the door being noisily locked. Moments later, Appan walked into view, following by the soldier. Zoltan watched the figures passing with relief. The next moment, his body tensed; was it by chance, or had Appan deliberately halted right underneath their loft? He raised his hand to demand total silence, and listened to the voices below. Appan was telling the soldier that he intended to commence production the following day. Zoltan understood that this information was meant for him, and sighed with relief. Their prayers had been answered. But another twenty-four hours were to pass before food was brought in.

Appan still had a problem. To be able to go freely into the factory was only one step towards overcoming it. How was he to carry even the bare minimum of food for so many people without arousing suspicion? His wife suggested he should choose very carefully among his past employees. He should choose only girls or women whom he could trust, and ask them for help to smuggle food into the factory. He knew from previous conversations he had had with Zoltan, that money was available to buy loyalty. The following day, Appan and three peasant workers arrived at the Ghetto gates. Appan presented his permit; nevertheless they were searched. Nothing was found except an unusually large amount of food between four people. Roszika, swinging her well padded hips, answered, "I like food, and since this is our first day back at work, we are having a celebration!" adding for good measure "This is a double celebration, because we are rid of the Jews!"

Up in the bunker, they could hear the voices of the women before they came into view. Weak from hunger and thirst, they became alarmed that Appan had not come alone. Does this mean another delay? Was it wise to trust these peasant women? Zoltan asked Dayan Weiss for advice. Should he go down and meet the girls or stay upstairs, in which case Appan would understand. Assuming they knew there were Jews hidden in the factory, Appan was unlikely to have told them exactly where they were. Dayan Weiss deliberated for a few moments, his eyes taking in the pitiful condition of his fellow sufferers, then turning to Zoltan, he told him "As it is written. It is better to die by the sword than by starvation!"

With money in his pocket, Zoltan crawled out of the bunker and descended the stairs to meet Appan and the girls. He took the bread and onions they had brought with immense gratitude. Though anxious to get back and distribute the food, he stayed to explain the need for complete secrecy, and promised each girl a beautiful villa with an income as payment for their loyalty. They agreed, and he handed each one a large sum of money. To them the dangers involved seemed a small price to pay for such undreamed of riches. After the war Zoltan kept his promise to the girls.

Reassured of their safety for the moment, though the women's loyalty had yet to be tested, Zoltan returned to the attic, wondering how he was going to share the food intended for twelve people among thirty.

How can one describe the secret well of strength and will power that human beings can draw on when tested to the limit, with only their faith to sustain them?

"How did you spend the long days?" I asked Miriam and Berish, "In fear!" was their simple answer.

Eli Schreiber answered; "The heat!"

In the days and weeks to come, time revolved around the moment when food was brought in. Its distribution was a major event, requiring the skills and wisdom of King Solomon. Every crumb was precious and carefully collected and shared. At the insistence of Tziviah, the little children were given tiny extra portions. It fell to Zoltan and his wife to provide other necessities for their survival. As Tziviah was to say. "We were all *lebedige mentschen* (living beings)."

Their sanitation arrangements were crude. Zoltan brought buckets from the factory and at night these would be emptied into the factory toilet. The movements of the night patrol were carefully checked, then the heavy buckets would be emptied with as little noise as possible, and the toilet flushed when the soldier was at the furthest point. Empty mineral bottles had to be re-filled with fresh water. This duty was shared by Tziviah, her maid Toby and Reb Moshe Leib.

Three more days passed. Although Appan and the women did not get searched every time they entered the Ghetto, they were too nervous to carry food every day, and assumed they had brought sufficient for several days. As a result they brought less than the minimum even for twelve people. No one had expected things to get so bad. Two weeks went by. They were all getting thinner and their strength was ebbing away. Zoltan advised everyone to sleep longer hours, thereby saving their energy. Those who snored when sleeping had a piece of string tied to their leg which could be pulled when necessary; this worked quite well. Tziviah was concerned with Rebbetzin Weiss' health; she seemed to be in pain, and too weak even to sit up most of the time. The smell from the waste buckets seemed to trouble her more than it did the stronger members. Someone gave her a tin of black shoe polish; the Rebbetzin would frequently smell the shoe polish, and this seemed to give her a little relief.

❦ ❦ ❦

The Ghetto was deserted except for the patients in the *Yarvan Korhaus* hospital, headed by a dedicated Gentile doctor. He used a variety of excuses to delay the deportation of his patients. His most successful ruse was to warn the Gestapo that a number of patients had developed a highly contagious form of diarrhea and for their own safety, he advised the Germans to stay clear. In this way, he was able to help many of the hospital patients to escape. Doctor Ferenc Kupfer was considered an eccentric by the Nazis. He was often observed walking his poodle through the streets of the Ghetto, in earnest conversation with his dog. The good doctor was an old friend of Zoltan. It happened that his daily walks would take him past the

The Jewish Hospital.

soap factory, frequently stopping outside the wall below the bunker, while keeping up a running commentary on current events. His poodle displayed a total lack of interest, stopping only to do what poodles are best at doing! In this way, Zoltan and the others in the bunker would be kept informed of all newsworthy items. The eagerly awaited 'doggy walks' came to an abrupt end three weeks later, when the remaining hospital patients were finally deported.

Chapter Twelve

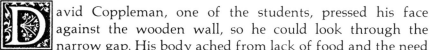avid Coppleman, one of the students, pressed his face against the wooden wall, so he could look through the narrow gap. His body ached from lack of food and the need to exercise his legs. Suddenly his thin pale face brightened, why had he not thought of it before! Under cover of darkness he would slip home. Their faithful servant of thirty years, Margit, had been left in charge of the house. He well remembered Margit reassuring his parents that she would take care of their home as if it were her own. Yes, he mused, he would enlist her help. Eager to put his plan into action he turned to his companion. "Chaim," he whispered hardly able to contain his excitement, "I have thought of an easy way to get food, we won't need to starve anymore." Seeing the skeptical look on his friend's face, he patiently explained. After spending the last three weeks incarcerated in this overcrowded bunker with no food, he was desperate to embrace any opportunity to get out. Respectfully, Chaim and David approached the Dayan with his plan. Dayan Weiss, however, advised against going and so did the other men he conferred with, but Chaim backed by David Coppleman, was very insistent. The two young men discounted all fears for their safety, assuring their elders, "We know how to be careful, and keep to the darkest part of the roads. We are all starving, and I know our faithful servant will help us with food, once I explain our predicament to her!" Against his better judgment, the Dayan reluctantly consented. How could he refuse these confident young men, with so many starving children present? He admonished them to take the utmost care and run no unnecessary risks, then watched heavy hearted as

they slipped through the passage. Fortunately, it was a moonless night. At an opportune moment, they slipped out of the building, stealthily running from doorway to doorway. Finally they arrived at the house. Panting, they crept around to the back which was shielded from the street. A light was on; the maid was still awake. They knocked gently on the kitchen window, heard her shuffle to the door, then a voice called out.

Quietly they answered, "It is us, please open the door!"

She seemed to take an inordinately long time opening it, and they ignored her look of dismay as she let them into the house. After all, it was very late and they did look very dirty and unkempt. Locking the door, she told them to go and bathe, then change into fresh clothing. In the meanwhile she would prepare something to eat.

The delicious smell of hot coffee and freshly cut bread with butter, totally disarmed them. The cunning old woman watched as they greedily ate their first meal in three weeks. In a tone of concern, she asked where they had been hiding and what brought them to risk being detected. They told her about the soap factory and all the starving people.

"We have come to ask for help. We need a regular supply of food."

She lowered her head so their eyes would not meet, and answered sweetly, "Of course I would like to help you, but you know how dangerous it is. If I suddenly start buying large quantities of food, it will attract suspicion. Unless, of course, I can afford to bribe the shopkeeper."

The boys were prepared, for they understood it would cost money to buy food and loyalty. "Don't worry about money," said David. "I know where my parents have hidden their valuables as well as a large amount of cash. They took great care the Nazis should not find them. We were told to use it if needed. What better use than to save lives!"

If only he had remembered his father's caution against putting total trust in their servant! When she was alone in the house she had searched every drawer and cupboard for the missing jewels without success. Now she would know! Jumping up from her chair she exclaimed, "Let us not waste time. We must help your starving friends as soon as possible."

Chaim and David were thrilled that she so readily agreed to help. Suddenly they felt very tired, and could hardly keep their eyes open. This was not lost on the old woman.

"Come," she said soothingly, "show me where the money is put away, then you can both go for a well deserved sleep. You will be perfectly safe. I will slip out to buy the food to take back with you, and wake you when I get back. You must return to the factory before daybreak."

How fortunate they were to have someone so caring Chaim remarked as they gratefully slipped into the freshly made beds. The next moment they were asleep. The old woman quietly closed the bedroom door, her face distorted with hatred. This was her house and she intended to keep it! She gave a chuckle of delight as she bent over the safe hidden behind the wash basin in the master bedroom. Now all this belonged to her alone!

Chapter Thirteen

Zoltan was the first to sense danger and alert the others. It was barely five o'clock in the morning; the first weak rays of the sun were pushing through the gaps, playfully flickering over the sleepers. Zoltan looked out into the yard. The soldier on guard duty passed at regular intervals; it was a long and boring watch with nothing to break the monotony. Zoltan wondered idly: did the soldier also long for the war to end, for the chance to sleep in his own bed, in his own home? Suddenly his heart missed a beat, his hands gripped the beam supporting the sloping wall, the knuckles whitened. Beads of sweat gathered on his forehead, and he motioned to Reb Yankel Schreiber, (when did he ever sleep)! They groaned quietly. Dayan Weiss, dozing with his back against the wall, was instantly alerted. Together they watched with mounting panic as a van disgorged its passengers in their courtyard. First out was a soldier in Gestapo uniform, followed by Appan and the three women. They seemed to Zoltan to be looking around, unsure and bewildered. The next to emerge was an old woman! The sickening realization dawned on the three men. This must be the old 'trusted' servant of the Coppleman family, for the boys had still not returned. Betrayed! Zoltan's heart ached for those two trusting young students. The old maid pointed towards the factory building overshadowing their bunker. Her shrill voice was full of malice, "In there, I know they are hiding in this building. Twenty-eight people altogether, the lads told me. Now go and find them!" she commanded, flushing with success.

The two Germans loathed this uncouth Hungarian peasant, and strongly resented her tone of voice. However, they held their peace, they would deal with her later. She had led them to the two sleeping boys. Now she promised to lead them to another twenty-eight!

Before entering the building the Nazis fired a few shots to scare anyone who might be in hiding. Everyone in the bunker was now awake. Shaking with fright, they huddled closer together. Parents gathered their children in close embrace. Rifke lay still in her mothers lap, one corner of the pillow firmly between her teeth, unable to comprehend yet sensing danger. Suddenly a different but equally menacing voice rent the air! It was Roszika. Having recovered from her initial uncertainty, she realized that unless they joined in the condemnation of the suspected Jews, they would draw suspicion on themselves. Taking up her cue, the other two women joined in. Appan walked towards the gate holding the keys to the lock, walking slightly ahead of the Gestapo, hoping they would not notice his shaking hands.

"Come, come hurry up, why is it taking you so long to open the doors! If those accursed Jews are in there then we want to find them!" Ilona shouted, looking menacingly at the old woman. Then just for good measure, once inside, she started banging doors and cupboards, lifting the lids of the soap vats, smashing packing cases.

"You cannot hide from me" shouted Evika, not to be outdone. "I will find you and hand you over to the nice German Gestapo, they know just what to do with you filthy Jews!"

Up in the rafters the tension was unbearable. Eyes bulged with terror. Had all their suffering been in vain? They could but pray . . . Then all went quiet. Not knowing was agony, why was it so still? A few moments went by, or was it an eternity? Then the sound of footsteps came even closer up the staircase. Zoltan felt his heart was ready to burst. The room contained a frozen tableau of terror. People were entering the attic. Now only a wall divided the hounds from their quarries. Someone began tapping the walls. Voices deliberated, empty packing cases were turned over . . . Suddenly the shrill voice of the old woman rose again. "I know where they are!" she spat out the words like the tongue of a rattle snake. Pounding the chimney stack with her fist, she shouted, "They are in there, in there! Those two Jew boys mentioned the chimney stack." She faced the more senior of the two Nazis, relishing her new found importance.

Behind the wall, the only sound was the quick in-drawing of breath and pounding of hearts. Surely, all was lost! Lips moved spontaneously as they silently recited the *Vidui* (confession), expecting at any moment the concealed entrance to be burst open. Beads of perspiration slowly rolled down grimy faces. Suddenly, all was quiet. A guttural voice, surely one of the Gestapo, asked in mocking tones "How many Jews did you say were hidden, inside this chimney? Twenty-eight you said, yes? Come, come, old woman, how can anyone, let alone twenty-eight people, hide in this narrow chimney?" Tapping it with his gloved hand, he added, "If they are in there, they are welcome to stay there!" Then, chuckling to himself, he yelled at her to be quiet, threatening to punish her for sending them on a fruitless exercise. He turned on his heel and descended the stairs, indicating to the others to follow him.

Appan signalled to his women: show disappointment at this unsuccessful search! Ilona took up the cry,

"Those lousy Jews! If the old woman is right, then they must have fled like the rats from the black plague! Someone must have warned them. You just wait till I find out who alerted the Jews that we were coming! Just wait till I find out!"

The two Gestapo men ignored her. They did not find these peasant women at all attractive, and wished to get back to their barracks. How coarse they were, compared with their own families back home in the 'Fatherland'!

❧ ❧ ❧

It was now Shabbos and those in hiding thanked Hashem for having saved their lives once more. *Kiddush* was recited on a *kezayis*, a morsel of bread they had saved up.

Three days passed before Appan and the girls returned to the factory to bring some more food. Since the last frightening episode they came less frequently, for fear of arousing suspicion. The Jews' intense hunger was made worse by lack of water, as the relentless sun beat down through the rafters, turning their bunker into a living hell. Veins protruded from bodies which were covered with weeping sores. Minds would wander and tempers flare. It was not an easy task to prevent arguments developing among people half crazed from lack of food and drink, the intense heat and constant close proximity. A dried up piece of moldy bread dipped in a few drops of water was considered a great delicacy.

The need to keep the peace among themselves at all cost was forcibly brought home to everyone one evening when they overheard two people in the courtyard. One voice declared he heard voices coming from the storage house, and suggested they should investigate. However, the other man suggested that it was probably the soldiers on guard duty behind the building.

To relieve the boredom and forget their constant hunger pains, Zoltan invited the Schreiber girls, Rochelle, Freidle and Miriam to go down to the factory. He explained the various stages in the production of soap, and the different methods of manufacture of domestic cleaning soap and the more refined and delicately scented toilet soap. He showed how the colors were mixed before being added to the main ingredients and how it was then poured into molds and left to solidify. As Miriam told me years later, it was a welcome diversion, a chance to stretch their legs. They could walk up and down and not stumble over people.

Once again their lives had been saved! But they must be more careful in the future. Dayan Weiss called a meeting, held in low whispers, where he allocated responsibility for keeping peace at any cost, but there were more ways to make a noise than by speaking. Sweat absorbed in their garments was irritating the skin, causing the open sores to become infected. A few buckets of water were brought up from the factory, and the inmates took turns washing their clothes. Great care was taken not to spill any water, and dispose of it as quietly as possible when dirty, but even that luxury came to halt when a police officer arrived, demanding the right to search the building because he had heard the sound of running water.

"Of course, you heard the sound of water," said a woman who was coming out of the factory, "this is a factory and the sound of water is normal!"

After this incident, they were afraid to wash any more clothes.

Chapter Fourteen

The Germans were in no hurry to dismantle the Ghetto wall. Systematically they searched each house, removing anything of value which had previously been overlooked. Nothing was left undisturbed. Occasionally they would inadvertently stumble on the greatest hidden treasures of all — Jewish souls! These isolated discoveries of hidden bunkers worried Appan. His mind dwelt increasingly on the consequences to his own family, should the Rothbart bunker be discovered. Heavy drinking sessions, followed by deep depression, left him unable to cope for days, while in the bunker the Jews waited ...

※　※　※

Appan's wife Maria became concerned, knowing that the Rothbart family had no other way of obtaining food. She could not let them starve. She would have to do something herself. Putting a loaf of bread and some onions in a shopping basket, she bravely walked to the Ghetto. If asked, she would explain that she had brought the workers' lunch, but no one stopped her. More confident, she walked quickly towards the factory. She had almost reached the gates, when she suddenly found her way barred by a gang of youths who seemed to have appeared from nowhere. Taunting her with anti-Semitic slogans, the leader shouted at her.

"You think we don't now where you are going? You are on your way to feed the 'Budus Zsido' (dirty Jews) who are hidden somewhere in this building!"

"Yes, we know all about it!" called his mate.

"You are a dirty Jew lover!" called another.

"Why don't we report her to the police?" shouted the leader.

Until that moment she had been paralyzed with shock at their apparent knowledge. The next instant she regained her wits and survival instinct. "What is this you said?" she barked. "You are going to report me for harboring Jews! Me harboring Jews! and that's not all, feeding them as well! Me, who hates their guts more than I detest you loitering louts! You dare accuse me!" she went on screaming, "Me the wife of the Chief Constable and the mother of the Chief of Police! I'll have you know, my husband has worked harder than anyone to rid this town of the accursed Jews, and you say that you are going to report me! Me!" Pausing to catch her breath and observe the effect this had, she continued, "I'll tell you what I think, it is *you* who are harboring the Jews. Come, let us go to the Police Station, I will ask my husband the Chief Constable to interrogate you all. They know how to get the truth out of you louts!" This had the desired effect: The boys quickly took off, running as fast as their feet would take them, well aware of the ruthless interrogation methods used. The thought of being accused was enough to put fear into their hearts.

Still shaken but pleased with the effect her tirade had on those youths, she hurried to deliver the food she had so bravely defended. She and Appan had never been inside the bunker; Zoltan and Tziviah would meet them in the attic of the factory or sometimes downstairs. It was not until after the war that they were to inspect the cavity in the rafters which had served so many people as a bunker, and marveled how anyone, let alone so many, could have survivedthere for eight weeks.

Chapter Fifteen

One event worth recording concerned Reb Moshe Leib Friedman Mendlovitch who did so much to help Zoltan and Tziviah with the daily chores. For even the few tasks that needed doing became major undertakings as their strength dwindled. His short thin body belied a strong character, immensely courageous and with an irrepressible sense of humor. He would slip in and out of the bunker to gather information. Hashem watched over him and his return with the news from the outside world was always eagerly awaited. On one of his excursions he learned of a 'flying bomb' the Germans had invented. He also told Dayan Weiss of the contact he had made with the underground movement. This news was received with great excitement and relief. So there were people on the outside working to snatch Jews from under the Nazis' noses! Vast sums of money were needed to bribe the border guards, and he heard of a woman from Arad, Rumania, who had already collected sufficient funds to ransom many Jewish lives. Eventually he met her through his underground contact and told her of their existence. He brought new hope and lifted the fugitives' spirits. Occasionally he brought information of missing family members who had managed to escape to Rumania, then everyone rejoiced. Sometimes his news was less joyful: yet another bunker uncovered by the Gestapo.

That Moshe Leib could come and go for so long, undetected, was truly a miracle. To leave, someone had to go down with him, unlock the front gate then lock it behind him. From then on, someone would take up vigil in the bunker watching the road through the slatted wall, never knowing when he would return. He was dressed to blend in with the normal passers-by, so they had to arrange a signal for the look-out to recognize him. He was to approach holding his hat in a certain manner; when she saw this, the lookout would go down and unlock the gate. The watcher was always a girl, because she was less likely to attract suspicion should anything go wrong.

So it came to pass one day, Miriam hurried down to unlock the door, and was horrified to discover a man standing with his hat in his hand in the manner of Moishe Leib, but it was a stranger! With commendable presence of mind she quickly slammed the door in his face. He banged and called for her to open up, but she ignored him and raced up the stairs as fast as she could. Between sobs she told the others what had happened. Once more they feared for their lives, and entreated the Almighty to spare them. In her panic Miriam had left the key in the lock, but they dared not go down to retrieve it. All that day and through the night they expected the Gestapo at any moment to circle the building.

I will quote from Dayan Weiss' own recollection of these events. 'Early next morning he distinctly heard a soft voice calling, "Open for me the gates of the righteous!" Dayan Weiss knew instantly that it was their friend Reb Moshe Leib. He personally hurried through the passage, (it was easier now, since he had lost so much weight) and down the stairs, then almost stumbled in his haste to unlock the door and welcome back Moshe Leib, who looked dumb-founded when the heavy door was opened. Stepping quickly inside, he told the Dayan that he had walked past with his hat in hand, but nobody had opened the gate and he feared that he was not expected back. To knock on the door, or even call out, would certainly have attracted attention, so after circling once more, he whispered the Biblical phrase as he approached the front of the building.'

Everyone rejoiced as the two men entered. Moshe Leib warned that the net was tightening; extra police patrols were drafted into this area, due to a new menace. Mobs of petty thieves were marauding the neighborhood, intent on snatching a few valuables from under the noses of the Nazis.

"Then you must remain here with us, and stop risking your life," the Dayan told him. Moshe Leib was adamant; it was important that he keep his clandestine meeting to arrange for their escape. This involved several groups working with utmost secrecy to protect each other, in the event that someone was captured. With the additional Gendarmes drafted into the Ghetto, the thieves were sure to be caught very soon, and the police would be back to their normal patrol.

The days dragged on endlessly in the bunker, revolving around their next meal, usually a small piece of bread with a slice of onion. One day, unexpectedly, Appan's girls smuggled in a large roasted goose! At first everyone refused to eat it because it was not kosher, but Dayan Weiss assured them that when life was threatened it was permissible, and left it to each individual to decide for himself. Days went by before any more food was brought in. Tziviah was worried about Reb Yankel Schreiber, who kept the little food he was allocated to give to his children. He seemed to exist almost without nourishment, even his water ration he would save for his youngest son Eli, retaining only enough for 'naigle wasser.' His eyes rarely strayed from the pages of his prayerbook.

The children and young people suffered most, but it was amazing how little even the children complained. When they cried it was only a whimper.

The long hot days dragged on. They watched the sun dip daily behind the trees with relief, but sunset would herald a different problem which tormented them through the night. Their bunker was the domain of a colony of mice and they proved their territorial claims by totally ignoring the humans and scurrying all over their bodies in their nocturnal quest for food. On more than one occasion this caused near panic. Zoltan, not a man easily ruffled, had dozed off in his usual floor space apparently near a nesting hole. He accepted the mice with resigned inevitability until the night he suddenly woke and jerked into a sitting position, too late to stifle a scream. Instantly everybody was awake, wondering what had happened, fearing some new catastrophe. All eyes turned on him as he put his hand down his shirt and pulled out two wriggling, squeaking mice!

Days passed; neither Appan nor the girls had been back with desperately needed food. Elke looked at the bag of dried beans she had brought with her. If only she could soak them to soften them, then they could be chewed and provide some nourishment. Tziviah went down into the factory, hoping to find a suitable container in which to soak the beans. Freidle eagerly offered to go down with Tziviah. She hoped it would ease the pain in her chest; the strain of stifling her cough was causing her great discomfort. With unsteady legs she slowly walked down the stairs gingerly holding on to the wall. Their voices never about a whisper, they searched among the discarded boxes and canisters, but most of the cans were badly eroded and no longer waterproof. At last they found an empty can which had been used for storing powered dyes. Carefully they scraped out the powder still clinging inside the canister, and Freidle was left to hold the can under the tap and with infinite patience let the water trickle in, drop by drop, so it could not be heard, while Tziviah went to collect candles stored in the office cabinet. She had not entered this room since they hid in the bunker. A thick layer of dust had settled on the ornate desk which dominated the room. This was the room where Zoltan would bring his important clients, where keen bargaining preceded the placing of large orders. Was it only a few weeks since she had surprised her husband when she walked in dressed as a peasant! Shaking her head, she went to the cabinet. Nothing had been disturbed, but why should it? All this was now the property of a Gentile, Appan! Taking a few boxes of candles she quickly went out closing the door behind her.

Tziviah had a bright idea and was anxious to try it out, to see if it would work. Back in the bunker she explained to Elke that she would try to cook the beans by holding the canister with the soaking beans over the lighted candles. Miriam was the first volunteer to hold the candle under the canister. She watched the brown specked beans as the first tiny air bubbles began forming, her arms and shoulders straining. She recalled with wistful longing, the steaming hot 'Cholent' which was the highlight of every Shabbos meal. The rich brown beans would be soaked overnight, then the following day, after her mother had added all the other ingredients, chicken fat, marrowbones, meat, vegetables, seasoning, it would be baked in the oven until the following day, lunchtime on Shabbos. Her eyes filled with tears; the very taste and smell of the baked cholent beans wafted about her. Would she ever again taste such delicacies? she wondered, as she watched the beans in water with bubbles rising to the top. Her arm ached and soon she had to support her elbow with her other hand. No amount of longing would speed the softening process. Hunger pains drove them to eat the beans long before they were cooked. They could not survive much longer without food.

Once again Reb Moshe Leib left the bunker on his mission of mercy. It was to be his last; he never returned. In vain they watched and waited, keeping a constant vigil, hoping, praying for his safety. His disappearance was a personal tragedy to each member of the bunker.

Afterwards, they learned the terrible story. Too late to return, Moshe Leib decided to spend the night in a hay loft. With more than the usual military activity in the neighborhood it seemed a good idea, and it was to be only for one night. Someone tipped off the Gestapo, and they stormed the building before dawn, expecting to find a Polish refugee. To quote Dayan Weiss; "Reb Moshe Leib gave up his life for the benefit of others. May Hashem avenge his blood!"

It was Miklos who told them of his capture. They learned that Moshe Leib had been instrumental in bringing their plight to the attention of the underground and negotiating the final details to ensure their safety.

Chapter Sixteen

o lift their spirits, Appan's workers arrived one morning with a giant loaf of bread weighing almost two kilos! They eagerly gathered around Mrs. Elsa Fuchs as she cut and distributed the loaf. Sadly, it seemed nowhere near as large, when sliced into twenty-eight pieces!

The sun had not yet risen on the following morning when Berish alerted his father. Someone was coming up the stairs! Fear and panic snaked through their ranks like a contagious disease. Who could it be? Had they been betrayed once more? By whom? From where? Questions flooded through their minds, numbing the icy panic gripping their hearts. Did this mean that the underground network had been betrayed, and with it their last shred of hope?

Hearts pounded inside their tortured bodies. Horror stricken and mesmerized, they watched as an invisible hand pushed a black suitcase through the entrance from the passage and it clattered to the floor, following by a pair of legs, and the next moment one young man emerged, then another. These were no Gestapo officers! "Shalom Aleichem" were the first words they uttered. The sudden release of tension was more than anyone could bear. Everyone began to cry, tears flowed unashamedly. After seven weeks of hunger and despair and frustration, the floodgates had opened. The sight of those two Jewish boys, when all hope had faded, was more than they could endure. For the two freedom fighters, who had witnessed so much misery and hunger, this proved harder to take. Nothing they had seen so far had been quite as bad as this. The children, were in a pitiful state, shrinking from them in fear.

Armin, tall and gaunt, spoke softly in fluent Hungarian with just a hint of an Austrian/German accent. He introduced his colleague simply as Ignacz. Forestalling any questions, he continued, "For obvious security reasons, we prefer to give you no information about ourselves, lest anyone is caught, while escaping." He paused, and looked at the solemn upturned faces. As always, when embarking on a new rescue operation, he worried about every detail; there was no room for mistakes, and misunderstandings often cost lives. The two men worked as a perfect team, Armin patiently asking questions; names, addresses, dates, and relatives or acquaintances in Rumania, etc. Occasionally he glanced at Ignacz, who was meticulously writing down the information. They gently explained that preparations for their escape were well in hand, but had been held up since Moshe Leib was apprehended. They spoke of the generosity of the Rumanian Jews who collected vast sums of money to save Jewish lives. False documents did not come cheaply, and the cooperation of border guards was even more expensive. Only ready cash was acceptable. The locals, who knew the hazardous terrain better than anyone else and acted as guides, also needed paying, asking for and getting exorbitant sums. Care had to be taken at every stage to avoid suspicion. Armin explained that, to minimize suspicion, no more than five at the most were to leave each time. Who were to be the first lucky ones was yet to be decided.

It was an emotional parting, with ardent prayers and blessings for their safety, and the safety of all those brave people who daily risked their lives to help their fellow human beings. The first stage of their deliverance had begun!

The Jewish Joint Organization helped to collect the large sums of money needed to finance this operation. $500 per head, a vast sum of money in those days, was paid to their Gentile helpers, who were mostly members of the banned Communist Party. Miklos was a leading member. He hired Hungarian speaking Rumanians as drivers. While deals were transacted and money changed hands, the families huddled in the bunker and anxiously waited for deliverance, praying that the Almighty should protect them.

Though in poor health, Appan readily offered his help. He would do all in his power to ensure the safety of his friends, and, eager to assist Miklos, he wished only to help Zoltan and his family. It was a great disappointment to him when he arrived in the factory, bringing with him the peasant clothing and disguises for the Rothbart family, to be greeted by Zoltan with a firm refusal. "No my friend, I am captain of this ship, and therefore the last to leave!" After saying these words, Zoltan suddenly felt a stab of fear. What if Appan, offended, should refuse further help? The next moment, a sigh of relief escaped his lips, as Appan shrugged his shoulders resignedly and handed him the clothes. Such selflessness only increased his admiration for his friend and employer.

Chapter Seventeen

ays passed, and no word had been received from Armin and Ignacz. Had they been unable to raise the money? Or worse, been apprehended?

Dayan Weiss called a meeting. "Sadly Reb Moshe Leib will not be coming back, but the work he had done and contacts made must be followed up." It was now their responsibility to make sure that he had not risked his life in vain. "We must contact Miklos, a gentile, the manager of Goldring's wholesale fishmarket. As a present owner, he is using the premises to hide Jews before they are smuggled out of the Ghetto, and he is a vital link in the Jewish underground network."

Zoltan asked Appan to contact Miklos. Eli and Freidle were both sick, and the others were desperate to get them out of the bunker. Their hopes now hinged on Appan and the girls arriving for work the following morning. And maybe, dared they hope, this would be a day when they could bring food with them!

It was Appan's wife who came with the workers. Taking the food the girls had smuggled in, she climbed the stairs. Mr. and Mrs. Rothbart were waiting for her in the attic. She handed over the food and impatiently brushed aside their words of gratitude. This situation could not continue, she said; her husband had changed from being an upright and reliable man, to an alcoholic wreck, threatening to commit suicide. Near to tears, she begged them to give themselves up and save her husband. Zoltan and Tziviah were dumbfounded — to give themselves up now! After all they had suffered! When help seemed so close! They begged her to have patience, and told her of the underground network, which was presumably still working for their escape, but since the disappearance of Moishe Leib, and Armin and Ignacz' visit they had no news of any progress. They asked her to contact Miklos and let him know their whereabouts. She hurried down into the factory to send a girl on this errand, and Roszika offered to go the Goldring house. As so many lives were at stake Zoltan would have preferred Maria to go herself. They watched Roszika walk out of the yard, and prayed silently. "May Hashem grant that Moshe Leib's work and effort will not have been in vain!"

As time crept by, the tension became unbearable, "Why is it taking so long for her to return?" Elke whispered.

"It is only half an hour since she left," someone reminded her. Only half an hour! Never since settling in the bunker had time passed so slowly. Tziviah watched the road below with mounting anxiety; her eyes strayed in the direction of the market. At last she called out excitedly, "She is coming, she is coming!" With a washing basket over his arm, Roszika heartily greeted the soldier on guard duty. Tziviah could hardly wait: what information might she have brought back, and why the basket? She emerged from the secret passage into the attic, and heard the girl's footsteps on the stairs. "Roszika!," she called, "Tell me what you have found out." By this time others had joined her, unable to wait any longer. Roszika explained that Miklos was arranging for the two sick children to be transferred shortly. He would take care of them and inform Elke's brother, who was at that time living as a Gentile and was in fact one of the couriers of the communist partisans. He had given Roszika the basket containing peasant clothing, including black kerchiefs for the woman's heads and flat caps for the men. The two children were both running high fevers. Elke gently stroked their heads — the only comfort she could give. She shot a anxious glance at her husband. His beautiful tailored suit now hung limp on his emaciated body; his dry cracked lips moved in constant prayer and supplication, entreating his Creator to have mercy on his children. Their eyes met; she saw the depth of his anguish. The next moment, his head bent once more over his open *sefer*.

At dusk Miklos came in a horse-drawn cart. Hesitating, a little unsteady, the two feverish children walked out of the gate and into the waiting wagon. It no longer mattered if they coughed. Miklos, sitting on the driver's seat, jerked at the reins; the aged horse reacted slowly, nodding his head from side to side, and clip-clopped out of the yard. Miklos cast an anxious glance at the coughing children. What they needed was a good wholesome meal. The cart stopped outside Goldring's old residence and he helped the children to alight. His genuine concern led him to waive his own strict rules. Instead of leading the children into the loft, he first brought them into the kitchen where his wife had prepared a hot stew. They sat down by the kitchen table. Eyes bulging in wonderment, the two children watched as he filled their plates with the rich brown stew. Never in all his experience had he seen anyone devour their food so fast! "Perhaps a little more?" They both nodded their heads, scarcely believing their good fortune. When the meal was over, Miklos explained he would have to take them to the attic. He dared not take the risk of letting them spend the night downstairs.

The first pangs from their digestive system, unaccustomed to food, were not long in coming. After more than two months of starvation, their shrunken stomachs could not cope with the rich meal. They managed only a few steps, before collapsing with severe cramps. This was followed by acute diarrhea which lasted for several agonizing hours. The two children clung to each other, silently crying for their mother until the early hours of the morning, when, exhausted, they finally fell asleep.

Still weak from their ordeal, they waited anxiously to be collected. Early that evening a surly youth arrived, wearing heavy walking shoes. He eyed the holes in the children's shoes as he explained that he had been instructed to smuggle them over the border into Rumania. With little enthusiasm Eli and Freidle followed him into a waiting van. To hide his uneasy feeling, Eli whispered to Freidle, "He is taking us to Uncle Aron; in this van it will not take us long to cross over the border and then he will drive us to Uncle Aron's house!" Freidle sighed, lost in thought, picturing their reunion with her favorite uncle.

The car stopped abruptly on the outskirts of the town. The driver jumped out and told them to follow him as he walked briskly right into a cornfield, trailing the two bewildered children behind him. He soon realized that they could not keep up with him. Reluctantly, he slowed a little but still had to stop and wait for them to catch up. It was only the fear of being abandoned that keep them going, hour after agonizing hour marching over difficult unpaved roads, through fields and even climbing mountains. Eli remembered walking through a forest, almost delirious from exhaustion. He held tight to his sister's hand, convinced that their guide was about to take them to some fearsome forest demon. Glancing furtively in all directions, he imagined every overhanging branch to be a long grasping arm. He wanted to scream, but no sound escaped his lips. Freidle felt his fear but could do no more than squeeze his hand reassuringly, as she wondered when this nightmare would end. Suddenly, they came upon a small clearing.

A man was dozing with his back against a chestnut tree, a weathered cape slung over one shoulder. His hand clasped something inside the cape, then relaxed when he saw the three travelers. He untied his rucksack and handed out chunks of black bread. Gratefully sinking to the ground, Freidle and Eli ate their bread, as they huddled together a small distance from the men. Reminding Eli of their ordeal the night before, Freidle warned him to eat slowly, chewing each bite. Their meal over, they stretched out and were soon asleep. The two men speaking rapidly in their native Rumanian tongue, carefully stubbed out their cigarette butts against the heel of their boots and they too were soon asleep.

It was still dark when the men woke the two children. The older one explained that they must try and cross the border before daybreak. He was beginning to feel sorry for these uncomplaining children; they looked so small and frail and gave him no trouble.

Refreshed from the food, and the sleep in the open air, instead of the stifling attic, Eli's fears and suspicions seemed childish to him now. Although the children's feet were sore with large blisters, they were no strangers to discomfort and were eager to continue their journey. Their guides assured them that they were indeed very close to the Rumanian border.

Aron Schreiber looked at his watch as he nervously paced up and down his room. Why was he so nervous? The Rumanian guides, all members of the outlawed Communist Party, knew every inch of the escape route far better then the soldiers patrolling the borders. He kept reminding himself of all the Jews who had successfully crossed the border, taking the same route that the two children were taking. He had personally chosen their guide, a fearless local youth. Taking his watch out again, he calculated that if all went well, they should have reached the forest. Here they would eat and rest until just before daybreak. Experience had taught that this was the safest hour to cross the frontier undetected. Why should this night be different? He would accomplish nothing by staying awake. Better to get some sleep and be ready for the children when they arrived in the morning. To make sure he did not oversleep, he lay down on his bed fully clothed. Utterly exhausted, he soon dozed off.

The room was in complete darkness and he had no idea how long he had been sleeping, but suddenly he was wide awake, his whole body drenched in perspiration. Had he been dreaming? He shook his head. It was too vivid for any dream, it was a nightmare. His friend had appeared to warn him that two children had been caught this night trying to cross the border illegally. Fully awake, his torment increased as he wondered on which side of the border they were caught. It was a well known fact that Hungarians took no prisoners. He longed to rush out into the street and find out the truth, but knew he would only arouse suspicion. Much better to wait until it was safe to contact certain people. He spent the next few hours praying that it might be only a bad dream.

Just after daybreak, as the first pale rays of the sun rose from the eastern side of the cornfield, he heard a soft knock of his door. Forgetting his usual safety drill, he unbolted it and flung it open. A gasp escaped his lips; was this another dream?

"Aron Batchy (Uncle Aron)!" called the little waif, holding on to her brother's hand. The next moment, having regained his presence of mind with overwhelming joy, he gathered the two pitiful children in his arms. Once they were all inside the room, he carefully locked the door and looked at them properly for the first time. He was aghast at the poor state they were in, emaciated, dirty and hardly able to stand. He gently led them to a bench, and disappeared into the little kitchen to prepare some food. How these children must have suffered! The need to get them to safety and care took on a new urgency. He asked many questions and was puzzled that Eli, whom he knew to be a lively, talkative child, never uttered a single word.

"We were not allowed to talk for the eight weeks we were hidden in the bunker," Freidle explained, "Maybe, he has forgotten how to talk!" As they ate, their uncle felt immense relief; fancy being upset by a mere dream!

Chapter Eighteen

The first complete family to leave the bunker was Dayan Weiss, his very sick wife and son. Having exchanged their distinctively Jewish clothes for those of a farm laborer's, they said a tearful farewell. Would they ever meet again was a sentiment everyone felt but dared not voice. Hearts pounding under their unfamiliar garments, the three watched with trepidation as Appan unlocked the factory gates. Eight weeks had gone by since they had entered through these gates: Eight weeks of imprisonment when the only air breathed was that which filtered through the gaps of the wooden structure. The plan had been for Miklos to hire a car which would take them to the Dayan's brother-in-law who was staying in the spa town of Felix.

To avoid suspicion, the Rebbetzin was to go first with Roszika. How strange it was, to be walking down Kopistran Street. A tense moment came when they noticed two soldiers coming towards them. Trembling with fear the Rebbetzin gripped her companion's arm, but mercifully her legs kept going. The soldiers drew nearer, then passed without even a glance. Phew! How close they had come!

Miklos was waiting in the timber yard. Roszika helped the Rebbetzin into the car, while Miklos settled into the driver's seat, the two men should be coming soon. The Rebbetzin closed her eyes and prayed that all should go well.

But all was not well! Inexplicably, the Dayan and Berish were left stranded on Kopistran Street, expecting someone to meet them. They were confused and at a loss — which way should they go? They must avoid attracting attention. Meanwhile, Miklos was waiting.

To their consternation, a man approached and speaking in German he asked for directions. The Dayan feared that his strong Polish accent was bound to arouse suspicion. Berish sensed his father's hesitation and quickly answered that they were in a great hurry and could not stop. To their amazement the man seemed not to have noticed the boy's strange tone. It was the first time in eight weeks that Berish had uttered a word louder than a whisper. His voice had a strange grating sound which alarmed the Dayan and shocked Berish into silence. It was several days later before he attempted to speak again.

The Dayan and his son dared not wait in the street, so they hastened to Goldring's house in the hope of meeting up with the Rebbetzin and Miklos. It is not easy to walk casually when you are in fear of your life and your feet want to run away! They reached the house but almost walked into a trap. Miklos Neni (Mrs.) was entertaining guests! Miraculously, she had noticed them coming, through the open window. She dashed out to meet them and signalled to them to follow her. Before the guests had time to miss her presence, she had returned, leaving the Dayan and Berish ensconced in the cellar, safe for the moment but deeply worried about the Rebbetzin.

In the meantime she had been sitting in the car getting more agitated as time ticked by and they did not appear. Leaving her in the car Miklos went to investigate. After searching the streets fruitlessly for two hours, he returned to his home and was very annoyed to find his two missing charges hiding in his house. Finally appeased with the promise of more money, he took them back to the waiting car, where the overwrought Rebbetzin was waiting. Because of the delays, it was no longer possible for Miklos to escort them to Felix as originally planned. Before leaving he gave the driver instructions on how to get to their destination.

The driver lost his way and they were in danger of attracting the attention of a policeman walking his beat through the almost deserted streets of Felix. Near panic, they circled the area once more. The driver, realizing the danger his passengers were exposed to, offered to drive them to a remote area and then search for the address where they were expected. They agreed to wait. Would the driver return? Was it too much to hope that he found the house? Fear and doubt filled their minds as the minutes ticked by. Suddenly he reappeared: the reassuring nod told them it was good news.

With renewed hope they drove to the house in Felix where the Rebbetzin's brother, Reb Aharon, lived — he was one of those Jews who successfully survived the war, masquerading as a Christian. They wept tears of joy and relief at their reunion and thanked Hashem to have come so far.

The night passed quickly as they exchanged news. They rejoiced to hear of those fortunate enough to have escaped across the border, and grieved for those left behind. At last, having exhausted all the news, they finally enjoyed their first undisturbed sleep in two months. They were still in danger from the Nazis, though disguised as Gentiles and in hiding, but at least they had a bed to sleep in.

The following day was Friday, when their next contact came to tell them that they would be collected on the following evening, Motzei Shabbos, to take them on the most difficult part of their journey. News had reached them of two Jews who had been killed that day, shot as they attempted to cross the border. But then, there was a sudden change of plan. The landlady decided she could no longer provide them with this safe shelter; she feared being caught, as the Nazis were tightening their security nets in her neighborhood. She would listen to no appeals, they had to leave that night.

This information was sent urgently to the underground agents. The Dayan was making Kiddush, when they received the signal to leave. As Dayan Weiss was to record; "There was no question of 'Chillul Shabbos' this was a matter of saving lives."

❀ ❀ ❀

At ten o'clock at night, the Hungarian woman arrived who was to escort Dayan Weiss, his wife, son and brother-in-law out of Felix. One last longing look around the sparsely furnished room, then the door closed behind them. The unwanted, and unwilling, wandering Jews were once again fleeing from their pursuers, through woods, fields and garden alleyways, fearful of being caught, with never a word spoken with their guide, who walked briskly with an occasional glance behind her to make sure they were still following. Suddenly, without warning, she disappeared. Had they been abandoned on the edge of this forest? Frightened and vulnerable they searched the undergrowth. Suppressing his own fear, Dayan Weiss tried to reassure his wife and son.

"There must be some simple explanation for her disappearance," he told them, with an optimism he did not feel.

As if in answer to his prayers, the woman suddenly reappeared, accompanied by two men. They were to be their guides for the remainder of the journey. It was indeed a miracle how their weakened legs and swollen feet could keep on going over the rough and unfamiliar paths. Their guides walked with the assurance of men who knew every stretch of the terrain, stopping only to allow the breathless and terrified fugitives to catch up. These hardy men of the mountains were unwilling to make allowances for the poor physical state of the fugitives. Only sheer willpower kept them going up the Apuseni mountain with its breathtaking view of the gorges and waterfalls and numerous caves, so popular with youth clubs during the long summer breaks. Now fearsome and daunting it seemed to mock them, as with hearts pounding ready to burst they climbed and climbed, before sliding and stumbling, they reached the valley on the other side.

At two o'clock in the morning, four agonizing hours since leaving the house, they came to a meadow bathed in tranquil moonlight. Their guide whispered, "A few more paces and we will be crossing the border!"

Their hearts throbbed with joy, though they could scarcely stand. Suddenly, without any warning, a menacing figure jumped out of the shadows formed by a line of trees, a gun was pointed at them.

"Stop, or I'll shoot!" the soldier shouted.

Terrified, they tried to run, but their legs no longer obeyed them. They collapsed helplessly to the ground with the gun still trained at their heads.

The Rebbetzin was wearing a treasured gold necklace. Hastily she unclasped it, and offered it to the soldier with a plea for mercy! He lowered his rifle, and examined the necklace, watching the moonlight play on its intricate pattern. At last, he silently pocketed the necklace, then prodded them with his rifle, indicating to get out of his way!

Walking as fast as their unsteady legs would take them, they crossed the unmarked frontier. Ignorant of the ordeals still ahead, they rejoiced at their good fortune. "It was as though a fresh breath of life was blown into us," Berish was to tell me. It was not long before they were reminded how vulnerable their position was. Their guides having brought them so far, now refused to take them any further unless they too received additional payment. They greatly resented the gift of a necklace to the soldier. After much arguing and pleading, for the travelers had nothing of value left to give, their escorts accepted a letter promising payment on reaching safety. As last they continued their journey, making arduous detours to avoid the Rumanian border police. It was Shabbos morning when they came across an abandoned barn, a perfect place to rest and sleep before continuing their journey. The Dayan and his troop climbed up into the loft, while their guides stretched out on the floor. Not long after, they were all sound asleep. It was quite dark when they woke up, refreshed.

They continued on foot through the night, through forests, over mountains and valleys, with just an occasional stop to rest, in an effort to cover as much ground as possible before daybreak. It is beyond the scope of my pen to explain the wonders of the human spirit. How anyone as frail and ill as the Rebbetzin could have endured and survived this incredible trek can only be by the grace of Hashem. The Dayan had on more than one occasion pleaded with their guides to find an alternative route when confronted with a steep mountain, but to no avail.

The following day, after a short rest and some food, they struggled and stumbled on, and that night finally arrived at the village of Dyanta. Having covered an incredible fifty miles of unknown terrain, they had successfully avoided being arrested.

Now, for the first time, they were welcomed on their arrival. Mr. Hertzman, a local dignitary, and Reb Yankel Friedman, the *shochet*, prepared a meal of freshly cooked meat and vegetables, an unbelievable delicacy to the wanderers. This was Monday — Parashas Matos-Masei. In this village they were reunited with others from the bunker. With gratitude and joy, they recounted their experiences, and thanked Hashem for bringing them this far.

Once rested, they were anxious to leave. A town with a large Jewish community could offer more security, where they could hopefully blend in with the rest of the population, but they had to find a way to travel onwards without being questioned. It was illegal for Jews to travel outside their own neighborhood.

A soldier in charge of a military vehicle was persuaded, with a suitable bribe to take a party of twenty people to Arad. In high spirits they boarded the van, in anticipation of joining the large, friendly community that was awaiting them. Their dreams were soon to be shattered. The police had been tipped off; the soldier had no choice but to obey when ordered to stop at the crossroad. Refusing their bribe, he ordered them to leave the lorry and marched them to the police station for interrogation. They were locked up for the night and told they would appear in court. The following morning a gendarme arrived to inspect the prisoners. Giving no explanation for his action, he chose three men and ordered their immediate deportation back to Hungary.

Mr. Hertzman, the leader of the Jewish community, requested a meeting with the chief of police. Over a large glass of *schnapps* he pleaded for the release of his friends, offering a large sum of money. The chief of police, though extremely tempted, explaining that he could do nothing, since the court had already been notified of the prisoners being held. Unless of course an alternative could be found! He thoughtfully rubbed his chin: it would be a shame to let this opportunity slip, so few came this way. Mr. Hertzman saw the greedy twinkle in his eye, and an idea came to him.

The plan was simple. Pouring the officer another drink, he suggested, "Why don't you round up some vagabonds and drunks to satisfy the court?"

The chief smiled and nodded. Wasting no time, he sent a policeman to round up the required number of vagrants. As they were brought in, the Jewish prisoners were freed. They sat in the fields as the substitutes were brought before the courts, awaiting the outcome. Since the court had no valid reason to prosecute these innocent people, they were free to go home.

News reached the Dayan that his *mechutan*, the Chimpa Rav, had also escaped from Hungary, and was now in Arad, and he was anxious to join him as soon as possible. The Joint again organized their journey with utmost care. Two gentiles dressed as train conductors were hired to escort them on their journey to Arad. They traveled unmolested until the train pulled into Michke station, where their escort noticed two inspectors stepping on board. Dayan Weiss and his entourage hurriedly alighted and hid in a field until the inspection was over, then they quickly jumped on the train as it slowly moved out of the station. Thankfully the rest of the journey was uneventful.

In Arad they were warmly greeted by the Jewish community. To their surprise, even here it was compulsory for every Jew to wear the Yellow Star. As long as we obey the new laws specifically made for Jews, restricting our freedom to travel etc., we are left unmolested, Dayan Weiss was told.

Shortly after their arrival Dayan Weiss received news from Reb Arye Leib Cimmetbaum, the Rebbetzin's nephew. He too had escaped from Hungary and was staying in Bucharest. He sent an urgent message to tell the Dayan that he had booked passage to Eretz Yisrael (then Palestine) on one of the boats docked in the harbor for himself, the Dayan and his family. In the letter, he pleaded with his uncle to join him in Bucharest without delay, for the ship was due to sail shortly. Once again money had to be raised to pay for the journey to Bucharest which was fraught with many difficulties as no one had legal traveling documents, and again the Joint came to their rescue. The following day, a soldier was hired to drive them to Bucharest. Their party had swelled to thirty people when the soldier arrived, driving a military van. They all piled in, eager to get to Bucharest, yet in dread of being stopped and searched. No one had traveling documents, only an unwavering faith that Hashem would protect them. The Dayan checked that everyone was on board, then looked anxiously at his ailing wife. Her condition had worsened, yet differently from the others. He hoped that in Bucharest he might find a doctor to treat her.

Turning to the driver, he said, "Do not stop under any circumstances! Just keep going."

The soldier nodded. He understood but would he be able to ignore the police? When challenged, he pressed his foot on the accelerator, and drove on at high speed. With the help of Hashem they arrived safely as far as Seben, but there the van developed a mechanical problem. The driver, helped by eager volunteers, attempted to repair it, but eventually he had to seek a mechanic. Many police and soldiers passed on the way, but incredibly not one stopped to investigate. At last the van was ready and they were able to continue their journey, but when they arrived in Bucharest, the ship had already sailed from the harbor.

To the Dayan's astonishment his nephew was standing on the quay side. "Arye Leib why did you not sail with this ship?" He exclaimed.

"Uncle Yitzchok, I did not want to go without you," was his simple reply. Later they learned that the ships were sunk by German U-boats.

In Bucharest, life was far from peaceful. During the next few weeks, the city was bombed relentlessly and many were killed and wounded. The refugees tried unsuccessfully to reach Bulgaria. On

August 23rd the situation greatly improved for the Jews, because the Rumanian king signed a peace pact with the Russians. This lifted the fear from the Jewish community of the German army marching into Rumania, but many people remained in their shelters for several years while sporadic bombing continued.

Amidst the national celebration of the peace pact, a personal tragedy struck Dayan Weiss and his son. On the tenth day of Kislev 1945 the righteous Alta Rifke Leah was gathered to her forebears. Loved and honored by all who knew her, she bore her illness with great courage and fortitude, setting an example few could follow. She merited burial with honor in a Jewish cemetery, when so many ended up in mass graves.

❈ ❈ ❈

Back in the Rothbart bunker, preparations were quietly going ahead for the next group to be removed. It was the turn of the Schreiber family. Yankel and Elke thanked Hashem when told by a contact that their two sick children were being take care of, and would join them in Rumania.

Suppressing their natural fear and anxiety of their ordeal ahead, they quietly removed their outer garments and donned their peasant clothes. Eight weeks, without a change of clothing and never able to wash! Miriam held her discarded dress at arm's length, and tried to recall the way it looked when freshly washed and starched. Even the coarse peasant clothes she was given seemed beautiful by comparison. She looked up and saw Rachele watching her. Their eyes met. How painfully thin they had become, how limply their dresses hung from their narrow shoulders! Their once beautiful auburn hair formed a matted mess hidden under a black kerchief.

Would they really fool the gendarmes?

Oh! to be free again, to walk in the street, to be able to smell flowers, pluck ripe plums from the trees, suck the juicy flesh from the skin, then eat that too!

To be able to enjoy all these simple priceless pleasures! Miriam sighed. Soon, soon, they would all be free!

That evening a covered wagon drew up outside the factory. Yankel Schreiber, his wife and family quickly piled into the back for the short journey to the Goldring house. Miklos was waiting and immediately took them up into the attic. He called softly and a head emerged, peeping from a bale of straw in the loft. A rope ladder dropped. So they were not the only ones being hidden in this loft.

"Are my two children up here?" Yankel asked.

"No," Miklos assured him, "they were collected by their guide last night and smuggled over the Rumanian border."

One by one, they climbed the swaying ladder, too frightened and bewildered to protest.

Up in the loft they settled down alongside the other fugitives. Too tired to exchange more than a few words, everyone was soon fast asleep.

The following morning, they were split into small groups for the last and most hazardous part of their journey. Miklos explained that they had been given two train tickets. It was decided that Rachele and her little brother Moishe would easily blend in with the train passengers; Moishe could hardly contain his excitement at this unexpected treat. Following a firm warning from his mother not to stray and to avoid attracting undue attention, he solemnly promised to remain at the side of Rachele. The next moment they climbed into the van and Miklos drove them to the station and watched them get onto the crowded train. The doors banged shut and it slowly steamed out of the station.

Rachele, unaccustomed to so much freedom, was relieved to find an empty seat on an otherwise crowded carriage; she sat down among the rough peasant women. Mercifully, no one took any notice, for even unwashed and cheap clothes could not hide her poise and natural dignity. She was worried about Moishe who had wandered off to the far end of the carriage. Curiosity held him spellbound as he listened to two peasants having a heated argument. Rachele's first impulse was to call him back, to be near her, but she decided against it. Watching his innocent young face, his eyes shining in merriment as he listened to the colorful exchange of insults, Rachele relaxed. She could keep an eye on him and leave him to enjoy the spectacle. She looked out of the window; soon they would cross the border to freedom. The terrible events of the last few months had given her a maturity far beyond her years.

Suddenly, her body stiffened, Moishe had cried out! Her eyes darted towards the group of women who had joined the original two still arguing, but to her horror, Moishe was no longer there. Throwing caution to the wind, she jumped up and raced down the corridor in pursuit of her little brother. She almost collided with a gendarme dragging a sobbing Moishe towards the guard's cubicle.

Moishe, having tired of watching the two peasants, had wandered off in pursuit of something to do. It was his misfortune to attract the attention of the guard as he wandered through the corridor. His distinctive long 'payot' (sidelocks), which he had secured under his cap with pins had loosened and dropped to there natural position making it obvious he was a little Jewish boy. Moishe burst into tears when the enormity of his indiscretion dawned on him. Disregarding her own safety, Rachele shouted, "What are doing with my brother?"

"Did you say, he is your brother?"

"Yes," Rachele answered.

"Then you too are under arrest!" Saying this, he marched them both into the guards' cubicle. Moishe was ashamed to look at his sister. Unable to cope with his outrageous folly, he once more burst into tears. This was more than Rachele could bear. Her anger melted away, she hugged him, gently stroking his head. They had been left in the small compartment under the watchful eye of a ticket collector, who explained that they would have to leave the train at the next station and be imprisoned, whereupon Moishe once more burst into tears. Rachele, however, knew they had reason to rejoice when their guard told her that the next stop would be on Rumanian soil! They were to remain in prison for the time it took their Uncle Aron to negotiate their release.

Uncle Aron's dream had indeed become something of a nightmare. But to Rachele and Moishe it was almost a treat; they were well fed, enjoying the luxury of three meals each day!

Chapter Nineteen

n the last stretch of their escape over the mountainous terrain into Rumania, Elke had stumbled and fallen into a ditch, breaking her arm. Miriam fastened a sling from her scarf to support the arm and ease the pain before they continued. Although in agony, she insisted they continue on without delay. When they finally reached Arad, she was rushed to the hospital at the expense of the Jewish community. The rest of the family were taken to a house which had been prepared for them.

Miriam would never forget that day, she told me. After all the deprivation they had endured, here they were, in a seemingly spotlessly clean house, the beds made up with sparkling white damask bedding. The day was intensely hot. How wonderful to be able to leave the doors and windows open, to fill a glass with clear cool water from the tap! A meal was on the kitchen table prepared by their neighbors whom they were yet to meet.

At last Elke was brought to the house. Her arm was in a sling, and she would not admit that it still hurt, but she could not hide her drawn face. Too tired to enjoy the food, they ate only a little, eager to get between the crisp cool sheets for their first proper sleep in months. The girls helped their mother to undress, then gently covered her with the top sheet. She closed her eyes. Rachel and Miriam tiptoed out of the room. The boys were already asleep when the girls hurriedly undressed; a few moments later they were all asleep. Suddenly, Miriam woke. Surely her mother had called out? Lying quietly she listened and almost froze with fear: Her mother was crying. She jumped out of bed and raced to her mother's room. The door was open and her mother was sitting on a chair looking extremely distressed, rocking her bad arm with her good one. "What is the matter?" asked Miriam.

Her father was nervously pacing up and down. "Is it giving you so much pain?"

Tears were swelling in her eyes, but her mother shook her head, as she cradled her arm. "No, my dear, it is not the injury, it is the bedbugs!"

Miriam looked bewildered, "Bedbugs? Surely not!"

In answer, her mother lifted the cover on her bed. Horrified, Miriam watched the bugs scurrying across the sheet! "There must be an army of these creatures inside my plaster," sighed Elke. "It was easy for them to crawl in, but now they cannot get out, and they are driving me crazy."

On checking, Miriam discovered that all the beds were infested, but not even a regiment of bedbugs feasting on the tired bodies could disturb the sleeping children.

Mrs. Schreiber had to endure her torment until the morning. Accompanied by a neighbor, she returned to the hospital where the plaster was removed and her arm cleansed from the bugs.

❦　❦　❦

The evacuation from the bunker continued. Each evening a new batch of "workers" would leave the factory.

The following Sunday, Appan arrived in high spirits; he had personally supervised the evacuation of the families so far, and now at last, it was the turn of his dear friends. To mark the occasion he had brought along some food for their journey. It had been a difficult and dangerous week for him, for he could never be sure that he could trust the Rumanian drivers who hated both the Nazis and their Hungarian allies. This made his association with them extremely precarious. But soon, it would be over! He hugged the small food parcel as he entered the factory. Zoltan and family would leave tonight. Tziviah watched Appan walk across the yard, an unaccustomed spring in his purposeful strides. She was well aware of the cause of his unfamiliar cheerfulness. By his calculation it was their turn to leave, and she felt guilty as she looked around the bunker. It was no longer crowded, but it was unthinkable to abandon even a single soul.

She turned to Zoltan, and was comforted by the understanding in his eyes. Together, they would break the news to Appan, and hope he would see their point of view. They emerged from their bunker, met Appan, and humbly confessed their deception. They could no longer pretend to be just twelve souls, they would have to enlist his help to get everyone out of the bunker. Zoltan explained that it had been beyond them to refuse the pleading of their friends. To hide her tears, Tziviah lowered her head and waited for Appan's protestation, but she was unprepared for his reaction. He threw up his hands, exclaiming "You poor, poor, starving souls, if only we had known! We would have tried to send you more food!"

Just over a week after the evacuation had begun, only ten people now remained, including the Rothbart family. It was arranged that they would all leave together.

It had been agreed that every woman in the bunker should contribute a piece of jewelry for Appan's wife Maria, as a token of their gratitude, assuring her that the promise of a villa and an income would be honored on their return to Grosswardein.

❦   ❦   ❦

With silent curiosity, Rifke sat watching as her mother applied black shoe polish to their hair. How strange and unpredictable grownups can be! She would have liked to know what caused her mother's strange behavior, but not having spoken for eight weeks, she could not express the question easily.

Tziviah looked at her little daughter. To suffer so much, so young, her shrunken little face now framed with this unattractive black mass. Would it be difficult to wash out?

"Just look at Rifke!" she murmured softly. "No-one would suspect her of being a Rothbart with her ginger hair dyed black."

Elsa nodded in agreement as Tziviah applied the shoe polish to Yonah's hair. Rifke's little face suddenly brightened; so that was the reason for their strange behavior! They had to be disguised. Would Mummy also change into those large peasant dresses? Rifke wondered without much enthusiasm. During the long weeks she had sometimes tried to recall their previous existence. The soft bed, her own room, and large slices of bread with butter. She even remembered being scolded for not finishing her bread.

Now Mummy was dressing her in these strange clothes; her hair felt even more itchy than before, but Mummy told her not to touch it. She watched everyone dress in the strange garments, then crawl through the hole in the wall. She and her Mummy, who was holding on to her hand, were the last to go through. It was strange and a little frightening, since it was much darker here than the place they had just come from.

Rifke wanted to go back, but her mother gently pulled her closer and told her to follow. Rifke hesitated, unsure on her feet, and Tziviah came to her rescue: She picked her up and slowly descended the stairs. Now they were in a vast hall which seemed vaguely familiar, here all the gypsies were crowding round a man they called Appan.

Rifke knew that they were not really gypsies, but they all reminded her of the wandering groups she had seen singing and playing violins. She gripped her mother tightly as they passed through the gate, and she hardly recognized her father who also seemed to be quite unsteady on his feet with two strange men holding him up. Suddenly they burst into song!

They swaggered past the guard on night duty, who did no more than give them a disdainful look. This part of Hungary was full of gypsies and vagabonds.

Never had this road appeared to be as long as it did now. Zoltan was surprised to find all the old landmarks still there, but with hardly anyone about, there was an unfamiliar strangeness. They kept up their acting and continued to stagger along the way, but once they reached the outskirts of the city, Appan and his companions slipped away, leaving the rest of the party to continue to their pre-arranged site where a van partially concealed from the road was waiting. Panting from the unaccustomed exertion, and lack of food, they thankfully piled into the vehicle. Zoltan was helping the children to climb in, when someone called, "Good evening, Zoltan Batchy!"

He froze for a moment, then asked, "How do you know my name?"

"We worked for you, and would have recognized you anywhere!" the man answered cheerfully, giving Zoltan a knowing wink.

At last they could relax and rest, sitting close together on the floor of the van as it swayed and bumped on the unpaved roads. They were leaving the Ghetto! They drove for hours, taking many unfamiliar roads to avoid detection. Their driver and his mate were seasoned travelers, knowing every inch of this terrain; they were

Rumanian farm hands, who in peace time supplemented their meager subsistence from casual farm work by assisting the smuggling fraternity. Nothing, however, had been as lucrative as the money they earned from smuggling Jews into Rumania. True, the borders were now being patrolled by trigger-happy storm troopers, but they even enjoyed the danger and the opportunity to outwit the self styled *Herrenfolk*. Suddenly, they came to a halt. The driver looked over his shoulder and grinned at his charges.

"Have we crossed the border?" someone inquired hopefully.

"No, it is not possible to cross the border undetected with a van."

"Not with a van full of Jews," his mate Horvat added. These were the first words he had spoken. Until now he had let Erno the obvious leader, do the talking. Parking the van at the edge of a field of maize, they signaled silently to the passengers to leave it.

Whispering, Erno explained that he hoped to guide them over the border by taking them through these cornfields, which would give them perfect cover.

"Follow me," he murmured, then he and Horvat marched off into the corn. It was not easy to keep up with the guides, who sometimes ran and ducked as if avoiding an unseen adversary. It was obvious that they were familiar with every turn and hedge they passed. Occasionally the group were allowed a few moments of rest, then the guides would resume their chase through the fields. Sometimes they had to cross a road, which they did with pounding hearts until they reached the safety of the next cornfield, bringing them nearer to their goal — Rumania!

During one of their short halts Tziviah noticed that her husband, who had carried Rifke on his shoulders, was no longer in their party. Unknown to her, he had accidentally slipped into a ditch, badly spraining his ankle. By the time he had managed to pull himself out, the rest of the party had disappeared from view and he was left to hobble along on his own. He tried to ignore the searing pain in his foot, as he lifted Rifke back onto his shoulders.

Tziviah was devastated; she did not want to go on without her husband, yet knew she could not stay behind. After hesitating for a moment she gripped Yonah's hand and hurried to catch up with the others. She soon reached Mr. Guttman who, having also injured his leg, had been unable to stay with the main party. Grateful not to be alone, they continued walking, hoping eventually to find the others and afraid to call out for fear of attracting the attention of the border guards. The tall stems of the maize made it impossible to detect where the others had gone. She dragged Yonah along, afraid to let go of his hand, then suddenly, they came to the end of the cornfield. A road ran parallel with railway lines. Neither Tziviah nor Mr. Guttman knew where they were or where the road would lead whether they were still on Hungarian soil or if they had unwittingly crossed into Rumania. It was too dangerous for them to remain in the open; it was late afternoon and would soon be dark. A wooden cabin stood a short distance away, so they walked towards it. On closer inspection, it seemed to be some kind of office; looking through the dusty window Tziviah could see a wooden table, some chairs, a small stove with a pan, nothing to indicate the identity of the cabin user. They were afraid to enter, so sat wearily on the ground, their backs pressed against the cabin wall, with no idea as to what to do next. They had been on the move for almost twenty-four hours without rest or food. Tziviah began reciting the special prayer that women say when the Sabbath ends and the new week starts. It gave her a warm feeling, and she forgot her misery for a few fleeting moments as she devoutly repeated the comforting words, *"G-tt fun Avrohom, fun Yitzchok und fun Yacov* (G-d of Abraham, of Isaac, and of Jacob) . . ."

Zoltan continued to hobble along in the direction of the border. He had walked for many hours with Rifke on his shoulders, though utterly exhausted; eight weeks in a restricted space on a starvation diet, followed by an unaccustomed marathon walk, was taking its toll. But for the child, he would have lain down in the field regardless of the consequences.

Towards midnight he came upon a clearing; straight ahead of him stood two dwelling houses. They seemed to be straight out of fairy tale. One was a beautiful villa, surrounded by a well kept garden; a light shone from a window. He longed to walk up and ask for help. Hesitantly he turned towards the other much smaller house, which had no garden. It was in almost total darkness: just a weak ray of light pierced through a gap in the curtains. He stood undecided. If he approached either house for help and they turned out to be hostile to Jews, then all the hardships he had endured would have been in vain. What was he to do? It was useless to go on when he was completely lost. He prayed for guidance, then, squaring his shoulders, he walked resolutely to the entrance of the smaller house. He knocked on the door. His heart pounding, what if the occupant is hostile to Jews? A window opened and he heard a woman call softly in Rumanian,

"Stay where you are, I am coming to open the door!" Immediately, she disappeared, closing the window behind her.

He did not have to wait long. Someone moved behind the door, the murmur of voices reached him, but he could not make out what was said. Abruptly but silently the door was opened and someone beckoned him to come inside. Hardly able to stand, he staggered into the room, and lifting Rifke from his back, he held her in his arms. Suddenly his hunger and tiredness were forgotten: there assembled before him were the other members of the party! But his joy soon turned to heartache when he was told that three were missing: his wife, son Yonah and their friend Mr. Guttman. He was assured that someone had been sent to search for them, and silently thanked the Almighty for guiding him to the right house. If only his dear wife and son were here! Looking at his swollen feet, he realized he could not help to search for them. He sat with his painful leg stretched out, Rifke sleeping soundly in his arms, and resigned himself to waiting patiently.

Tziviah, her back to the cabin wall, still held Yonah's frail little hand, as she contemplated the hopelessness of their situation. Mr. Guttman sat a few paces away, his hunched shoulders and troubled face portrayed his feelings. Neither had spoken much during the weary hours since being separated from the rest of the party. It was important to preserve what little energy they had left. Mr. Guttman forced himself to stand up; he must shake off this strong desire to sleep. He looked down at the two figures sitting huddled together. Tziviah was crying, the tears running silently down her cheeks.

Suddenly, a man appeared from nowhere. "What a place for you to stop!" he exclaimed gently in Rumanian. "Can't you see how easily you could have been detected! The railway lines are here, the police station over there and the cabin you are leaning against belongs to the railway guard!"

He took some bread from a bag and watched the hungry trio eating. Since joining the rescue party he had become accustomed to tracking down Jews who had not eaten for days. He could always tell by the way they ate the bread he gave them. After the bread was finished, they walked on.

Breathlessly, trying to keep up, Mr. Guttman asked, "Who are you and who sent you?"

"Don't talk. Follow me, the others are all safe and waiting for you. We must make haste because this is a dangerous area" the man replied. "Once we reach the forest, I will let you rest."

Many hours later, in the safety of the forest, he finally allowed them to rest. "You can lie down here and sleep awhile, before daybreak we will be joined by the rest of your party." Saying this he took off his coat, exposing a gun slung over his shoulder. When he saw the fear in Tziviah's eyes he tried to reassure her. "I am not about to kill you. I carry this gun in self-defense. I have been sentenced to be hanged, and there is a warrant out for my arrest," he stated matter of factly. "I am wanted for murder here in Hungary, and carry the gun to defend myself against being captured."

Not quite convinced of this explanation and still fearful for their safety, Tziviah asked him, "Well, if you are wanted in Hungary, and you say you are Rumanian, what are you doing here? Why don't you go back to the safety of Rumania?"

At this he slapped his broad hand across the barrel of his gun, grinning at them, "Why am I here? To make money, of course! Lots of money; the Jews in Rumania pay us a very handsome fee for every Jew we take across the border. This won't last forever, you know!" he concluded ruefully. "Now get some sleep, we have a day's march ahead of us."

Having rolled his jacket to make a pillow for his head, he promptly fell asleep and was soon snoring, his hand still clasping his gun. Mr. Guttman urged Tziviah to put her trust in Hashem and sleep too. Yonah was already fast asleep with his head resting against his mother's arm. She gently stroked his head; how pale and thin he was! Was it only eight weeks ago, when she had watched him playing boisterously in the garden chasing the butterflies? The buttons on his trousers had strained against his bulging waistline then; now it pained her to see his sunken cheeks. She once again let her tears flow freely and silently while she entreated the Almighty to protect them. At last she too fell asleep.

The sun had risen high in the cloudless sky before any of them stirred. One by one they stretched, picking the bits of bracken from their clothes. Once fully awake, both Tziviah and Mr. Guttman spoke at once. "What happened to the rest of our party? You said they would join us before daybreak. It must be almost noon time, so where are they? What do we do now?"

With studied deliberation, the stranger pulled a tin of tobacco out of his trouser pocket, then slowly rolled himself a cigarette before replying. "We wait here until they come."

"What if no one comes?" suggested Mr. Guttman.

"We wait," was the stubborn reply.

So they waited. They remained seated or dozing right through the day in an effort to conserve their strength. Still, there was no sign of the others. The sun was setting once more, their spirits at their lowest ebb, when they finally heard someone approaching.

Tziviah was instantly on her feet; all feelings of hunger and despair evaporated at the sight of the others. She greeted each like a loved one, and when finally her husband came through the densely growing trees, still carrying Rifke on his back, Tziviah's joy knew no bounds. After a few moments of rest they were ready for their final march to freedom. They trudged steadily through that night, silently following their leader through fields and more forests; sometimes they were told to take off their shoes, so as not to be heard. Dawn was breaking when they finally reached a river bank. They waded straight into the swiftly flowing water to cool their aching feet.

Their guide's voice boomed out. "You may talk now, as loud as you wish, we have just crossed the border! We are now in Rumania!"

It would be difficult to describe the emotions of the jubilant group of refugees. I can but quote Tziviah: "Reborn! We all felt suddenly reborn! We would have danced for joy, but no one had enough energy!"

The Rumanian authorities did not exactly prepare a welcoming party. Some Jews were caught, but a few days spent in the local prison, called Tarquju, was but a small price to pay for the privilege of staying in the country. Later they learned that Rachele and Moishe Schreiber had been caught at the border and were later released after the leaders of the local Jewish community had paid a fine.

The travelers' ordeal was not yet over. After a short rest, they resumed their march, trudging behind their guide, like a group of wandering gypsies. Finally they arrived at an isolated farm house. The old farmer and his daughter were obviously expecting the weary, footsore travelers. They were taken through the farm yard, past a flock of chickens fighting over yellow corn. Chasing the dog out of the cow shed, the farmer motioned them to go inside. A feeding trough stretched the length of one wall, divided into sections for each cow. A three legged milking stool hung from a rusty spike on the wall. The galvanized buckets still held a few drops of milk. It could not have been long since milking time.

It was more than eight weeks since they had last tasted milk! "Milk," they whispered as they gratefully sank onto the stone floor, just avoiding the odd patch of cow dung. Milk! Could they possibly ask for some milk? As if in answer the maid came in, carrying a coarse linen sling bag over her shoulder and a pan of milk with several tin cups in her hands. Setting everything down on the floor, she opened the bag and distributed cobs of homebaked black bread. She poured each one a cup of milk. No gourmet banquet served on silver dishes could ever compare with this meal! Tziviah studied this peasant girl; her hair was plaited and tied in a semi circle over the crown of her head, an attractive method of keeping her long tresses out of the way.

Anouska had become resigned to the pitiful state of fugitives, who arrived almost daily in her father's barn, but it always upset her to watch the children's faces as she handed out the food. She silently watched the emaciated children brighten while savoring the creamy taste of fresh milk, but no one realized the effect it would have on their starved digestive systems! The marvelous feeling was soon replaced with bloated discomfort and severe swelling of the abdomen, which was wrongly treated as an infection. The symptoms of malnutrition often went unrecognized, until the release of the concentration camp survivors made everyone familiar with them.

They remained in the barn, sleeping on the floor, happy to have escaped from Hungary, resigned to share their sleeping quarters with an assortment of livestock belonging to the farmer.

The following morning, two young men arrived to take them on the next stage of their journey. As members of the underground rescue team, they were well aware of the fears and heartaches of the fugitives and their desire for news from loved ones. Laslo and Armin patiently listened to a barrage of questions, answering each as best they could. Then it was time to leave the farm. They piled into the van waiting in the farm yard, and after a short but bumpy journey they arrived in Gyarta, a small rural town. Here they were first treated with insecticide, then, oh, joy, a bath and clean clothes, their first in eight weeks! Clean and refreshed, they traveled to Arad, a much larger town with its own small Jewish community.

The Joint Distribution Committee had arranged a reception at the local community center. Tables were laid with food and drinks for the refugees, who arrived at intervals throughout the day. Arrangements were made to house them temporarily with local Jewish families, while efforts were being made to find places on a more permanent basis. After spending three weeks in Arad, Zoltan and his family, including Mundy and Ernsty Fuchs, were offered hospitality by a wonderful couple in Bucharest, the capital of Rumania.

The Joint Committee promised to have their travel documents ready for the following day. At that time the law prohibited Jews from traveling beyond their own restricted neighborhood, and anyone caught breaking it was sent to prison.

The Joint had seen to everything. Zoltan was introduced to a high ranking army officer, under whose protection they were to travel to Bucharest. He was well paid for his services. They arrived at their destination without the constant need to produce their documents for inspection, and for the next five months they remained in the spacious home of Mr. and Mrs. . . . where they were treated as members of the family. Slowly, with the help of this kind couple, their shattered minds and bodies began to mend.

Chapter Twenty

Bucharest, June, 1945. Now that the war was over, Zoltan was anxious to return home and see if there was anything to salvage from his home and business. He discussed his plans with their hosts, who encouraged him to go first by himself and prepare the place for his family.

The following day he boarded the train that would take him back to Grosswardein. The hallmarks of a defeated nation were all too evident, as he traveled through the countryside. His heart beat faster as he stepped off the train; pausing a moment, he looked around the neglected station concourse. Bitter memories flooded back.

The presence of the Nazis pervaded everywhere. Their ghosts stalked the deserted streets. He shuddered as he recalled the last time he had walked these same streets, in disguise, like a hunted criminal. Revulsion welled up inside him, and he resisted with difficulty the strong urge to run away.

Squaring his shoulders he resolved to put the past behind him and start again. The Nazis could not break his spirit now. His mind firmly made up, he walked with renewed courage in the direction of the factory.

He strode along the length of Kopistran Utca Street, oblivious to the people he encountered. He reached the factory gate, now totally deserted. There he stopped abruptly; memories flooded back: No, they were not mere memories, but immediate reality. He could not control the pounding of his heart, the blood rushing to his head, his temples throbbing. Would he ever again be able to walk through these doors without recoiling?

Once inside the vast, deserted hall, he slowly walked through, his footsteps echoing across the emptiness. The Nazis had plundered everything that could be moved. The long rows of coloring powders, the bottles of scents, the packing materials — all gone. The newly installed machines for shaping and wrapping, also gone! It must have taken an army of lorries to move all that machinery. This factory had grown to its present size from years of hard work. How could he consider starting anew he wondered, casting his experienced eye over the vacant spaces. He felt his earlier resolve slipping, but pulled himself together. He must not succumb to despair now. There must be a way to start afresh, and he would find it! There was a shortage of soaps both for domestic and personal use, so selling would be no problem; manufacture would be much more difficult.

After some thought, his spirits lifted. They might have taken the machinery, but they could not rob him of his expertise! Continuing his rounds, he entered the section which had housed the giant mixing drums, each the size of a large room, in which the soap ingredients were mixed and boiled, then poured into molds to set. To Zoltan's astonishment nothing had been disturbed. A quick glance at the panel of switches showed they had not been touched. For the moment everything was useless, these giant kettles designed for huge quantities could not be used for the small amounts he hoped to start production with. However, he still had some valuable equipment for future use. He must concentrate on the immediate present. How many of his old suppliers of raw material would still be in business?

He mounted the ladder which was bolted on to the side of one of the drums, and peered over the edge. What he saw as he peered over the edge of the drum, almost made him lose his grip. Was he imagining it? No! Inside the drum walls was a thick layer of solidified soap. He estimated it was quite sufficient to set him up in business.

Quickly he descended the ladder. Praised be Hashem! In one magical moment, his despair had turned to joy.

He decided to visit his friends Appan and Maria. Their delight at seeing each other was mutual. He stayed a while discussing past events and plans for their return. Reluctantly taking his leave, he took the train back to Bucharest, anxious to share the good news with Tziviah.

How could they ever repay their generous hosts Tziviah wondered, they had opened their home and their hearts to the Rothbart family for the past five months. Mrs. Reich helped Tziviah prepare for their departure, buying and packing into cases the few essentials they needed. After an emotional farewell from their benefactors, they boarded the train that would take them back to their home town in Grosswardein. Doors slammed, the whistle blew, slowly the train gathered speed. With mixed emotions and new found confidence, Tziviah settled down in the noisy carriage. With maternal affection, she watched the children in animated chatter. She smiled indulgently — how comforting to hear Rifke's voice rising above the others. She marveled at the childrens' resilience, even their nightmares were becoming less frequent. She wondered uneasily, could it possibly disturb the children, to come back to Grosswardein? She turned to Zoltan, unsure whether to confide her fear.

"Don't worry about the children," he answered her unspoken question. Not for the first time, she marveled at his perception.

Ensconced in the swaying overcrowded carriage, Zoltan confided his concern for the health of his dear friend Appan. It was Tziviah's turn to reassure her husband.

"Don't worry, we will make sure he has the best medical care, and help Maria nurse him back to health."

❧ ❧ ❧

Their beautiful home had been looted and vandalized, only the carpets were left. Zoltan suggested they move into the factory premises for the moment and Tziviah readily agreed; this way she could help her husband and still be near her children. They began to clear away the mess and rubbish left by the looters. Tziviah swept the floors and scrubbed the workbenches. She searched through the rubbish heap in the yard, to see if anything could be salvaged, reclaiming many seemingly useless articles: strings, tapes and discarded molds. Crumpled wrapping paper she spread on the work bench, and patiently smoothed each sheet. With her practical mind she found ways to use much that lay on the scrap heap. It was there that Tziviah found tools that Zoltan used to scrape the soap from the walls of the giant drums. They spent long days lifting the soap into buckets, then molding it by hand into saleable bars. A ready market would eagerly snap up all they could produce.

It was well past midnight when Zoltan finally stopped work. Exhausted but elated he slowly descended the ladder, carefully wiping his precious tools, and reflected on his good fortune. He had survived with his family and been given the opportunity to provide for their needs! Walking through the hall towards their temporary living quarters, Zoltan noticed the freshly scrubbed workbenches with the first batch of raw soap which Tziviah had worked into attractive molds. His face softened; how well she combined the roles of helper, wife and mother! The children were fast asleep, their pale little faces barely visible under their feather covers. Tziviah had prepared a modest meal, which they ate in silence, their first meal, under their own roof. They praised the Almighty for having brought them this far.

With his expert knowledge and ability to improvise, the plant was soon running smoothly and profitably. Zoltan and Tziviah overcame every drawback and were soon employing a team of workers to cope with the growing production. But they were unaware that their progress was being closely monitored!

Chapter Twenty-One

ayan Weiss contemplated his future. He would have liked to emigrate to *Eretz Yisroel*; to leave the past with all its tragic, painful memories behind and rebuild his life away from Rumania, away from Europe. He wanted to go to a place where he would once again be able to serve the community and lead a congregation in the path of the righteous. A place where his dear son would have an opportunity to develop his fertile mind in a Torah true way. That was his fervent wish, but to quote from the Dayan's own pen: 'Man may have his plans, but Hashem has His own master plan which He carries out!'

A deep sigh escaped his lips as he extracted a letter from his pocket bearing the Grosswardein postmark. It was one of many he had received, entreating him to return and lead the community once more. He had intended to return, but only to salvage something of his collection of treasured manuscripts and other holy *seforim* (books).

Carefully folding the letter, he slipped it back in his pocket. No he could not ignore their pleading. Setting aside his own personal wishes, he made the decision to return to Grosswardein without further delay.

He packed his few belongings and boarded the train, accompanied by Berish. Sitting close together on the hard bench they relived those terrible events which had driven them into hiding and eventual escape. Berish closed his eyes, trying to hide his tears. If only his mother could have been with them! But nothing would ever be the same again.

At last the train steamed into the station. In vain, they searched the platform for familiar faces. Hesitating for a moment, Dayan Weiss looked at Berish, giving him an affectionate pat on his arm. He understood only too well the anguish the boy was feeling.

The streets were strangely deserted. Gone were the carefree, excitable crowds of the pre-Nazi occupation; gone too were the dreaded storm-troopers, their mission so very nearly successful! Of 30,000 Jewish souls who had lived in pre-war Grosswardein, barely 2,000 had survived! Few were prepared to return to settle in this town; the very bricks of the houses must surely weep from what they had witnessed!

Evidence of the brutal occupation was everywhere in the Jewish sector. Wanton destruction and desecration of the synagogues filled the Dayan with sadness. Strips of parchment from the Holy Scrolls littered the streets, leaves from prayer books were trodden underfoot and scattered in the gutters. Father and son bent down, picking up fragments of the holy books as they walked towards their home.

Flushed with excitement, Berish started to run up the path as they reached the house. The door was not locked! He pushed it open, how desolate it was! Where were the warm, familiar objects of his childhood! He sadly rejoined the Dayan who was standing in his study, gazing at the empty shelves, stripped of their books and manuscripts. Without a word, they left the house.

❦ ❦ ❦

Zoltan met Dayan Weiss and Berish walking away from the house. They warmly embraced, in joyous reunion. Then Zoltan insisted they should be his guests. "Tziviah will be overjoyed to see you," he said, adding wistfully, "we have a little celebration with each returning survivor." In animated conversation, they stopped outside an imposing apartment block. Berish edged closer to his father as he turned to look towards the nearby soap factory. The painful memories of those terrifying eight weeks came flooding back. His throat went dry at the memory of those scorching hot waterless days.

"Come, let me show you our apartment," Zoltan called, mercifully dispelling these thoughts. All at once, Berish felt ravenously hungry, and eagerly followed their host up the wide staircase. Tziviah was delighted to see them and welcomed them into their new home.

"Come with me!" she said, and he followed her into the kitchen. Jonah and Rifke were sitting on the kitchen floor, absorbed in a game of dominoes. Berish watched the game progress as Tziviah hastily prepared two additional meals.

Berish marveled how well the children looked in contrast to their last meeting. He looked around the cozy kitchen; here, he did not feel a stranger. Soon he too was absorbed in a game of dominoes. Jonah and Rifke set up a wail of protest when Berish was summoned to join the adults at the supper table.

The Dayan and Zoltan continued their discussion long after Tziviah had cleared away the supper dishes. Berish was now peacefully asleep in the armchair, the combined effect of a delicious hot meal and convivial atmosphere having proved too much for him.

Tziviah, humming softly to herself, while she cleared up the kitchen, looked at the wall clock. It was past the children's bedtime. How quietly they played together at bedtime, hoping to avoid their mother's attention! Ignoring their protestation, she propelled them into the bathroom. Tears turned into laughter when she promised to read to them their favorite children's story.

A little while later, Tziviah closed the book she had been reading; the children, were now fast asleep. She chuckled indulgently, Hanzel and Gretel were her favorites too! Switching off the light, she tiptoed out of the room. Now she must prepare the spare room for her guests; Berish had been so tired at supper. He needed a good night's rest. In the doorway of the dining room she looked at the sleeping boy. How he resembled his mother! She had never noticed it before. The delicate features, the high forehead and the same ready smile. Did he have the Rebbetzin's strength of character? Quickly turning away, her tears spilled over.

❧ ❧ ❧

In the weeks following, a constant flow of Holocaust survivors streamed into Grosswardein. The magnitude of the unspeakable atrocities that came to light defies description and it is impossible to exaggerate. The survivors were mainly young people and children, vainly searching for parents, brothers, sisters or just a familiar face from the past.

To their eternal credit, the American Joint set up distribution centers and spared no effort to help survivors. Grosswardein became an important distribution center, attracting many homeless and penniless Jewish souls. Zoltan was invited to take charge. With

Tziviah's support and encouragement he accepted this new burden, for which he needed wisdom, patience and deep compassion.

One by one the apartments started filling up. Zoltan and his family had been one of the first to move in, followed by many other members of the Rothbart "bunker family." The building became a magnet which drew them together, and each new returnee caused fresh rejoicing. Reb Leibel Stempel, Reb Chaim Katz, the Lefcovitch family and the Zupnick family, to mention but a few of the damaged survivors, temporarily returned to Grosswardein, but could not settle there. Eventually they set their hopes on emigrating to 'De Goldena Medina,' America, to rebuild their shattered lives.

Shortly after his return, Dayan Weiss married the widow Malke, daughter of Reb Chaim Dov Halpern a member of the Rizhiner dynasty. She was a gracious lady who with but a few words could make even the most reticent feel at ease in her company. She was held in great esteem by all who were privileged to know her. Eventually she and the Dayan settled in Manchester, he having accepted the leadership of the Greater Manchester Orthodox Community. He held this post with distinction for over twenty years, before taking up his last position as the head of the *Eidah Hacharedis* community in Jerusalem.

The Schreiber family also returned soon after the 'liberation' as Miriam was to tell me.

"By a miracle, we found our villa just as we had left it, nothing had been touched!"

With a characteristic gesture of gratitude to the Almighty, Mr. Schreiber offered his home to the Vizhnitzer Dayan, Rabbi Schnee-balg and his large family. Reb Yankel and his family joined the rest of the 'bunker family' in the apartment block. He rented the ground floor apartment, facing that of the Rothbart's across the courtyard. For a while it seemed that Grosswardein might once again blossom into a thriving Jewish center, though most of the survivors preferred to emigrate rather than return. Many newcomers remained only while awaiting exit visas to far away places.

Efforts were being made to bring back a semblance of normality: Schools, Shuls, yeshivos, the kosher bakery and slaughter house were re-opened. *Mikvah* amenities essential for an orthodox community were also arranged. With Dayan Weiss at the helm, it was hoped to tempt others to settle in Grosswardein. Dayan Weiss wrote in his book *Minchas Yitzchok*, that he felt it his duty to save the many young people and orphaned children from assimilation, and find solutions to a multitude of problems and heartaches. With the support of other well known rabbis, they were able to assist the tragic cases of *agunim* and *agunos* (those whose spouses were missing but not actually proven to be deceased).

The local sanatorium was ill-equipped to cope with the sudden influx of tuberculosis cases from camp survivors ravaged with consumption. The hospital resources were also stretched beyond their limits with the many psychiatric cases arriving — those tragic souls who managed to survive the horrors of concentration camps only to succumb to total mental breakdown on their release. These were mostly the sole survivors of large families who could no longer cope with the reality and scope of the tragedy. Alas, they were not an uncommon phenomenon. It was left to the 'healthy' survivors to help with rehabilitation and instill a spark of hope and the will to fight for their recovery.

Soon after their arrival, Elke Schreiber organized her daughters into a routine for visiting the sanatorium patients. Rochel Schreiber was seen daily with a wicker basket over her arm entering the sanatorium, her visits eagerly awaited. She cheered the patients with her sunny disposition as she distributed food. She knew instinctively how to lift the spirits of even the most depressed with a few encouraging words. Freidle and Miriam followed her example, becoming regular visitors in the crowded hospital wards which had been set aside for the many psychiatric patients. In these ways this deeply caring, but fragmented community did much to help.

❀   ❀   ❀

Valiant efforts were made to rekindle this once proud and prosperous Jewish center to a semblance of its former glory. Each returning survivor was greeted with genuine warmth, often with tears of joy.

Among the early arrivals were Lola (Erika) and Yidel Weinberger with their younger son Moishe. Lola and the boy had remained in Budapest. Having acquired a new identity, they lived in comparative safety, though always in fear of detection and betrayal.

Suddenly the war was over! The defeated Nazis fled. Now a new fear gripped Lola's heart — the fear of the unknown. Horrendous stories were filtering through Budapest as the first survivors returned. Not knowing the fate of her husband and that of her son Shuli, she agonized over what to do; to return to Grosswardein or wait for her husband to come. Tormented with uncertainty, she remained in Budapest, praying for their safe return.

She recalled the day the boys were entrusted to a Hungarian gentile, to join her as soon as it was safe, but only Moishe came.

At last her husband did come, but their joy was marred by the absence of Shuli. As Yidel told Lola, "I was among the lucky few who had managed to slip over the border into Rumania, joining the Bobover Rebbe's entourage in Bucharest. I thought the two children were safely with you!"

Now they were back in Grosswardein. Their house stood empty awaiting their return, but it was no longer 'home,' Lola paced slowly through the elegant rooms, which once held so much joy and laughter, then turned abruptly and walked out of the house. It took all the patience and persuasion Yidel could muster to change her mind. "Will you let the Nazis triumph over you?" he pleaded. "They chased us out of our property, and with the grace of Hashem it has been restored to us!"

Three weeks later, however, their tears changed from sorrow to joy. Their missing son Shuli returned to their welcoming arms. Pale and emaciated with a maturity far beyond his age, he haltingly told them what had happened. He and his grandparents were herded into a wagon and deported to Auschwitz. He carefully avoided answering his parents' probing questions, not wishing to inflict unnecessary anguish. He owed his life, he told them, to a Polish Jew; on their arrival at the death camp, this man whispered to him on his way to be interrogated:

"How old are you?"

Shuli whispered, "13."

"Tell them you are 18!" he answered, before melting into the crowd which watched the new arrivals lining up for the infamous 'selection.' Shuli later discovered that all the young children were taken directly into the gas chambers. May Hashem avenge their blood.

The Weinbergers could not adjust to a life in Grosswardein. Lola's sister in New York besieged her with letters, begging them to join her. So they moved to Prague, to await their visas, and finally sailed for a new life, where they could live and work and raise their children in a Torah true way. It took time to shed the traumas and nightmares, the legacies of the 'Old Country.' With the blessing of their first daughter dawned a new identity, a feeling of belonging, they were no longer 'greenhorns' but parents of a new generation of Americans.

Chapter Twenty-Two

ife in postwar Grosswardein, now part of Rumania, was becoming increasingly difficult. The communist overlords were making their presence felt in every sphere of life.

The efforts of dedicated Rabbonim and lay leaders to kindle a religious objective into the young survivors were thwarted when the authorities outlawed the teaching and observance of religion. Private enterprise, and freedom of speech were also forbidden. These oppressive decrees struck fear into the newly emerging Jewish community, but for a while, with a resilience born from a long history of persecutions, the community grew and prospered.

The Rothbart household was blessed with the birth of a new baby. The Schreiber household was agog with the preparations for their eldest daughter Rochel's marriage to Reb Herzle Schapiro, who later settled in Antwerp.

This post-holocaust community which arose from the ashes of the gas chambers, led by its outstanding leaders, was slowly losing heart as the noose of an oppressive regime was perceptibly tightening its grip, hostile to anyone who did not embrace its faithless, secularist society. To the Jews, however, to succumb to the Communist doctrine was unthinkable.

Emigration was once again the main topic of conversation, whispered in low tones since even to mention it was to attract hostile attention:

"I can give you the name of an official who will supply exit visas. For a fee, of course."

"Of course!"

Fortunately, for the many Jews wishing to emigrate, there were in those early post war days government officials willing to supply the necessary documents for a large fee. Escape to any part of the globe was preferred to remaining in a totalitarian state. The Jewish community worked hard and long with but a single aim; when their time came to emigrate, they should not be penniless. Quietly and secretly people were studying maps of South America, Uruguay, Paraguay, Venezuela etc; these far away exotic places became household names through their willingness to accept Jewish refugees.

Outwardly life continued as normal within the community, the steady flow of newcomers needing shelter and food were quietly absorbed. With the newly acquired prosperity, there was no shortage of money when it was needed for a specific cause. Many families befriended young children left orphaned, taking them into their homes.

One day, Zoltan watched with indifference as an open lorry carrying Russian troops drove past. Suddenly his attention was riveted by the figure of a little girl standing in the lorry, her little hands gripping the edge of the truck. Their eyes met, 'What is a little Jewish girl doing in that lorry?' flashed through his mind! At the same instant he heard her calling "Zoltan Batchy!" Her arms stretched out towards him as the truck drove past. All his senses now mobilized, he sprinted forward, chasing the truck. Luckily it came to a halt at the next crossroad, only a short distance ahead. Catching up just as the driver slammed into first gear, Zoltan snatched the child from the lorry as the driver released the brake. Before the soldiers had time to react, the lorry had crossed the intersection and rolled out of sight. Zoltan held the girl close as she let her tears flow, her little body shaking. At last she calmed down and looked up in gratitude: He caught his breath, she was the daughter of his friend Mr. Honig. Why was she on that lorry, and where had she come from?

"Sheindy, where are your parents?" She shrugged her shoulders.

"Are you alone?" She nodded.

He wanted to ask many more questions, but decided it would be better to let Tziviah deal with the child.

"Come," he said, taking her by the hand. "I will take you home with me, until your parents return."

Alas, that was not to be. Later it was confirmed that Sheindy was the only member of the Honig family to survive. With the resilience of the very young, and endowed with a happy disposition, she captured the hearts of everyone. She remained with the Rothbarts and would often visit the Schreibers, who treated her as one of their own. But they never discovered how she came to be on the military lorry. Sheindy was determined not to talk about it.

When the Lefcovitch family emigrated to New York, they offered to take the little waif. She left Grosswardein and set sail for New York as one of the Lefcovitch family, sharing the joys and frustrations of starting a new life in a strange new world.

Forty years passed before Sheindy met the Rothbarts again.

Chapter Twenty-Three

The marketplace in the heart of the Jewish quarters in Grosswardein became a popular place for buying second hand furniture and other household goods. These items, once plundered from Jewish homes, were now offered for sale. In some cases they were offered to the previous owners of the property! No one complained; they were too thankful for the opportunity to buy back such items as their beautiful household linen, carpets, and ornaments at a fraction of their true value. To the local peasants these were useless items, which did not feed hungry mouths nor pay the rent. Life had become increasingly more difficult for the impoverished farmers and laborers. Since the Russian occupation, they had confiscated all local grown produce, and the movement of livestock was closely monitored.

Of course, not all Jews returned and of those who did, not everyone could afford to buy back their goods, so much of the looted property remained on the market stalls awaiting buyers.

Miriam was walking through the market. It held a special fascination for her, and she stopped to admire the bric-a-brac on display. The goods were of fine quality, items such as one would expect to find in the homes of the wealthy. Picking up an exquisite silver box she held it up to admire the intricate enamel and filigree pattern. The stallholder, her weather-beaten face framed with a black scarf, looked up. Her eyes darted from the silver box in Miriam's hand to her face, anticipating a sale. She knew that Jews were fond of silver articles. She watched Miriam lift the hinged lid, and give a stifled gasp of delight: cradled inside the box was a magnificent diamond brooch. Hiding her excitement, Miriam took the brooch and placed the box back on the table. The woman looked at her with obvious dismay; she had hoped to sell the silver box and make a handsome profit, but this girl had lost interest in the silver box and only wanted the trinket inside it! They finally agreed on a price and, handing the brooch to Miriam, she did not hide her disappointment at her choice of purchase.

Miriam hurried away unable to contain her excitement any longer. She had never seen a more beautiful brooch! She could not wait to get home and show it to her mother. Every member of the household admired it.

"Mama," Miriam said, holding the brooch in the palm of her hand, "do you think it would be a nice gift for Tziviah Neni as a token of our appreciation?"

"But of course, it is a lovely gift" Elke answered, smiling. She was immensely proud of her generous, caring daughters.

Tziviah was to treasure this gift above all others, and wore it for every occasion. It is a sad reflection of the times we live in, that it was stolen from her with many other items, when her home in Manchester was burgled. Needless to say, it was never traced. But, that was in the far distant future . . .

❊ ❊ ❊

Zoltan paused at the factory gate, watching his workers arriving for the morning shift. They touched their caps as a sign of respect, and he returned their cheerful 'Good Morning' greeting. So much had been achieved these last two years. Gone were the days when he and Tziviah worked all hours to rebuild the factory from the little they had salvaged. The factory was running smoothly and profitably. His order books were full, the demand even outstripping his increased production. Being in a 'sellers market,' profit was high, so he could afford to employ a production manager, leaving him with more time to devote to the many charitable causes, and help in the important task of rebuilding the various amenities essential in the running of a orthodox community.

Zoltan was standing at the entrance of the factory, now back in full production. Casually watching as his work force entered through the gate, touching their cap in respectful greeting as they passed through. The irony of it did not escape him, these were the same men and women who, not so long ago, at best stood by as the Jews were being hounded out of their homes.

He turned away, irritated at allowing these unwelcome images to surface in his mind. After all he reasoned, he and many other Jews owed their lives to a gentile couple. He walked away from the gate, he was due to meet the Appans that morning to finalize the sale of a magnificent villa in their name, together with a trust fund to provide a comfortable income. Zoltan felt a deep affection for this couple and remained in close contact throughout the years. The Appans were treated with great respect and received a constant stream of visitors from their extended family. Though scattered in many parts of the world: the Rothbarts settled in Paris, the Dayan in Manchester, the Schreibers in London, New York and Antwerp, they all retained their link with Appan. They sent him gifts and expensive medicines, but his health continued to deteriorate. Maria continued to enjoy the loving attention of the survivors until her death in the early 1980's. To this day, Berish cherishes a postcard they received from Maria shortly before her death.

He absentmindedly glanced into the factory. "Ah, good day to you!" he called to the commissar who introduced himself as Ignacs and his assistant Gyuri. Zoltan knew them by sight; he had often

Thank you card from the Appans to Weiss family.

seen them drinking with his workers at the open air wine bar. He knew they were part of the Communist "Brotherhood" now in charge at the town hall and government offices, but they seemed likable enough and eager to make friends with the community.

"Are you here on official business?" Zoltan asked, holding out his hand.

"Yes, Rothbart Batchy, let us go inside" smiled Ignacs.

Zoltan, puzzled but not unduly concerned, took them into his office.

After accepting a cigarette, Ignacs explained that he was employed by the local taxation office. "Naturally there are going to be changes. We are here to help and explain a few new rules." Noticing the look of alarm on Zoltan's face he hastily continued, "You have nothing to fear. I will be here to oversee the smooth running of your business."

Zoltan wanted to protest that his business was running smoothly, but Ignacs had not yet finished.

"As from today, you employ me as your security man," he concluded, drawing hard on his cigarette.

Zoltan was outraged, "I have no security problems! My employees work hard and diligently for a fair wage. Besides, I employ a manager, therefore, I see no need for a security guard," he added, hoping this would end the strange conversation. He started to rise from his seat, but Ignacs ignored the gesture.

"Of course you need a full time security man. How else do you stop your workers from pilfering?"

"My workers don't pilfer!" he retorted. "It has always been my policy to sell to them at cost price. They are not tempted to steal."

"Well, I was coming to that," Ignacs continued. "You will have to stop selling to your workers. From now on, you will sell your entire production to Russia at a price to be agreed upon. Now let me have your order books and work sheets. An inspector is on his way to advise on ways to improve efficiency."

In stunned silence Zoltan complied.

The following day he was informed that for the purpose of increasing production, the factory would have to be open on Saturday.

"Work on Saturday! Never!" he declared.

"You have no choice!" he was told.

From that time on, Zoltan knew that he was being watched. Within days of the unofficial take-over, his previous application for an exit visa was refused. He was valued not only for his standing in the community and the influence he could exert, but also for his technical knowledge and experience.

It was dangerous to clash with the town hall dictators; but to open his factory on Shabbos was unthinkable! He had no illusions of the battle ahead. Dare he jeopardize the lives of his loved ones?

❁ ❁ ❁

Yankel Schreiber came to his rescue.

It was past midnight, but Zoltan had no thought of sleep. Deeply troubled by the recent turn of events, he nervously paced up and down in his carpet slippers.

Two years had gone by since they returned to Grosswaardein, in the winter of 1945. With nothing but an abundance of enthusiasm and a burning desire to forget the past, they had worked incredibly hard to overcome every difficulty. He looked around the comfortable room: not pretentious or extravagant, just comfortable and above all, a home. He sat down on the edge of a chair, then rose; he resumed his restless pacing. All his hopes and plans for the future had vanished. He could not forget the cruel glint in the inspector's eyes, when told that the factory would remain closed on the Sabbath.

The baby was crying in the adjoining room. He heard Tziviah croon to him, then all was quiet again: 'Sholom Boruch' was asleep. Sholom — Peace, because the war was over, and Boruch after his grandfather. Suddenly Zoltan's body stiffened. Was that a knock on the door? He waited, the knock came again. He hurriedly unlocked the door as he recognized the voice of Yankel Schreiber.

"Reb Yankel, what brings you here at this late hour, and in this manner? Is someone chasing you?"

"No, no," Reb Yankel whispered, closing the door behind him. "We are all right, praised be Hashem, but you are in grave danger. You are to be arrested in the morning." Putting his hand on Zoltan's arm, he said urgently, "You know what that means — Siberia! — Come, we must hurry, I have a horse-drawn carriage waiting outside. We must not waste time, be quick, wake your wife and children. The driver will take you over the border into Hungary. Now Hurry!"

After his first reaction of stunned disbelief, Zoltan sprang into action. He shook Tziviah awake with the news and she dressed in a moment. She wrapped the sleeping child in his warm bedclothes and packed some food into a basket. With the sleepy children, Rifke and

Jonah wrapped up in several layers of clothes, they silently left their hard won home, never to return. Tziviah fought back her tears as she watched the little crowd gathered in the courtyard to wish them a safe journey. The news had traveled fast among this close and caring community.

"A horse-drawn carriage attracts less attention along the country roads," Reb Yankel commented, as he lifted Jonah into the coach. Once again, stealthily and by night, they were fleeing from pursuers. Years later Tziviah told me:

"I will never forget that night, all of us bundled into the carriage. We clung to our frightened and bewildered children. The rhythmic clip-clop of the horses' hoofs mingled with the sound of footsteps alongside the carriage with words of encouragement coming from all sides, then fading into the distance. At last only the solitary figure of Reb Yankel remained, striding alongside the carriage, showering us with a stream of blessings."

Two hours after leaving their home, they were safely over the Hungarian border.

At dawn, their home was raided by the Communist Secret Police. They would certainly have been arrested but for the timely intervention of Reb Yankel.

Chapter Twenty-Four

nce safely over the border, the coachman pulled up at the roadside. He dismounted and, respectfully touching his cap, assured them that it was now quite safe to alight and stretch their legs if they so wished. How ironic that, after the war, it was the Hungarians who were more tolerant towards the Jews!

The pale rays of the wintry sun broke through the clouds as their carriage rolled along the main thoroughfare into Tokay, a town renowned for the wine of that name. Zoltan hoped to find temporary shelter with his old friends, the Freankel family, manufacturers of the famous 'Freankel Matches,' whose name was a household word.

Their daughter, Elsa Fuchs, now a widow, had returned to Tokay with her boys, Moishe and Ernsty.

The Rothbarts were welcomed into their home with open arms. This last ordeal had been too much for Tziviah's already strained nerves; she needed all the patience and loving care they lavished on her to help her regain her health.

Grateful for their hospitality, yet not wishing to impose, Zoltan arranged to leave Tziviah and the children in Tokay, which would enable him to travel onward to Prague, which, at that time was the distribution center of the American Joint. Hardworking and dedicated, they helped thousands of refugees, providing food, clothing, traveling documents and money. With nowhere else to go, the "Joint" was their only hope!

Once Tziviah was sufficiently recovered, she arranged for herself and the children to join Zoltan in Prague. The children had thrived during their two months stay in Tokay. The time came to bid their generous hosts an emotional farewell. In Prague, they exchanged their former spacious living accommodations for a one roomed apartment, but Zoltan assured her that they were extremely lucky to find even one room in this overcrowded city!

To their surprise and delight, they were reunited with Dayan Weiss, his family, Yankel Schreiber's family and many other acquaintances. Everyone was anxious to emigrate before it was too late. Dayan Weiss explained to Zoltan how he had left Grosswardein. "I was resolved to remain as head of the community. We worked so hard to rebuild the schools, the synagogues, slaughter house etc., against formidable odds, as you well know." He sighed.

It was not just the hostile Communist influence, but the rebellious young survivors of the many evil death camps who caused him problems. Having suffered beyond belief while still so very young, they needed infinite patience and tender guidance. "The religious survival of the orphaned youngsters is at stake!" The new schools for boys and for girls had proved a great success. Dayan Weiss was resolved these should not suffer when Zoltan had to flee. With a nucleus of willing helpers, the schools continued to thrive, but not for long. New laws came into effect restricting private ownership of businesses and private schools, in particular religious schools were outlawed. Once again fear filled the hearts of the Jewish population, as they watched the erosion of their time honored values.

Still the Dayan, loath to leave his people, resolved to stay and lead them as best he could.

Once again, fate extended a hand to guide his destiny, as the Dayan so aptly wrote, "Man may have his plans, but Hashem has a master plan which He carries out!"

One day, a high ranking officer, bedecked with rows of military medals called on the Dayan, demanding an audience. He was accompanied by a young woman whom he introduced as his daughter. Coming quickly to the purpose of his visit, he explained that his daughter was married to a man who had been sent to Dachau, the forced labor camp. He had not returned and was listed 'missing, presumed dead.' His wife was now betrothed to an officer in the Rumanian Army.

"This young man has a brilliant future in the army," the father concluded with pride.

Though religion had no place in their present lifestyle, he wanted the marriage service performed by a Rabbi.

The Dayan studied the documents which the father presented. Father and daughter exchanged anxious glances, as they waited in silence. Shaking his head, the Dayan sighed. Handing the papers back to the officer, he commented sadly, "At the moment, there is insufficient evidence to declare your daughter free to remarry."

Enraged at this unwelcome decision, the father jumped to his feet, shouting, "But, I have told you, she is betrothed, the wedding date has been fixed, you cannot refuse now."

The Dayan was shaken by this unexpected reaction, but he replied calmly, "I feel your pain, but I cannot bend the halachah. The law is quite clear, you must wait." Thumping the table, the father shouted, "I demand you sanction this marriage!"

"I cannot go against the Torah law!" the Dayan retorted.

"I have powerful friends! Agree to this marriage, or you forfeit your life!" raged the other.

Undaunted, the Dayan replied, "The law is the law!"

Ominous threats still ringing in his ear, he watched the officer storm out of the room, followed by the daughter.

The ever watchful *shammas* (beadle) rushed into the room. "Are you all right?" he asked. "We could not help but overhear the conversation. Those were no idle threats," he continued. "We must find a place for you to hide, you are in grave danger!"

With great reluctance, the Dayan finally agreed to go into hiding, until it was safe for him to travel to Prague. Before leaving, he insisted on saying farewell to the congregation he had worked so hard to establish. Struggling to contain his emotions, he stood on the *bimah* in the crowded shul hall. His eyes scanned the eager upturned faces, some unashamedly crying. How many would he ever see again? His farewell message was, to remain steadfast to their religious commitments, and to reject the Communist way of life, which was cruel and Godless. Lucidly he compared their present struggle to that of a ship floundering in a storm, but once the tempest subsides, the ship can once again glide over the rippling waters. In contrast, a fortress which seems so much stronger and more solid could collapse like a pack of cards in an earthquake. Then it was time to go.

Now here they were in this great city of Prague, but to the many refugees, its only attraction was the Joint Distribution Committee Center. Most refugees hoped to emigrate to the Holy Land, but this dream was soon to be cruelly shattered. Yankel Schreiber moved his family to Marienbad, and a few months later they were granted visas to Belgium. They stayed in Antwerp for the next two years, before putting down their final roots in Boro Park, New York.

Chapter Twenty-Five

Dayan Weiss and his family were still in Prague when Foreign Minister Masaryk was murdered. Thousands of Jews felt their hearts sink at the news. Though officially his death was an accident (he allegedly fell out of a window), few were deceived, and shock waves traveled throughout the war-weary free world.

❀ ❀ ❀

It was at the height of these tense and unsettling times that help arrived in the guise of a British Officer!

Dayan Weiss had returned to his lodgings from yet another fruitless visit to the consulate, one more forlorn figure in a long line of hopefuls. He was sipping a lemon tea the Rebbetzin had prepared for him, when there was a knock on the door. Without much enthusiasm he watched his wife open the door. Framed in the doorway, smiling broadly, stood a British Captain.

He held out his hand, saying, "My name is Rabbi Dr. Solomon Schonfeld. I am from London, and I am looking for a Rabbi Yitzchok Weiss." Mystified, the Dayan extended his hand in greeting.

Rabbi Schonfeld should need no introduction from me. Few did more to save the lives of the Jews in Europe, particularly children, than this warm courageous man. He now explained that Rabbi Weingarten, better known as the 'Liegge Rav,' had asked him to find the Dayan and arrange for him to come to England.

Shortly after their meeting, the Dayan received his travel papers for the journey to England. Rabbi Schonfeld had accomplished his mission: the Dayan, his wife and son were able to travel unhindered. With no worldly possessions, but a brilliant mind with an unmatched store of Torah Wisdom, he would soon make his mark among the Torah luminaries in England.

Victoria Railway Station, on a cold wet morning, is not the most cozy place, but in May 1947 it was the beginning of a new life and new hope. With not a single English coin between them and not a word of English, they sat on a bench, hoping someone would come to collect them.

Berish told me later, "The first to greet us was a total stranger. 'Shalom Aleichem,' he called extending his hand, 'Where are you from?' and without waiting for an answer, 'Can I give you a lift?' This was England! I will never forget Mr. Itzinger, and his warm welcoming words!"

❧ ❧ ❧

Zoltan yearned to settle in Palestine. Where else but in the Jewish homeland could he hope to find peace and safety for his family? It was not to be, yet, they had come so very close to realizing their dream. With the traveling papers 'Lese Pasee,' safely in his pocket, he walked out of the consulate building. Striding along the busy street, a new spring in his walk, he ran over in his mind the things he must see to. Provisions, clothing, but, first priority, to contact a shipping agent. He smiled wryly, as he recalled the comment of the counter clerk in the consulate when handing him his papers.

"The whole world is *Auf reder* (on wheels)!"

Passing a news stand, his attention was drawn to the crowd gathered around the display stand. His curiosity aroused, he edged closer. Shocked and horrified, he read the Reuter News Bulletin, scrawled in capital letters on the board "WAR IN PALESTINE!"

He read and reread the offending words. Suddenly he felt much older than his years. What was he to tell Tziviah? This was a blow to the thousands of homeless survivors which would send them reeling. Which country would still want to take them in? Their health also caused concern: many were still suffering from the effects of prolonged malnutrition and harsh treatment, and were ill equipped to withstand the rigors of winter in the unheated, overcrowded living conditions.

Once again, the American Joint stepped in to ease the plight of the refugees. Hoteliers in the holiday resorts of Marienbad and Carlsbad were only too pleased to open their doors to the refugees, who in turn greatly benefited from their new environment.

In these beautiful resorts the refugees slowly regained their health. Leaders tried to bind them into a community, with a shul for prayers and a place for those who wished to learn and also provided various activities. This was important, as Mrs. Rothbart was to tell me: "Resorts are wonderful places for vacations, and do wonders to restore a tired tycoon. But they become altogether less attractive when people are in limbo, with an uncertain future stretching from days, to weeks, into months!"

In the Autumn of 1947, Zoltan and his family, together with a group of displaced persons, arrived in Carlsbad. They were warmly greeted by the small Orthodox community, led by Rabbi Shloime Josefovits, a tall, handsome, scholarly man with a ready smile. A veteran, having arrived the previous year, he provided some permanency to the ever changing community. He acted as their Cantor, Shochet and Mohel, helped and supported by his pretty, young wife Sara. Their home was a magnet for those seeking advice or just someone to confide in. He possessed the rare combination of wit and discretion.

Zoltan was overjoyed to meet Reb Shloime again, and they formed a deep and lasting friendship. Sara and Tziviah too enjoyed their new found friendship, sharing in their joys of motherhood. This peaceful existence continued for almost a year.

Rabbi Dr. Schonfeld arrived one day to offer Rabbi Josefovits a post as rabbi to another Orthodox congregation in the industrial city of Sheffield.

Shortly after their departure, the Rothbart family were offered visas to France.

Life is so much stranger than fiction. Thirty years later, they would meet again, when both families finally settled in Manchester.

Zoltan had never envisioned settling in France, but Tziviah, always the optimist, reassured her husband.

"As soon as we reach Paris, we can apply for emigration to America. From France it must be much easier!"

"You are right. Hashem has brought us this far, and will continue to guide us." Zoltan remarked.

On a cold windy day in September 1948, together with a group of thirty other refugees, Zoltan and Tziviah stood on the platform in Carlsbad. Taking leave of their friends was not easy; they had lived together for the last nine months in this town; now they wondered when they would ever meet again. Those who boarded the train to Paris were the lucky ones.

At two o'clock in the morning, cold and bewildered, they alighted. With no roots and few possessions, they huddled close together, anxiously scanning the deserted station.

Promised by the Joint that someone would come to meet them on their arrival, Zoltan suggested they wait inside the heated hall until they were collected. They had hardly settled inside, when a guard informed them that since the last train had left, the station was now closed.

"*S'il vous plait, mesdames et monsieur,* You will have to wait outside!"

No amount of pleading helped. They were marched out into the cold morning air, stamping their feet on the unwelcoming pavement to keep warm. Not until two hours had passed did anyone come to collect them.

Chapter Twenty-Six

ife was very difficult for the new arrivals, shuttled from hotel to hotel, a family to each room, using a small Primus stove to prepare food, but no one considered this a hardship. It was the 'gateway' to a new life, away from Europe — a temporary base. Though most of their friends did emigrate to America and Canada, the Rothbarts settled in Paris, where they remained for the next thirty years. They formed a close-knit orthodox community, determined to protect their growing children from unacceptable outside influence. Friendships forged in Carlsbad and old friends from Grosswardein provided a nucleus, with the continuity and sense of belonging which was so precious to everyone. Each new arrival from the Communist Bloc received the same warm welcome and was drawn into the circle. The Stemple, Frishwasser, and Meisels families are warmly remembered by Tziviah; she also recalls the Lubavitcher Rebbe, the Margareten Rav and Reb Itzikel who officiated at many post war weddings.

Zoltan, always the optimist, wasted no time in setting up a small plant to manufacture soap, but he soon discovered that hard work and enthusiasm were not enough. He could not compete against the established, mass-produced, attractively packaged soap.

"They were not exactly queuing up waiting to buy our soap!" Tziviah remarked.

Not easily beaten, Zoltan tried his hand at other projects; importing carpets from Spain, was just one of his abortive ventures. In the spring of 1950 he was introduced to the lucrative trade in nylon stockings. Never one to miss an opportunity, he started commuting between Paris and Dusseldorf in Germany. Though the work was financially rewarding, Zoltan was away all week, returning to Paris for most weekends. Tziviah was expecting her fourth child, so she was delighted when Zoltan was offered a partnership in a small local quilting factory. It was a difficult decision to make, to give up his present earning powers for the uncertainty of manufacturing. However, it was his consideration for Tziviah which helped him decide.

This proved a turning point for both partners. Just three years after arriving penniless in the great cosmopolitan city of Paris, they started manufacturing quilts. From this most modest of beginnings, the firm grew into a well run modern factory providing employment for many people

With the birth of their precious daughter Chanelle, Zoltan became increasingly involved with local Jewish affairs. Together with Dr. Naftalis he was voted Joint Gabai in the Shul. His efforts to improve the amenities for their members were warmly applauded by the elders on the governing board. When, a short time later, the town hall planners submitted an offer to buy the synagogue and adjoining land as part of a redevelopment plan, Zoltan was overwhelmingly voted to be their official negotiator, and it was a decision which proved invaluable.

Zoltan and Dr. Naftalis succeeded in negotiating a brilliant package. Included in the deal was a new, greatly enlarged synagogue, with an imposing hall to be hired out for social functions. There was also to be an apartment block and a *mikvah* at the back of the shul. Their aim was to provide an adequate income from the apartments to make the shul financially self-sufficient.

This proved to be no mere idle dream. To this day the rental from the apartment block goes a long way to meet the expenses of the magnificent shul on the Rue Bastfoi.

❧ ❧ ❧

Refugees arriving from Rumania brought news of worsening conditions for the Jews. Living conditions were rapidly deteriorating and famine was rampant. Zoltan organized the collection of food, clothing and money. Women did the door to door collections. The response from both Jewish businesses and private donations was tremendous, but more was needed to provide continued sustenance for the many families. Soon the cry for help from the Russian continent stretched their resources.

The late Satmar Rebbe was asked for his help in making known the plight of their brethren, to the Jews in the free world. He immediately organized relief operations, establishing distribution centers in many cities around the globe. One grateful recipient told Tziviah many years later in Israel, "Many of us owe our lives to the parcels we received from abroad. The contents of a single parcel, when sold on the black market, was enough to sustain a family for three months!"

Tziviah smiled happily. It made all the hard work and long hours trudging through the streets in all types of weather well worthwhile. She recalled times when she had not been too well, or the children demanded attention, times when she had felt unhappy at leaving the children in the care of others. Suddenly, here was proof that it had not been in vain! Their prompt and sustained action had helped to save lives!

❦   ❦   ❦

On their last visit to Israel, shortly before his death, Zoltan and Tziviah had traveled to Jerusalem for a family celebration. Zoltan had suffered a stroke some years previously, from which he had only partially recovered. Frail and in poor health he was confined to a wheelchair. Tziviah never far from his side, was dozing in the lounge waiting for Zoltan to wake from his midday nap. Someone knocked on her apartment door. It was a middle aged lady dressed in a floral cotton dress, her hair covered with a matching scarf.

"Frau Rothbart?" she inquired.

Tziviah nodded wondering at the intrusion. The woman smiled broadly, unable to contain her excitement she said:

"You don't know my married name, but you might remember a little girl called Sheindy Honig!"

Pleased with the effect it had on Tziviah, she gladly accepted the invitation to enter. Tziviah looked at her in wonderment as she tried to equate in her mind the little waif of forty years past with this jolly well endowed lady . . . It was so long ago, but she never forgot the little girl her husband brought home. Of course they did correspond occasionally, but somehow their paths had never crossed.

Sheindy gently interrupted her thoughts, "Yes, I am a grandmother now, not a little girl." She sighed, "I have dreamed of the day

I would meet you and Mr. Rothbart and thank you personally for saving me," she murmured. "Is Mr. Rothbart at home?" she asked.

"He is," Tziviah answered, "He is not very well."

Gently opening the door to the bedroom, she beckoned Sheindy to look inside, holding her finger to her lips, indicating silence. Sheindy tiptoed to the door, tears filled her eyes as she watched Zoltan sleeping peacefully. He looked much older then she had imagined, his waxen complexion in stark contrast to the crisp pink pillows. The years seemed to fall away, and she was once more the frightened child he had rescued. Stepping back, she let Tziviah gently close the door. There is so much she would have liked to say, to thank them both, but words failed her. The older woman understood and gave her an affectionate hug in parting, Two days later, Zoltan Rothbart's soul was gathered to his rightful place in *Gan Eden*.

Part Three
Ilonka

Chapter One

May 1945. Ilonka slowly walked out of the building into the dusty cobble-stoned yard. She looked around her at the decayed old warehouse which had been converted into a prison. An eerie silence prevailed, a strangeness she could not comprehend. What was different? Her mind reacted with painful slowness as she tried to understand this strange feeling. The barbed wire encircling the camp, the turreted lookout posts at regular intervals, the searchlight, all was in place; nothing had changed. And yet it was different. Two days had passed without food. The previous evening they had not been collected for their shift in the ammunition factory. Lacking the energy to sustain her interest, she hardly cared.

Since the prisoners' transfer from Auschwitz to Zittau in the Sudetanland, conditions had improved. The wanton beatings were less frequent, the vicious dogs held mainly on a leash. With only two girls to each bunk, it was less crowded than Auschwitz, but with food becoming scarcer, it hardly left room to rejoice.

Yet she had been among the lucky ones to have escaped the gas chamber. It had been a miracle she would never forget.

The last terrifying days in Auschwitz remained burnt into her memory. Allied planes attacked the compound; they hid from the rain of bombs as best they could. Rumors filtered through that the Russians were closing in.

While the demoralized soldiers of the self-styled "Herrenfolk" were fighting on all fronts to hold their crumbling defense, the Nazis never faltered in their resolve to annihilate the Jews. With increased urgency they intensified their efforts to implement the 'Final Solution.'

"The infamous crematorium and gas chambers were working to full capacity." Ilonka recalled those terrifying days.

"There were just a few girls left in 'Block 8.' All others were emptied. We were told to join the girls in the 'Schreib Stube' — administration." These Jewish girls had been the 'privileged ones'; now they were destined to be the last to enter the so-called 'bath house' whence no one emerged alive. But to these terrified young girls it was just another unquestionable command they had to obey. Their minds no longer reacted.

They were told to strip before entering the 'shower room,' painfully aware of the consequences of even a moment's hesitation. Trembling, acutely conscious of the cruel, cold eyes watching through the peepholes, they began to obey. Suddenly, a tremendous blast rocked the very foundation. A bomb had exploded just outside the gas chamber, killing and injuring the guards. The blast activated the automatic sirens, drowning their screams. In the confusion that followed a Nazi guard rushed in and ordered the terrified girls towards a loaded carriage, prodding them with a stick, shouting "Shneller, Shneller!" The wheels began to roll as they scrambled on board.

Ilonka's mind blocked out all memory of the journey to Zittau. It was late October, 1944. The girls were immediately taken to the ammunition factory and ordered to work through the night. At dawn next morning, exhausted and starving, they were taken to their barracks, where they were given a portion of bread. This became their daily routine. They were never allowed out in daylight. Ilonka recalls working with the other Jewish slave laborers alongside British and Russian prisoners of war, only a cord strung across to separate the two gangs. The British soldiers were often distressed by the brutal beatings endured by the Jews and used to smuggle food to the girls.

Ilonka never tired of telling me, "One day when the hated supervisor's attention was diverted for a moment, a British soldier slipped an apple into my hand. I was stunned at this unexpected gift! I recovered in time, and hid it inside my dress before the guard noticed anything. Why was I the lucky one?" Back in the dormitory, she held up the apple; smooth, shining and rosy, it was the most beautiful fruit they had ever seen. "First, we feasted on it with our eyes. Then it was handed round, and everyone took a small bite. Never will I forget the gorgeous taste of that beautiful apple!"

❦ ❦ ❦

A short time later, as they were being driven back to camp from their factory night shift, the Nazi guard who traveled with them suddenly remarked, "Have I not always been kind to you? I never beat you like the other guards did!" Puzzled and frightened by this outburst, the girls did not respond. They stared at the floor and pretended not to hear. His eyes darted from one to the other and he repeated his question, adding, "When the Russians come, will you help to hide me?" The girls did not immediately understand the significance of the question, and nodded their heads. You did not disagree with a SS guard! It was a relief when the lorry swung into the compound and jolted to a halt. There was no food for the inmates that day.

❦ ❦ ❦

Ilonka was shaken out of her reverie. Someone shouted, "Look, no guards!" Next moment the cry reverberated from different parts of the compound, "The guards are gone, we are free! free!" Ilonka looked about her. Emaciated figures clothed in rags shuffled in all directions, some listless, too weak to care, others darting suspicious glances about, fearful of finding a hated guard in every corner.

Sometime later lorry-loads of Russian soldiers drove into the camp, to be greeted as conquering heroes. At last — freedom! The prisoners' joy and relief knew no bounds in those first exhilarating moments. Scores of young girls surged forward to embrace the troops, overwhelmed with gratitude towards their saviors. They watched jubilantly as the Russians systematically rounded up those guards who had left it too late to flee. The girls momentarily forgot their own pain as they watched their tormentors being prodded with rifle butts into the waiting lorries. Was it only yesterday these same men had arrogantly strutted around the compound, whip in one had and pistol in the other!

Not all the inmates cared to watch this triumph; their craving for food was greater than their desire for revenge. In moments, by sheer force of numbers, hunger-crazed survivors broke down the doors of the store houses where shelves carried neatly stacked provisions. They surged forward, ripping open bags of flour, sugar, potatoes, onions. If it was edible, it was devoured. In contrast to their own starvation diet, here was ample proof that the food shortage did not affect the guards. Unfortunately, the prisoners' digestive systems, shrunk and weakened from prolonged starvation, could not cope with this sudden bounty, and the consequences were often tragic.

Once the German guards had been rounded up, the Russians began distributing loaves of bread to the Jewish prisoners who were now free to move about. Grateful for their kindness and generosity, many girls were happy to accept an offer from the Russian soldiers. "Come with us into the German houses, and you can take anything you want from them!" Delighted at this, few girls were willing to listen to the older women who urged them to refuse. Ilonka, an innocent thirteen year old, did not understand. She watched in puzzlement as the lorries reversed and, with the lighthearted laughter of the girls ringing in her ears, she watched the lorries disappear down the dusty country road. Would they all come back dressed in beautiful clothes?

❧   ❧   ❧

It was dark in the bunker. Ilonka lay on her wooden, coverless bed, afraid to move. All around her she could hear girls crying. Some sobbed uncontrollably, others just moaned softly. She was not sure which was the more distressing. It made her cry too; something terrible had happened to the girls and now she knew she must never trust a Russian soldier.

Chapter Two

he war was over, the hated German guards taken into captivity. But what was to become of the prisoners? No one came to their rescue, and they did not want to risk another night's encounter with the Russians. Ilonka joined a group of girls from various parts of Czechoslovakia. With nothing but the tattered clothes they were wearing, they marched out of the liberated camp. With only the vaguest knowledge of the direction to take, they kept walking, intent on putting as much distance as possible between themselves and the place of their slavery.

At last their painful, swollen legs would carry them no farther, and they rested in a field. Hunger pangs racked their bodies. A vehicle approached; as it drew nearer they could see it was a military car. Russian personnel! The next instant they had all dived into the bushes. As Ilonka was the youngest, the other girls pushed her forward.

"Go on, they won't harm you," they pleaded. "Stand in the road and ask them for food." She was given a hefty push from behind, which catapulted her forward. She stumbled trembling towards the road; hissing behind her, she could hear the girls' whispered threats. With a boldness which surprised herself, she shouted, "Gleba, Gleba!" (bread, bread). The car slowed down and stopped. Terror held her transfixed. The driver looked at the officer seated beside him, and they conferred in Russian, then he issued a sharp command. Next moment the soldiers in the back of the truck took some loaves of bread from a rack and threw them to where Ilonka was standing. They landed almost at her feet.

She grabbed them and without a backward glance, holding tightly to her precious booty, she raced back to the girls. Anxious faces peeped round the hedges, cropped heads accentuating burning expectant eyes. Only when they heard the lorry start its engine and speed away did the girls jump out from their hiding places. The next instant Ilonka was overwhelmed by hands pulling at the loaves. She lost her balance and they all rolled laughing on the ground, breathless from the exertion. Quickly dividing the bread, they ate their first meal since the previous afternoon. They all agreed it was the most delicious food they had ever enjoyed. Overcome with fatigue, they stretched out and slept, blissfully unaware of the difficult weeks ahead before they finally reached their destination: Ten destitute girls with not a penny or possession between them, no one to help or guide them, only an intense longing to return home. They were undaunted by the distance: They needed to cover perhaps 400 miles with no more than an idea of the direction in which they had to march. But having suffered much worse conditions, they were content to keep going. Each secretly hoped to meet a friend or loved one, and it was this longing to be reunited with their families which gave them the willpower to keep going during the long arduous trek.

Sometimes they were able to hitch a lift on a military convoy and were given food. At other times, they were glad just to steal into an unused barn at night, watch as the lights went out in the farmhouse, then quietly raid the farmer's dustbin for discarded kitchen refuse. Occasionally they encountered a farmer who did not chase them away, but would offer food. Their progress was painfully slow, and not always in the right direction. Days blurred into weeks but Providence came to their rescue and they finally reached Brno, a thriving town on the main railway line running through the length of the country and into Hungary. Still a long way from their homes, disoriented and suffering acutely from fatigue and starvation, they decided to jump on a train slowly moving out of the station — not even pausing to consider if it was going in the right direction. Once safely on board, they debated where it would take them. What was to become of them? Ilonka didn't care, she closed her eyes for a moment as she stretched out her swollen aching legs. At least she did not have to walk. How comforting it was to see the houses and fields flash past her windows!

Blanka had been listening to the women talking on the opposite bench in the carriage, and gathered they were on their way to a market at the next stop. On an impulse she called out cheerfully, "Do you know where this train goes?"

"Budapest."

"Budapest!" the girls whispered to each other, hardly able to believe their luck. If left unchallenged, they could possibly end up in that exciting city which none of the girls had yet seen. So many Jewish people lived in Budapest, perhaps someone would help them.

They huddled close together, hoping to be overlooked, but they need not have worried. No one came to check their papers or demand payment. The hours went by with constant diversions claiming their attention. The beautiful, ever-changing rural landscape was punctuated by innumerable halts at small stations, no more than wooden platforms in the midst of the fields, teeming with a mixture of peasants, geese, goats or other farm animals all scrambling to get on the train; while those wishing to alight were struggling to get off. The result was a multi-tongued exchange of insults from these excitable Slavic races. They did not seem to have problems understanding each others' profanity.

Chapter Three

At last, Budapest! Overwhelmed at the unexpected size and grandeur of the buildings, the girls gingerly stepped onto the platform. They felt acutely conscious of their shabby appearance, even among this impoverished postwar crowd. They stayed close together, trying to ignore the stares of the urbane citizens: it hardly mattered if the stares were caused by pity or revulsion. Unwashed, lice infested, with bodies bloated from malnutrition, they well knew how conspicuous they looked.

"Shalom Aleichem!"

They all spun around together. Unable to utter a sound, they stared at the man greeting them so unexpectedly. He was clean shaven, in his mid-thirties, wearing a brown derby hat. He smiled benignly at them. "Shalom Aleichem," he patiently repeated. A sigh of relief sufficed for an answer.

"Have you anywhere to go?"

They shook their heads.

"Come with me, we have here an organization to help survivors. You will be given food and clothing." he said kindly.

Still no one spoke. Glancing at each other, they eagerly followed him out into the bustling crowded street of this beautiful ancient city. They were oblivious to the people passing or the tree lined streets. Suddenly, they were no longer alone! Someone had offered to help!

It all seemed like a wonderful dream, but they were awake, trying to keep up with his brisk pace, until he noticed their difficulty in following. Then he stopped, allowing the girls a few moments rest before he continued at a more leisurely pace.

"Here we are," he said stopping abruptly outside an ancient building. "This is the Joint Distribution Committee's headquarters. Just walk in, they are here to help you!" He watched as they mounted the stairs. Halfway up, the girls realized they had not thanked him, and turned around, but he was gone. "We never saw him again. He came from nowhere, like a guardian angel, and later just melted away!"

A look of disbelief and shock greeted the bewildered girls as they stumbled into the Joint office. The officials quickly recovered, however, and welcomed them with genuine warmth. The girls responded with a flood of tears, tears of relief. Having been despised and rejected for so long, the unexpected hospitality proved too much. They never forgot those wonderful caring people.

The Joint's task was to provide for the immediate needs of all survivors who arrived daily — food, clothing, a bed to sleep in and, most important, bathing facilities. Ilonka and her party of girls were infested with head and body lice, sucking at their lifeblood. The hostels set up for the survivors were equipped to deal with this common plague, a legacy from concentration camps and aggravated by their living conditions.

To the girls this was paradise! Food to begin with, then their first hot bath. Clean and refreshed, they were given a new set of clothing. They looked in wonderment at each other, as they came out of the baths — what a transformation! The incomparable feeling of being reborn! Afterwards they went into the dining hall for a meal served by caring, warmhearted women, who also wanted to know about missing relatives. In the dormitories each girl was given her own bed. Ilonka could not contain her delight, she exclaimed, "A bed and even a cover all to myself!" It was an undreamed-of luxury. It did not take long before they were peacefully asleep in blissful oblivion. The nightmares that were to plague them were still to come and would last a lifetime, but on this first night, they slept peacefully, their hair, no longer matted with dirt and lice, softly framing their pale, thin faces.

They stayed in the hostel for a few weeks, slowly regaining a little strength and with it the desire to get 'home.' They were unwilling to even consider the possibility that 'home' was no more: cruel reality was still to come. When the time came to go, each was given some money. But it was not easy to leave the warmth and companionship of the other girls; having shared their lives so intimately for so long it was difficult to part. Ilonka and four other girls set off together for the first part of their journey, all heading in a northeasterly direction. They had agreed to stay together as long as possible. Trudging the endless roads, begging free rides whenever possible, they were able to save their money to buy food.

They bypassed the town of Mishkolz, not realizing that this once vibrant center of Jewish life now struggling to rebuild its community, extended a warm welcome to every survivor coming into its town. With no one to guide or give directions, they slept the night in a field, unaware that only a short distance away, a comfortable bed and a cooked meal awaited each survivor.

They had reached the town of Ungvar, nestled on the border with Ukraine. Not even their physical exhaustion could dampen their excitement at the prospect of reaching their respective homes. It had been a long haul from Zittau. The hardships, the hunger, pain and frustrations would soon fade into the past as they would be reunited with their very own loved ones. The girls hugged and kissed and cried, promising to keep in touch. At last the time came to part, to go their separate ways. Instinctively they turned around to wave at each other . . .

Chapter Four

Ilonka looked about her. Suddenly, for the first time in her life, she was totally alone! After all the hardships and pain she had endured, it was always the thought of reaching Ungvar that had kept her going. Sometimes it had seemed an impossible dream. Yet here she was expecting to feel elated and happy at her own achievement, but all she felt was an oppressive loneliness.

Quickening her steps, she tried to run but was soon out of breath. How frightening this loneliness was! Her father was sure to be waiting for her; she would run into his arms. Would her two brothers and little sister be waiting for her too? Oblivious to all around her, gasping for breath, she hurried along the road that would take her home. Just one more street, then a right turn ... Perhaps her father was looking out of the window, waiting impatiently for her. She stopped abruptly, a little cry escaped her lips. Her home! Where was her home? This pile of charred rubble? In disbelief, she looked about her, perhaps she had come to the wrong house in the wrong street? But no, this vacant space was where their home had been. In shock, her eyes noticed for the first time other devastated areas. All her pent up pain and frustration welled up inside her. Leaning against a tree stump, she cried bitterly ...

❀   ❀   ❀

What was to become of her? Where was she to go? Overwhelmed by loneliness, she longed for someone to talk to, someone who would comfort her. Suddenly she brightened. Pappa too, must have returned, only to find the house no longer standing. She could just picture his dear face, how disappointed he must have been! He would have wanted to prepare for their homecoming! Pappa must have gone on to Sobranc, to her grandmother's house. The next moment her mind was made up: she too would go on to Sobranc. Hungry and desperately tired, she walked on, never thinking of rest.

Ilonka told me, "I was alone and frightened, but convinced that my father was waiting for me in his mother's house. So I forced myself to walk. It was not the seventeen kilometers which worried me. I was terrified of being unable to reach it before nightfall!"

Once out of town, she was so overcome with fatigue, that she could not go on. Selecting a tree, she sat down on a low branch, with her back resting against the main trunk. She felt safe there, knowing she could not be seen from the roadside. She closed her eyes, shutting out the alien, indifferent world around her. What had became of the other girls? Had they been more fortunate? Were any by now reunited with their families, or had they fared no better than she? She squeezed her eyelids tightly together in concentration, sending a fervent prayer to the Almighty, entreating Him to help. Inexplicably, she felt suddenly less alone, as if a comforting hand touched her shoulder. Somewhat refreshed she continued on her way.

Though dazed and numb from fatigue, her feet and hands badly swollen, her spirits suddenly soared as she neared Sobranc. From this once peaceful town they had been forcibly evicted, to be herded like cattle into wagons which were subsequently sealed. "No!" she scolded herself, she must not dwell in the past. She was free, she would soon arrive at her grandmother's home, and Pappa would be waiting, and maybe Mamma too.

Growing more confident, she recalled her last meeting with her father in Auschwitz, when she had cried out to him across the barbed wire, "Where is Mamma?"

"*Die mamma ist auf ein gutten platz* (Mamma is in a good place)," he answered. Had she misunderstood? Yes, surely she had.

Not even the anticipation of their reunion could make her weary legs walk faster. Urging her body forward, ignoring the pain, she stumbled on.

The house was still there! Even from afar she was reassured, for it looked the same as before, crisp white net curtains at the windows. Excitement and joy rose within her, at last she too would be home, with her own family! She stopped outside the door, her heart pounding. Fleetingly she wondered why no one had come to open the door, did they not see her coming? Perhaps everyone was in the backyard. Dismissing her unwelcome thoughts, she knocked on the door. A few moments later it was opened by their old maid. Ilonka was over the threshold before the woman had recognized her, and did not notice her hostile look. Ilonka rushed into the living room.

"Get out of my house!" the "maid" shouted. Looking around the room, Ilonka noticed an elaborately embroidered cloth spread on the polished sideboard; she remembered watching her mother sewing it. It was a Chanukah gift for her grandmother.

Her shoulders were gripped by a pair of powerful hands like steel clamps. Instantly her own hand shot out and grabbed the embroidered cloth from the dresser. Clutching the precious object, she winced from the pain as she was swung around; the next moment she had been hurled out of the house and flung into the road. Dazed, she remained squatting on the ground, devastated by the unexpected turn of events. She gently tried to smooth out the crumpled cloth, stroking the silken flowers, tracing the intricate pattern, stem linked to flowering stem, to form a graceful bouquet, each flower stitched to perfection.

Closing her eyes tightly, she felt herself transported into an altogether different world: to her previous home from which she had been so cruelly snatched. She was back in their warm friendly living room, her mother sitting near the table lamp, absorbed with the embroidery she was working. She was back in that magical world where one ate regular meals and slept in clean beds, where Pappa would wake you with *negil vassar* and the smell of coffee wafted through the house. Ilonka pressed the crumpled cloth closer to her chest, to keep the vision alive. Hot tears spilled down her sunken cheeks.

"Ilonka, why are you sitting on the ground?" Through her sobs, she became aware of someone calling her name. Reluctantly, she lifted her head up. "Ilonka!" A woman was bending down, her eyes pleading, "Have you seen our daughter?" The man standing beside her added, "You must remember our Anicka, she was taken away in the same transport as you. Do you know what happened to her?" His voice broke into a sob. Ilonka looked at the two people. Could this pathetic, ill-clothed couple really be the elegant, wealthy Mr. and Mrs. Erno Moritz?

She did indeed remember Anicka; they had gone to school together, and had been together in Auschwitz, but she did not know what had become of her since. Their eyes pleaded for news she couldnot give. She felt sorry for this couple. "I don't know what happened to Anicka," she answered. The broken-hearted couple turned reluctantly away. Ilonka was still squatting on the ground when Mr. and Mrs. Moritz turned round and came back. They touched Ilonka on the shoulder, and said softly, "Please come with us! We will take care of you. You can be our daughter."

Ilonka jumped to her feet, "No, I don't want to be your daughter!" she blurted out, then lowered her eyes, when she saw the pain in theirs. She had not meant to hurt them, so she hastily added, "I want to stay here and wait until my father comes back. I know he will come back!" she added fervently.

The Moritzes continued to plead with her.

"We want to lavish all our love on you. We have no one left from our family, and you have no one from your family. We will treasure you and take care of you. It is not safe for you to stay alone in this hostile town."

But Ilonka was adamant, she was going to be there when her father returned. She wiped her tear-stained face with the back of her hand.

Sadly, the couple walked away, aching to stretch out their arms and hold a child.

With daytime turning to dusk, Ilonka began in earnest to look for a place to spend the night. She considered herself lucky to come across a vacant house which was used by other survivors as a temporary shelter. Grateful for the companionship, she lay down on the bare floorboards. After staying a few days in Sobranc, she decided to return to Ungvar, a larger town with its own railway station. It would be easier not to miss anyone coming back, she reasoned. Back in Ungvar, she joined other young people, like herself, alone and destitute.

There was little to keep them occupied, in those early postwar days, and no one to take charge of the precious young survivors. They roamed the streets and railway stations. There was no greater joy than finding a relative.

At night they slept in deserted houses, on the bare floorboards. "On reflection," Ilonka said to me, "it seems strange that it never entered our minds to feel sorry for ourselves. We were provided daily with a hot meal, from the newly opened soup kitchen; we feared no one, and could sleep as long as we liked."

Ilonka, an early riser, would make her way to the station to await the first train of the day. With mounting excitement she would watch the train steam into the station, her eyes scanning the crowd ... Anger and hurt welled up inside her. Why was her father not coming? She had spoken to him in Auschwitz, what was keeping him? Well, maybe tomorrow!

Chapter Five

lowly the Jewish survivors were returning, life had to be rebuilt. Nothing was the same. Her school friends were gone. She longed for those orderly bygone days, when everyone seemed to have parents, grandparents and numerous other relatives, who always seemed to be coming to visit bringing presents. This was especially true in the summertime, when this peaceful rural town would spring to life with the influx of holiday guests, who came every year to bathe in the local sulfur spring water, famous for its healing properties. Ilonka could never understand how one could enjoy bathing in the foul smelling water, and watched with distaste as the bathers paid the hired attendants to cover their bodies with slimy mud from the lake.

Without realizing it, her steps had taken her to this famous beauty spa. How calm and peaceful it was, with just a couple strolling by! She slowly turned towards the decaying cabins; she could almost hear her mother and aunty calling as they emerged from a mud session. "Mamma, Mamma" she murmured softly. Tears stung in her eyes, as she turned away. She could not bear to stay in this place any longer, where the nostalgic past seemed as if suspended in the very air she breathed.

✿ ✿ ✿

She watched a marriage being solemnized in the time honored way, outside in the square, under a newly erected *Chuppah* — canopy. Ilonka gazed in wonderment. The pretty widow of a wealthy banker was marrying a butcher; she had been to school with his daughters, but not one of the children had survived. With Hashem's blessing, it was time to rebuild their lives. Many survivors married before emigrating.

Ilonka became restless, like many other lonely youngsters. Suddenly she longed to get away from this town with its painful memories lurking from every corner. On an impulse, she set out. Time had no meaning and distances were irrelevant. The fact that the balmy summer evenings might soon turn into bitter cold and hostile nights, never even crossed her mind. She simply walked, passing through villages, begging for food on the way.

It was on a dusty country lane, that she suddenly came face to face with her cousin Ignazs. Walking aimlessly, she idly watched a donkey cart approaching. Casually, without enthusiasm, she observed its laborious progress. The donkey nodded its head in rhythmic movement. A solitary figure was perched on the narrow wooden seat. They had almost passed each other, when she suddenly cried out "Ignazs!" The man jerked his head around; the next moment, he jumped off the buggy and they hugged each other.

"Ignazs, tell me, have you seen Apuka (Father)?" she asked.

He hesitated and she dropped her arms. She waited patiently while he stared into the distance, "Your father is not coming back," he said gently.

"Liar," she hissed, "I saw him myself in Auschwitz, we spoke a few words!"

"I know," he whispered, his voice breaking.

She pleaded with him to tell her how he had died, but he firmly refused. He did not wish to torment her with the details. He never did! It took Ilonka some time to absorb the truth. Nothing she had endured so far matched the total devastation she now felt, her whole world had suddenly collapsed. She had always clung to the hope of finding her father, but now the last vestige of hope was gone! The tears so bravely not shed at the loss of all her loved ones — for mamma and grandmamma, brothers and sister, now spilled over in a torrent of grief, anger and black despair. She sobbed and sobbed. Ignazs could offer no comfort, he understood the depth of her suffering, the loneliness of her soul. He too was grieving for the loss of his young bride, and his parents.

"Come with me. I have a farm house, not far from here."

"No, thank you, but would you take me back to Ungvar?"

"Hop on, I am going that way to buy some provisions and pick up a few people."

They drove in silence, each absorbed with his own thoughts. At last they clip-clopped into town. Ilonka jumped off, ignoring his pleas to come with him, and hurried away. Her overwhelming desire to be alone, blurred all other considerations. He, understanding, made no attempt to follow her.

Weeks went by, in aimless existence. The station was still a magnet for missing relatives: perhaps Ilonka was not the only survivor who refused to accept that not one of their loved ones would ever return. They continued to wait at the railway station, watching, scanning every person who alighted.

The money she had been given by the Joint Office in Budapest was gone. Ilonka relied on the soup kitchen for her meals. It was there, standing in the queue, that Ignazs found her. Her pale thin face creased into a smile as he walked towards her; for a fleeting moment she was afraid he would ignore her. How could she have been so rude to him? Her only surviving relative and she had refused his help! As if in answer to her prayer, he approached as she stood in the queue.

"Ilonka, you have no need to stand in a food line! I have turned my farm into a guest house, and I want you to be my cook."

"But I can't cook," she protested.

"You don't need a degree in cooking to satisfy starving people!" he assured her. She eagerly accepted his offer.

"Shall we pick up your belongings?" he asked as she settled into the horse-drawn buggy.

"I have none" she answered, simply.

Chapter Six

Her first glimpse of the farmhouse was from a distance as they jolted over the tortuous dirt track, stretching for endless kilometers, the only road which led to the farmhouse. This was surrounded by overgrown fields lying fallow, since Jews had been prohibited from owning land. Ilonka saw only a place which was to be her home, and to her it was beautiful. She stepped off the cart, eager to explore. Young people seemed to materialize from all sides — from inside the house and from the back yard — all showing genuine delight in welcoming back their host. They milled around Ignazs, firing questions at him in three different languages. He listened, good humoredly, then answered each one, slipping effortlessly from Hungarian to Rumanian and the various Slovak dialects. Ignazs was a shrewd man and since the war had been involved in the lucrative trade of contraband, that ancient trade that flourishes in wartime and wherever severe restrictions and embargoes are in force. Ilonka soon learned that her cousin was rarely at home; his main income came from smuggling people to and fro over the borders, which enabled him also to smuggle commodities from one country to another. American cigarettes, the most acceptable form of payment, were eagerly sought after. Inflation being rampant, the country's currency was almost worthless. Unearthed family treasures, jewels and antiques, were changing hands for cigarettes.

In the floor of the buggy, Ignazs showed her the hidden recess under the coconut matting. He pried off the wooden planks which covered the cavity. It looked deceptively small, but held a surprising quantity of contraband cigarettes and valuables.

Ilonka marveled at his ingenuity, thrilled to be sharing his confidence. As if reading her mind, he said, "Go and look through the cottage, but be quick! We are all hungry and are waiting for you to cook our supper!"

This was her introduction to a new way of life. From being a waif in limbo, she was placed in charge of a guest house. Experience she had none, but she did possess an abundance of enthusiasm to prove herself in the task her cousin had entrusted to her. Rising early the following morning, she scrubbed the floor in the kitchen, then using all her strength she attempted to remove the accumulated grime and grease from the solid wooden kitchen table.

Pleased with the result she sat down to rest, the chairs would have to be washed down later. At the moment her strength was limited, but she was impatient to wash years of neglect away.

From one of his trips, Ignazs returned with a crate of lively chickens. They were to provide the welcome addition of fresh eggs to their restricted diet. Ilonka's culinary skills were limited to the most basic dishes of potatoes, cooked, mashed or baked in their skins, but no guests ever complained; they were only too grateful to be given a hot, freshly cooked meal. She was eager to learn cookery hints from the constant new arrivals, some of whom only stayed overnight. In a surprisingly short time, she was adept at preparing the meals, even baking her own bread. A goat provided fresh milk and cheese, but this, of course, increased Ilonka's work load.

One day Ignazs came into the kitchen carrying a parcel which he sheepishly deposited on the table, inviting Ilonka to open it. Unwrapping the bundle under his watchful eyes, she lifted a stunning dirndl dress from its wrapping. She admired it, brushing her hand over the soft gathered material. "Beautiful," she remarked, folding it back into the paper.

"Don't you want to try it on, and see if it fits you?" he inquired casually.

"Try it? Fit me? Why?"

"Because it's yours!"

She stared at him incredulously, not believing what she heard. This beautiful creation — hers! It had never entered her mind that she was deserving of anything in return for her work. That evening in the privacy of her bedroom she shyly slipped into the dress, and walked to the window admiring her reflection. How beautiful! Thrilled with her own image, she let her imagination take over. Humming a tune, she pirouetted around her bedroom, then threw herself on the bed as the room continued to spin.

Chapter Seven

Ilonka was gingerly gathering the eggs from the chicken coop, shooing away the indignant hens, when she heard the horse and buggy grinding to a halt in the yard.

"Ilonka I have a surprise for you!" Ignazs called.

"Coming," she answered, intent on finishing her battle with her feathered adversaries. She never lost her distaste for this messy chore. Emerging from the hut, she saw Ignazs approaching, accompanied by a young woman. The next moment she was transfixed "Pirrie" she cried, almost dropping the basket with the eggs and ran to embrace her cousin.

They hugged and kissed and cried, holding onto each other. "Isn't it incredible," Pirrie marveled, "the person I paid to smuggle me over the Ukrainian border was none other than our mutual cousin Ignazs!"

After supper, Pirrie helped with the dishes and tidied the kitchen. Later they sat on the rustic bench outside, breathing in the heady scent of a magnolia tree while shadows drifted across the yard on the warm summer evening. They talked until late into the night. Ilonka was elated when she finally succeeded in persuading her cousin to remain at the farm for the time being. Since he had an additional helper, Ignazs decided to invest in a cow. He knew a farmer who would trade him a cow for whiskey and schnapps. Now they enjoyed butter and other dairy products.

The arrival of her cousin made Ilonka happy and contented, and, for a while her life revolved around the daily work, which the two girls now shared. In addition to the normal running of the house, they started to make jam from the heavily laden plum trees. Apples and pears needed sorting and careful storing. Their days were filled with simple, satisfying chores.

However, Pirrie was getting restless. A born city dweller, she could never be reconciled to a life of farming. She longed to stretch her intellectual resources, to mix and socialize and of course, to rebuild her life. She had been engaged, and the marriage date fixed, before the world had come crashing down.

"It is time for us to leave this farm and move to the city before the winter sets in," Pirrie told Ilonka one day as they prepared to clean the vegetables. Ilonka looked at her cousin in utter amazement.

"Why do you want to leave here? I like it here! Oh, please stay!" she pleaded, horrified at the prospect of either leaving or losing the company of her cousin. "What about Ignazs, how can we do this to him?" she said, fighting back the tears. Ilonka could not bear the thought of having her idyllic life disrupted once more.

Reluctantly, she had to concede that this was no place for her cousin, a vivacious girl with a sharp intellect. Pirrie was grateful to Ignazs for allowing her the opportunity to regain her strength, yet felt under no obligation to remain, for she had worked hard for her keep. She told Ignazs that she was leaving, and taking Ilonka with her. To her relief, he did not object.

"Don't worry," he said reassuringly," I can always find women willing to work for food and a roof over their heads." She discussed with Ignazs her plan to go back to Michelovce over the Ukrainian border. Ilonka listened to her cousin discussing the best and safest route to cross the heavily guarded borders, and tried to stifle the fear rising inside her. Why did she have to become a fugitive once more, risking imprisonment when she was perfectly content to stay at the farm! And yet she grudgingly had to admit that this was not the life for a religious Jew, cut off as they were from the mainstream of Jewish life.

Her mind went back over the turbulent events of the past two years. She was no longer the pampered and protected young girl, who, barely in her teens, had been so cruelly snatched from her sheltered home. Many a lonely sleepless night she lay in bed fondly recalling happier times, when their life was centered around the synagogue; the festivals, marriages and even engagements were happy events shared with all the neighbors. Yes, she often missed the orderly regulated life of the Orthodox Jew. In her mind's eyes, she could see her mother busy in the kitchen, putting the final touches to the meat platter, then removing her apron. She would re-tie the bow on her silken head scarf before going to light the candles, prepared in gleaming silver candlesticks on the dining room table. Her father, she sighed at her recollection, would be preparing to go to the synagogue with her brothers, Chaim and David, dressed in their best suits, their faces shining, their *payot* neatly curled. Suddenly, her mind was made up: she too must leave the comparative security of the farm. She would go with her cousin.

A few days later, the two girls huddled together in the cart against the chilly autumn night, the solitary figure of Ignazs silhouetted against the inky black moonless sky. With a few encouraging words, pulling at the reins, he gently urged the donkey forward.

Chapter Eight

And so ended another chapter in Ilonka's short life. Here in this remote farm house, she had begun to create her life. She had built up her strength and health and learned to trust people again. The cart wheels crunched on the pebble strewn ground, rolling out onto the winding dirt track, heading once more for the unknown. Ignazs had warned them of the possible dangers ahead. It was considered undemocratic to leave your country according to the laws of the Russians who now ruled it. Guards were posted along the borders between the Ukraine and Slovakia, with orders to shoot at anyone caught trying to leave, yet most of the surviving Jews were willing to risk their lives in their effort to improve their precarious existence.

They came to an abrupt halt. Ahead, in the distance, was a brightly lit building.

"You see that house?" Ignazs said. "It is a Crisma-tavern, very popular with the Russian soldiers who are stationed in this area. They come here every night. To relieve their boredom, they get drunk and look for mischief." He looked at the two young women. "You must understand, of course for your own safety, you must not be seen by these Cossacks. Be very careful not to attract attention as you walk to the house, keep well out of the light. Make your way to the back of the tavern; I will alert the landlord." Ignazs waited for the girls to alight. He knew they were frightened and tried to reassure them. "My arrival at the tavern should help you. I will divert the Russians' attention with a bottle of red wine; that will allow the landlord time to slip out through the back to see to you."

Uneasily they watched him drive away. Pirrie whispered, "Let's follow the cart — with that noise, no one can hear our footsteps."

They cautiously stepped forward, keeping to the dark side of the road, close to the hedges, scurrying like frightened rabbits across every gap in the fence. Ilonka moved closer to Pirrie. "This is not as bad as being alone!" she whispered. Pirrie took her hand and squeezed it reassuringly.

The lights seemed to recede as they darted in and out of the shadows, then suddenly the tavern loomed ahead, its bright lights beckoning. Pirrie instinctively drew back into the shadow, holding Ilonka's hand tightly. She knew only too well the danger at which Ignazs had hinted. Slowly, with the utmost caution, she led the way to the back of the building. She froze for a moment as the sound of merriment floated through the air, then they quickly covered the last stretch and leaned against the wall in the back of the building with hearts pounding. Pirrie gently knocked on the kitchen door. Immediately it was opened and someone beckoned them inside. Not a word was spoken as they were hustled up the stairs. The sound of men's voices floated upwards. They were obviously in a merry mood. At last the girls reached the loft. Once used for storing hay, it was a perfect place to hide. For the moment, they were safe and warm. Curling up on a bed of straw, Ilonka was soon fast asleep, oblivious of the rowdy Cossacks drinking the night away.

❧   ❧   ❧

"Wake up, wake up," Pirrie was shaking her by the shoulder. "We must hurry." Stretching and yawning, Ilonka tried to linger a little longer in her cozy lair. The next moment she was wide awake when she saw Pirrie going through the trap door. Instantly, she followed her out of the loft.

Downstairs all was quiet; deserted, except for the old retainer sweeping the saloon, and throwing fistfuls of fresh wood shavings across the stone floor. He seemed unaware of their presence, having learned long ago not to notice the strange comings and goings.

After a hearty breakfast of crusty black bread and scalding hot coffee, which the landlord's wife prepared for the two girls, it was time to leave.

Their guide was a morose man, of stocky build, who walked with the assured confidence of those used to pitting their wits against the harsh elements of the Carpathian mountains. No lovers of their new Bolshevik masters, they were easily bribed to help outwit the hated border patrol.

Ignazs had chosen an excellent guide. He seemed to sense when the soldier on patrol would stop and light a cigarette, which was the moment he had been waiting for. Waving his hand he signalled to the girls to edge cautiously forward through the under-growth. Now they were almost over the border! They had to wait once more until the soldier resumed his watch. Eventually they crossed the border.

To their joy, they met Pirrie's sister Lenka in Michelovce. She had recently married and welcomed them both into her tiny apartment. Ilonka will never forget the day when Pirrie, by a miracle, was reunited with her fiancé! Each thought the other had perished. A few weeks later they were married, and after the wedding, they secretly traveled to Vienna and eventually emigrated to Canada.

Ilonka tried to be brave when the time came to part. She had never felt the same closeness with Lenka as she enjoyed with Pirrie. The two sisters were very different and Ilonka had always found it easy to confide in Pirrie — she understood her fears and her uncertainties, her constant need for reassurance, yet at the same time her wish to remain fiercely independent. Fighting back her tears, for she must not let her cousin know how unhappy she was at being left behind, she hugged and kissed her, then watched sadly as the new Mrs. Sondheim eagerly followed her husband on board the train. She was alone once more. However, she resolved not to depend on others again: she must be more independent. From now on, she would look after and support herself.

A friend of Lenka's offered her the job of mother's helper, which she gladly accepted. A deep sigh escaped her lips; how she missed her own little brothers. She even missed the times she would be rudely awakened, with their high pitched voices calling to each other across the bedroom, when the clock on her bedside table told her it was too early to get up. No amount of pleading could dampen their early morning exuberance. Alas, never again would their voices disturb her sleep.

Now at last she had an opportunity to be part of a real home where the voices of children reverberated through the house. Lenka looked up from her sewing machine at the unfamiliar sound, Ilonka was humming a tune as she peeled the potatoes for their evening meal. Lenka resumed her sewing, how comforting to see the sudden change in her young cousin, teenager's could be so unpredictable she mused.

The following day she moved in with the family, but cruel disillusion was soon to follow. From the start, it was made clear to her that it was never intended for her to be treated as one of the family. When not looking after the children, her place was in the kitchen. The parents constantly criticized her, and they would not allow their high spirited youngsters to be disciplined, but were quick to scold Ilonka if the children misbehaved. Ilonka's only pleasure was her daily excursion to the park with the children; they liked her, and were eager to please her. They loved to play in the grass and chase the ball which Ilonka threw.

One day, as she sat in the park watching the children and contemplating her own unhappy position, she was startled to hear someone call her name. Looking up, she saw a girl approaching.

"Blanka!" she cried, jumping up and running towards her friend. They embraced closely, both crying unashamedly.

To meet at last one of the girls!

"It is so good to see you, so good to see you!" Ilonka kept repeating in between sobs. They were tears of joy at finding each other, and for Ilonka, all the heartache she had endured came spilling out with the flood of tears. Blanka cradled the younger girl in her arms, as she listened to her outpouring, waiting for her sobs to subside. They sat on the bench and talked and talked. Blanka, too, had much to tell.

"Yes, I am married." she said, adjusting the turban she wore on her head. "Wigs are expensive," she added. "What are you doing here in Michelovce? There are no religious people here."

Ilonka looked at her in surprise, "Where else shall I go?"

"Have you not tried to emigrate?"

"Emigrate, where to, and how?" Ilonka answered. She did not really want to be uprooted once more. The mere contemplation of change filled her with uneasiness.

Blanka understood. Putting her arm around Ilonka's shoulder, she spoke to her softly.

"I have heard of special rescue operations funded by Jews from England and America. They are looking for orphans like yourself. Their aim is to save destitute children." She waited, but Ilonka remained silent so she went on, "If you go to one of these hostels, they will arrange for you to join a 'Kinder-transport' leaving for England or America. It is a wonderful opportunity to start a new life, in a country where Jews are free, the same as everyone else!"

Ilonka just shook her head. Though desperately unhappy, she was afraid to leave. To go into a hostel among people she did not know filled her with dread. Blanka persisted. "Ilonka, my dear child, this is no place for you. You, who shamed me in Auschwitz when you refused bread on Pesach and lived on potato peelings! I often listened to you reciting *Avinu Malkeinu* by heart. Can I ignore your plight and let you waste your precious young life with these uncaring, irreligious people?" Getting no reaction, she continued, "My child, I will arrange everything for you. You have no future here." Suddenly she brightened, as a new idea occurred to her. "Ilonka, I will come with you — I will introduce you myself."

Ilonka looked up, "Would you really?" she asked in disbelief. She rose, and called the children. It was time to go home. "Let me think about it."

"Ilonka, will you be coming to the park tomorrow?"

"I come here every day with the children," she answered, then taking Sariky and Erno by the hand, she hurried home.

Not until she had settled the children for the night and was curled up on her bed in the room she shared with them, was Ilonka able to think with any clarity. Why was she hesitating? Anger rose inside her, she longed to be part of an Orthodox home once more, where she could keep the laws of Shabbos openly, without fear of being ridiculed. Wryly she recalled the lonely Friday nights since her employment, waiting until the children were asleep, when she too would settle in her bed, and softly sing the beloved *zemiros*-songs to herself, ever careful not to wake the children. Doubts and uncertainties flooded her mind. Would she really be happier in a hostel? Perhaps the girls would resent a newcomer? Ever since Pirrie had emigrated, no one had wanted her. She recalled with nostalgia their times together, when neither minded working hard, they shared the work with good humor, and there were plenty of occasions for laughter, and even heated arguments were soon forgotten. Ah, and the times when they just talked and talked, reminiscing about their previous carefree lives!

One of the children coughed, bringing her abruptly back to her present predicament. It was no use dwelling on the past, and Pirrie was not coming back. Dare she trust her old friend Blanka? She had no passport and no identification papers. How difficult and insurmountable seemed the problems which came to torment her through the night. It was long after midnight, when she finally fell asleep.

The following morning she wondered if it had all been just a bad dream. With her mind preoccupied, she washed and dressed the children, occasionally glancing out of the window.

Breakfast over, she cleared away the dishes then helped with the chores, with one eye on the old alarm clock on the mantlepiece. What was the matter with that clock? Never had time dragged on so painfully slow. At last it was time to take the children to the park. Would Blanka be waiting for her? But Blanka did not come.

Days passed by and still no word from Blanka. If only she could contact her, to tell her she was ready to leave! How could she have hesitated to seize the opportunity to escape from her present misery? If only she could be given another chance! Everyday, she prayed to Hashem that Blanka would be waiting for her on her daily excursions to the park. She let the children run ahead towards the pond where they watched the ducks being fed. Ilonka looked idly towards the curved tree-lined pedestrian way, as if in answer to the prayer, she saw Blanka coming towards her.

"It is all arranged!" she called from afar. Ilonka stared in astonishment.

"How did you know I would accept?"

Grinning broadly Blanka answered, "Because, you are not stupid! In any case your conscience would not allow you to stay in this irreligious environment."

A flicker of a smile flitted across Ilonka's face; she could have added that another reason for wanting to leave was her dislike of the couple she lived with, but it did not matter anymore.

"When are we going?" she asked.

"Tomorrow morning. I will meet you at the station."

"Tomorrow? So soon?" Ilonka gasped.

Blanka retorted, "Why not?"

"But of course, and why not!" Ilonka laughed.

The following morning, she dressed early, then prepared the children's breakfast. Afterwards, leaving a short note for the parents, she quietly slipped out of the house.

How would the parents react when they found she had gone? With the logic of the young, she felt perfectly justified in repaying the pain and humiliation she had endured, by walking out of their lives, leaving just a note. Empty-handed, without a backward glance, she hurried to the station. She began to run, a heavy burden seemed to have lifted from her young shoulders.

Blanka was waiting for her. "Where are your belongings?"

"I have none." Why do people always ask her that? Ilonka wondered. She had only one treasure, her grandmother's embroidered cloth, which was neatly folded and pinned inside her skirt. Having no luggage was a distinct advantage when trying to board a crowded train.

Blanka watched her young friend, who, oblivious to the melee around her sat staring wistfully out of the window. The cares of the world seemed to have settled on this child. She leaned across and patted her hand reassuringly.

"Don't worry, you are no longer alone." Startled, Ilonka turned toward her. Their eyes met; in the swaying crowded train, she suddenly felt at peace.

Chapter Nine

ll too soon it seemed to Ilonka, the train screeched to a halt in Kosice, a town that had had a large Jewish community before the war. Being not far from the Hungarian border, it had become a temporary haven for many fleeing from the communist regimes. Blanka took her protege by the arm and guided her out of the station. She paused for a moment to allow the traffic to pass, then confidently crossed the road in the direction of the old Jewish quarter.

Ilonka clung to Blanka as they entered the hostel. The sight of girls laughing, giggling and arguing all at the same time bewildered her. She felt intimidated, when a group surrounded her with undisguised curiosity. In the weeks to come, she too would join in appraising every newcomer, but now, frightened and bewildered, she closely followed Blanka who was walking towards a door marked 'Office.' Before she could knock, it opened, a young woman in her early thirties emerged. With a quick glance at Ilonka, she quietly but firmly told the girls milling around. "Please, leave the hall, you are upsetting our new girl." Without a murmur they disappeared. Mrs. Lefcovitch held out her hand to greet them. "Welcome to our hostel. You see what great excitement there is every time a new girl arrives!" She sighed, and added wistfully, "You must excuse their behavior, they are always hoping to meet someone whom they know! We all rejoice when that happens. Alas, it is not very often."

They followed her into the office. Some time was spent with the necessary formality of filling in a questionnaire. Why do they have to know all these details? Ilonka wondered irritably. Is it really necessary for anyone to know when she last saw her mother, and the place and birth date of her father? It brought tears to her eyes.

As if in answer, Frau Lefcovitch put down her pen, and with a reassuring smile, she patiently explained. "These questions are important to confirm your identity, and will help us to get you a passport."

Ilonka looked at her in surprise. Without uttering a word, this lady watching her across the table, seemed to be able to read her thoughts.

In the weeks and months to come, Ilonka was to discover that this deeply caring woman, herself a holocaust survivor, had developed a gift for understanding the bewildered and frightened minds of a great many motherless girls.

Infinite patience, love and understanding was needed to help these girls over these difficult times. When tormented by nightmares and despairing moods, when overcome by prolonged bouts of crying, Frau Lefcovitch was always there: She understood when a girl needed to be alone, or when she could not bear her own company. She knew how to defuse a potential quarrel, with a few soothing words. Tempers could so easily get out of control among so many troubled young people, but Frau Lefcovitch seemed to turn even the bitterest opponents into friends, bringing out the best qualities in each girl.

To help them become future useful members of society, each girl had to learn a trade — dressmaking, hairdressing, wig-making, typing and shorthand, or book-keeping. Ilonka in a party of ten girls went to work in a local embroidery factory, where they were taught to operate the machines that sewed the intricate designs onto tablecloths. They soon settled down to the discipline of a regulated life, going to work every morning and working until six in the evening, taking sandwiches for their lunch. After supper, they would listen to lectures on Jewish Laws. Ilonka enjoyed these lectures, especially when given by survivors of the world famous teachers' training college, established in Poland, by the much revered Sara Shneerer. These lectures had a special fascination for these culture-starved girls.

The rest of the evenings and weekends were often spent together, with everyone joining in a sing-along and forging close bonds, which would last a lifetime. The weeks and months passed by. Sometimes, they would celebrate a marriage. As the girls were settling down, Frau Lefcovitch would take on the role of matchmaker. Many a girl who arrived at the Internat Hostel at Kosice, destitute and alone, would leave it some months later to start life as a married woman. There are to this day happily married elderly couples in many far flung

Wedding of one of the girls from the Kosice Hostel.

countries who started their married life from the hostel in Kosice. The girls looked forward to these happy events in their lives. These were not lavish weddings, food was scarce, but the joy and happiness was shared by everyone. The singing and dancing went on into the night.

But the greatest event was the summer camp. Ilonka remembers it fondly as the happiest time; they were taken to a summer camp in the spa town of Trencin, in the breathtakingly beautiful Carpathian mountains. Here they were joined by another group of girls from a hostel in Bratislava. All this was paid for by the American Joint Distribution Committee. They spent the long summer weeks forging lasting friendships with the other girls, going for long walks and participating in other outdoor activities. In the evenings there was singing and dancing to their hearts content. Then finally after the summer, back to Kosice and the factory routine.

The following April 1948, just before Pesach, Ilonka was among the excited group of girls who were part of the 'Kinder-transport' leaving for England under the auspices of Rabbi Dr. Schonfeld.

Now they are parents and grandparents, experiencing the joy of watching their grandchildren growing up. However, even the sound of their melodious voices learning Torah reaching up to heaven, cannot erase the scars or dim the sound of distant crying. Only the coming of *Mashiach* will turn the anguish into joy. May it come speedily in our time.

This volume is part of
THE ARTSCROLL SERIES®
an ongoing project of
translations, commentaries and expositions
on Scripture, Mishnah, Talmud, Halachah,
liturgy, histroy, the classic Rabbinic writings,
biographies, and thought.

For a brochure of current publications
visit your local Hebrew bookseller
or contact the publisher:

Mesorah Publications, ltd

4401 Second Avenue
Brooklyn, New York 11232
(718) 921-9000